NIGHT WORLD

More from L.J. Smith:

Night World

Volume 1: *Secret Vampire, Daughters of Darkness*
and *Enchantress*
Volume 2: *Dark Angel, The Chosen* and *Soulmate*
Volume 3: *Huntress, Black Dawn* and *Witchlight*

Beautiful Dead
by Eden Maguire

1: *Jonas*
2: *Arizona*
3: *Summer*
4: *Phoenix*

Darke Academy
by Gabrielle Poole

1: *Secret Lives*
2: *Blood Ties*
3: *Divided Souls*

NIGHT WORLD

VOLUME THREE

HUNTRESS
BLACK DAWN
WITCHLIGHT

L. J. SMITH

Hodder
Children's
Books

A division of Hachette Children's Books

Night World copyright © 1996 Lisa J. Smith

Huntress first published in the USA in 1996, *Black Dawn* first published in
1997 and *Witchlight* first published in 1997 as three separate paperbacks
by Pocket Books, a division of Simon & Schuster Inc.

The Night World: Huntress first published in Great Britain in 1997
by Hodder Children's Books

The Night World: Black Dawn first published in
Great Britain in 1997 by Hodder Children's Books

The Night World: Witchlight first published in Great Britain
in 1997 by Hodder Children's Books

This bind-up edition published in 2009
by Hodder Children's Books

ISBN-13: 978 0 340 99664 5

Typeset in Meridien and Neuland by Avon DataSet Ltd,
Bidford on Avon, Warwickshire

Printed in the UK by CPI Bookmarque, Croydon, CR0 4TD

The paper and board used in this paperback by Hodder Children's
Books are natural recyclable products made from wood grown in
sustainable forests. The manufacturing processes conform to the
environmental regulations of the country of origin.

Hodder Children's Books
a division of Hachette Children's Books
338 Euston Road, London NW1 3BH
An Hachette UK Company
www.hachette.co.uk

The Night World . . . love was never so scary.

The Night World isn't a place. It's all around us. It's a secret society of vampires, werewolves, witches, and other creatures of darkness that live among us. They're beautiful and deadly and irresistible to humans. Your high school teacher could be one, and so could your boyfriend.

The Night World laws say it's OK to hunt humans. It's OK to toy with their hearts, it's even OK to kill them. There are only two things you can't do with them.

1) Never let them find out the Night World exists.
2) Never fall in love with one of them.

These are stories about what happens when the rules get broken.

HUNTRESS

For Brian Nelson and Justin Lauffenburger

CHAPTER

1

'It's simple,' Jez said on the night of the last hunt of her life. 'You run. We chase. If we catch you, you die. We'll give you three minutes head start.'

The skinhead gang leader in front of her didn't move. He had a pasty face and shark eyes. He was standing tensely, trying to look tough, but Jez could see the little quiver in his leg muscles.

Jez flashed him a smile.

'Pick a weapon,' she said. Her toe nudged the pile at her feet. There was a lot of stuff there – guns, knives, baseball bats, even a few spears. 'Hey, take *more* than one. Take as many as you want. My treat.'

There was a stifled giggle from behind her and Jez made a sharp gesture to stop it. Then there was silence. The two gangs stood facing each other, six skinhead thugs on one side and Jez's gang on the other. Except that Jez's people weren't exactly normal gang members.

The skinhead leader's eyes shifted to the pile. Then he made a sudden lunge and came up with something in his hand.

A gun, of course. They always picked guns. This particular gun was the kind it was illegal to buy in

California these days, a large calibre semi-automatic assault weapon. The skinhead whipped it up and held it pointed straight at Jez.

Jez threw back her head and laughed.

Everyone was staring at her – and that was fine. She looked great and she knew it.

Hands on her hips, red hair tumbling over her shoulders and down her back, fine-boned face tipped to the sky – yeah, she looked good. Tall and proud and fierce . . . and very beautiful. She was Jez Redfern, the huntress.

She lowered her chin and fixed the gang leader with eyes that were neither silver nor blue but some colour in between. A colour he never could have seen before, because no human had eyes like that.

He didn't get the clue. He didn't seem like the brightest.

'Chase this,' he said, and he fired the gun.

Jez moved at the last instant. Not that metal through the chest would have seriously hurt her, but it might have knocked her backward and she didn't want that. She'd just taken over the leadership of the gang from Morgead, and she didn't want to show any weakness.

The bullet passed through her left arm. There was a little explosion of blood and a sharp flash of pain as it fractured the bone before passing on through. Jez narrowed her eyes, but held on to her smile.

Then she glanced down at her arm and lost the smile, hissing. She hadn't considered the damage to her sleeve. Now there was a bloody hole in it. Why didn't she ever think about these things?

'Do you know how much leather costs? Do you know how much a North Beach jacket costs?' She advanced on the skinhead leader.

He was blinking and hyperventilating. Trying to figure

out how she'd moved so fast and why she wasn't yelling in agony. He aimed the gun and fired again. And again, each time more wildly.

Jez dodged. She didn't want any more holes. The flesh of her arm was already healing, closing up and smoothing over. Too bad her jacket couldn't do the same. She reached the skinhead without getting hit again and grabbed him by the front of his green and black Air Force flight jacket. She lifted him, one handed, until the steel toes of his Doc Marten boots just cleared the ground.

'You better run, boy,' she said. Then she threw him.

He sailed through the air a remarkable distance and bounced off a tree. He scrambled up, his eyes showing white with terror, his chest heaving. He looked at her, looked at his gang, then turned and started running through the redwoods.

The other gang members stared after him for a moment before diving for the weapons pile. Jez watched them, frowning. They'd just seen how effective bullets were against people like her, but they still went for the guns, passing by perfectly good split-bamboo knives, yew arrows, and a gorgeous snakewood walking stick.

And then things were noisy for a while as the skinheads came up from the pile and started firing. Jez's gang dodged easily, but an exasperated voice sounded in Jez's head.

Can we go after them now? *Or do you want to show off some more?*

She flicked a glance behind her. Morgead Blackthorn was seventeen, a year older than she, and her worst enemy. He was conceited, hotheaded, stubborn, and power-hungry – and it didn't help that he was always saying she was all those things, too.

'I told them three minutes,' she said out loud. 'You

3

want me to break my word?' And for that instant, while she was snarling at him, she forgot to keep track of bullets.

The next thing she knew Morgead was knocking her backward. He was lying on top of her. Something whizzed over both of them and hit a tree, spraying bark.

Morgead's gem-green eyes glared down into hers. 'But . . . they're . . . not . . . running,' he said with exaggerated patience. 'In case you hadn't noticed.'

He was too close. His hands were on either side of her head. His weight was on her. Jez kicked him off, furious with him and appalled at herself.

'This is *my* game. *I* thought of it. We play it my way!' she yelled.

The skinheads were scattering anyway. They'd finally realized that shooting was pointless. They were running, crashing through the sword fern.

'OK, now!' Jez said. 'But the leader's mine.'

There was a chorus of shouts and hunting calls from her gang. Val, the biggest and always the most impatient, dashed off first, yelling something like 'Yeeeeeehaw.' Then Thistle and Raven went, the slight blonde and the tall dark girl sticking together as always. Pierce hung back, staring with his cold eyes at a tree, waiting to give his prey the illusion of escaping.

Jez didn't look to see what Morgead was doing. Why should she care?

She started off in the direction the skinhead leader had taken. But she didn't exactly take his path. She went through the trees, jumping from one redwood to another. The giant sequoias were the best; they had the thickest branches, although the wart-like bulges called burls on the coastal redwoods were good landing places, too. Jez jumped and grabbed and jumped again, occasionally doing acrobatic flips when she caught a branch just for the fun of it.

She loved Muir Woods. Even though all the wood around her was deadly – or maybe because it was. She liked taking risks. And the place was beautiful: the cathedral silence, the mossy greenness, the resinous smell.

Last week they'd hunted seven gang members through Golden Gate Park. It had been enjoyable, but not really private, and they couldn't let the humans fight back much. Gunshots in the park would attract attention. Muir Woods had been Jez's idea – they could kidnap the gang members and bring them here where nobody would disturb them. They would give them weapons. It would be a real hunt, with real danger.

Jez squatted on a branch to catch her breath. There just wasn't enough real danger in the world, she thought. Not like the old days, when there were still vampire hunters left in the Bay Area. Jez's parents had been killed by vampire hunters. But now that they'd all been eliminated, there wasn't anything really scary anymore . . .

She froze. There was an almost inaudible crunching in the pine needles ahead of her. Instantly she was on the move again, leaping fearlessly off the branch into space, landing on the spongy pine-needle carpet with her knees bent. She turned and stood face-to-face with the skinhead.

'Hey there,' she said.

CHAPTER 2

The skinhead's face was contorted, his eyes huge. He stared at her, breathing hard like a hurt animal.

'I know,' Jez said. 'You ran fast. You can't figure out how I ran faster.'

'You're – not – human,' the skinhead panted. Except that he threw in a lot of other words, the kind humans liked to use when they were upset.

'You guessed,' Jez said cheerfully, ignoring the obscenities. 'You're not as dumb as you look.'

'*What – the hell – are you?*'

'Death.' Jez smiled at him. 'Are you going to fight? I hope so.'

He fumbled the gun up again. His hands were shaking so hard he could scarcely aim it.

'I think you're out of ammo,' Jez said. 'But anyway a branch would be better. You want me to break one off for you?'

He pulled the trigger. The gun just clicked. He looked at it.

Jez smiled at him, showing her teeth.

She could feel them grow as she went into feeding mode. Her canines lengthening and curving until they were as sharp and delicate and translucent as a cat's. She liked the feel of them lightly indenting her lower lip as she half-opened her mouth.

That wasn't the only change. She knew that her eyes were turning to liquid silver and her lips were getting redder and fuller as blood flowed into them in anticipation of feeding. Her whole body was taking on an indefinable charge of energy.

The skinhead watched as she became more and more beautiful, more and more inhuman. And then he seemed to fold in on himself. With his back against a tree, he slid down until he was sitting on the ground in the middle of some pale brown oyster fungus. He was staring straight ahead.

Jez's gaze was drawn to the double lightning bolt tattooed on his neck. Right . . . there, she thought. The skin seemed reasonably clean, and the smell of blood was enticing. It was running there, rich with adrenaline, in blue veins just under the surface. She was almost intoxicated just thinking about tapping it.

Fear was good; it added that extra spice to the taste. Like Sweetarts. This was going to be good . . .

Then she heard a soft broken sound.

The skinhead was crying.

Not loud bawling. Not blubbering and begging. Just crying like a kid, slow tears trickling down his cheeks as he shook.

'I thought better of you,' Jez said. She shook her hair out, tossed it in contempt. But something inside her seemed to tighten.

He didn't say anything. He just stared at her – no, *through* her – and cried. Jez knew what he was seeing. His own death.

'Oh, come on,' Jez said. 'So you don't want to die. Who

does? But you've killed people before. Your gang killed that guy Juan last week. You can dish it out, but you can't take it.'

He still didn't say anything. He wasn't pointing the gun at her anymore; he was clutching it with both hands to his chest as if it were a teddy bear or something. Or maybe as if he were going to kill himself to get away from her. The muzzle of the gun was under his chin.

The thing inside Jez tightened more. Tightened and twisted until she couldn't breathe. What was wrong with her? He was just a human, and a human of the worst kind. He *deserved* to die, and not just because she was hungry.

But the sound of that crying . . . It seemed to pull at her. She had a feeling almost of déjà vu, as if this had all happened before – but it *hadn't*. She knew it hadn't.

The skinhead spoke at last. 'Do it quick,' he whispered.

And Jez's mind was thrown into chaos.

With just those words she was suddenly not in the forest anymore. She was falling into nothingness, whirling and spinning, with nothing to grab hold of. She saw pictures in bright, disjointed flashes. Nothing made sense; she was plunging in darkness with scenes unreeling before her helpless eyes.

'Do it quickly,' somebody whispered. A flash and Jez saw who: a woman with dark red hair and delicate, bony shoulders. She had a face like a medieval princess. 'I won't fight you,' the woman said. 'Kill me. But let my daughter live.'

Mother . . .

These were her memories.

She wanted to see more of her mother – she didn't have any conscious memory of the woman who'd given birth to her. But instead there was another flash. A little girl was huddled in a corner, shaking. The child had flame-bright hair and eyes that were neither silver nor blue. And she was so frightened . . .

Another flash. A tall man running to the child. Turning around, standing in front of her. 'Leave her alone! It's not her fault. She doesn't have to die!'

Daddy.

Her parents, who'd been killed when she was four. Executed by vampire hunters . . .

Another flash and she saw fighting. Blood. Dark figures struggling with her mother and father. And screaming that wouldn't quite resolve into words.

And then one of the dark figures picked up the little girl in the corner and held her up high . . . and Jez saw that he had fangs. He wasn't a vampire hunter; he was a vampire.

And the little girl, whose mouth was open in a wail, had none.

All at once, Jez could understand the screaming.

'Kill her! Kill the human! Kill the freak!'

They were screaming it about *her*.

Jez came back to herself. She was in Muir Woods, kneeling in the ferns and moss, with the skinhead cowering in front of her. Everything was the same . . . but everything was different. She felt dazed and terrified.

What did it *mean*?

It was just some bizarre hallucination. It had to be. She knew how her parents had died. Her mother had been murdered outright by the vampire hunters. Her father had been mortally wounded, but he'd managed to carry the four-year-old Jez to his brother's house before he died. Uncle Bracken had raised her, and he'd told her the story over and over.

But that screaming . . .

It didn't mean anything. It *couldn't*. She was Jez Redfern, more of a vampire than anyone, even Morgead. Of all the lamia, the vampires who could have children, her family was the most important. Her uncle Bracken was a vampire, and so was his father, and his father's father, all the way back to Hunter Redfern.

But her mother . . .

What did she know about her mother's family? Nothing. Uncle Bracken always just said that they'd come from the East Coast.

Something inside Jez was trembling. She didn't want to frame the next question, but the words came into her mind anyway, blunt and inescapable.

What if her mother had been human?

That would make Jez . . .

No. It wasn't possible. It wasn't just that Night World law forbade vampires to fall in love with humans. It was that there was no such thing as a vampire-human hybrid. It couldn't be *done*; it had never been done in twenty thousand years. Anybody like that would be a freak . . .

The trembling inside her was getting worse.

She stood up slowly and only vaguely noticed when the skinhead made a sound of fear. She couldn't focus on him. She was staring between the redwood trees.

If it were true . . . it *couldn't* be true, but if it were true . . . she would have to leave everything. Uncle Bracken. The gang.

And Morgead. She'd have to leave Morgead. For some reason that made her throat close convulsively.

And she would go . . . where? What kind of a place was there for a half-human half-vampire freak?

Nowhere in the Night World. That was certain. The Night People would have to kill any creature like that.

The skinhead made another sound, a little whimper. Jez blinked and looked at him.

It couldn't be true, but all of a sudden she didn't care about killing him anymore. In fact, she had a feeling like slow horror creeping over her, as if something in her brain was tallying up all the humans she'd hurt and killed over the years. Something was taking over her legs, making her knees rubbery. Something was crushing her chest, making her feel as if she were going to be sick.

'Get out of here,' she whispered to the skinhead.

He shut his eyes. When he spoke it was in a kind of moan. 'You'll just chase me.'

'No.' But she understood his fear. She was a huntress. She'd chased so many people. So many humans . . .

Jez shuddered violently and shut her eyes. It was as if she had suddenly seen herself in a mirror and the image was unbearable. It wasn't Jez the proud and fierce and beautiful. It was Jez the murderer.

I have to stop the others.

The telepathic call she sent out was almost a scream. *Everybody! This is Jez. Come to me, right now! Drop what you're doing and come!*

She knew they'd obey – they were her gang, after all. But none of them except Morgead had enough telepathic power to answer across the distance.

What's wrong? he said.

Jez stood very still. She couldn't tell him the truth. Morgead hated humans. If he even knew what she suspected . . . the way he would look at her . . .

He would be sickened. Not to mention that he'd undoubtedly have to kill her.

I'll explain later, she told him, feeling numb. *I just found out – that it's not safe to feed here.*

Then she cut the telepathic link short. She was afraid

he'd sense too much of what was going on inside her.

She stood with her arms wrapped around herself, staring between the trees. Then she glanced at the skinhead, who was still huddled in the sword fern.

There was one last thing she had to do with him.

Ignoring his wild flinching, she stretched out her hand. Touched him, once, on the forehead with an extended finger. A gentle, precise contact.

'Remember . . . nothing,' she said. 'Now go.'

She felt the power flow out of her, wrapping itself around the skinhead's brain, changing its chemistry, rearranging his thoughts. It was something she was very good at.

The skinhead's eyes went blank. Jez didn't watch him as he began to crawl away.

All she could think of now was getting to Uncle Bracken. He would answer her questions; he would explain. He would prove to her that none of it was true.

He'd make everything all right.

CHAPTER
3

Jez burst through the door and turned immediately into the small library off the front hall. Her uncle was sitting there at his desk, surrounded by built-in bookcases. He looked up in surprise.

'Uncle Bracken, who was my mother? How did my parents die?' It all came out in a single rush of breath. And then Jez wanted to say, 'Tell me the truth,' but instead she heard herself saying wildly, 'Tell me it's not true. It's not possible, is it? Uncle Bracken, I'm so scared.'

Her uncle stared at her for a moment. There was shock and despair in his face. Then he bent his head and shut his eyes.

'But how is it possible?' Jez whispered. 'How am I here?' It was hours later. Dawn was tinting the window. She was sitting on the floor, back against a bookcase, where she'd collapsed, staring emptily into the distance.

'You mean, how can a vampire-human halfbreed exist? I don't know. Your parents never knew. They never expected to have children.' Uncle Bracken ran both hands through his hair, head down. 'They didn't even realize you could live as a vampire. Your father brought you to me because he was dying and I was the only person he could trust. He knew I wouldn't turn you over to the Night World elders.'

'Maybe you should have,' Jez whispered.

Uncle Bracken went on as if he hadn't heard her. 'You lived without blood then. You looked like a human child. I don't know what made me try to see if you could learn how to feed. I brought you a rabbit and bit it for you and let you smell the blood.' He gave a short laugh of reminiscence. 'And your little teeth sharpened right up and you knew what to do. That was when I knew you were a true Redfern.'

'But I'm not.' Jez heard the words as if someone else was speaking them from a distance. 'I'm not even a Night Person. I'm vermin.'

Uncle Bracken let go of his hair and looked at her. His eyes, normally the same silvery-blue as Jez's, were burning with a pure silver flame. 'Your mother was a good woman,' he said harshly. 'Your father gave up everything to be with her. She wasn't vermin.'

Jez looked away, but she wasn't ashamed. She was numb. She felt nothing except a vast emptiness inside her, stretching infinitely in all directions.

And that was good. She never wanted to feel again. Everything she'd felt in her life – everything she could remember – had been a lie.

She wasn't a huntress, a predator fulfilling her place in the scheme of things by chasing down her lawful prey. She was a murderer. She was a monster.

'I can't stay here anymore,' she said.

Uncle Bracken winced. 'Where will you go?'

'I don't know.'

He let out his breath and spoke slowly and sadly. 'I have an idea.'

CHAPTER

4

Rule Number One of living with humans. Always wash the blood off before coming in the house.

Jez stood at the outdoor faucet, icy-cold water splashing over her hands. She was scrubbing – carefully – a long, slim dagger made of split bamboo, with a cutting edge as sharp as glass. When it was clean, she slipped it into her right knee-high boot. Then she daubed water over several stains on her T-shirt and jeans and scrubbed them with a fingernail. Finally she whipped out a pocket mirror and examined her face critically.

The girl who looked back didn't much resemble the wild, laughing huntress who had leaped from tree to tree in Muir Woods. Oh, the features were the same; the height of cheekbone, the curve of chin. They had even fined out a bit because she was a year older. The red flag of hair was the same, too, although now it was pulled back in an attempt to tame its fiery disorder. The difference was in the expression, which was sadder and wiser than Jez had ever imagined she could be, and in the eyes.

The eyes weren't as silvery as they had been, not as dangerously beautiful. But that was only to be expected. She had discovered that she didn't need to drink blood as long as she didn't use her vampire powers. Human food kept her alive – and made her look more human.

One other thing about the eyes. They were scarily vulnerable, even to Jez. No matter how she tried to make them hard and menacing, they had the wounded look of a deer that knows it's going to die and accepts it. Sometimes she wondered if that was an omen.

Well. No blood on her face. She shoved the mirror back in her pocket. She was mostly presentable, if extremely late for dinner. She turned the faucet off and headed for the back door of the low, sweeping ranch house.

Everyone looked up as she came in.

The family was in the kitchen, eating at the oak table with the white trim, under the bright fluorescent light. The TV was blaring cheerfully from the family room. Uncle Jim, her mother's brother, was munching tacos and leafing through the mail. He had red hair darker than Jez's and a long face that looked almost as medieval as Jez's mother's had. He was usually off in a gentle, worried dream somewhere. Now he waved an envelope at Jez and gazed at her reproachfully, but he couldn't say anything because his mouth was full.

Aunt Nanami was on the phone, drinking a diet Coke. She was small, with dark shiny hair and eyes that turned to crescents when she smiled. She opened her mouth and frowned at Jez, but couldn't say anything, either.

Ricky, who was ten, had carroty hair and expressive eyebrows. He gave Jez a big smile that showed chewed-up taco in his mouth and said, 'Hi!'

Jez smiled back. No matter what she did, Ricky was there for her.

Claire, who was Jez's age, was sitting primly, eating bits of taco with her fork. She looked like a smaller version of Aunt Nan, but with a very sour expression.

'Where have you *been*?' she said. 'We waited almost an hour for you and you never even called.'

'Sorry,' Jez said, looking at all of them. It was such an incredibly normal family scene, so completely typical, and it struck her to the heart.

It was over a year since she had walked out of the Night World to find these people, her mother's relatives. It was eleven and a half months since Uncle Jim had taken her in, not knowing anything about her except that she was his orphaned niece and that her father's family couldn't handle her anymore and had given up on her. All these months, she had lived with the Goddard family – and she still didn't fit in.

She could look human, she could act human, but she couldn't *be* human.

Just as Uncle Jim swallowed and got his mouth clear to speak to her, she said, 'I'm not hungry. I think I'll just go do my homework.'

Uncle Jim called, 'Wait a minute,' after her, but it was Claire who slammed down her napkin and actually followed Jez through the hall to the other side of the house.

'What do you *mean*, "Sorry"? You do this every day. You're always disappearing; half the time you stay out until after midnight, and then you don't even have an explanation.'

'Yeah, I know, Claire.' Jez answered without looking back. 'I'll try to do better.'

'You say that every time. And every time it's exactly the same. Don't you realize that my parents worry about you? Don't you even care?'

'Yes, I care, Claire.'

'You don't act like it. You act like rules don't apply to you. And you say sorry, but you're just going to do it again.'

Jez had to keep herself from turning around and

snapping at her cousin. She liked everyone else in the family, but Claire was a royal pain.

Worse, she was a *shrewd* royal pain. And she was right; Jez was going to do it again, and there was no way she could explain.

The thing was, vampire hunters have to keep weird hours.

When you're on the trail of a vampire-and-shapeshifter killing team, as Jez had been this evening, chasing them through the slums of Oakland, trying to get them cornered in some crack house where there aren't little kids to get hurt, you don't think about missing dinner. You don't stop in the middle of staking the undead to phone home.

Maybe I shouldn't have become a vampire hunter, Jez thought. But it's a little late to change now, and *somebody's* got to protect these stupid— these innocent humans from the Night World.

Oh, well.

She'd reached the door of her bedroom. Instead of yelling at her cousin, she simply half turned and said, 'Why don't you go work on your Web page, Claire?' Then she opened the door and glanced inside.

And froze.

Her room, which she had left in military neatness, was a shambles. The window was wide open. Papers and clothes were scattered across the floor. And there was a very large ghoul standing at the foot of the bed.

The ghoul opened its mouth menacingly at Jez.

'Oh, very funny,' Claire was saying, right behind her. 'Maybe I should help you with your homework. I hear you're not doing so great in chemistry—'

Jez moved fast, stepping nimbly inside the door and slamming it in Claire's face, pressing the little knob in the handle to lock it.

'Hey!' Now Claire sounded *really* mad. 'That's rude!'

'Uh, sorry, Claire!' Jez faced the ghoul. What was it *doing* here? If it had followed her home, she was in bad trouble. That meant the Night World knew where she was. 'You know, Claire, I think I really need to be alone for a little while – I can't talk *and* do my homework.' She took a step toward the creature, watching its reaction.

Ghouls were semi-vampires. They were what happened to a human who was bled out but didn't get quite enough vampire blood in exchange to become a true vampire. They were undead but rotting. They had very little mind, and only one idea in the world: to drink blood, which they usually did by eating as much of a human body as possible. They liked hearts.

This ghoul was a new one, about two weeks dead. It was male and looked as if it had been a body-builder, although by now it wasn't so much buff as puffed. Its body was swollen with the gas of decomposition. Its tongue and eyes were protruding, its cheeks were chipmunklike, and bloody fluid was leaking from its nose.

And of course it didn't smell good.

As Jez edged closer, she suddenly realized that the ghoul wasn't alone. She could now see around the foot of the bed, and there was a boy lying on the carpet, apparently unconscious. The boy had light hair and rumpled clothes, but Jez couldn't see his face. The ghoul was stooping over him, reaching for him with sausage-shaped fingers.

'I don't think so,' Jez told it softly. She could feel a dangerous smile settling on her face. She reached into her right boot and pulled out the dagger.

'What did you say?' Claire shouted from the other side of the door.

'Nothing, Claire. Just getting out my homework.' Jez

jumped onto the bed. The ghoul was very big – she needed all the height she could get.

The ghoul turned to face her, its lackluster bug-eyes on the dagger. It made a little hissing sound around its swollen tongue. Fortunately that was all the noise it could make.

Claire was rattling the door. 'Did you *lock* this? What are you doing in there?'

'Just studying, Claire. Go away.' Jez snapped a foot toward the ghoul, catching it under the chin. She needed to stun it and stake it fast. Ghouls weren't smart, but like the Energizer Bunny they kept going and going. This one could eat the entire Goddard family tonight and still be hungry at dawn.

The ghoul hit the wall opposite the bed. Jez jumped down, putting herself between it and the boy on the floor.

'What was that *noise*?' Claire yelled.

'I dropped a book.'

The ghoul swung. Jez ducked. There were giant blisters on its arms, the brownish colour of old blood.

It rushed her, trying to slam her against the chest of drawers. Jez flung herself backward, but she didn't have much room to manoeuvre. It caught her in the stomach with an elbow, a jarring blow.

Jez wouldn't let herself double over. She twisted and helped the ghoul in the direction it was already going, giving it impetus with her foot. It smacked into the window seat, face down.

'*What is going on in there?*'

'Just looking for something.' Jez moved before the ghoul could recover, jumping to straddle its legs. She grabbed its hair – not a good idea; it came off in clumps in her hand. Kneeling on it to keep it still, she raised the slim bamboo knife high and brought it down hard.

There was a puncturing sound and a terrible smell. The

knife had penetrated just under the shoulder blade, six inches into the heart.

The ghoul convulsed once and stopped moving.

Claire's voice came piercingly from behind the closed door. 'Mum! She's *doing* something in there!'

Then Aunt Nan's voice: 'Jez, are you all right?'

Jez stood, pulling her bamboo dagger out, wiping it on the ghoul's shirt. 'I'm just having a little trouble finding a ruler . . .' The ghoul was in a perfect position. She put her arms around its waist, ignoring the feeling of skin slipping loose under her fingers, and heaved it up onto the window seat. There weren't many human girls who could have picked up almost two hundred pounds of dead weight, and even Jez ended up a little breathless. She gave the ghoul a shove, rolling it over until it reached the open window, then she stuffed and manoeuvered it out. It fell heavily into a bed of impatiens, squashing the flowers.

Good. She'd haul it away later tonight and dispose of it.

Jez caught her breath, brushed off her hands, and closed the window. She drew the curtains shut, then turned. The fair-haired boy was lying perfectly still. Jez touched his back gently, saw that he was breathing.

The door rattled and Claire's voice rose hysterically. 'Mum, do you smell that *smell*?'

Aunt Nan called, 'Jez!'

'Coming!' Jez glanced around the room. She needed something . . . there. The bed.

Grabbing a handful of material near the head of the bed, she flipped comforter, blankets and sheets over so they trailed off the foot, completely covering the boy. She tossed a couple of pillows on top of the pile for good measure, then grabbed a ruler off the desk. Then she opened the door, leaned against the doorframe casually, and summoned her brightest smile.

'Sorry about that,' she said. 'What can I do for you?'

Claire and Aunt Nan just stared at her.

Claire looked like a rumpled, angry kitten. The fine dark hair that framed her face was ruffled; she was breathing hard, and her almond-shaped eyes were flashing sparks. Aunt Nan looked more worried and dismayed.

'Are you OK?' she said, leaning in slightly to try and get a look at Jez's room. 'We heard a lot of noise.'

And you'd have heard more earlier if you hadn't been watching TV. 'I'm fine. I'm great. You know how it is when you can't find something.' Jez lifted the ruler. Then she stepped back and opened the door father.

Aunt Nan's eyes widened as she took in the mess. 'Jez . . . this does not happen when you can't find a ruler. This looks like *Claire's* room.'

Claire made a choked sound of indignation. 'It does not. My room's *never* been this bad. And what's that *smell*?' She slipped by Aunt Nan and advanced on Jez, who sidestepped to keep her from getting to the pile of blankets.

Claire stopped dead anyway, her face wrinkling. She put a hand to cover her nose and mouth. 'It's *you*,' she said, pointing at Jez. '*You* smell like that.'

'Sorry.' It was true; what with all the contact she'd had with the ghoul, and the dirty knife in her boot, she was pretty ripe. 'I think I stepped in something on the way home.'

'I didn't smell anything when you came in,' Claire said suspiciously.

'And that's another thing,' Aunt Nan said. She had been glancing around the room, but there was nothing suspicious to see except the unusual clutter – the curtains hung motionless over the shut window; the pile of bedding on the floor was still. Now she turned to face Jez again. 'You didn't call to say you were going to miss dinner again. I need to know where you go after school, Jez. I need to know when you're going to be out late. It's common courtesy.'

'I know. I'll remember next time. I really will.' Jez said it as sincerely as possible, and in a tone she hoped would close the subject. She needed to get rid of these people and look at the boy under the blankets. He might be seriously hurt.

Aunt Nan was nodding. 'You'd better. And you'd better take a shower before you do anything else. Throw your clothes in the laundry room; I'll put them in the wash.' She made as if to kiss Jez on the cheek, but stopped, wrinkled her nose, and then just nodded again at her.

'And that's it? That's all?' Claire was looking at her mother in disbelief. 'Mum, she's *up* to something, can't you see that? She comes in late, smelling like dead skunk and sewage and I don't know what, and then she locks herself in and bangs around and lies, and all you're going to say is "Don't do it again"? She gets away with *everything* around here—'

'Claire, quit it. She said she was sorry. I'm sure she won't let it happen again.'

'If *I* did something like that you'd skin me, but, no, if Jez does it, it must be OK. Well, I'll tell you something else. She cut school today. She left before sixth period.'

'Is that true, Jez?' a new voice asked. Uncle Jim was standing in the doorway, pulling at his chin with long fingers. He looked sad.

It was true. Jez had left early to set up a trap for the vampire and shapeshifter. She looked at her uncle and made a regretful motion with her head and shoulders.

'Jez, you just can't *do* that. I'm trying to be reasonable, but this is only the second week of school. You can't start this kind of behaviour again. It can't be like last year.'

He thought. 'From now on, you leave your motorcycle at home. You drive to school and back with Claire, in the Audi.'

Jez nodded. 'OK, Uncle Jim,' she said out loud. Now go away, she added silently. Thin curls of anxiety were churning in her stomach.

'Thank you.' He smiled at her.

'See?' Claire jumped in, her voice hitting a note to shatter glass. 'This is just what I'm talking about! You never yell at her, either! Is it because you're afraid she'll run away, like she did from her dad's relatives? So everybody has to walk on eggshells around her because otherwise she'll just take off—'

'OK, that's it. I'm not listening to any more of this.' Aunt Nan waved a hand at Claire, then turned around to shoo Uncle Jim out of her path. 'I'm going to clean up the dinner table. If you two want to fight, do it quietly.'

'No, it's better if they do their homework,' Uncle Jim said, moving slowly. 'Both of you, do your homework, OK?' He looked at Jez in a way that was probably meant to be commanding, but came out wistful. 'And tomorrow come home on time.'

Jez nodded. Then both adults were gone, but Claire was staring after them. Jez couldn't be sure, but she thought there were tears in her eyes.

Jez felt a pang. Of course, Claire was dead on about the leeway Aunt Nan and Uncle Jim gave her. And of course, it *wasn't* fair to Claire.

I should say something to her. Poor little thing. She really feels bad . . .

But before she could open her mouth, Claire whirled around. The eyes that had been wet a moment ago were flashing.

'You just wait,' she said. 'They don't see through you,

but *I* do. You're up to something, and I'm going to find out what it is. *And don't think I can't do it.'*

She turned and stalked out the door.

Jez stood for an instant, speechless, then she blinked and closed the door. She locked it. And then for the first time since she'd seen the ghoul, she allowed herself to let out a long breath.

That had been close. And Claire was serious, which was going to be a problem. But Jez didn't have time to think about it now.

She turned the clock radio on her nightstand to a rock station. A loud one. Then she flipped the covers off the foot of the bed and knelt.

The boy was lying face down, with one arm stretched over his head. Jez couldn't see any blood. She took his shoulder and carefully rolled him over.

And stopped breathing.

'*Hugh.'*

CHAPTER 5

The boy's light hair was longish, falling over his forehead in disarray. He had a nice face, serious, but with an unexpected dimple in his chin that gave him a slightly mischievous look. His body was nicely muscled but compact; standing, Jez knew, he'd be no taller than she. There was a large bump coming up on his forehead, just under the falling hair. The ghoul had probably slammed him against something.

Jez jumped up and got a blue plastic cup full of water from her nightstand. She grabbed a clean T-shirt from the floor and dipped it into the water, then she gently brushed back the hair from the boy's forehead.

It was silky under her fingers. Even softer than she would have thought. Jez kept her face expressionless and began to wipe his face with the damp cloth.

He didn't stir. Jez's heart, which was already thumping distinctly, sped up. She took a deep breath and kept wiping.

Finally, although it probably didn't have anything to do with the water, the boy's dark eyelashes moved. He coughed, breathed, blinked, and looked at her.

Relief spread through Jez. 'Don't try to sit up yet.'

'That's what they all say,' he agreed, and sat up. He put a hand to his head and groaned. Jez steadied him.

'I'm fine,' he said. 'Just tell the room to stop moving.' He looked around the room, blinked again and suddenly seemed to focus. He grabbed her arm, his eyes wide. 'Something followed me—'

'A ghoul. It's dead.'

He let out his breath. Then he smiled wryly. 'You saved my life.'

'And I don't even charge,' Jez said, embarrassed.

'No, I mean it.' His smile faded and he looked straight at her. 'Thank you.'

Jez could feel heat trying to rise to her face, and she had a hard time holding his gaze. His eyes were grey and so intense – fathomless. Her skin was tingling.

She looked away and said evenly, 'We should get you to a hospital. You might have a concussion.'

'No. I'm OK. Let me just see if I can stand up.' When she opened her mouth to protest, he added, 'Jez, you don't know why I'm here. It can't wait.'

He was right; Jez had been so intent on getting him conscious that she hadn't even wondered what he was doing here. She looked at him for a moment, then nodded. She helped him up, and let go of his arm when she saw he could stand without falling over.

'See, I'm fine.' He took a few steps, then made a circuit of the room, loosening his muscles. Jez watched him narrowly, ready to grab him if he fell. But he walked steadily except for a slight limp.

And that wasn't from his encounter with the ghoul tonight, Jez knew. He'd had the limp from childhood, from when the werewolves took his family.

How he'd been able to get over that and join Circle Daybreak, Jez would never know.

He'd lost his parents almost as young as she had. He'd lost his two sisters and his brother, too. His entire family had been on a camping trip at Lake Tahoe, when in the middle of the night they'd been attacked by a pack of werewolves. Renegade 'wolves, hunting illegally because Night World law wouldn't let them kill as often as they liked.

Just like Jez's old gang.

The 'wolves had ripped through the Davis family's tents and killed the humans, one, two, three. Easy as that. The only one they left alive was seven-year-old Hugh, because he was too little to have much meat on his body. They had just settled down to eat the hearts and livers of their victims, when suddenly the one too little to be worth eating was dashing at them with a homemade torch constructed of kerosene-soaked underwear wrapped around a stick. He was also waving a silver cross on a chain the werewolves had torn from his sister's neck.

Two things werewolves don't like: silver and fire. The little boy was attacking with both. The 'wolves decided to kill him.

Slowly.

They almost did it. They managed to chew one of his legs almost off before a park ranger arrived, attracted by the spreading fire from the dropped torch.

The ranger had a gun, and the fire was getting out of control. The 'wolves left.

Hugh almost died of blood loss on the way to the hospital.

But he was a tough kid. And a very smart one. He didn't even try to explain to anybody what he'd been doing with the silver necklace. He knew they would never believe him if he said he'd suddenly remembered a bunch of past lives, including one where he'd seen a werewolf killed.

Hugh Davis was an Old Soul.

And a *wakened* Old Soul, which was even more rare. It scared Jez a little. He was human and she was from the Night World, but she didn't pretend to understand the magic that brought some humans back again and again, reincarnating them in new bodies. Letting them remember all their past lifetimes, making them smarter and more clear-headed every time they were born.

In Hugh's case, also gentler every time. In spite of the attack on his family, when he got out of the hospital the first thing he did was try to find some Night People. He knew they weren't all bad. He knew some of them would help him stop the werewolves from hurting anyone else.

Fortunately, the first people he found were from Circle Daybreak.

Circles were witch organisations, but Circle Daybreak was for humans and vampires and shapeshifters and werewolves, too. It was an underground society, as secret within the Night World as the Night World was secret within the human world. It went against the most basic tenets of Night World law: that humans were not to be told about the Night World, and that Night People shouldn't fall in love with humans. Circle Daybreak was fighting to unite everybody, to stop the killings, and to bring peace between the races.

Jez wished them luck.

She suddenly realized that Hugh had stopped walking and was looking at her. She blinked and focussed, furious with herself for her slip in concentration. As a huntress – of vampires or anything else – you stayed alert all the time, or you were dead.

'You were miles away,' Hugh said softly. His grey eyes were calm but intense as always. That look Old Souls get when they're reading you, Jez thought.

She said, 'Sorry. Um, do you want some ice for that bump?'

'No, I like it. I'm thinking of getting one on the other side, to match.' He sat on the bed, serious again. 'Really, I've got some stuff to explain to you, and it's going to take a while.'

Jez didn't sit. 'Hugh, I think you need it. And I need to take a shower or my aunt will get suspicious about what I'm doing in here for so long. Besides, the smell is driving me crazy.' Although she couldn't use her vampire powers without bringing on the bloodlust, her senses were still much more acute than a human's.

'Eau de Ghoul? And I was just starting to enjoy it.' Hugh nodded at her, switching from gentle humour to gentle gravity as always. 'You need to do what will keep your cover here. I shouldn't be so impatient.'

Jez took the fastest shower of her life, then dressed in clean clothes she'd brought to the bathroom. As she returned carrying a glassful of ice from the kitchen and a washcloth, she saw that Claire's bedroom door was ajar and Claire was watching her narrowly.

Jez raised the glass in a mock toast, and slipped into her own bedroom.

'Here.' She made an ice pack and handed it to Hugh. He accepted it docilely. 'Now, what is it that's so urgent? And how come you're so popular with ghouls all of a sudden?'

Instead of answering, Hugh looked into a middle distance. He was bracing himself for something. Finally he lowered the ice pack and looked straight at her.

'You know I care about you. If anything happened to you, I don't know what I'd do. And if anything happened because of *me* . . .' He shook his head.

Jez told her heart to get down where it belonged. It was

pounding in her throat, choking her. She kept her voice flat as she said, 'Thanks.'

Something like hurt flashed in his eyes and was gone instantly. 'You don't think I mean it.'

Jez still spoke flatly, in a clipped, hurried voice. She wasn't good at talking about emotional stuff. 'Hugh, look. You were my first human friend. When I came to live here, nobody at Circle Daybreak would have anything to do with me. I don't blame them – not after the things my gang did to humans. But it was hard because they wouldn't even talk to me, much less trust me, and they wouldn't believe I wanted to help them. And then you showed up that day after school. And you *did* talk to me—'

'And I did trust you,' Hugh said. 'And I still do.' He looked distant again. 'I thought you were the saddest person I'd ever seen, and the most beautiful – and the bravest. I knew you wouldn't betray Circle Daybreak.'

And that's why I love you, Jez thought before she could stop herself. It was easier to live with if she didn't put it into words.

Because it was hopeless, of course. You couldn't hang on to an Old Soul. Nobody could – not unless they were one of those tiny fraction of people who were soulmates. Wakened Old Souls were too . . . old. They knew too much, had seen too much to get attached to any one person.

Much less a person who was tainted with vampire blood.

So all she said was 'I know. That's why I work with Circle Daybreak. Because *you* convinced them I wasn't some kind of spy for the Night World. I owe you, Hugh. And – I believe you care about me.' Because you care about everybody, she added silently.

Hugh nodded, but he didn't look any happier. 'It's about something dangerous. Something I don't want to ask you to do.' He dug into his jeans pocket and came up with a thick packet of what looked like folded newspaper articles. He held it out to her.

Jez took it, frowned, then paged through the first few articles. Headlines jumped out at her.

' "Four-year-old dies in coyote attack." "Record heatwave in Midwest; hundreds hospitalized." "Mother confesses: I killed my babies." "Mystery virus erupts in eastern U.S.: Scientists baffled." '

There were lots more, but she didn't look at them. She looked at Hugh, her eyebrows drawn together. 'Thanks for sharing this. Am I supposed to fight the coyote or the virus?'

His lips smiled, but his eyes were bottomless and frighteningly sad. 'Nobody can fight what's happening – at least not in the ordinary way. And all that's just the beginning.'

'Of *what*?' She loved Hugh, but sometimes she wanted to strangle him. Old Souls loved being mysterious.

'Have you noticed the weather lately? It's either floods or droughts. Record cold days in winter, record heat in the summer. Record number of hurricanes and tornadoes. Record snowfall and hail. It just gets weirder and weirder every year.'

'Well – sure.' Jez shrugged. 'They talk about it on TV all the time. But it doesn't mean any—'

'And the earth's being disturbed, too. Earthquakes. Volcanoes. Last year four dormant volcanoes erupted and there were dozens of major quakes.'

Jez narrowed her eyes. 'OK . . .'

'And there's another weird thing, even though it's not as obvious. You have to kind of dig a little to get to the statistics. There's been an increase in animal attacks all over the world. All kinds of animals.' He tapped the pile of newspaper articles. 'This coyote attack – a couple of years ago you never heard about coyotes killing kids. Just like you never heard of mountain lions attacking adults. But now it's happening, and it's happening everywhere.'

Prickles of unease were going up Jez's arms. It was true, what Hugh was saying. Not that she'd paid much attention to the human news when she was a vampire – but it did seem as if animal attacks were getting more frequent.

'A bunch of elephants stomped their trainers last year,' she said slowly.

'Dog attacks are up four hundred percent,' Hugh said. 'According to the California state police. In New Mexico there's an epidemic of rabid bats. In Florida they've had *seven* tourists killed by alligators since last January – and believe me, that information was hard to find. Nobody wanted to report it.'

'I bet.'

'Then there are the insects. We're seeing more and more people get attacked by them. Killer bees. Fire ants. Tiger mosquitoes – and, no, I'm not joking. They're for real, and they carry dengue fever, a really nasty disease.'

'Hugh . . .'

'Which brings me to diseases. You have to have noticed that. There are new diseases popping up all over. Ebola. Mad cow disease. That flesh-eating bacteria. Hanta viruses. Lassa. Crimean-Congo haemorrhagic fever. You bleed from your ears and nose and mouth and into the whites of your eyes—'

Jez opened her mouth to say 'Hugh' again, but he was racing on, his chest rising and falling quickly, his grey eyes almost feverish.

'And they're resistant to antibiotics the same way that the insects are resistant to pesticides. They're all *mutating*. Changing. Getting stronger and more deadly. And—'

'Hugh.' She got it in while he took a breath.

'—there's a hole in the ozone.' He looked at her. 'What?'

'What does it all *mean*?'

'It means that things are changing. Spiraling out of control. Heading for . . .' He stopped and looked at her. 'Jez, it's not those things themselves that are the problem. It's what's behind them.'

'And what *is* behind them?'

Hugh said simply, 'The Old Powers are rising.'

Chills swept over Jez. The Old Powers. The Ancient Magic that had controlled the universe in the old days of the Night World. No one could see or know the Old Powers; they were forces of nature, not people. And they had been sleeping like giant dragons for thousands of years ever since humans had gained control of the world. If they were waking up again now . . .

If magic was coming back again, everything would change.

'It shows in different weird ways,' Hugh went on. 'Night People are getting more powerful. Lots of them have noticed it. And they say the soulmate principle is back.'

The soulmate principle. The idea that for every person there was one destined soulmate, one true love, and that the two souls were bound for eternity. Jez lifted her shoulders and dropped them without meeting Hugh's eyes. 'Yeah, I heard. Don't believe it, though.'

'I've seen it,' Hugh said, and for a moment Jez's heart stopped. Then it started again as he continued, 'In other people, I mean. I've seen people our age who found their soulmate, and it's really true; you can see it in their eyes. The Old Powers really *are* rising, Jez . . . for good and for evil. That's what's behind all these other changes.'

Jez sat very still. 'And so what happens if they keep rising?'

'What happens is . . .' Hugh paused and then looked at her. 'It means a time of darkness is coming,' he said simply.

'A time—?'

'Of serious darkness. The worst. We're talking the end of the world, here.'

Jez could feel gooseflesh on the back of her neck, where her wet hair touched her skin. She might have been tempted to laugh if it were anybody else telling her this. But it was Hugh, and he wasn't joking. She had no desire to laugh.

'But then it's all over,' she said. 'There's nothing we can do. How can anybody stop the end of the world?'

'Well.' He ran a quick hand through his hair, pushing it off his forehead. 'That's why I'm here. Because I'm hoping *you* can.'

CHAPTER
6

'Me?'

Hugh nodded.

'*I'm* supposed to stop the end of the world? *How?*'

'First, I ought to tell you that it's not just me that believes all this about the millennium. It's not even Circle Daybreak that believes it. It's the Night World Council, Jez.'

'The joint Council? Witches *and* vampires?'

Hugh nodded again. 'They had a big meeting about it this summer. And they dug up some old prophecies about what's going to happen this time.'

'Like?'

Hugh looked slightly self-conscious. 'Here's one. It used to rhyme in the original, I think, but this is the translation.' He took a breath and quoted slowly:

'In blue fire, the final darkness is banished.
In blood, the final price is paid.'

Great, Jez thought. Whose blood? But Hugh was going on.

'Four to stand between the light and the shadow,
Four of blue fire, power in their blood.
Born in the year of the blind Maiden's vision;
Four less one and darkness triumphs.'

Jez blinked slowly. 'What's blue fire?'

'Nobody knows.'

' "Four to stand between the light and the shadow . . ."
Meaning to hold off the end of the world?'

'That's what the Council thinks. They think it means
that four people have been born, four Wild Powers who're
going to be instrumental in whatever's coming, whatever
battle or disaster that's going to destroy us. Those four can
stop the end of the world – but only if all of them fight
together.'

' "Four less one and darkness triumphs," ' Jez said.

'Right. And that's where you come in.'

'Sorry, I don't think I'm one of them.'

Hugh smiled. 'That's not what I meant. The fact is,
somebody around here has already reported finding a
Wild Power. Circle Daybreak intercepted a message from
him to the Council saying that he'll hand the Wild Power
over to them if they make it worth his while. Otherwise
he'll just sit tight until they're desperate enough to agree
to his terms.'

Jez had a sinking feeling. She said one word. 'Who?'

Hugh's expression was knowing and regretful. 'It's one
of your old gang, Jez. Morgead Blackthorn.'

Jez shut her eyes.

Yeah, that *sounded* like Morgead, trying to shake down
the Night World Council. Only *he* was crazy and nervy
enough to do that. He was stubborn, too – perfectly
capable of letting disaster come if he didn't get his way.
But of all the people in the world, why did it have to be

him? And how had he found a Wild Power, anyway?

Hugh was speaking again softly. 'You can see why we need you. Somebody has to get to him and find out who the Wild Power is – and you're the only one who stands a chance of doing that.'

Jez pushed hair off her face and breathed slowly, trying to think.

'I don't need to tell you how dangerous it is,' Hugh said, looking into the distance again. 'And I don't want to ask you to do it. In fact, if you're smart, you'll tell me to get lost right now.'

Jez couldn't tell him to get lost. 'What I don't understand is why we can't just let the Council take care of it. They'll want the Wild Powers *bad*, and they have a lot more resources.'

Hugh glanced back at her, startled. His grey eyes were wide with an expression that Jez had never seen before. Then he smiled, and it was an incredibly sad smile.

'That's just what we can't do. You're right, the Council wants the Wild Powers. But not so they can fight the end of the world. Jez . . . they only want them so they can kill them.'

That was when Jez realized what his expression was. It was gentle regret for innocence – *her* innocence.

She couldn't believe how stupid she had been.

'Oh, Goddess,' she said slowly.

Hugh nodded. 'They want it to happen. At least the vampires do. If the human world ends – well, that's their chance, isn't it? For thousands of years the Night People have had to hide, to live in the shadows while the humans spread all over the world. But the Council wants that to change.'

The reason Jez had been so slow was that it was hard for her to imagine anybody actually wanting to bring on the

Apocalypse. But of course it made sense. 'They're willing to risk being destroyed themselves,' she whispered.

'They figure that whatever happens, it'll be worse on the humans, since the humans don't know it's coming. Hell, some of the Night People think *they're* what's coming. Hunter Redfern is saying that vampires are going to wipe out and enslave the humans and that after that the Night World is going to reign.'

Jez felt a new chill. Hunter Redfern. Her ancestor, who was over five hundred years old but looked about thirty. He was bad, and he practically ran the Council.

'Great,' she muttered. 'So my family's going to destroy the world.'

Hugh gave her a bleak smile. 'Hunter says the Old Powers are rising to make vampires stronger so they can take over. And the scary thing is, he's right. Like I said before, the Night People *are* getting stronger, developing more powers. Nobody knows why. But most of the vampires on the Council seem to believe Hunter.'

'So we don't have much time,' Jez said. 'We have to get the Wild Power *before* Morgead makes a deal with the Night World.'

'Right. Circle Daybreak is fixing up a safe place to keep the Wild Powers until we get all four. And the Council knows we're doing it – that's probably why that ghoul was following me. They're watching us. I'm just sorry I led it here,' he added absently, with a worried look around the room.

'Doesn't matter. He's not telling anybody anything.'

'No. Thanks to you. But we'll meet someplace different next time. I can't endanger your family.' He looked back at her. 'Jez, if the Night World manages to kill even one of the Wild Powers – well, if you believe the prophecy, it's all over.'

Jez understood now. She still had questions, but they could wait. One thing was clear in her mind.

'I'll do it. I have to.'

Hugh said very quietly, 'Are you sure?'

'Well, *somebody* has to. And you were right; I'm the only one who can handle Morgead.'

The truth was that she thought nobody could handle Morgead – but she certainly had a better chance than any Circle Daybreaker. Of course, she wouldn't survive the assignment. Even if she managed to steal the Wild Power out from under Morgead's nose, he'd hunt her down and kill her for it.

That was irrelevant.

'He hates me, and I hate him, but at least I *know* him,' she said out loud.

There was a silence and she realized that Hugh was looking at her oddly. 'You think he hates you?'

'Of course. All we ever did was fight.'

Hugh smiled very faintly – an Old Soul look. 'I see.'

'What's that supposed to mean?'

'It means – I don't think he hates you, Jez. Maybe he has strong emotions for you, but from what I've heard I don't think hate is one of them.'

Jez shook her head. 'You don't understand. He was always gunning for me. And if he found out I'm half human – well, that would be the end. He hates humans worse than anything. But I think I can fool him for as long as it takes to get the Wild Power.'

Hugh nodded, but he didn't look happy. His eyes were bruised and tired. 'If you can pull it off, you'll save a lot of lives.'

He knows, too, Jez thought. That I'll die doing this.

It was some comfort that he cared – and more comfort that he didn't understand *why* she was doing it. Sure, she wanted to save lives. But there was something else.

The Council had tried to mess with Hugh. They'd sent a stinking *ghoul* after him. They would probably send something different tomorrow – certainly, they'd keep trying to kill him.

And for that, Jez was going to wipe the floor with them. Hugh wasn't any kind of fighter. He couldn't defend himself. He shouldn't be a target.

She realized that Hugh was still looking at her, with pain in his eyes. She smiled to show him that she wasn't afraid of dying.

'It's a family affair,' she told him – and that was true, too. 'Hunter's my great-great-great-great-great-grandfather. It's only right that I stop him. And if anything happens to me – well, one Redfern less is probably a blessing to the world.'

And that was the last part of the truth. She came from a tainted family. No matter what she did, who she saved, or how hard she tried, there would always be vampire blood running in her veins. She was a potential danger to humanity by her very existence.

But Hugh was looking horrified. 'Don't you ever say that.' He stared at her for another moment and then took her by the shoulders, squeezing. 'Jez, you're one of the best people I know. What you did before last year is—'

'Is part of me,' Jez said. She was trying not to feel his warm grip through her T-shirt, trying not to show that his little squeeze sent a shock through her entire body. 'And nothing can change that. I know what I am.'

Hugh shook her slightly. 'Jez—'

'And right now, I have to get rid of that ghoul. And you'd better be getting home.'

For a moment she thought he was going to shake her again; then he slowly let go of her. 'You're officially accepting the assignment?' The way he said it sounded as if he were giving her one last chance not to.

'Yes.'

He nodded. He didn't ask *how* she planned on getting back into a gang that she'd abandoned, or getting information from Morgead, who hated her. Jez knew why. He simply trusted that she could do it.

'When you know something, call this number.' He dug in a different pocket and handed her a square of paper like a business card. 'I'll give you a location where I can meet you – someplace away from here. We shouldn't talk about anything on the phone.'

Jez took the card. 'Thanks.'

'Please be careful, Jez.'

'Yes. Can I keep the articles?'

He snorted. 'Sure.' Then he gave her one of those sad Old-Soul smiles. 'You probably don't need them, though. Just look around. Watch the news. You can see it all happening out there.'

'We're going to stop it,' Jez said. She reconsidered. 'We're going to try.'

Jez had a problem the next morning. The problem was Claire.

They were supposed to drive to school together, to ensure that Jez didn't cut school. But Jez had to cut school to go find Morgead. She didn't want to imagine the kind of trouble that was going to get her in with Uncle Jim and Aunt Nanami – but it was crucial to get to Morgead as soon as possible. She couldn't afford to waste time.

At the first major stop light – and there weren't a lot of them in Clayton – she smacked her forehead with her palm.

'I forgot my chemistry book!' She unfastened her seat

belt and slid out of the Audi just as the light turned green. 'You go ahead!' she shouted to Claire, slamming the door and leaning in the open window. 'I'll catch up to you.'

Claire's expression showed her temperature was reaching the boiling point. 'Are you crazy? Get in; I'll drive back.'

'You'll be late. Go on without me.' She made a little fluttery encouraging motion with her fingers.

One of the three cars behind Claire honked.

Claire opened her mouth and shut it again. Her eyes were shooting sparks. 'You did this on purpose! I know you're up to something, Jez, and I'm going to find out—'

Honk. Honk.

Jez stepped back and waved goodbye.

And Claire drove off, as Jez had known she would. Claire couldn't stand the peer pressure of cars telling her to get moving.

Jez turned and began to jog for home, in a smooth, steady, ground-eating lope.

When she got there, she wasn't even breathing hard. She opened the garage and picked up a long, slim bundle that had been concealed in a corner. Then she turned to her bike.

Besides Hugh, it was the love of her life. A Harley. An 883 Sportster hugger. Just twenty-seven inches tall and eighty-seven inches long, a lean, light, mean machine. She loved its classic simplicity, its cold clean lines, its spare body. She thought of it as her steel and chrome thoroughbred.

Now she strapped the long bundle diagonally on her back, where it balanced nicely despite its odd size. She put on a dark full-face helmet and swung a leg over the motorcycle. A moment later she was roaring away, heading out of Clayton toward San Francisco.

She enjoyed the ride, even though she knew it might be her last one. Maybe because of that. It was a dazzling end-of-summer day, with a sky of September blue and a pure-white sun. The air that parted for Jez was warm.

How can people ride in cages? she thought, twisting the throttle to shoot past a station wagon. What good are cars? You're completely isolated from your surroundings. You can't hear or smell anything outside; you can't feel wind or power or a slight change in the temperature. You can't jump out to fight at an instant's notice. You certainly can't stake somebody at high speed while leaning out of a car window.

You could do it from a bike, though. If you were fast enough, you could skewer somebody as you roared by, like a knight with a lance. She and Morgead had fought that way once.

And maybe will again, she thought, and flashed a grim smile into the wind.

The sky remained blue as she continued west, instead of clouding up as she approached the ocean. It was so clear that from Oakland she could see the entire bay and the skyline of San Francisco. The tall buildings looked startlingly close.

She was leaving her own world and entering Morgead's.

It was something she didn't do often. San Francisco was an hour and fifteen minutes away from Clayton – assuming there was no traffic. It might as well have been in another state. Clayton was a tiny rural town, mostly cows, with a few decent houses and one pumpkin farm. As far as Jez knew, the Night World didn't know it existed. It wasn't the kind of place Night People cared about.

Which was why she'd managed to hide there for so long.

But now she was heading straight for the heart of the fire. As she crossed the Bay Bridge and reached the city, she was acutely aware of how vulnerable she was. A year ago Jez had broken the laws of the gang by disappearing. If any gang member saw her, they had the right to kill her.

Idiot. Nobody can recognize you. That's why you wear the full-face helmet. That's why you keep your hair up. That's why you don't custom-paint the bike.

She was still hyper-alert as she cruised the streets heading for one of the city's most unsavoury districts.

There. She felt a jolt at the sight of a familiar building. Tan, blocky, and unlovely, it rose to three storeys plus an irregular roof. Jez squinted up at the roof without taking off her helmet.

Then she went and stood casually against the rough concrete wall, near the rusty metal intercom. She waited until a couple of girls dressed like artists came up and got buzzed in by one of the tenants. Then she detached herself from the wall and calmly followed them.

She couldn't let Morgead know she was coming.

He'd kill her without waiting to ask questions if he got the jump on her. Her only chance was to jump him first, and then make him listen.

The building was even uglier inside than it was outside, with empty echoing stairwells and faceless industrial-sized hallways. But Jez found her heart beating faster and something like longing twisting in her chest. This place might be hideous, but it was also freedom. Each one of the giant rooms behind the metal doors was rented by somebody who didn't care about carpets and windows, but wanted a big empty space where they could be alone and do exactly what they wanted.

It was mostly starving artists here, people who needed large studios. Some of the doors were painted in gemlike colours and rough textures. Most had industrial-sized locks on them.

I don't miss it, Jez told herself. But every corner brought a shock of memory. Morgead had lived here for years, ever since his mother ran off with some vampire from Europe. And Jez had practically lived here, too, because it had been gang headquarters.

We had some good times . . .

No. She shook her head slightly to break off the thought and continued on her way, slipping silently through the corridors, going deeper and deeper into the building. At last she got to a place where there was no sound except the humming of the naked fluorescent lights on the ceiling. The walls were closer together here. There was a sense of isolation, of being far from the rest of the world.

And one narrow staircase going up.

Jez paused, listened a moment, then, keeping her eyes on the staircase, removed the long bundle from her back. She unwrapped it carefully, revealing a stick that was a work of art. It was just over four feet long and an inch in diameter. The wood was deep glossy red with irregular black markings that looked a little like tiger stripes or hieroglyphics.

Snakewood. One of the hardest woods in the world, dense and strong, but with just the right amount of resilience for a fighting stick. It made a striking and individual weapon.

There was one other unusual thing about it. Fighting sticks were usually blunt at either end, to allow the person holding it to get a grip. This one had one blunt end and one that tapered to an angled, narrow tip. Like a spear. The point was hard as iron and extremely sharp.

It could punch right through clothing to penetrate a vampire heart.

Jez held the stick in both hands for a moment, looking down at it. Then she straightened, and, holding it in a light grip ready for action, she began up the stairs.

'Ready or not, Morgead, here I come.'

CHAPTER

7

She emerged on the rooftop.

There was a sort of roof garden here – anyway, a lot of scraggly plants in large wooden tubs. There was also some dirty patio furniture and other odds and ends. But the main feature was a small structure that sat on the roof the way a house sits on a street.

Morgead's home. The penthouse. It was as stark and unlovely as the rest of the building, but it had a great view and it was completely private. There were no other tall buildings nearby to look down on it.

Jez moved stealthily toward the door. Her feet made no noise on the pitted asphalt of the roof, and she was in a state of almost painfully heightened awareness. In the old days sneaking up on another gang member had been a game. You got to laugh at them if you could startle them, and they got to be furious and humiliated.

Today it wasn't a game.

Jez started toward the warped wooden door – then stopped. Doors were trouble. Morgead would have been an idiot not to have rigged it to alert him to intruders.

Cat-quiet, she headed instead for a narrow metal ladder that led to the roof of the wooden structure. Now she was on the real top of the building. The only thing higher was a metal flagpole without a flag.

She moved noiselessly across the new roof. At the far edge she found herself looking four storeys straight down. And directly below her there was a window.

An open window.

Jez smiled tightly.

Then she hooked her toes over the four-inch lip at the edge of the roof and dropped gracefully forward. She grabbed the top of the window in middive and hung suspended, defying gravity like a bat attached upside down. She looked inside.

And there he was. Lying on a futon, asleep. He was sprawled on his back, fully clothed in jeans, boots, and a leather jacket. He looked good.

Just like the old days, Jez thought. When the gang would stay out all night riding their bikes and hunting or fighting or partying, and then come home in the morning to scramble into clothes for school. Except Morgead, who would smirk at them and then collapse. He didn't have parents or relatives to keep him from skipping.

I'm surprised he's not wearing his helmet, too, she thought, pulling herself back up to the roof. She picked up the fighting stick, manoeuvered it into the window, then let herself down again, this time hanging by her hands. She slid in without making a noise.

Then she went to stand over him.

He hadn't changed. He looked exactly as she remembered, except younger and more vulnerable because he was asleep. His face was pale, making his dark hair seem even darker. His lashes were black crescents on his cheeks.

Evil and dangerous, Jez reminded herself. It annoyed her that she *had* to remind herself of what Morgead was.

For some reason her mind was throwing pictures at her, scenes from her childhood while she was living here in San Francisco with her Uncle Bracken.

A five-year-old Jez, with shorter red hair that looked as if it had never been combed, walking with a little grimy-faced Morgead, hand in hand. An eight-year-old Jez with two skinned knees, scowling as a businesslike Morgead pulled wood splinters out of her legs with rusty tweezers. A seven-year-old Morgead with his face lit up in astonishment as Jez persuaded him to try the human thing called ice cream . . .

Stop it, Jez told her brain flatly. You might as well give up, because it's no good. We were friends then – well, some of the time – but we're enemies now. He's changed. I've changed. He'd kill me in a second now if it would suit his purpose. And I'm going to do what has to be done.

She backed up and poked him lightly with the stick. 'Morgead.'

His eyes flew open and he sat up. He was awake instantly, like any vampire, and he focussed on her without a trace of confusion. Jez had changed her grip on the stick and was standing ready in case he went straight into an attack.

But instead, a strange expression crossed his face. It went from startled recognition into something Jez didn't understand. For a moment he was simply staring at her, eyes big, chest heaving, looking as if he were caught in between pain and happiness.

Then he said quietly, 'Jez.'

'Hi, Morgead.'

'You came back.'

Jez shifted the stick again. 'Apparently.'

He got up in one motion. 'Where the hell have you *been*?'

Now he just looked furious, Jez noted. Which was easier to deal with, because that was how she remembered him.

'I can't tell you,' she said, which was perfectly true, and would also annoy the life out of him.

It did. He shook his head to get dark hair out of his eyes – it was always dishevelled in the morning, Jez remembered – and glared at her. He was standing easily: not in any attack posture, but with the relaxed readiness that meant he could go flying in any direction at any moment. Jez kept half her mind on watching his leg muscles.

'You can't *tell* me? You disappear one day without any kind of warning, without even leaving a *note* . . . you leave the gang and me and just completely vanish and nobody knows where to find you, not even your uncle . . . and now you reappear again and *you can't tell me where you were?*' He was working himself into one of his Extremely Excited States, Jez realized. She was surprised; she'd expected him to stay cooler and attack hard.

'What did you think you were doing, just cutting out on everybody? Did it ever occur to you that people would be *worried* about you? That people would think you were *dead*?'

It didn't occur to me that anyone would *care*, Jez thought, startled. Especially not you. But she couldn't say that. 'Look, I didn't mean to hurt anybody. And I can't talk about why I went. But I'm back now—'

'You can't just come back!'

Jez was losing her calm. Nothing was going the way she'd expected; the things she'd scripted out to say weren't getting said. 'I know I can't just come back—'

'Because it doesn't work that way!' Morgead was pacing now, tossing hair out of his eyes again as he turned to glare at her. 'Blood in, blood out. Since you're apparently not dead, you abandoned us. You're not allowed to do that! And you certainly can't expect to just walk back in and become my second again—'

'I *don't*!' Jez yelled. She had to shut him up. 'I have no intention of becoming your second-in-command!' she said when he finally paused. 'I came to challenge you as leader.'

Morgead's jaw dropped.

Jez let her breath out. That wasn't exactly how she'd planned to say it. But now, seeing his shock, she felt more in control. She leaned casually against the wall, smiled at him, and said smoothly, 'I was leader when I left, remember.'

'You . . . have got to be . . . joking.' Morgead stared at her. 'You expect to waltz back in here as *leader*?'

'If I can beat you. I think I can. I did it once.'

He stared for another minute, seeming beyond words. Then he threw back his head and laughed.

It was a scary sound.

When he looked at her again, his eyes were bright and hard. 'Yeah, you did. I've gotten better since then.'

Jez said three words. 'So have I.'

And with that, everything changed. Morgead shifted position – only slightly, but he was now in a fighting stance. Jez felt adrenaline flow through her own body. The challenge had been issued and accepted; there was nothing more to say. They were now facing each other ready to fight.

And this she could deal with. She was much better at fighting than at playing with words. She knew Morgead in this mood; his pride and his skill had been questioned and he was now absolutely determined to win. This was very familiar.

Without taking his eyes from her, he reached out and

picked a fighting stick from the rack behind him.

Japanese oak, Jez noted. Heavy, well-seasoned, resilient. Good choice.

The fire-hardened end was very pointy.

He wouldn't try to use that first, though. First, he would go for disarming her. The simplest way to do this was to break the wrist of her dominant hand. After that he'd go for critical points and nerve centres. He didn't play around at this.

A minute change in Morgead's posture alerted her, and then they were both moving.

He swung his stick up and down in a perfect arc, aiming for her right wrist. Jez blocked easily with her own stick and felt the shock as wood clashed with wood. She instantly changed her grip and tried for a trap, but he whipped his stick out of the way and was facing her again as if he'd never moved in the first place.

He smiled at her.

He's right. He's gotten better. A small chill went through Jez, and for the first time she worried about her ability to beat him.

Because I have to do it without *killing* him, she thought. She wasn't at all sure he had the same concern about not killing her.

'You're so predictable, Morgead,' she told him. 'I could fight you in my sleep.' She feinted toward his wrist and then tried to sweep his legs out from underneath him.

He blocked and tried for a trap. 'Oh, yeah? And you hit like a four-year-old. You couldn't take me down if I stood here and let you.'

They circled each other warily.

The snakewood stick was warm in Jez's hands. It was funny, some distant part of her mind thought irrelevantly, how the most humble and lowly of human weapons was the most dangerous to vampires.

But it was also the most versatile weapon in the world. With a stick, unlike a knife or gun or sword, you could fine-tune the degree of pain and injury you caused. You could disarm and control attackers, and – if the circumstances required it – you could inflict pain without permanently injuring them.

Of course if they were vampires, you could also *kill* them, which you couldn't do with a knife or gun. Only wood could stop the vampire heart permanently, which was why the fighting stick was the weapon of choice for vampires who wanted to hurt each other . . . and for vampire hunters.

Jez grinned at Morgead, knowing it was not a particularly nice smile.

Her feet whispered across the worn oak boards of the floor. She and Morgead had practised here countless times, measuring themselves against each other, training themselves to be the best. And it had worked. They were both masters of this most deadly weapon.

But no fight had ever mattered as much as this one.

'Next you're going to try for a head strike,' she informed Morgead coolly. 'Because you always do.'

'You think you know everything. But you don't know me anymore. I've changed,' he told her, just as calmly – and went for a head strike.

'Psyche,' he said as she blocked it and wood clashed with a sharp *whack*.

'Wrong.' Jez twisted her stick sharply, got leverage on his, and whipped it down, holding it against his upper thighs. 'Trap.' She grinned into his face.

And was startled for a moment. She hadn't been this close to him in a long time. His eyes – they were *so* green, gem-coloured, and full of strange light.

For just an instant neither of them moved; their weapons down, their gazes connected. Their faces were so close their breath mingled.

Then Morgead slipped out of the trap. 'Don't try *that* stuff,' he said nastily.

'What stuff?' The moment her stick was free of his, she snapped it up again, reversing her grip and thrusting toward his eyes.

'You know what stuff!' He deflected her thrust with unnecessary force. 'That "I'm Jez and I'm so wild and beautiful" stuff. That "Why don't you just drop your stick and let me hit you because it'll be fun" stuff.'

'Morgead . . . what are you . . . talking about?' In between the words she attacked, a strike to his throat and then one to his temple. He blocked and evaded – which was just what she wanted. Evasion. Retreat. She was crowding him into a corner.

'That's the only way you won before. Trying to play on people's feelings for you. Well, it won't work anymore!' He countered viciously, but it didn't matter. Jez blocked with a whirlwind of strikes of her own, pressing him, and then he had no choice but to retreat until his back was against the corner.

She had him.

She had no idea what he meant about playing on people's feelings, and she didn't have time to think about it. Morgead was dangerous as a wounded tiger when he was cornered. His eyes were glowing emerald green with sheer fury, and there was a hardness to his features that hadn't been there last year.

He does hate me, Jez thought. Hugh was wrong. He's hurt and angry and he absolutely *hates* me.

The textbook answer was to use that emotion against him, to provoke him and get him so mad that he gave her an opening. Some instinct deep inside Jez was worried about that, but she didn't listen.

'Hey, all's fair, right?' she told him softly. 'And what do you mean, it won't work? I've got you, haven't I?' She flashed out a couple of quick attacks, more to keep him occupied than anything else. 'You're caught, and you're going to have to let down your guard sometime.'

The green eyes that had been luminous with fury suddenly went cold. The colour of glacier ice. 'Unless I do something unexpected,' he said.

'Nothing you do is unexpected,' she said sweetly.

But her mind was telling her that provoking him had been a mistake. She had hit some nerve, and he was stronger than he'd been a year ago. He didn't lose his temper under pressure the way he'd used to. He just got more determined.

Those green eyes unnerved her.

Move in hard, she thought. All out. Go for a pressure point. Numb his arm—

But before she could do anything, a wave of Power hit her.

It sent her reeling.

She'd never felt anything exactly like it. It came from Morgead, a shockwave of telepathic energy that struck her like a physical thing. It knocked her back two steps and made her struggle for balance. It left the air crackling with electricity and a faint smell of ozone.

Jez's mind spun.

How had he *done* that?

'It's not hard,' Morgead said in a calm, cold voice that went with his eyes. He was out of the corner by now, of course. For a moment Jez thought he was reading her thoughts, but then she realized her question must be written all over her face. 'It's something I discovered after you left,' he went on. 'All it takes is practice.'

If you're telepathic, Jez thought. Which I'm not anymore.

The Night People are getting stronger, developing more powers, she thought. Well, Hugh had been right on that one.

And she was in trouble now.

Whack! That was Morgead going for a side sweep. He'd noticed her lack of balance. Jez countered automatically, but her head wasn't clear and her body was ringing with pain. He'd shaken her, distracted her.

'As you said, all's fair,' Morgead said, with a small, cold smile on his lips. 'You have your weapons. I have mine.'

And then he threw another of those shockwaves at her. Jez was better braced for it now, but it still rocked her on her feet, took her attention off her weapon –

Just long enough for her to screw up and let him in.

He drove upward to catch her stick from below. Then he twisted, sweeping her stick in a circle, forcing her off balance again, trying to topple her backward. As Jez fought to recover, he struck to her elbow. Hard.

Wham!

It was a different sound from the crisp *whack* when wood hit wood. This was softer, duller, the sound of wood hitting flesh and bone.

Jez heard her own involuntary gasp of pain.

Fire shot up her arm, into her shoulder, and for a moment she lost her grip on the stick with her right hand. She forced her fingers to close on it again, but they were numb. She couldn't feel what she was holding.

She couldn't block properly with one arm useless.

And Morgead was advancing, that deadly cold light in his eyes. Absolutely merciless. His movements were relaxed and easy; he knew exactly what he was doing now.

Two more whacks and he got through her guard again. The oak stick slammed into her ribs and she felt another wave of sickening pain. Grey dots danced in front of her eyes.

Fractured? Jez wondered briefly. She hoped not. Vampires could break each other's ribs in fun and know that everything would heal in a day or two. But Jez wouldn't recover like that. Morgead might kill her without even meaning to.

She couldn't let him keep striking her – but she couldn't retreat, either. If he got her into a corner, she'd be lost.

Whack-wham. He got her on the knee. Pain sparked up and down her leg, lighting every nerve. She had no choice but to back up. He was crowding her relentlessly, forcing her to the wall.

Morgead flashed a smile at her. Not the cold smile. This one was brilliant, and very familiar to Jez. It made him look devastatingly handsome, and it meant that he was in absolute command of the situation.

'You can give up anytime, now,' he said. 'Because I'm going to win and we both know it.'

CHAPTER

8

I can't lose this fight.

Suddenly that was the only thought in Jez's mind. She couldn't afford to be hurt or scared – or stupid. There was too much riding on it.

And since Morgead had the advantages of telepathy and strength on her at the moment, she was going to have to come up with some clever way to beat him.

It only took a moment to come up with a plan. And then Jez was carrying it out, every ounce of her concentration focussed on tricking him.

She stopped backing up and took a step sideways, deliberately putting herself in a position where she could make only a clumsy block. Then she gave him an opening, holding her stick awkwardly, its tip toward him but drooping too far down.

You see – it's my elbow, she thought to him, knowing he couldn't hear her, but willing him to take the bait. My elbow hurts too much; I'm distracted; the stick is no longer an extension of me. My right side is unprotected.

She was as good at it as any mother bird who pretends to have a broken wing to lure a predator away from her nest. And she could see the flash of triumph in Morgead's eyes.

That's it; don't waste time injuring me anymore . . . come in for the kill.

He was doing it. He'd stopped trying to get her into a corner. With his handsome face intent, his eyes narrowed in concentration, he was manoeuvering for a single decisive strike; a takedown to end the combat.

But as he raised his fighting stick to make it, Jez pulled her own stick back as if she were afraid to block, afraid of the jarring contact. This was the moment. If he caught on now, if he realized why she was positioning her stick this way, he'd never make the move she wanted him to. He'd go back to disarming her.

I'm too hurt to block properly; my arm's too weak to raise, she thought, letting her shoulders droop and her body sway tiredly. It wasn't hard to pretend. The pain in various parts of her body was real enough, and if she let herself *feel* it, it was very nearly disabling.

Morgead fell for it.

He made the strike she wanted; straight down. At that instant Jez slid her leading foot back, shifting just out of range. His stick whistled by her nose – missing. And then, before he could raise it again, while he was unguarded, Jez lunged. She put all the power of her body behind it, all her strength, slipping in between Morgead's arms and driving the stick to his midsection.

The air in his lungs exploded out in a harsh gasp and he doubled over.

Jez didn't hesitate. She had to finish him instantly, because in a second he would be fully recovered. By the time he was completely bent over she was already whipping her stick out and around to strike him behind the knee. Again, she put her whole weight behind the blow, following through to scoop him onto his back.

Morgead landed with a thud. Before he could move, Jez snap-kicked hard, catching his wrist and knocking his stick away. It clattered across the floor, oak on oak.

Then she held the pointed end of her own stick to his throat.

'Yield or die,' she said breathlessly, and smiled.

Morgead glared up at her.

He was even more breathless than she was, but there was nothing like surrender in those green eyes. He was *mad*.

'You tricked me!'

'All's fair.'

He just looked at her balefully from under the disordered hair that fell across his forehead. He was sprawled flat, long legs stretched out, arms flung to either side, with the tip of the snakewood fighting stick resting snugly in the pale hollow of his throat. He was completely at her mercy – or at least that was how it seemed.

Jez knew him better.

She knew that he never gave up, and that when he wasn't too mad to think, he was as smart as she was. And as sneaky. Right now the helpless act was about as sincere as her wounded bird routine.

So she was ready when he threw another blast of Power at her. She saw his pupils dilate like a cat's about to pounce, and she braced herself, shifting the stick minutely to push into his collarbone as she leaned forward.

The energy smashed into her. She could almost see it now, with the sixth sense that was part of her vampire heritage. It was like the downrush of a nuclear cloud, the part that went flowing along the ground, destroying everything in its path, spreading in a circle from the point of impact. It seemed to be faintly green, the colour of Morgead's eyes. And it packed quite a punch.

Jez gritted her teeth and hung on to the fighting stick, keeping it in place, letting the Power wash through her. It blew her hair back to stream in a hot wind and it seemed to last forever.

But finally it was over, and she was tingling with pain, with a metallic feeling in her teeth. And Morgead was still trapped.

He hissed at her, an amazingly reptilian sound.

'Got anything else?' Jez said, grinning down at him with narrowed eyes. Every bruise on her body hurt afresh in the aftermath of the blast – but she wasn't going to let him see that. 'No? I didn't think so.'

Morgead's upper lip lifted. 'Drop dead, Jezebel.'

Nobody was allowed to use her full name. 'You first, Morgy,' she suggested, and leaned harder on the stick.

The green eyes were beautifully luminous now, with sheer anger and hatred. 'So kill me,' he said nastily.

'Morgead—'

'It's the only way you're going to win. Otherwise I'm just going to lie here and wait to recharge. And when I've got enough Power I'll hit you again.'

'You never know when it's over, do you?'

'It's never over.'

Jez bit down on a rush of fury and exasperation. 'I didn't want to have to do this,' she snarled, 'but I will.'

She didn't kill him. Instead, she hurt him.

She grabbed his wrist and locked it, with her hand holding his and her stick on top of his wrist. She could use leverage here to cause severe pain – or to break the bone.

'Give up, Morgead.'

'Bite me.'

'I'm going to break your wrist.'

'Fine. I hope you enjoy it.' He kept glaring.

Like a little kid threatening to play on the freeway, Jez thought, and suddenly, inexplicably she was almost overcome by laughter. She choked it back.

She didn't *want* to break his wrist. But she knew she had to. And she had to do it soon, before he regenerated enough Power to hit her again. She couldn't take another of those blasts.

'Morgead, give!' She put enough pressure on his wrist that it really hurt.

He gave her the evil eye through dark lashes.

'You're so stubborn!' Jez put on more pressure.

She could tell it was hurting him. It was hurting *her* to keep the steady pressure up. Shooting stars of pain were zinging in her elbow.

Jez's heart was beating hard and her muscles were beginning to tremble with fatigue. This was much more difficult for both of them than a clean break would have been. And he was a vampire – his wrist would heal in a few days. She wouldn't be injuring him permanently.

I *have* to do it, she told herself. She tensed her muscles—

And Morgead took a little quick breath, an indrawn hiss of pain. For just an instant his green eyes lost their gemlike clarity, unfocussing a bit as he winced.

Jez let go of his wrist and collapsed to sit beside him, breathing hard.

You are *so* stupid, her mind told her. She shook her hair out and shut her eyes, trying to deal with the fury.

Beside her, Morgead sat up. 'What are you doing?'

'I don't know!' Jez snarled without opening her eyes. Being weak and idiotic, she answered herself. She didn't even know *why* she couldn't go through with it. She killed vampires – and less obnoxious ones than Morgead – all the time.

'I didn't yield,' Morgead said. His voice was flat and dangerous. 'So it's not over.'

'Fine, blast me.'

'I'm going to.'

'So do it.'

'What, you like it so much?'

Jez snapped. She grabbed her stick off the ground and turned to look at him for the first time since she'd sat down. 'Yeah, I love it, Morgead! I'm crazy about pain! So do it, and then I'm going to hit you over your thick head so hard you won't wake up until next week!' She might have said more, but the look in his eyes stopped her.

He was staring at her intently, not simply belligerently as she'd imagined. His green eyes were narrow and searching.

'You're just crazy period,' he said, sitting back, his gaze still probing. In a different tone he said softly, 'So why didn't you do it?'

Jez lifted her shoulders and dropped them. There was a pit of anger and misery in her stomach. 'I suppose because then I'd have to break every bone in your body, you jerk. You'd never give up, not with that new power you've got.'

'I could teach it to you. The others aren't strong enough to learn it, but you are.'

That forced a short laugh out of Jez. 'Yeah, right.' She shut her eyes briefly, wondering what Morgead would say if she were to tell him *why* she could never learn it.

He'd squash me like a bug, she thought, and laughed again.

'You laugh weird, Jez.'

'I have a twisted sense of humour.' She looked at him, blinking wetness out of her lashes. Where had that come from? There must be something in her eye. 'So. Want to start this fight again?'

He was staring at her hand gripping the snakewood stick. Jez tried to keep that hand steady, but she could feel the fine tremors in the muscles. She took a deep breath and clenched her teeth, making her gaze challenging.

I can fight again. I can do it because I have to, and this time I won't let any stupid sympathy get in the way of beating him. I *have* to win. Everything depends on it.

Morgead looked back at her face. 'No,' he said abruptly. 'We don't have to do it again. I yield.'

Jez blinked in shock. It was the last thing she'd expected. Morgead's expression was cold and unreadable.

Jez got mad.

'Why?' she blazed at him. 'Because I'm tired? Because you don't think I can take you?' She whipped the stick up, ready to split his stupid skull.

'Because you're crazy!' Morgead yelled. 'And because—' He stopped dead, looked furious. Then he said curtly, 'Because you won fair the first time.'

Jez stared at him.

Slowly she lowered the stick.

Morgead's expression was still distinctly unfriendly. But he'd just made an almost unbelievable admission.

'You just don't want me to whop you anymore,' she said.

He gave her a sideways look that would kill pigeons in midair.

Jez let out her breath. Her heart was just beginning to settle down and relief was spreading through her.

I did it. I really did it. I'm not going to die today.

'So it's over,' she said. 'I'm back in.'

'You're leader,' Morgead said sourly. 'Enjoy it, because I'm going to be right behind you every step, just waiting for my chance.'

'I wouldn't expect anything else,' Jez said. Then she

blinked. 'What are you doing?'

'What do you think?' His face set, his eyes on the far wall, Morgead was tugging his shirt away from his neck, and leaning his head back.

'I have no idea—' Then Jez realized. She went cold to the tips of her fingers.

I didn't think. I should have remembered, but I didn't, and I didn't plan for this . . .

'Blood in, blood out,' Morgead said shortly.

Why didn't I remember? Panic was stirring inside Jez. She couldn't see any way to get out of it.

For human gangs 'blood in, blood out' meant you got beat up when you were jumped in, and you didn't leave until you were dead. But for vampire gangs . . .

I can't bite him.

The most frightening thing was that something inside her wanted to do it. Her entire skin was tingling, and it suddenly seemed as if it was only yesterday that she'd had her last blood meal. She could remember exactly how it felt, sinking her teeth into smooth skin, piercing it easily, feeling the warm flow start.

And Morgead's blood would be dark and sweet and powerful. Vampire blood wasn't life-sustaining like human blood, but it was rich with the hidden promise of the Night World. And Morgead was one of the strongest vampires she'd ever met. His blood would be full of the mastery of that new attack, full of raw, vital young energy.

But I don't drink blood. I'm not a vampire! Not anymore.

Jez was trembling in shock. In the entire year since she'd stopped drinking blood, she'd never been so tempted. She had no idea why it had come on like this now, but it was almost out of her control. She pressed her tongue against one sharpening canine, trying to restrain it, trying to get some relief from the stress. Her upper and lower jaws were aching fiercely.

I can't. It's unthinkable. If I do it once, I'll never be able to stop. I'll become – what I was back then.

I'll be lost.

I can't – but I have to. I need to get back in the gang.

Morgead was staring at her. 'Now what's wrong with you?'

'I . . .' Jez was dizzy with fear and longing and the sense of danger. She couldn't see any way out . . .

And then she saw it.

'Here,' she said, unbuttoning the collar of her shirt. 'You bite me.'

'*What?*'

'It satisfies the requirement. Blood has to be spilled. And it's the leader who does it.'

'*You're* the leader, idiot.'

'Not until I'm back in the gang. And I'm not back in the gang until blood is spilled.'

He was staring at her, his eyes hard and demanding and not amused at all. 'Jez . . . that's ridiculous. *Why?*'

He was too smart. She didn't dare let him keep thinking about it. 'Because I think it's the proper procedure. And because – I overfed last night. I don't want anymore.' She stared straight into his eyes, not allowing a muscle to quiver. Trying to force her version of the truth into his brain.

Morgead blinked and looked away.

Jez allowed herself to relax minutely. She had one advantage over Morgead; there was no way he could even imagine her real motives. She just hoped he wouldn't discern the human flavour to her blood.

'If you won't tell me, I give up.' He shrugged. 'So, fine. If that's the way you want it . . .'

'It is.'

'Whatever.' He turned back to her and reached for her shoulders.

A new shock rocked Jez. Morgead never hesitated once he made up his mind, but this was a little unnerving. His grip was a bit too firm and authoritative; Jez felt out of control.

And how am I going to shield myself? she thought wildly, clamping down on a new wave of fear. He's already a powerful telepath and sharing blood increases rapport. How am I supposed to block *that*—?

Everything was happening too fast; she didn't have time to plan or think. All she could do was try not to panic as Morgead drew her close.

Jerk . . . he's had too much experience at this, part of her thought furiously. At subduing any kind of prey. At gentling scared girls – human girls.

He was holding her lightly and precisely; he was tilting her chin back. Jez shut her eyes and tried to blank her mind.

And now she could feel the warmth of his face near her skin; she could feel his breath on her throat. She knew his canine teeth were extending, lengthening, thinning to needle points. She tried to control her breathing.

She felt a swathe of warmth as he licked her throat once, and then a pain that made her own teeth ache. His teeth had pierced her skin, sharp as obsidian.

Then the release of blood flowing. Her life, spilling out. The instinctive twinge of fear Jez felt had nothing to do with him invading her mind.

No vampire liked to make this kind of submission. Letting someone drink your blood meant you were weaker, it meant you were willingly making yourself prey.

Everything inside Jez protested at just relaxing and letting Morgead do this.

And maybe that was the answer, she thought suddenly. A wall of turmoil to cover her thoughts. Pretend to be too agitated to let him make contact . . .

But his lips were surprisingly soft on her throat, and the pain was gone, and he was holding her more like a lover than like a predator. She could feel his mind all around her, strong, demanding.

He wasn't trying to hurt her. He was trying to make it not-terrible for her.

But I want it to be terrible. I don't want to feel like this . . .

It didn't matter. She felt as if she were being pulled by a swift current, dragged and tumbled into some place she had never been before. Sparkling lights danced behind her closed eyelids. Electricity crackled through her body.

And then she felt his mouth moving gently on her throat, and the world fell away . . .

CHAPTER 9

No. This can't be happening.

Jez had never felt anything like this before, but she knew instinctively that it was dangerous. She was being pulled into Morgead's *mind*. She could feel it surrounding her, enfolding her, a touch that was light but almost irresistible, that was trying to draw out the most secret part of herself.

And the most frightening thing was that Morgead wasn't doing it.

It was something outside both of them, something that was trying to mix them together like two pools of water being stirred. Jez could feel that Morgead was as startled and astonished as she was. The only difference was that he didn't seem to be resisting the force. He didn't seem terrified and unhappy about it, as Jez was. He seemed . . . exhilarated and wondering, like somebody skydiving for the first time.

That's because he's *crazy*, Jez thought dizzily. He loves danger and he enjoys courting death—

I enjoy you, a voice said in her mind.

Morgead's voice. Soft as a whisper, a feather-touch that shook Jez to her soul.

It had been so long since she'd heard that voice.

And he had heard *her*. Sharing blood made even humans telepathic. Jez hadn't been able to talk mentally since—

She managed to cut the thought off as panic surged through her. While one part of her mind gabbled desperately, 'He's here, he's here, he's *inside*, what are we going to do now?' another part threw up a smokescreen, flooding her thoughts with visions of mist and clouds.

There was something like a swift gasp from Morgead.

Jez, don't. Don't hide from me—

You're not allowed here, she snapped back, this time directing the thought straight at him. *Go away!*

I can't. For just a moment his mental voice sounded confused and scared. She hadn't realized Morgead could *be* confused and scared. *I'm not doing this. It's just – happening.*

But it shouldn't be happening, Jez thought, and she didn't know whether she was talking to him or just to herself. She was beginning to shake. She couldn't resist the pull that was trying to bring her soul to the surface and intermingle it with Morgead's – she *couldn't*. It was stronger than anything she'd ever experienced. But she knew that if she gave in, she was dead.

Don't be afraid. Don't, Morgead said in a voice she had never heard from him before. A voice of desperate gentleness. His mind was trying to wrap around hers protectively, like dark wings shielding her, touching her softly.

Jez felt her insides turn to water.

No. *No* . . .

Yes, Morgead's voice whispered.

She had to stop this – now. She had to break the contact. But although Jez could still feel her physical body, she seemed powerless to control it. She could sense Morgead's arms supporting her and his lips on her throat and she knew that he was still drinking. But she couldn't so much as move a finger to push him away. The muscles that she'd trained so ruthlessly to obey her under any circumstances were betraying her now.

She had to try another way.

This shouldn't be happening, she told Morgead, putting all the energy of her terror behind the thought.

I know. But that's because you're fighting it. We should be somewhere else by now.

Jez was exasperated. *Where else?*

I don't know, he said, and she could feel a tinge of sadness in his thought. *Some place – deeper. Where we'd really be together. But you won't open your mind . . .*

Morgead, what are you talking about? What do you think is going on?

He seemed genuinely surprised. *Don't you know? It's the soulmate principle.*

Jez felt the floor drop away beneath her.

No. That's not possible. That can't *be*. She wasn't talking to Morgead anymore; she was desperately trying to convince herself. I'm not soulmates with Morgead. I can't be. We hate each other . . . he hates me . . . all we ever do is fight . . .

He's impossible and dangerous and hotheaded and stubborn . . . he's crazy . . . he's angry and hostile . . . he's frustrating and infuriating and he loves to make me miserable . . .

And I don't even believe in soulmates. And even if I did, I wouldn't believe it could happen like this, just bang, out of the blue, like getting hit by a train when you're not looking, without any warning or even any attraction to the person beforehand . . .

But the very hysteria of her own thoughts was a bad sign. Anything that could tear away her self-control like this was powerful almost beyond imagination. And she could still feel it pulling at her, trying to strip off the layers of cloud she was hiding behind. It wanted Morgead to *see* her as she truly was.

And it was trying to show her Morgead. Flashes of his life, of himself. Glimpses that hit her and seemed to cut cleanly through her, leaving her gasping with their intensity.

A little boy with a mop of tousled dark hair and eyes like emerald, watching his mother walk out the door with some man – again. Going to play alone in the darkness, amusing himself. And then meeting a little redheaded girl, a girl with silvery-blue eyes and a flashing smile. And not being alone anymore. And walking on fences with her in the cool night air, chasing small animals, falling and giggling . . .

A slightly older boy with longer hair that fell around his face, uncared-for. Watching his mother walk out one last time, never to come back. Hunting for food, sleeping in an empty house that got messier and messier. Learning to care for himself. Training himself. Getting harder, in mind and body, seeing a sullen expression when he looked in the mirror . . .

A boy even older watching humans, who were weak and silly and short-lived, but who had all the things he didn't have. Family, security, food every night. Watching the Night People, the elders, who felt no responsibility to help an abandoned vampire child . . .

I never knew, Jez thought. She still felt dizzy, as if she couldn't get enough air. The images were dazzling in their clarity and they tore at her heart.

A boy who started a gang to create a family, and who went first to the little girl with red hair. The two of them grinning wickedly, running wild in the streets, finding others. Collecting kids the adults couldn't control or wouldn't miss. Walking around the worst parts of town, unafraid – because they had one another now.

The images were coming faster, and Jez could hardly keep up with them.

Dashing through the metal scrap yard . . . with Jez . . . Hiding under a fish-smelling wharf . . . from Jez . . . His first big kill, a stag in the hills of San Rafael . . . and Jez there to share the hot blood that warmed and intoxicated and brought life all at once. Fear and happiness and anger and arguments, hurt and sadness and exasperation – but always with Jez interwoven into the fabric. She was always there in his memories, fire-coloured hair streaming behind her, heavy-lashed eyes snapping with challenge and excitement. She was everything bright and eager and brave and honest. She was haloed with flame.

I didn't know . . . how could I know? How could I realize I meant so much to him . . . ?

And who would have thought it would mean so much to her when she found out? She was stunned, overcome – but something inside her was singing, too.

She was *happy* about it. She could feel something bubbling up that she hadn't even realized was there; a wild and heady delight that seemed to shoot out to the palms of her hands and the soles of her feet.

Morgead, she whispered with her mind.

She could sense him, but for once he didn't answer. She felt his sudden fear, his own desire to run and hide. He hadn't meant to show her these things. They were being forced out of him by the same power that was dragging at Jez.

I'm sorry. I didn't mean to look, she thought to him. *I'll go away . . .*

No. Suddenly he wasn't hiding anymore. *No, I don't want you to go. I want you to stay.*

Jez felt herself flow toward him, helplessly. The truth was that she didn't know if she could turn away even if he'd wanted her to. She could feel his mind touching hers – she could taste the very essence of his soul. And it made her tremble.

This was like nothing she'd ever felt before. It was so strange . . . but so wonderful. A pleasure that she couldn't have dreamed of. To be this close, and to be getting closer, like fire and bright darkness merging . . . To feel her mind opening to him . . .

And then the distant echo of fear, like an animal screaming a warning.

Are you insane? This is *Morgead*. Let him see your soul . . . pry open your innermost secrets . . . and you won't live long enough to regret it. He'll tear your throat out the instant he finds out . . .

Jez flinched wildly from the voice. She didn't want to resist the pull to Morgead any longer. But fear was shivering through her, poisoning the warmth and closeness, freezing the edges of her mind. And she knew that the voice was the only rationality left in her.

Do you want to die? it asked her point-blank.

Jez, Morgead was saying quietly. *What's wrong? Why won't you let it happen?*

Not just you dying, the voice said. All those others. Claire and Aunt Nan and Uncle Jim and Ricky. Hugh . . .

Something white-hot flickered through her. Hugh. Whom she loved. Who couldn't fight for himself. She hadn't even *thought* of him since she'd entered Morgead's mind – and that terrified her.

How could she have forgotten him? For the last year Hugh had represented everything good to her. He'd awakened feelings in her that she'd never had before. And he was the one person she would never betray.

Jez, Morgead said.

Jez did the only thing she could think of. She threw an image at him, a picture to stir his memories. A picture of her walking out, leaving the gang, leaving him.

It wasn't a real picture, of course. It was a symbol.

It was bait.

And she felt it hit Morgead's mind and clash there, and strike memories that flew like sparks.

The first meeting of the gang with her not there. Questions. Puzzlement. All of them searching for her, trying to find a hint of her unique Power signature on the streets. At first laughing as they called for her, making it a game, then the laughter turning into annoyance as she stayed missing. Then annoyance turning into worry.

Her uncle Bracken's house. The gang crowded on the doorstep with Morgead in front. Uncle Bracken looking lost and sad. 'I don't know where she is. She just – disappeared.' And worry turning into gut-wrenching fear. Fear and anger and sorrow and betrayal.

If she wasn't dead, then she'd abandoned him. Just like everyone else. Just like his mother.

And that grief and fury building, both perfectly balanced because Morgead didn't know which was the truth. But always with the knowledge, either way, that the world was cold because she was gone.

And then . . . her appearing in his room today. Obviously alive. Insultingly healthy. And unforgivably casual as she told him he would never know why she'd left.

Jez felt Morgead's outrage swelling up, a dark wave inside him, a coldness that felt no mercy for anyone and only wanted to hurt and kill. It was filling him, sweeping everything else away. Just being in contact with it started her heart pounding and shortened her breath. Its raw violence was terrifying.

You left me! he snarled at her, three syllables with a world of bitterness behind them.

I had to. And I'll never tell you why. Jez could feel her own eyes stinging; she supposed he could sense how it hurt her to say that. But it was the only thing that would work. The pull between them was weakening, being smashed away by his anger.

You're a traitor, he said. And the image behind it was that of everyone who'd ever betrayed a friend or a lover or a cause for the most selfish of reasons. Every betrayer from the history of the human world or the Night World. That was what Morgead thought of her.

I don't care what you think, she said.

You never cared, he shot back. *I know that now. I don't know why I ever thought differently.*

The force that had been trying to drag them together had thinned to a silver thread of connection. And that was good – it was *necessary*, Jez told herself. She made an effort and felt herself slide away from Morgead's mind, and then further, and then further.

You'd better not forget it again, she said. It was easier to be nasty when she couldn't feel his reactions. *It might be bad for your health.*

Don't worry, he told her briefly. *I can take care of myself. And you'd better believe I'll never forget.*

The thread was so fine and taut that Jez could hardly sense it now. She felt an odd lurch inside her, a pleading, but she knew what needed to be done.

I do what I want to, for my own reasons, she said. *And nobody questions me. I'm leader, remember?*

Snap!

It was a physical sensation, the feeling of breaking

away, as Morgead was carried off on a wave of his own black anger. He was retreating from her so fast that it made her dizzy . . .

And then her eyes were open and she was in her own body.

Jez blinked, trying to focus on the room. She was looking up at the ceiling, and everything was too bright and too large and too fuzzy. Morgead's arms were around her and her throat was arched back, still exposed. Every nerve was quivering.

Then suddenly the arms around her let go and she fell. She landed on her back, still blinking, trying to gather herself and figure out which muscles moved what. Her throat stung, and she could feel dampness there. She was giddy.

'What's wrong with you? Get up and get out,' Morgead snarled. Jez focussed on him. He looked very tall from her upside-down vantage point. His green eyes were as cold as chips of gemstone.

Then she realized what was wrong.

'You took too much blood, you jerk.' She tried to put her usual acidity into the words, to cover up her weakness. 'It was just supposed to be a ritual thing, but you lost control. I should've known you would.'

Something flickered in Morgead's eyes, but then his mouth hardened. 'Tough,' he said shortly. 'You shouldn't have given me the chance.'

'I won't make the same mistake again!' She struggled to a sitting position, trying not to show the effort it cost her. The problem – again – was that she wasn't a vampire. She couldn't recover as quickly from loss of blood . . . but Morgead didn't know that.

Not that he'd care, anyway.

Part of her winced at that, tried to argue, but Jez

brushed it aside. She needed all her strength and every wall she could build if she was going to get past what had happened.

It *shouldn't* have happened, whatever it had been. It had been some horrible mistake, and she was lucky to have gotten away with her life. And from now on, the only thing to do was try to forget it.

'I probably should tell you why I'm here,' she said, and got to her feet without a discernable wobble. 'I forgot to mention it before.'

'Why you came back? I don't even want to know.' He only wanted her to leave; she could tell that from his posture, from the tense way he was pacing.

'You will when I tell you.' She didn't have the energy to yell at him the way she wanted. She couldn't afford the luxury of going with her emotions.

'Why do you always think you know what I want?' he snapped, his back to her.

'OK. Be like that. You probably wouldn't appreciate the chance anyway.'

Morgead whirled. He glared at her in a way that meant he could think of too many nasty things to say to settle on one. Finally he just said almost inaudibly, 'What chance?'

'I didn't come back just to take over the gang. I want to *do* things with it. I want to make us more powerful.'

In the old days the idea would have made him grin, put a wicked sparkle in his eyes. They'd always agreed on power, if nothing else.

Now he just stood there. He stared at her. His expression changed slowly from cold fury to suspicion to dawning insight. His green eyes narrowed, then widened. He let out his breath.

And then he threw back his head and laughed and laughed and laughed.

Jez said nothing, just watched him, inconspicuously testing her balance and feeling relieved that she could stand without fainting. At last, though, she couldn't stand the sound of that laughing anymore. There was very little humour in it.

'Want to share the joke?'

'It's just . . . of course. I should have known. Maybe I *did* know, underneath.' He was still chuckling, but it was a vicious noise, and his eyes were distant and full of something like hatred. Maybe self-hatred. Certainly bitterness.

Jez felt a chill.

'There's only one thing that could have brought you back. And I should have realized that from the instant you turned up. It wasn't concern for anybody here; it's got nothing to do with the gang.' He looked her straight in the face, his lips curved in a perfect, malevolent smile. He had never been more handsome, or more cold.

'I know what it is, Jez Redfern. I know exactly why you're here today.'

CHAPTER 10

Jez held herself perfectly still, keeping her face expressionless. Her mind was clicking through strategies. Two exits – but to go out the window meant a three-storey drop, and she probably wouldn't survive that in her condition. Although, of course, she couldn't leave anyway without doing something to silence Morgead – and she wouldn't survive a fight, either . . .

She suppressed any feeling, returned Morgead's gaze, and said calmly, 'And why is that?'

Triumph flashed in his eyes. 'Jez *Redfern*. That's the key, isn't it? Your family.'

I'll have to kill him somehow, she thought, but he was going on.

'Your family sent you. Hunter Redfern. He knows that I've really found the Wild Power, and he expects you to get it out of me.'

Relief spread slowly through Jez, and her stomach muscles relaxed. She didn't let it show. 'You idiot! Of course not. I don't run errands for the Council.'

Morgead's lip lifted. 'I didn't say the Council. I said Hunter Redfern. He's trying to steal a march on the Council, isn't he? He wants the Wild Power himself. To

81

restore the Redferns to the glory of old. You're running errands for *him*.'

Jez choked on exasperation. Then she listened to the part of her mind that was telling her to keep her temper and think clearly.

Strategy, that part was saying. He's just *handed* you the answer and you're trying to smack it away.

'All right; what if that is true?' she said at last, her voice curt. 'What if I do come from Hunter?'

'Then you can tell him to get bent. I told the Council my terms. I'm not settling for anything less.'

'And what were your terms?'

He sneered. 'As if you didn't know.' When she just stared at him, he shrugged and stopped pacing. 'A seat on the Council,' he said coolly, arms folded.

Jez burst out laughing. 'You,' she said, 'are out of your mind.'

'I know they won't give it to me.' He smiled, not a nice smile. 'I expect them to offer something like control of San Francisco. And some position after the millennium.'

After the millennium. Meaning after the apocalypse, after the human race had been killed or subjugated or eaten or whatever else Hunter Redfern had in mind.

'You want to be a prince in the new world order,' Jez said slowly, and she was surprised at how bitterly it came out. She was surprised at how *surprised* she was. Wasn't it just what she expected of Morgead?

'I want what's coming to me. All my life I've had to stand around and watch humans get everything. After the millennium things will be different.' He glared at her broodingly.

Jez still felt sick. But she knew what to say now.

'And what makes you think the *Council* is going to be around after the millennium?' She shook her head.

'You're better off going with Hunter. I'd bet on him against the Council any day.'

Morgead blinked once, lizardlike. 'He's planning on getting rid of the Council?'

Jez held his gaze. 'What would *you* do in his place?'

Morgead's expression didn't get any sweeter. But she could see from his eyes that she had him.

He turned away sharply and went to glower out the window. Jez could practically see the wheels turning in his head. Finally he looked back.

'All right,' he said coldly. 'I'll join Hunter's team – but only on my terms. After the millennium—'

'After the millennium you'll get what you deserve.' Jez couldn't help glaring back at him. Morgead brought out all her worst traits, all the things she tried to control in herself.

'You'll get a position,' she amended, spinning the story she knew he wanted to hear. She was winging it, but she had no choice. 'Hunter wants people loyal to him in the new order. And if you can prove you're valuable, he'll want you. But first you have to prove it. OK? Deal?'

'If I can trust you.'

'We can trust each other because we have to. We both want the same thing. If we do what Hunter wants, we both win.'

'So we cooperate – for the time being.'

'We cooperate – and we see what happens,' Jez said evenly.

They stared at each other from opposite sides of the room. It was as if the blood sharing had never happened. They were back to their old roles – maybe a little more hostile, but the same old Jez and Morgead, enjoying being adversaries.

Maybe it'll be easy from now on, Jez thought. As long

as Hunter doesn't show up to blow my story.

Then she grinned inwardly. It would never happen. Hunter Redfern hadn't visited the West Coast for fifty years.

'Business,' she said crisply, out loud. 'Where's the Wild Power, Morgead?'

'I'll show you.' He walked over to the futon and sat down.

Jez stayed where she was. 'You'll show me what?'

'Show you the Wild Power.' There was a TV with a DVR at the foot of the bed, sitting on the bare floor. Morgead was whizzing through some footage.

Jez settled on the far end of the futon, glad for the chance to sit.

'You've got the Wild Power *recorded*?'

He threw her an icy glance over his shoulder. 'Yeah, on *America's Funniest Home Movies*. Just shut up, Jez, and watch.'

Jez narrowed her eyes and watched.

What she was looking at was a TV movie about a doomsday asteroid. A movie she'd seen – it had been awful. Suddenly the action was interrupted by the logo of a local news station. A blonde anchorwoman came on screen.

'Breaking news in San Francisco this hour. We have live pictures from the Marina district where a five-alarm fire is raging through a government housing project. We go now to Linda Chin, who's on the scene.'

The scene switched to a dark-haired reporter.

'Regina, I'm here at Taylor Street, where firefighters are trying to prevent this spectacular blaze from spreading—'

Jez looked from the TV to Morgead. 'What's this got to do with the Wild Power? I saw it live. It happened a couple weeks ago. I was watching that stupid movie—'

She broke off, shocked at herself. She'd actually been about to say 'I was watching that stupid movie with Claire and Aunt Nan.' Just like that, to blurt out the names of the humans she lived with. She clenched her teeth, furious.

She'd already let Morgead know one thing: that a couple of weeks ago she'd been in this area, where a local news station could break in.

What was *wrong* with her?

Morgead tilted a sardonic glance at her, just to show her that he hadn't missed her slip. But all he said was 'Keep watching. You'll see what it's got to do with the Wild Power.'

On screen the flames were brilliant orange, dazzling against the background of darkness. So bright that if Jez hadn't known that area of the Marina district well, she wouldn't have been able to tell much about it. In front of the building firefighters in yellow were carrying hoses. Smoke flooded out suddenly as one of the hoses sprayed a straight line of water into the flames.

'Their greatest fear is that there may be a little girl still inside this complex—'

Yes. That was what Jez remembered about this fire. There had been a kid . . .

'Look here,' Morgead said, pointing.

The camera was zooming in on something, bringing the flames in close. A window in the pinky-brown concrete of the building. High up, on the third floor. Flames were pouring up from the walkway below it, making the whole area look too dangerous to approach.

The reporter was still talking, but Jez had tuned her out. She leaned closer, eyes fixed on that window.

Like all the other windows, it was half covered with a

wrought-iron screen in a diamond pattern. Unlike the others, it had something else: On the still there were a couple of plastic buckets with dirt and scraggly plants. A window box.

And a face looking out between the plants.

A child's face.

'There,' Morgead said.

The reporter was speaking. 'Regina, the firefighters say there is definitely someone on the third floor of this building. They are looking for a way to approach the person – the little girl—'

High-powered searchlights had been turned on the flames. That was the only reason the girl was visible at all. Even so, Jez couldn't distinguish any features. The girl was a small blurry blob.

Firefighters were trying to manoeuver some kind of ladder toward the building. People were running, appearing and disappearing in the swirling smoke. The scene was eerie, otherworldly.

Jez remembered this, remembered listening to the barely suppressed horror in the reporter's voice, remembered Claire beside her hissing in a sharp breath.

'It's a kid,' Claire had said, grabbing Jez's arm and digging her nails in, momentarily forgetting how much she disliked Jez. 'Oh, God, a kid.'

And I said something like, 'It'll be OK,' Jez remembered. But I knew it wouldn't be. There was too much fire. There wasn't a chance . . .

The reporter was saying, 'The entire building is involved . . .' And the camera was going in for a close-up again, and Jez remembered realizing that they were actually going to *show* this girl burning alive on TV.

The plastic buckets were melting. The firemen were trying to do something with the ladder. And then there was a sudden huge burst of orange, an explosion, as the flames below the window *poofed* and began pouring themselves upward with frantic energy. They were so bright they seemed to suck all the light out of their surroundings.

They engulfed the girl's window.

The reporter's voice broke.

Jez remembered Claire gasping, 'No . . .' and her nails drawing blood. She remembered wanting to shut her own eyes.

And then, suddenly, the TV screen flickered and a huge wall of smoke billowed out from the building. Black smoke, then grey, then a light grey that looked almost white. Everything was lost in the smoke. When it finally cleared a little, the reporter was staring up at the building in open amazement, forgetting to turn toward the camera.

'This is astonishing . . . Regina, this is a complete turnaround . . . The firefighters have – either the water has suddenly taken effect or something else has caused the fire to die . . . I've never seen anything like this . . .'

Every window in the building was now belching white smoke. And the picture seemed to have gone washed-out and pale, because there were no more vivid orange flames against the darkness.

The fire was simply gone.

'I really don't know what's happened, Regina . . . I think I can safely say that everybody here is very thankful . . .'

The camera zoomed in on the face in the window. It was still difficult to make out features, but Jez could see coffee-coloured skin and what seemed to be a calm expression. Then a hand reached out to gently pick up one of the melted plastic buckets and take it inside.

The picture froze. Morgead had hit Pause.

'They never did figure out what stopped the fire. It went out everywhere, all at once, as if it had been smothered.'

Jez could see where he was going. 'And you think it was some sort of Power that killed it. I don't know, Morgead – it's a pretty big assumption. And to jump from that to the idea that it was a Wild Power—'

'You missed it, then.' Morgead sounded smug.

'Missed *what*?'

He was rewinding the footage, going back to the moment before the fire went out. 'I almost missed it myself when I saw it live. It was lucky I was recording it. When I went back and looked again, I could see it clearly.'

The playback was in slow motion now. Jez saw the burst of orange fire, frame by frame, getting larger. She saw it crawl up to engulf the window.

And then there was a flash.

It had only showed up as a flicker at normal speed, easily mistaken for some kind of camera problem. At this speed, though, Jez couldn't mistake it.

It was blue.

It looked like lightning or flame; blue-white with a halo of more intense blue around it. And it *moved*. It started out small, a circular spot right at the window. In the next frame it was much bigger, spreading out in all directions, fingers reaching into the flames. In the next frame it covered the entire TV screen, seeming to engulf the fire.

In the next frame it was gone and the fire was gone with it. White smoke began to creep out of windows.

Jez was riveted.

'Goddess,' she whispered. 'Blue fire.'

Morgead quickly rewound to play the scene again.

' "In blue fire, the final darkness is banished; In blood, the

final price is paid." If that girl isn't a Wild Power, Jez . . .
then what is she? You tell me.'

'I don't know.' Jez bit her lip slowly, watching the
strange thing blossom on the TV again. So the blue fire in
the poem meant a new kind of energy. 'You're beginning
to convince me. But—'

'Look, everybody knows that one of the Wild Powers is
in San Francisco. One of the old hags in the witch circle –
Grandma Harman or somebody – had a dream about it.
She saw the blue fire in front of Coit Tower or something.
And everybody knows that the four Wild Powers are
supposed to start manifesting themselves around now. I
think that girl did it for the first time when she realized
she was going to die. When she got that desperate.'

Jez could picture that kind of desperation; she'd
pictured it the first time, when she'd been watching the
fire live. How it must feel . . . being trapped like that.
Knowing that there was no earthly help for you, that you
were about to experience the most terrible pain
imaginable. Knowing that you were going to feel your
body char and your hair burn like a torch and that it
would take two or three endless minutes before you died
and the horror was over.

Yeah, you would be desperate, all right. Knowing all
that might drag a new power out of you, a frantic burst of
strength, like an unconscious scream pulled from the
depths of yourself.

But one thing bothered her.

'If this kid is the Wild Power, why didn't her Circle
notice what happened? Why didn't she tell them, "Hey,
guys, look; I can put out fires now?" '

Morgead looked annoyed. 'What do you mean,
her Circle?'

'Well, she's a witch, right? You're not telling me

vampires or shapeshifters are developing new powers like *that*.'

'Who said anything about witches or vampires or shapeshifters? The kid's *human*.'

Jez blinked.

And blinked again, trying to conceal the extent of her astonishment. For a moment she thought Morgead was putting her on, but his green eyes were simply exasperated, not sly.

'The Wild Powers . . . can be human?'

Morgead smiled suddenly – a smirk. 'You really didn't know. You haven't heard all the prophecies, have you?' He struck a mocking oratorical pose. 'There's supposed to be:

One from the land of kings long forgotten;
One from the hearth which still holds the spark;
One from the Day World where two eyes are watching;
One from the twilight to be one with the dark.'

The Day World, Jez thought. Not the Night World, the human world. At least one of the Wild Powers had to be human.

Unbelievable . . . but why not? Wild Powers were supposed to be weird.

Then she thought of something and her stomach sank.

'No wonder you're so eager to turn her in,' she said softly. 'Not just to get a reward—'

'But because the little scum deserves to die – or whatever it is Hunter has in mind for her.' Morgead's voice was matter-of-fact. 'Yeah, vermin have no right developing Night World powers. Right?'

'Of course right,' Jez said without emotion. I'm going to have to watch this kid every minute, she thought. He's got no pity at all for her – Goddess knows what he might do before letting me have her.

'Jez.' Morgead's voice was soft, almost pleasant, but it caught Jez's full attention. 'Why didn't Hunter tell you that prophecy? The Council dug it up last week.'

She glanced at him and felt an inner shiver. Suspicion was cold in the depths of his green eyes. When Morgead was yelling and furious he was dangerous enough, but when he was quiet like this, he was deadly.

'I have no idea,' she said flatly, tossing the problem back at him. 'Maybe because I was already out here in California when they figured it out. But why don't you call him and ask yourself? I'm sure he'd love to hear from you.'

There was a pause. Then Morgead gave her a look of disgust and turned away.

A good bluff is priceless, Jez thought.

It was safe now to move on. She said, 'So what do the "two eyes watching" mean in the prophecy?'

He rolled his own eyes. 'How should I know? *You* figure it out. You've always been the smart one.'

Despite the heavy sarcasm, Jez felt a different kind of shiver, one of surprise. He really believed that. Morgead was so smart himself – he'd seen that flicker on the TV screen and realized what it was, when apparently none of the adults in the Bay Area had – but he thought she was smarter.

'Well, you seem to be doing all right yourself,' she said.

She had been looking steadily at him, to show him no weakness, and she saw his expression change. His green eyes softened slightly, and the sarcastic quirk of his lip straightened.

'Nah, I'm just blundering along,' he muttered, his gaze shifting. Then he glanced back up and somehow they were caught in a moment when they were just looking at each other in silence. Neither of them turned away, and Jez's heart gave a strange thump.

The moment stretched.

Idiot! This is ridiculous. A minute ago you were scared of him – not to mention sickened by his attitude toward humans. You can't just suddenly switch to *this*.

But it was no good. Even the realization that she was in danger of her life didn't help. Jez couldn't think of a thing to say to break the tension, and she couldn't seem to look away from Morgead.

'Jez, look—'

He leaned forward and put a hand on her forearm. He didn't even seem to know he was doing it. His expression was abstracted now, and his eyes were fixed on hers.

His hand was warm. Tingles spread from the place where it touched Jez's skin.

'Jez . . . about before . . . I didn't . . .'

Suddenly Jez's heart was beating far too quickly. I *have* to say something, she thought, fighting to keep her face impassive. But her throat was dry and her mind a humming blank. All she could feel clearly was the place where she and Morgead touched. All she could see clearly was his eyes. Cat's eyes, deepest emerald, with shifting green lights in them . . .

'Jez,' he said a third time.

And Jez realized all at once that the silver thread between them hadn't been broken. That it might be stretched almost into invisibility, but it was still *there*, still pulling, trying to make her body go weak and her vision blur. Trying to make her fall toward Morgead even as he was falling toward her.

And then came the sound of someone kicking in the front door.

CHAPTER
11

'**H**ey, Morgead!' the voice was shouting even as the door went slamming and crashing open, sticking every few inches because it was old and warped and didn't fit the frame anymore.

Jez had jerked around at the first noise. The connection between her and Morgead was disrupted, although she could feel faint echoes of the silver thread, like a guitar string vibrating after it was strummed.

'Hey, Morgead—'

'Hey, you still asleep—?' Several laughing, raucous people were crowding into the room. But the yelling stopped abruptly as they caught sight of Jez.

There was a gasp, and then silence.

Jez stood up to face them. She couldn't afford to feel tired anymore; every muscle was lightly tensed, every sense alert.

She knew the danger she was in.

Just like Morgead, they were the flotsam and jetsam of the San Francisco streets. The orphans, the ones who lived with indifferent relatives, the ones nobody in the Night World really wanted. The forgotten ones.

Her gang.

They were out of school and ready to rumble.

Jez had always thought, from the day she and Morgead began picking these kids up, that the Night World was making a mistake in treating them like garbage. They might be young; they might not have families, but they had power. Every one of them had the strength to be a formidable opponent.

And right now they were looking at her like a group of wolves looking at dinner. If they all decided to go for her at once, she would be in trouble. Somebody would end up getting killed.

She faced them squarely, outwardly calm, as a quiet voice finally broke the silence.

'It's really you, Jez.'

And then another voice, from beside Jez. 'Yeah, she came back,' Morgead said carelessly. 'She joined the gang again.'

Jez shot him the briefest of sideways glances. She hadn't expected him to help. He returned the look with an unreadable expression.

'. . . she came back?' somebody said blankly.

Jez felt a twinge of amused sympathy. 'That's right,' she said, keeping her face grave. 'I had to go away for a while, and I can't tell you where, but now I'm back. I just fought my way back in – and I beat Morgead for the leadership.' She figured she might as well get it all over with at once. She had no idea how they were going to react to the idea of her as leader.

There was another long moment of silence, and then a whoop. A sound that resembled a war cry. At the same instant there was a violent rush toward Jez – four people all throwing themselves at her. For a heartbeat she stood frozen, ready to fend off a four-fold attack.

Then arms wrapped around her waist.

'Jez! I missed you!'

Someone slapped her on the back almost hard enough to knock her down. 'You bad girl! You beat him *again*?'

People were trying to hug her and punch her and pat her all at once. Jez had to struggle not to show she was overwhelmed. She hadn't expected this of them.

'It's good to see you guys again,' she said. Her voice was very slightly unsteady. And it was the truth.

Raven Mandril said, 'You scared us when you disappeared, you know.' Raven was the tall, willowy one with the marble-pale skin. Her black hair was short in back and long in front, falling over one eye and obscuring it. The other eye, midnight blue, gleamed at Jez.

Jez allowed herself to gleam back, just a bit. She had always liked Raven, who was the most mature of the group. 'Sorry, girl.'

'*I* wasn't scared.' That was Thistle, still hugging Jez's waist. Thistle Galena was the delicate one who had stopped her ageing when she reached ten. She was as old as the others, but tiny and almost weightless. She had feathery blonde hair, amethyst eyes, and little glistening white teeth. Her speciality was playing the lost child and then attacking any humans who tried to help her.

'You're never scared,' Jez told her, squeezing back.

'She means she knew you were all right, wherever you were. I did, too,' Pierce Holt said. Pierce was the slender, cold boy, the one with the aristocratic face and the artist's hands. He had dark blond hair and deep-set eyes and he seemed to carry his own windchill factor with him. But just now he was looking at Jez with cool approval.

'I'm glad somebody thought so,' Jez said, with a glance at Morgead, who just looked condescending.

'Yeah, well, *some* people were going crazy. They thought you were dead,' Valerian Stillman put in, following Jez's look. Val was the big, heroic one, with deep russet hair, grey-flecked eyes, and the build of a linebacker. He was usually either laughing or yelling with impatience. 'Morgead had us scouring the streets for you from Daly City to the Golden Gate Bridge—'

'Because I was hoping a few of you would fall off,' Morgead said without emotion. 'But I had no such luck. Now shut up, Val. We don't have time for all this class-reunion stuff. We've got something important to do.'

Thistle's face lit up as she stepped back from Jez. 'You mean a hunt?'

'He means the Wild Power,' Raven said. Her one visible eye was fixed on Jez. 'He's told you already, hasn't he?'

'I didn't need to tell her,' Morgead said. 'She already knew. She came back because Hunter Redfern wants to make a deal with us. The Wild Power for a place with him after the millennium.'

He got a reaction – the one Jez knew he expected. Thistle squeaked with pleasure, Raven laughed huskily, Pierce gave one of his cold smiles, and Val roared.

'He knows we've got the real thing! He doesn't wanna mess with us!' he shouted.

'That's right, Val; I'm sure he's quaking in his boots,' Morgead said. He glanced at Jez and rolled his eyes.

Jez couldn't help but grin. This really was like old times: she and Morgead trading secret looks about Val. There was a strange warmth sweeping through her – not the scary tingling heat she'd experienced with Morgead alone, but something simpler. A feeling of being with people who liked her and knew her. A feeling of belonging.

She never felt that at her human school. She'd seen things that would drive her human classmates insane even to imagine. None of them had any idea of what the real world was like – or what Jez was like, for that matter.

But now she was surrounded by people who understood her. And it felt so good that it was alarming.

She hadn't expected this, that she would slip back into the gang like a hand in a glove. Or that something inside her would look around and sigh and say, 'We're home.'

Because I am *not* home, she told herself sternly. These are not my people. They don't really know me, either . . .

But they don't have to, the little sigh returned. You don't ever need to tell them you're human. There's no reason for them to find out.

Jez shoved the thought away, scrunched down hard on the sighing part of her mind. And hoped it would stay scrunched. She tried to focus on what the others were saying.

Thistle was talking to Morgead, showing all her small teeth as she smiled. 'So if you've got the terms settled, does that mean we get to do it now? We get to pick the little girl up?'

'Today? Yeah, I guess we could.' Morgead looked at Jez. 'We know her name and everything. It's Iona Skelton, and she's living just a couple buildings down from where the fire was. Thistle made friends with her earlier this week.'

Jez was startled, although she kept her expression relaxed. She hadn't expected things to move this fast. But it might all work out for the best, she realized, her mind turning over possibilities quickly. If she could snatch the kid and take her back to Hugh, this whole masquerade could be over by tomorrow. She might even live through it.

'Don't get too excited,' she warned Thistle, combing some bits of grass out of the smaller girl's silk-floss hair. 'Hunter wants the Wild Power alive and unharmed. He's got plans for her.'

'Plus, before we take her, we've got to test her,' Morgead said.

Jez controlled an urge to swallow, went on combing Thistle's hair with her fingers. 'What do you mean, test her?'

'I'd think that would be obvious. We can't take the chance of sending Hunter a dud. We have to make sure she *is* the Wild Power.'

Jez raised an eyebrow. 'I thought you *were* sure,' she said, but of course she knew Morgead was right. She herself would have insisted Hugh find a way to test the little girl before doing anything else with her.

The problem was that Morgead's testing was likely to be . . . unpleasant.

'I'm sure, but I still want to test her!' Morgead snapped. 'Do you have a problem with that?'

'Only if it's dangerous. For us, I mean. After all, she's got some kind of power beyond imagining, right?'

'And she's in elementary school. I hardly think she's gonna be able to take on six vampires.'

The others were looking back and forth between Morgead and Jez like fans at a tennis match.

'It's just as if she never left,' Raven said dryly, and Val bellowed laughter while Thistle giggled.

'They always sound so – married,' Pierce observed, with just a tinge of spite to his cold voice.

Jez glared at them, aware that Morgead was doing the same. 'I wouldn't marry him if every other guy on earth was dead,' she informed Pierce.

'If it were a choice between her and a human, I'd pick the human,' Morgead put in nastily.

Everyone laughed at that. Even Jez.

The sun glittered on the water at the Marina. On Jez's left was a wide strip of green grass, where people were flying huge and colourful kites, complicated ones with dozens of rainbow tails. On the sidewalk people were rollerblading and jogging and walking dogs. Everybody was wearing summer clothing; everybody was happy.

It was different on the other side of the street.

Everything changed over there. A line of pinky-brown concrete stood like a wall to mark the difference. There was a high school and then rows of a housing project, all the buildings identically square, flat, and ugly. And on the next street beyond them, there was nobody walking at all.

Jez let Morgead take the lead on his motorcycle as he headed for those buildings. She always found this place depressing.

He pulled into a narrow alley beside a store with a dilapidated sign proclaiming 'Shellfish De Lish'. Val roared in after him, then Jez, then Raven with Thistle riding pillion behind her, and finally Pierce. They all turned off their motors.

'That's where she lives now; across the street,' Morgead said. 'She and her mum are staying with her aunt. Nobody plays in the playground; it's too dangerous. But Thistle might be able to get her to come down the stairs.'

'Of course I can,' Thistle said calmly. She showed her pointed teeth in a grin.

'Then we can grab her and be gone before her mum even notices,' Morgead said. 'We can take her back to my place and do the test where it's private.'

Jez breathed once to calm the knot in her stomach. '*I'll* grab her,' she said. At least that way she might be able to whisper something comforting to the kid. 'Thistle, you try to get her right out to the sidewalk. Everybody else, stay behind me – if she sees a bunch of motorcycles, she'll probably freak. But be ready to gun it when I pull out and grab her. The noise should help cover up any screams. Raven, you pick up Thistle as soon as I get the kid, and we all go straight back to Morgead's.'

Everyone was nodding, looking pleased with the plan – except Morgead.

'I think we should knock her out when we grab her. That way there won't *be* any screams. Not to mention any blue fire when she figures out she's being kidnapped—'

'I already said how we're going to do it,' Jez cut in flatly. 'I don't want her knocked out, and I don't think she'll be able to hurt us. Now, everybody get ready. Off you go, Thistle.'

As Thistle skipped across the street, Morgead let out a sharp breath. His jaw was tight.

'You never could take advice, Jez.'

'And you never could take orders.' She could see him starting to sizzle, but only out of the corner of her eye. Most of her attention was focussed on the housing building.

It was such a desolate place. No graffiti – but no grass, either. A couple of dispirited trees in front. And that playground with a blue metal slide and a few motorcycles-on-springs to ride . . . all looking new and untouched.

'Imagine growing up in a place like this,' she said.

Pierce laughed oddly. 'You sound as if you feel sorry for her.'

Jez glanced back. There was no sympathy in his deep-set dark eyes – and none in Raven's midnight blue or Val's hazel ones, either. Funny, she didn't remember them being *that* heartless – but of course she hadn't been sensitive to the issue back in the old days. She would never have stopped to wonder about what they felt for human children.

'It's because it's a kid,' Morgead said brusquely. 'It's hard on any kid growing up in a place like this.'

Jez glanced at him, surprised. She saw in his emerald

green eyes what she'd missed in the others; a kind of bleak pity. Then he shrugged, and the expression was gone.

Partly to change the subject, and partly because she was curious, she said, 'Morgead? Do you know the prophecy with the line about the blind Maiden's vision?'

'What, this one?' He quoted:

'Four to stand between the light and the shadow,
Four of blue fire, power in their blood.
Born in the year of the blind Maiden's vision;
Four less one and darkness triumphs.'

'Yeah. What do you think "born in the year of the blind Maiden's vision" *means*?'

He looked impatient. 'Well, the Maiden has to be Aradia, right?'

'Who's that?' Val interrupted, his linebacker body quivering with interest.

Morgead gave Jez one of his humouring-Val looks. 'The Maiden of the Witches,' he said. 'You know, the blind girl? The Maiden part of the Maiden, Mother, and Crone group that rules all the witches? She's only one of the most important people in the Night World—'

'Oh, yeah. I remember.' Val settled back.

'I agree,' Jez said. 'The blind Maiden has to be Aradia. But what does the "year of her vision" mean? How old is this kid we're snatching?'

'About eight, I think.'

'Did Aradia have some special vision eight years ago?'

Morgead was staring across the street, now, his eyebrows together. 'How should I know? She's been having visions since she went blind, right? Which means, like, seventeen years' worth of 'em. Who's supposed to tell which one the poem means?'

'What *you* mean is that you haven't even tried to figure it out,' Jez said acidly.

He threw her an evil glance. 'You're so smart; you do it.'

Jez said nothing, but she made up her mind to do just that. For some reason, the poem bothered her. Aradia was eighteen now, and had been having visions since she lost her sight at the age of one. Some particular vision must have been special. Otherwise, why would it be included in the prophecy?

It had to be important. And part of Jez's mind was worried about it.

Just then she saw movement across the street. A brown metal door was opening and two small figures were coming out.

One with feathery blonde hair, the other with tiny dark braids. They were hand in hand.

Something twisted inside Jez.

Just stay calm, *stay calm*, she told herself. It's no good to think about grabbing her and making a run for the East Bay. They'll just follow you; track you down. Stay cool and you'll be able to get the kid free later.

Yeah, after Morgead does his little 'test'.

But she stayed cool and didn't move, breathing slowly and evenly as Thistle led the other girl down the stairs. When they reached the sidewalk, Jez pressed the starter button.

She didn't say 'Now!' She didn't need to. She just peeled out, knowing the others would follow like a flock of well-trained ducklings. She heard their engines roar to life, sensed them behind her in tight formation, and she headed straight for the sidewalk.

The Wild Power kid wasn't dumb. When she saw Jez's motorcycle coming at her, she tried to run. Her mistake was that she tried to save Thistle, too. She tried to pull the little blonde girl with her, but Thistle was suddenly strong, grabbing the chain-link fence with a small hand like steel, holding them both in place.

Jez swooped in and caught her target neatly around the waist. She swooped the child onto the saddle facing her, felt the small body thud against her, felt hands clutch at her automatically for balance.

Then she whipped past a parked car, twisted the throttle to get a surge of speed, and flew out of there.

Behind her, she knew Raven was snagging Thistle and the others were all following. There wasn't a scream or even a sound from the housing project.

They were roaring down Taylor Street. They were passing the high school. They were making it away clean.

'Hang on to me or you'll fall off and get hurt!' Jez yelled to the child in front of her, making a turn so fast that her knee almost scraped the ground. She wanted to stay far enough ahead of the others that she could talk.

'Take me back home!' The kid yelled it, but not hysterically. She hadn't shrieked even once. Jez looked down at her.

And found herself staring into deep, velvety brown eyes. Solemn eyes. They looked reproachful and unhappy – but not afraid.

Jez was startled.

She'd expected crying, terror, anger. But she had the feeling that this kid wouldn't even be yelling if it hadn't been the only way to be heard.

Maybe I should have been more worried about what she'll do to us. Maybe she *can* call blue fire down to kill people. Otherwise, how can she be so composed when she's just been kidnapped?

But those brown eyes – they weren't the eyes of

somebody about to attack. They were – Jez didn't know what they were. But they wrenched her heart.

'Look – Iona, right? That's your name?'

The kid nodded.

'Look, Iona, I know this seems weird and scary – having somebody just grab you off the street. And I can't explain everything now. But I promise you, you're not going to get hurt. Nothing's going to hurt you – OK?'

'I want to go home.'

Oh, kid, so do I, Jez thought suddenly. She had to blink hard. 'I'm going to take you home – or at least someplace safe,' she added, as honesty unexpectedly kicked in. There was something about the kid that made her not want to lie. 'But first we've got to go to a friend of mine's house. But, look, no matter how strange all this seems, I want you to remember something. I won't let you get hurt. OK? Can you believe that?'

'My mum is going to be scared.'

Jez took a deep breath and headed onto the freeway. 'I promise I won't let you get hurt,' she said again. And that was all she could say.

She felt like a centaur, some creature that was half person and half steel horse, carrying off a human kid at sixty miles an hour. It was pointless to try to make conversation on the freeway, and Iona didn't speak again until they were roaring up to Morgead's building.

Then she said simply, 'I don't want to go in there.'

'It's not a bad place,' Jez said, braking front and back. 'We're going up on the roof. There's a little garden there.'

A tiny flicker of interest showed in the solemn brown eyes. Four other bikes pulled in beside Jez.

'Yeeehaw! We got her!' Val yelled, pulling off his helmet.

'Yeah, and we'd better take her upstairs before

somebody sees us,' Raven said, tossing her dark hair so it fell over one eye again.

Thistle was climbing off the back of Raven's motorcycle. Jez felt the small body in front of her stiffen. Thistle looked at Iona and smiled her sharptoothed smile.

Iona just looked back. She didn't say a word, but after a minute Thistle flushed and turned away.

'So now we're going to test her, right? It's time to test her, isn't it, Morgead?'

Jez had never heard Thistle's voice so shrill – so disturbed. She glanced down at the child in front of her, but Morgead was speaking.

'Yeah, it's time to test her,' he said, sounding unexpectedly tired for somebody who'd just pulled off such a triumph. Who'd just caught a Wild Power that was going to make his career. 'Let's get it over with.'

CHAPTER

12

Jez kept one hand on the kid as they walked up the stairs under the dirty fluorescent bulbs. She could only imagine what Iona must be thinking as they shepherded her to the top.

They came out on the roof into slanting afternoon sunlight. Jez gave Iona's shoulder a little squeeze.

'See – there's the garden.' She nodded toward a potted palm and three wooden barrels with miscellaneous wilted leaves in them. Iona glanced that way, then gave Jez a sober look.

'They're not getting enough water,' she said as quietly as she said everything.

'Yeah, well, it didn't rain enough this summer,' Morgead said. 'You want to fix that?'

Iona just looked seriously at him.

'Look, what I mean is, you've got the Power, right? So if you just want to show us right now, anything you want, be my guest. It'll make things a lot simpler. Make it rain, why don't you?'

Iona looked right at him. 'I don't know what you're talking about.'

'I'm just saying that there's no reason for you to get

106

hurt here. We just want to see you do something like what you did the night of the fire. Anything. Just show us.'

Jez watched him. There was something incongruous about the scene: Morgead in his high boots and leather jacket, iron-muscled, sleek, sinewy, on one knee in front of this harmless-looking kid in pink pants. And the kid just looking back at him with her sad and distant eyes.

'I guess you're crazy,' Iona said softly. Her pigtails moved as she shook her head. A pink ribbon fluttered loosely.

'Do you remember the fire?' Jez said from behind her.

'Course.' The kid turned slowly around. 'I was scared.'

'But you didn't get hurt. The fire got close to you and then you did something. And then the fire went away.'

'I was scared, and then the fire went away. But I didn't do anything.'

'OK,' Morgead said. He stood. 'Maybe if you can't tell us, you can show us.'

Before Jez could say anything, he was picking up the little girl up and carrying her. He had to step over a line of debris that stretched like a diagonal wall from one side of the roof to the other. It was composed of telephone books, splintery logs, old clothes, and other odds and ends, and it formed a barrier, blocking off a corner of the roof from the rest.

He put Iona in the triangle beyond the debris. Then he stepped back over the wall, leaving her there. Iona didn't say anything, didn't try to follow him back out of the triangle.

Jez stood tensely. The kid's a Wild Power, she told herself. She's already survived worse than this. And no matter what happens, she's not going to get hurt.

I promised her that.

But she would have liked to be telepathic again just for

a few minutes, just to tell the kid one more time not to be scared. She especially wanted to as Val and Raven poured gasoline on the wall of debris. Iona watched them do it with huge sober eyes, still not moving.

Then Pierce lit a match.

The flames leaped up yellow and blue. Not the bright orange they would have been at night.

But hot. They spread fast and Jez could feel the heat from where she was standing, ten feet away.

The kid was closer.

She still didn't say anything, didn't try to jump over the flames while they were low. In a few moments they were high enough that she couldn't jump through them without setting herself on fire.

OK, Jez thought, knowing the kid couldn't hear her. Now, *do it*! Come on, Iona. Put the fire out.

Iona just looked at it.

She was standing absolutely still, with her little hands curled into fists at her sides. A small and lonely figure, with the late afternoon sun making a soft red halo around her head and the hot wind from the fire rippling her pink-trimmed shirt. She faced the flames dead-on, but not aggressively, not as if she were planning to fight them.

Damn; this is *wrong*, Jez thought. Her own hands were clenched into fists so tightly that her nails were biting into her palms.

'You know, I'm concerned,' Pierce said softly from just behind her. 'I have a concern here.'

Jez glanced at him quickly. Pierce didn't talk a lot, and he always seemed the coldest of the group – aside from Morgead, of course, who could be colder than anyone. Now Jez wondered. Could he, who never seemed to be moved by pity, actually be the most sensitive?

'I'm worried about this fire. I know nobody can look

down on us, but it's making a lot of smoke. What if one of the other tenants comes up to investigate?'

Jez almost hit him.

This is *not* my home, she thought, and felt the part of her that had sighed and felt loved and understood wither away. These are not my people. I don't belong with them.

And Pierce wasn't worth hitting. She turned her back on him to look at Iona again. She was dimly aware of Morgead telling him to shut up, that other tenants were the least of their worries, but most of her attention was focussed on the kid.

Come on, kid! she thought. Then she said it out loud.

'Come on, Iona! Put out the fire. You can do it! Just do what you did before!' She tried to catch the child's eye, but Iona was looking at the flames. She seemed to be trembling now.

'Yeah, come on!' Morgead said brusquely. 'Let's get this over with, kid.'

Raven leaned forward, her long front hair ruffling in the wind. 'Do you remember what you did that night?' she shouted seriously. 'Think!'

Iona looked at her and spoke for the first time. 'I didn't do anything!' Her voice, so composed before, was edging on tears.

The fire was full-blown now, loud as a roaring wind, sending little bits of burning debris into the air. One floated down to rest at Iona's foot and she stepped backward.

She's got to be scared, Jez told herself. That's the whole point of this test. If she's not scared, she'll never be able to find her Power. And we're talking about saving the world, here. We're not just torturing this kid for fun . . .

It's still wrong.

The thought burst out from some deep part of her. Jez had seen a lot of horrible things as a vampire and a vampire hunter, but suddenly she knew she couldn't watch any more of *this*.

I'm going to call it off.

She looked at Morgead. He was standing tensely, arms folded over his chest, green eyes fixed on Iona as if he could will her into doing what he wanted. Raven and Val were beside him, Raven expressionless under her fall of dark hair; Val frowning with his big hands on his hips. Thistle was a step or so behind them.

'It's time to stop,' Jez said.

Morgead's head whipped around to look at her. 'No. We've gotten this far; it would be stupid to have to start all over again. Would that be any nicer to her?'

'I said, it's time to *stop*. What do you have to put out the fire – or did you even think of that?'

As they were talking, Thistle stepped forward. She moved right up to the flames, staring at Iona.

'You'd better do something fast,' she shouted. 'Or you're going to burn right up.'

The childish, taunting tone caught Jez's attention, but Morgead was talking to her.

'She's going to put it out any minute now. She just has to be frightened enough—'

'Morgead, she's absolutely terrified already! Look at her!'

Morgead turned. Iona's clenched fists were now raised to chest-level; her mouth was slightly open as she breathed far too fast. And although she wasn't screaming or crying like a normal kid, Jez could see the tremors running through her little body. She looked like a small trapped animal.

'If she's not doing it now, she's never going to,' Jez told

Morgead flatly. 'It was a stupid idea in the first place, and it's over!'

She saw the change in his green eyes; the flare of anger and then the sudden darkness of defeat. She realized that he was going to cave.

But before he could say anything, Thistle moved forward.

'You're gonna die!' she shrilled. 'You're gonna burn up right now!' And she began kicking flaming debris at Iona.

Everything happened very fast after that.

The debris came apart in a shower of sparks as it flew toward Iona. Iona's mouth came open in horror as she found fiery garbage swirling around her knees. And then Raven was yelling at Thistle, but Thistle was already kicking more.

A second deluge of sparks hit Iona. Jez saw her put up her hands to protect her face, then fling her arms out as a piece of burning cloth settled on her sleeve. She saw the sleeve spurt with a tiny flame. She saw Iona cast a frantic look around, searching for a way to escape.

Morgead was dragging Thistle back by her collar. Thistle was still kicking. Sparks were everywhere and Jez felt a hot pain on her cheek.

And then Iona's eyes went enormous and blank and fixed and Jez could see that she'd made some decision, she'd found some way to get out of this.

Only not the right one.

She was going to jump.

Jez saw Iona turn toward the edge of the roof, and she knew in that same instant that she couldn't get to the child in time to stop her.

So there was only one thing to do.

Jez only hoped she would be fast enough.

She very nearly wasn't. But there was a two-foot wall

at the roof's perimeter, and it delayed Iona for a second as she scrambled onto it. That gave Jez a second to leap through the fire and catch up.

And then Iona was on the wall, and then she was launching her small body into empty space. She jumped like a flying squirrel, arms and legs outspread, looking down at the three-storey drop.

Jez jumped with her.

Jez! The telepathic shout followed her, but Jez scarcely heard it. She had no idea who had even said it. Her entire consciousness was focussed on Iona.

Maybe some part of her was still hoping that the kid had magic and could make the wind hold her up. But it didn't happen and Jez didn't waste time thinking about it. She hit Iona in midair, grabbing the small body and hanging on.

It was something no human could have done. Jez's vampire muscles instinctively knew how to handle this, though. They twisted her as she fell, putting her underneath the child in her arms, putting her legs below her like a cat's.

But of course Jez didn't have a vampire's resistance to injury. She knew perfectly well that when she hit, the fall would break both her legs. In her weakened state it might well kill her.

It should save the kid, though, she thought unemotionally as the ground rushed up to meet her. The extra resiliency of Jez's flesh would act as a cushion.

But there was one thing Jez hadn't thought of.

The trees.

There were discouraged-looking redbud trees planted at regular intervals along the cracked and mossy sidewalk. None of them had too much in the way of foliage even in late summer, but they certainly had a lot of little branches.

Jez and the kid crashed right into one of them.

Jez felt pain, but scratching, stabbing pain instead of the slamming agony of hitting the side-walk. Her legs were smashing through things that cracked and snapped and poked her. Twigs and branches. She was being flipped around as some of the twigs caught on her jeans and others snagged her leather jacket. Every branch she hit decreased her velocity.

So when she finally crashed out of the tree and hit concrete, it merely knocked the wind out of her.

Black dots danced in front of her eyes. Then her vision cleared and she realized that she was lying on her back with Iona clutched to her stomach. Shiny redbud leaves were floating down all around her.

Goddess, she thought. We made it. I don't believe it.

There was a dark blur and something thudded against the sidewalk beside her.

Morgead. He landed like a cat, bending his knees, but like a *big* cat. A three-storey jump was pretty steep even for a vampire. Jez could see the shock reverberate through him as his legs hit concrete, and then he fell forward.

That must hurt, she thought with distant sympathy. But the next instant he was up again, he was by her side and bending over her.

'*Are you all right?*' He was yelling it both aloud and telepathically. His dark hair was mussed and flying; his green eyes were wild. '*Jez!*'

Oh. It was you who yelled when I jumped, Jez thought. I should have known.

She blinked up at him. 'Of course I'm all right,' she said hazily. She tugged at the kid lying on her. 'Iona! Are *you* all right?'

Iona stirred. Both her hands were clutching Jez's jacket in front, but she sat up a little without letting go. There was a burned patch on her sleeve, but no fire.

Her velvety brown eyes were huge – and misty. She looked sad and confused.

'That was really scary,' she said.

'I know.' Jez gulped. She wasn't any good at talking about emotional things, but right now the words spilled out without conscious effort. 'I'm sorry, Iona; I'm so sorry, I'm so sorry. We shouldn't have done that. It was a very bad thing to do, and I'm really sorry, and we're going to take you home now. Nobody's going to hurt you. We're going to take you back to your mum.'

The velvety eyes were still unhappy. Tired and unhappy and reproachful. Jez had never felt like more of a monster; not even that night in Muir Woods when she had realized she was hunting her own kind.

Iona's gaze remained steady, but her chin quivered.

Jez looked at Morgead. 'Can you erase her memory? I can't see any reason why she should have to remember all this.'

He was still breathing quickly, his face pale and his pupils dilated. But he looked at Iona and nodded. 'Yeah, I can wipe her.'

'Because she's not the Wild Power, you know,' Jez said levelly, as if making a comment about the weather.

Morgead flinched. Then he shoved his hair back with his knuckles, his eyes shutting briefly.

'She's an extraordinary kid, and I don't know exactly what she's going to be – maybe President or some great doctor or botanist or something. Something special, because she's got that inner light – something that keeps her from getting mad or mean or hysterical. But that's got nothing to do with being a Wild Power.'

'All right! I know, already!' Morgead yelled, and Jez realized she was babbling. She shut up.

Morgead took a breath and put his hand down. 'She's not it. I was wrong. I made a bad mistake. OK?'

'OK.' Jez felt calmer now. 'So can you please wipe her?'

'Yes! I'm doing it!' Morgead put his hands on Iona's slender shoulders. 'Look, kid, I'm – sorry. I never thought you'd – you know, jump like that.'

Iona didn't say anything. If he wanted forgiveness, he wasn't getting it.

He took a deep breath and went on. 'This has been a pretty rotten day, hasn't it? So why don't you just forget all about it, and before you know it, you'll be home.'

Jez could feel him reach out with his mind, touching the child's consciousness with his Power. Iona's eyes shifted, she looked at Jez uncertainly.

'It's OK,' Jez whispered. 'It won't hurt.' She hung on to Iona's gaze, trying to comfort her as Morgead's suggestions took hold.

'You don't ever have to remember this,' Morgead said, his voice soothing now. Gentle. 'So why don't you just go to sleep? You can have a little nap . . . and when you wake up, you'll be home.'

Iona's eyelids were closing. At the last possible second she gave Jez a tiny sleepy smile – just the barest change of expression, but it seemed to ease the tightness in Jez's chest. And then Iona's lashes were lying heavy on her cheeks and her breathing was deep and regular.

Jez sat up and gently put the sleeping child on the sidewalk. She smoothed back one stray pigtail and watched the little chest rise and fall a couple of times. Then she looked up at Morgead.

'Thanks.'

He shrugged, exhaling sharply. 'It was the least I could do.' Then he gave her an odd glance.

Jez thought of it at the same instant. She was the one

so concerned about the child – why had she asked Morgead to wipe her memory?

Because I can't do it, she thought dryly. Out loud she said, 'I'm really kind of tired, after everything that's happened today. I don't have much Power left.'

'Yeah . . .' But his green eyes were slightly narrowed, searching.

'Plus, I hurt.' Jez stretched, gingerly testing her muscles, feeling every part of her protest.

The searching look vanished instantly. Morgead leaned forward and began to go over her with light, expert fingers, his eyes worried.

'Can you move everything? What about your legs? Do you feel numb anywhere?'

'I can move everything, and I only wish I felt numb somewhere.'

'Jez – I'm sorry.' He blurted it out as awkwardly as he had to the child. 'I didn't mean . . . I mean, this just hasn't turned out the way I planned. The kid getting hurt – you getting hurt. It just wasn't what I had in mind.'

The kid getting hurt? Jez thought. Don't tell me you care about that.

But there was no reason for Morgead to lie. And he did look unhappy – probably more unhappy than Jez had ever seen him. His eyes were still all pupil, as if he were scared.

'I'm not hurt,' Jez said. It was all she could think of. She felt dizzy suddenly – uncertain and a little giddy, as if she were still tumbling off the roof.

'Yes, you are.' He said it with automatic stubbornness, as if it were one of their arguments. But his hand reached out to touch her cheek.

The one that had been hit by burning debris. It hurt, but Morgead was touching so lightly . . . Coolness seemed to flow from his fingers, seeping into the burn and making it feel better.

Jez gasped. 'Morgead – what are you doing?'

'Giving you some Power. You're low and you need it.'

Giving her Power? She'd never heard of such a thing. But he was *doing* it. She could feel her skin healing itself faster, could feel his strength pour into her.

It was a strange sensation. It made her shiver inwardly. 'Morgead . . .'

His eyes were fixed on her face. And suddenly they were all Jez could see; the rest of the world was a blur. All she could hear was the soft catch in his breath; all she could feel was the gentleness of his touch.

'Jez . . .'

They were leaning toward each other, or falling. It was that silver thread between them, shortening, pulling. They had nothing to grab on to but each other. And then Morgead's arms were around her and she felt his warm mouth touch hers.

CHAPTER
13

The kiss was warm and sweet. Not frightening. Jez felt herself relax in Morgead's arms before she knew what she was doing. His heart was beating so fast against hers. She felt dizzy, but safe, too; a wonderful feeling.

But the approach of his mind was another thing. It was just like the first time: that terrible, irresistible pull trying to suck her soul out and mix it with Morgead's until they were both one person. Until he knew her every secret and she had no place to hide.

And the worst thing was that she knew it wasn't Morgead doing it. It was that outside force doing it to both of them, carrying them along helplessly.

Whether we want it or not. And we *don't* want it, Jez told herself desperately. We both hate it. Neither of us wants to share our souls . . .

But then why was he still holding her, still kissing her? And why was she letting him?

At that instant she felt his mind touch hers, reaching through the smoke-screen of protection she'd thrown around herself to brush her thoughts as lightly as a moth's wing. She recognized Morgead's essence in it; she could feel his soul, dark and bright and full of fierce emotion for her. He was opening himself to her; not trying to fight this or even holding back. He was going farther than the pull forced him to, giving himself to her freely . . .

It was a gift that sent her reeling. And she couldn't resist it. Her mind flowed out of its own accord to touch his, tendrils of thought wrapping around his gratefully. The shock of pleasure when she let it happen was frightening – except that she couldn't be frightened anymore, not now.

And then she felt him respond, felt his happiness, felt his thoughts enfolding hers, holding her mind as gently as his arms held her body. And white light exploded behind her eyes . . .

Jez! Morgead! What's wrong with you two?

The thought was foreign, cold, and unwanted. It broke into Jez's warm little world and rattled around annoyingly. Jez tried to push it away.

Hey, look; I'm just trying to help. If you guys are alive, then, like give us a sign, OK?

Morgead made a sound like a mental groan. *It's Val. I have to kill him.*

I'm going to help, Jez told him. Then something occurred to her. *Oh – wait. Where are we . . . ?*

It was a good question. A weird but necessary question. It took them a moment to untangle their thoughts from each other and rise back to the real world.

Where they seemed to be sitting under the ruins of a redbud tree, arms around each other, Jez's head on Morgead's shoulder, Morgead's face pressed into Jez's hair.

At least we weren't still kissing, Jez thought abstractedly. She could feel herself flushing scarlet. The rest of the gang was standing around them, looking down with worried expressions.

'What do you guys want?' Morgead said brusquely.

'What do we *want*?' Raven leaned forward, dark hair swinging. Jez actually saw both her midnight blue eyes underneath. 'You three jumped off the roof just as the fire got out of control. We put it out and came down to see if you were still alive – and then we find you here hanging on to each other and totally out of it. And you want to know what we *want*? We want to know if you're *OK*.'

'We're fine,' Morgead said. He didn't say anything more, and Jez understood. Neither of them had any desire to talk about it in front of other people. That could wait until they were alone, until it was the right time.

They didn't need to express this to each other. Jez simply knew, and knew that he knew.

'What about *her*?' Thistle pointed to Iona, still asleep on the sidewalk.

Jez was already moving to the child. She checked the little body over, noted the even breathing and the peaceful expression.

'She's fine, too,' she said, settling back. She held Thistle's gaze. 'No thanks to you.'

Thistle's cheeks were pink. She looked angry, embarrassed, and defensive. 'She's just a human.'

'She's a kid!' Morgead yelled, shooting up to his feet. He towered over Thistle, who suddenly looked very small. 'Which *you're* not,' he went on unsympathetically. 'You're just a – a sixteen-year-old Shirley Temple wannabe.'

'All right, both of you!' Jez said sharply. She waited until they shut up and looked at her before continuing. 'You – be quiet and let me take care of things,' she said to Morgead. 'And *you* – if you ever try to hurt a kid again, I'll knock your head off.' This to Thistle, who opened her mouth, but then shut it again without speaking.

Jez nodded. 'OK, that's settled. Now we've got to get this girl home.'

Val stared at her. 'Home?'

'Yeah, Val.' Jez picked the child up. 'In case you missed something, she's not the Wild Power.'

'But . . .' Val wriggled his broad shoulders uncomfortably and looked at Morgead. 'You mean you were wrong?'

'There's a first time for everything, right?' Morgead glared at him.

'But, then – who *is* the Wild Power?' Raven put in quietly.

'Who knows?' It was the first time Pierce had spoken, and his voice was low and distantly amused.

Jez glanced at him. His blond hair glinted in the red light of the sunset, and his dark eyes were mocking.

I really don't think I like you much, she thought.

But of course he was right. 'If this kid isn't the one – well, I guess it could have been anybody at the scene,' she said slowly. 'Anybody worried enough to want to save her. One of the firefighters, a neighbour – anybody.'

'Assuming the blue flash on the tape really was evidence of a Wild Power,' Pierce said.

'I think it was.' Jez glanced at Morgead. 'It sure looked like blue fire. And it certainly was some kind of Power.'

'And Grandma Harman dreamed about the Wild Power being in San Francisco,' Morgead added. 'It all fits too well.' He looked at Jez slyly. 'But it couldn't have been anybody at the scene, you know.'

'Why not?'

'Because of what you said about that line in the prophecy. "Born in the year of the blind Maiden's vision." That means it has to be somebody born less than eighteen years ago. Before that, Aradia couldn't have visions because she wasn't alive.'

Goddess, I'm slow today, Jez thought. I should have thought of that. She gave him a wry nod of respect and he returned it with a grin. Not maliciously.

'It's still not much to go on,' Raven said in her pragmatic way. 'But don't you think we should go back inside to discuss it? Somebody's going to come along eventually and see us with an unconscious kid.'

'Good point,' Jez said. 'But I'm not going up with you. I'm taking the kid home.'

'Me, too,' Morgead said. Jez glanced at him; he had his stubborn expression on.

'OK, but just us. Two motorcycles are going to be conspicuous enough.' She turned to Raven. 'The rest of you can do what you want tonight; try to figure out who the Wild Power is or whatever. We'll meet again tomorrow and see what we've come up with.'

'Why wait?' Val said. 'It's only dusk. We could meet tonight—'

'I'm tired,' Jez cut in. 'It's enough for the day.' And Goddess knows how I'm going to explain being gone *this* long to Aunt Nan, she thought wearily. Not to mention missing school.

Pierce was watching her with an odd expression. 'So you'll have to report to Hunter that we failed,' he said, and there was a probing tone in his voice that Jez didn't like.

'Yeah, I'll tell him you screwed up,' she said heavily. 'But that we still have some options. Unless you'd rather I just tell him that you're all idiots and not worth giving a second chance.' She kept looking at Pierce until he looked away.

When she turned to Morgead he was scowling, but he

didn't say anything. He silently started toward their bikes.

They couldn't talk while they were riding. Jez was too full of her own thoughts anyway.

She was finally free to consider those last minutes with Morgead.

It had been . . . amazing. Electrifying. But also enlightening.

She knew now what had happened to them, what was happening. He had been right. It was the soulmate principle.

So we're soulmates. Morgead and I. After all our fighting and challenging each other and everything. It's so strange, but in a way it makes sense, too . . .

And it's really a pity that even if we both survive the next week or so, we're never going to see each other again.

The thought came from some deep part of her that was utterly heartless and practical and saw everything in the cold light of truth.

Because unfortunately the universe had picked the wrong person for Jez to be soulmates with. It had picked one that would hate her and want to kill her once he realized what she really was.

Bad mistake, universe, Jez thought, biting down on a laugh. She realized, dimly, that she was verging on being hysterical.

It had been such a long day, and she was so tired, and so hurt, and she'd failed in her mission, and now Morgead was in love with her, but there was just no hope. Small wonder she was punchy and an emotional wreck. She was lucky not to be falling off her bike.

There really was no hope. Even in that last encounter, even when Morgead had been revealing his soul to her, Jez had managed to keep her own secrets buried. He didn't know. He had no idea that the girl he was in love with was vermin. Was working with Circle Daybreak. Was lying to him to steal the Wild Power out from under his nose and end the hopes of the vampires for a world without humans.

He was ambitious, she had always known that. All he'd ever cared about was climbing higher and getting more power. She'd promised him a position in the new world order – while all the time she was working as hard as she could to make sure that the new world order never came.

He would never forgive that deception. He would never even be able to understand why she had done it.

So you have to forget about him, the cold-and-practical part of her mind said quietly. And there was nothing inside Jez that even tried to argue.

It was dark by the time they reached the Marina district. As they approached the housing project, Jez saw flashing lights ahead.

Police car lights. Well, that wasn't unexpected. Iona's mother would have notified them by now. Jez just hoped she wasn't too worried . . .

Idiot! her mind said sarcastically. How worried do you expect her to be, with it getting dark and her eight-year-old missing?

She turned into an alley and Morgead followed her.

'We'll have to do a drive-by,' she said over the thrum of the engines. 'Drop her by the police cars and then shoot out of there. They'll probably chase us. Are you up for it?'

He nodded. 'We should go separate ways. That'll make it harder for them to catch us.'

'Right. You go on home once you lose them. So will I.'

She couldn't see his features clearly in the dark alley, but she knew he was looking at her. 'So will you? Go home?'

'I mean I'll go to the place where I'm staying.'

She expected him to ask about that, try to find out where it was, what she was doing. He didn't. Instead he said, 'Do you have to?'

She blinked at him, startled. Then she frowned. 'Yes, I have to. I *want* to. I'm tired, Morgead, and anyway I'm not ready to be spending the night with a guy.'

'I didn't mean *that*—'

Jez waved a hand. 'I know. I'm sorry. But I'm still tired, and—' And I've got other responsibilities that you don't understand. And if I stick around you any longer, while I'm this tired, I'm afraid that you're going to find out what they are.

'And you're still mad,' he said bleakly.

'I'm not mad—'

'Or disgusted or whatever.'

What was he talking about? 'I'm just tired,' she said firmly. 'Now let's drop the kid off, and I'll see you tomorrow.'

'I—' He let out his breath violently. 'All right.'

Jez didn't waste any more time. She unzipped her jacket, which had been holding Iona firmly against her. Then she sped out into the street.

One block, two blocks. And now she was right beside the dark and deserted playground, and now she was almost level with the police cars. There were several officers standing around talking, and several other bystanders who might be neighbours.

Jez targeted one of the neighbours.

She swooped in toward the woman, who was on the outside edge of the sidewalk. She came up fast, then hit the brakes.

'Hey,' she said. 'Here.'

The woman turned around and her jaw dropped. Jez didn't hesitate, just bundled Iona into her arms. The woman grabbed the child's weight automatically.

'Give her to her mum, OK?'

And then Jez was roaring out and away. She could hear Morgead behind her, and shouts from the housing project. Then a police siren.

She glanced back. Morgead was just turning on a side street. He waved once at her, and then he was speeding off.

Jez could hear more sirens now. She twisted the throttle and headed for the Bay Bridge.

At least a pursuit was something she could enjoy.

When she finally shook the police cars tailing her, she turned toward Clayton. She would have been worried about what her aunt and uncle were going to say if she hadn't already been too worried about Iona.

She'll be all right, she told herself. She shouldn't remember anything, and her mum will take care of her.

But Jez couldn't help but feel guilty . . . and just plain sad. There was some sort of bond between her and the child. She felt – responsible for her, and not just because she'd kidnapped and terrorized her.

Nobody should have to grow up in that kind of place. I may have run around on the streets when I was little, but at least I had Uncle Bracken, and a nice home to go to if I wanted. Iona – she doesn't even have a safe playground.

I should do something for her, but what can I do that would matter?

I don't know; maybe I can visit her sometime. Maybe I can buy her a plant . . .

There weren't any easy answers, and she was drawing up to a neat yellow frame house.

Home.

Time, Jez thought, to face the music. Uncle Jim and Aunt Nan and nasty little Claire. She just hoped they left enough of her alive so that she could call Hugh afterward.

She pulled her motorcycle into the garage, climbed off, and went inside.

'. . . at all is bad enough. But to do it the day after you make us a promise – well, what are we supposed to think? How are we supposed to trust you again?'

Jez was sitting on the blue floral couch in the living room. The Goddard living room didn't get used much, only for very formal occasions.

This was one of them. It was a court martial.

And there wasn't really a thing that Jez could say to the humans she lived with. She certainly couldn't give them any excuse that would make sense.

'First, ditching Claire even though you swore to us that you'd let her drive you to school.' Aunt Nanami was ticking items off on her fingers. 'Second, ditching school after you swore to us you weren't going to skip again. Third, going off some place you won't even tell us about. Fourth, not even calling to let us know you were still alive. Fifth, getting home at almost ten o'clock at night—'

Uncle Jim cleared his throat. 'Nan, I think we've been over this already.'

A couple of times, Jez thought. Oh, well, at least Claire is enjoying it. Her cousin was standing at the entrance to the living room, openly listening. When she happened to catch Jez's eye she smiled brilliantly, her small face actually glowing with smug satisfaction.

Aunt Nan was shaking her head. 'I just want to make sure she *understands*, Jim. I thought she understood last night, but obviously . . .' She threw her hands up.

'Well, the thing is—' Uncle Jim cleared his throat again and looked at Jez. He looked uncomfortable; he wasn't very good at discipline, but Jez could see that he'd reached his limit. 'The thing is that we can't just keep yelling at you. We have to *do* something, Jez. So we've decided to lock up your motorcycle. You can't ride it anymore, not until you learn to be more responsible.'

Jez sat stunned.

Not her bike. They couldn't take her bike from her.

How would she *get* anywhere?

She had to be mobile. She had to get to Morgead tomorrow – she had to get to *Hugh* sometime. She had to be able to track down the Wild Power. And she couldn't do any of that without transportation.

But she could see from Uncle Jim's face that he was serious. He'd finally decided to put his foot down, and Jez had got caught underneath it.

She let out her breath. Part of her wanted to yell and storm and rage about this, to lose control and make a big noisy fuss.

But it wouldn't do any good. Besides, she'd managed to keep her temper for almost a year with these people, to live her double life as a student and vampire hunter and make it all work. To blow that now would be stupid.

And another part of her was scared that she was even verging on losing control. That was what even a day with Morgead did to her. It cut through all her careful discipline and changed her back into a raving barbarian.

Morgead . . . she couldn't think about him now.

'OK, Uncle Jim,' she said out loud. 'I understand. You do what you have to.'

'If you can just show us that you're learning to be responsible, then you can have the bike back. You have to learn to take life more seriously, Jez.'

That forced a tired snort out of her. She was laughing before she knew it, and her aunt and uncle were looking shocked and displeased.

'I'm sorry,' she said. 'I'll try harder.'

And I'll just have to take public transportation tomorrow, she thought when the lecture was over and she was free to go to her room. Even though that's a lot more dangerous. I could get hunted down so easily . . .

'You messed with the wrong person, you know?' Claire said as Jez reached her door. 'You shouldn't have dumped me like that. You shouldn't make me mad.'

'Yeah, Claire; well, now I know better. I'm terrified.'

'You're *still* not taking things seriously, are you?'

'Claire—' Jez rounded on the smaller girl. Then she stopped dead. 'I don't have time for this,' she muttered. 'I have to make a call. You just run along and harass somebody else.'

She shut the bedroom door in Claire's face.

Which, she realized later, was a mistake. At the time, though, she was too tired to think about it.

She was too tired to think properly at all. Tired and distraught, with the feeling that everything was closing in and happening too fast.

And so when she picked up the phone to dial Hugh she hardly noticed the little click on the line, and she didn't stop for even a second to consider what it meant.

CHAPTER

14

'Did you have trouble getting away?' Hugh said.

It was the next morning, a very different sort of day from yesterday. The sky was overcast and the air was heavy. Everyone Jez had passed at the Concord BART station looked a little depressed.

'Eh, a little,' she said, and sat down by Hugh on the platform. They were at the far end of the station, beyond the covered area with benches, beside a little concrete security house. It was a safe and private meeting place since the station was almost deserted after the morning commute. 'They chained up my bike with this huge chain. Claire drove me to school – she's been watching me like a werewolf guarding dinner. And Aunt Nan called the office to make sure I didn't cut.'

Hugh shifted in concern. There was a tiny breath of warm wind, and it stirred his fair hair. 'So what did you do?'

Jez grinned. 'I cut.' She shrugged and added, 'I got a guy from my auto shop class to drive me here. It wasn't hard.'

He smiled at her sadly, his grey eyes distant. 'But they're going to find out. Jez, I'm really sorry for completely messing up your life.'

She shrugged again. 'Yeah, but if I don't do it, everybody's life is going to be even more completely messed up. Every human's.'

'I know.' He shivered slightly. Then he drew up his legs, clasping his arms around them. He looked at her with his chin on his knees. 'So what did you find out?'

'That the girl Morgead thought was the Wild Power isn't.' He looks so cute that way, Jez thought helplessly. So – compact. Morgead would never sit like that.

Hugh winced. 'Great. You're sure?'

'Yeah. It was a little kid, eight years old, and she was something special – but not that. She was . . .' Jez tried to think of a way to describe it. Hugh watched her with eyes that were clear and fathomless, sad and wry and gentle all at once. And suddenly Jez got it. She gasped.

'Goddess – I know! She was like *you*. That kid was an Old Soul.'

Hugh's eyebrows went up. 'You think?'

'I'm sure of it. She had that same way of looking at you as if she's seen all of history and she knows that you're just a little part. That . . . "big picture" look. As if she were beyond stupid human things.'

'But not a Wild Power,' Hugh said softly. He looked half discouraged and half relieved. 'So then the Morgead connection is useless.'

'Actually, no. Because he's got evidence for the Wild Power recorded.' Jez explained about the movie and the fire and the blue flash. 'So somebody around that kid is probably it. I know that area and so does Morgead. We may be able to find out who.'

Hugh chewed his lip. Then he looked directly at her. 'It sounds dangerous. Just how is Morgead taking this – you coming back and all?'

Jez stared out across the BART tracks. They looked like

regular train tracks, except for the big one labelled DANGER ELECTRIC THIRD RAIL. There was a sound like faraway thunder, and then a train came whizzing up like a sleek futuristic white dragon. It stopped and a few people got on and off in the distance. She waited until it left again to answer.

'He . . . wasn't very happy at first. But then he kind of got used to it. I don't think he's going to make any trouble – unless he finds out, you know.'

She wasn't sure what else to say. She didn't want to talk to Hugh about Morgead – and she certainly didn't want to explain what had happened. Especially not when she was so confused about it all herself.

'You still think he'd hate you if he found out you were half human?' Hugh's voice was quiet.

Jez laughed shortly. 'Believe it. He would.'

There was a silence, while Hugh looked at her. Suddenly Jez found her mind posing an odd question. If it were Hugh or Morgead, which would she take?

Of course, it was a completely *ridiculous* question. She couldn't have either of them. Hugh was an Old Soul, and beyond her reach. Not to mention that he only thought of her as a friend. And Morgead might be her soulmate, but he would murder her if he ever discovered the truth.

But still, if she did have a choice . . . Hugh or Morgead?

A day ago she'd have said Hugh without question. How strange that now it came up the other way.

Because, impossible as it was, deadly as she knew it to be, it was Morgead she was in love with. And she had only just understood that this moment.

What a pity that there was no hope in the world for them.

Jez found herself giving another short laugh – and then she realized that Hugh was still looking at her. She could feel colour rise to her cheeks.

'You were miles away again.'

'I'm just foggy. Not enough sleep, I guess.' Plus all that fun yesterday. She was still sore from the stick fight and the fall with Iona. But that wasn't Hugh's problem.

She took a breath, groping for another subject. 'You know, there was something I wanted to ask you. Morgead said the Council had dug up another prophecy – about where each of the Wild Powers is from. Have you heard it?' When he shook his head, she quoted:

'One from the land of kings long forgotten;
One from the hearth which still holds the spark;
One from the Day World where two eyes are watching;
One from the twilight to be one with the dark.'

'Interesting.' Hugh's grey eyes had lit up. ' "One from the hearth" . . . that's got to be the Harman witches. Their last name was originally "Hearth-Woman." '

'Yeah. But the line about the one from the Day World – that one's a human, right?'

'It sounds like it.'

'That's what Morgead thought – that's why he thought the little girl might be a Wild Power even though she was human. But what I can't figure out is what it means by "where two eyes are watching".'

'Mmm . . .' Hugh gazed into the distance, as if he liked the challenge. 'The only thing I can think of that combines the idea of "Day" and "eyes" is a poem. It goes something like "The Night has a thousand eyes, and the Day only one." The one eye being the sun, you know, and the thousand eyes the stars at night.'

'Hmpf. What about the moon?'

Hugh grinned. 'I don't know. Maybe the author wasn't good at astronomy.'

'Well – that doesn't help much. I thought it might be a clue. But the truth is that we don't even know if it's the human Wild Power we're after.'

Hugh put his chin on his knees again. 'True. But I'll let Circle Daybreak know about that prophecy. It might help eventually.' He was silent a moment, then added, 'You know, they dug up something interesting, too. Apparently the Hopi Tribe predicted the end of the world pretty accurately.'

'The Hopi?'

'I should say, the ends of the worlds. They knew that it had happened before their time, and that it would happen again. Their legend says that the first world was destroyed by fire. The second world was destroyed by ice. The third world ended in water – a universal flood. And the fourth world – well, that's ours. It's supposed to end in blood and darkness – and end soon.'

Jez murmured, 'The first world—?'

'Don't remember your Night World history?' He *tched* at her, with a smile that didn't reach his eyes. 'The first civilization was the shapeshifters'. Back when humans were scared to go out of their caves, the shapeshifters ruled and the humans thought of them as gods. Animal spirits, totems. It was Shapeshifter World. That lasted for about ten thousand years, until a bunch of volcanoes suddenly became active—'

'Fire.'

'Yeah. The weather changed, people migrated, and the shapeshifters lost control. After that it was really Witch World. The witches did better than everybody else for ten thousand years, but then there was an Ice Age—'

'And the Night Wars,' Jez said, remembering. 'When the vampires fought the witches.'

'Right. And after all that, the vampires were in control;

it was Vampire World. Which lasted about another ten thousand years, until the flood. And after the flood, human civilization really started. It was Human World, and it has been for a long time. The Night People have just been hanging on around the edges, hiding. But . . .' He paused and straightened. 'That started about eight thousand B.C.'

'Oh.'

'Yeah. The millennium marks the end of our ten thousand years.' He gave his gentle, half-mocking smile. 'We humans are about to lose our lease. Something's going to happen to bring blood and darkness and then there'll be a whole new world.'

'Only if we don't stop it,' Jez said. 'And we will – because we have to.'

Hugh's smiled changed, softening. 'I think we're lucky to have people like you trying.' Then he lost the smile completely. He looked uncertain. 'Jez – you know, Old Souls aren't really beyond "stupid human things." We're as human as anybody. And we . . . I mean, and I . . .'

Jez's heart was beating uncomfortably fast. The way he was looking at her – she'd never seen Hugh look like that at anything or anyone.

Another rumble in the distance, and then a train came rushing in.

Hugh blinked, glanced up at the digital clock display above the platform, then checked his watch. He cursed.

'I'm supposed to be somewhere. I'm late.'

Jez's heart gave a strange thump. But not of disappointment. Weirdly, it was more like relief.

'Me, too,' she said. 'I'm supposed to meet Morgead before everybody else gets out of school. I ought to take the next train to San Francisco.'

He still hesitated. 'Jez—'

'Go on,' she said, standing up. 'I'll call you if I turn up anything. Wish me luck.'

'Be careful,' he said instead, and then he was hurrying away.

Jez watched him go. She couldn't help wondering what he had been about to say.

Then she turned to walk back to the central part of the station. She was partway around the concrete guardhouse when she heard a noise on the other side.

A stealthy, sneaking noise. Not the kind a security guard would make.

Jez didn't hesitate. Smoothly, completely soundless herself, she changed course, turning back and going around the structure the other way to get behind the sneaker. The instant she had a clear view of the intruder's back, she jumped.

She landed on top of her quarry, with a control hold on the person's wrist. But she already knew that this wasn't going to be a fight to the death.

'Jez – ow – it's me!' Claire spluttered.

'I know it's you, Claire.'

'Let go of my arm!'

'I don't think so, Claire. You having an interesting morning? Hear any good jokes?'

'Jez!' Claire struggled, hurting herself, then got mad and hurt herself more trying to hit Jez. Jez allowed her to sit up, still keeping hold of her.

Claire's face was flushed and wrathful, her dark hair sticking in strands to her cheeks. Her eyes were shooting sparks.

'OK, so I'm sorry for eavesdropping. I followed you when Greg Ludlum drove you here. I wanted to know what you were doing. I didn't know that you were completely freaking insane!'

'Well, it's too bad you didn't figure it out earlier. Because unfortunately I have to kill you now to keep you from talking.'

Claire's eyes widened and she choked. Jez suddenly realized that underneath all the sparks and the yelling her cousin was terrified.

She let go of Claire's arm and Claire slumped away from her, rubbing it.

'You – you *are* insane, aren't you?' Claire looked at her sideways, through clinging strands of hair. 'I mean, all that stuff about the world ending – it's some kind of bizarre game you're playing with your weird friends, isn't it? Some kind of Dungeons and Dragons stuff . . .'

'What do you think, Claire?' Jez stood up and offered Claire a hand, worried that someone might notice them. She kept that hand on Claire as she herded Claire back behind the guard house.

The truth was that this situation wasn't funny. Claire really was in trouble – because Jez was in trouble.

Her entire cover was blown. Everything she'd worked for in the past year – Claire could destroy it all. Claire knew way too much, and Claire hated her enough to use it.

'I think . . . I don't know what to think.' Claire swallowed. 'Who was that guy?'

'One of my weird friends. Right?'

'He didn't seem so weird. When he said things – I don't know. They sounded . . .' Claire's voice trailed off. Finally it came back, almost inaudibly. 'Real.'

'Great.' I *am* going to have to kill her. What else can I do?

'It's not a game, is it?' Claire said, looking at her. All the anger was gone from the dark eyes now. They were simply bewildered and frightened.

Then Claire shook her head. 'But, I mean, it's impossible. Vampires and shapeshifters and witches – it's all just . . .' Her voice trailed off again.

Jez was simply looking at her, with eyes that might be less silvery than a year ago, but that she knew were still pretty strange. And after a few moments Claire's gaze lost its focus and her whole body seemed to fall in on itself, as if it had lost something vital. Innocence maybe, Jez thought grimly.

'Oh, God, it *is* true,' Claire whispered. 'I mean, it's *really true*. That's why you're gone all the time, isn't it? You're off – doing something.'

Jez said, 'Yeah.'

Claire sagged against the guardhouse. 'Oh, God. I . . . God. I feel so strange. It's like – nothing is what I thought.'

Yeah, I know the feeling, Jez thought. When the whole world turns around and you have to adjust in two seconds flat. It happened to me, too, a year ago.

But none of that was going to help Claire. All she could say was 'I'm sorry.'

Claire didn't seem to hear her. She was speaking in a voice that was just a breath. 'That's why . . . that's why all that weird stuff with your father. Nobody knowing anything about his family and all. I knew from the beginning that there was something about you; I just couldn't tell what it was.'

Oh, great, Jez thought. Here it comes. She tried to keep her face impassive as Claire faced her squarely, raising her eyes with a look somewhere between wonder and dread.

'That guy – he said you were only half human. Which means you're half . . . something else?'

'I'm half human and half vampire,' Jez said quietly. The interesting thing was that it was so easy to get out. She'd only ever spoken the words aloud to one person before: Hugh.

Now she looked to see if Claire would actually faint or just fall down.

Claire did neither. She just shut her eyes. 'You know the really insane thing? I believe that.' She opened her eyes again. 'But – I didn't know you *could* be. Half and half.'

'Neither did anybody else, till I was born. I'm the only one.' Jez examined her cousin, realized that she really wasn't going to faint. When she spoke again, her voice came out more challenging than she meant it to. 'So now that you know, Claire, what are you going to do about it?'

'What do you mean, what am I going to do?' Claire glanced around, then her voice dropped as her eyes glinted with interest. 'Look – do you, like, have to drink blood and everything?'

'Not anymore,' Jez said shortly. What was this? Who would have thought that studious, straitlaced Claire would have such an interest in vampires?

'But you mean you used to?'

'Before I came to live with you guys. I thought I was a full vampire then. But I found out that I could live without it, as long as I didn't use my powers.'

'You've got powers? Really? What kind?'

'No kind. Look, enough with the questions. I told you, I'm not a vampire anymore.'

'And you're not evil.' Claire said it flatly.

Jez looked at her, startled. 'What makes you say *that*?'

'I heard what you were talking about, saving the world and all. I didn't understand it, but it sounded like you were on the right side. And—' Claire hesitated, then shrugged. 'And I know *you*, OK? I mean, you're arrogant and stubborn and you never explain anything, but you're not *evil*. You just aren't – inside. I can tell.'

Jez laughed. A real laugh. She couldn't help it.

Of all people, Claire. She'd misjudged this girl who was her own age but had nothing else in common with her. Her cousin had unexpected depths.

'Well, thanks,' she said. 'I try not to be too evil – these days.' Then she sobered. 'Look, Claire, if you really think that, and if you really believe that the stuff you heard was true—'

'About the end of the world? I don't believe it. I mean, I heard it, and I believe you believe it – and when I first heard it I kind of believed it, but—'

'Just – skip the rest and plain believe it, Claire. It happens to be the truth. And I'm trying to do something about it.'

'Something about a Wild Power, right?' Claire wasn't sagging anymore. She looked almost excited. 'But what's a—'

'You don't need to know. The point is that if you want to, you can help me.'

'I can? Really?'

'You can help me by going back to school and forgetting that this ever happened. You can help me by keeping my secret and not ever saying a word about this to anybody. And, incidentally, you'll be keeping your family safe at the same time.'

Claire looked away, worked her jaw. 'This stuff you're doing is pretty dangerous.' It wasn't a question.

'Very dangerous.' Jez stepped back. 'And I'm late for it right now. So do we have a deal? Will you help me or not? Can I trust you?'

'Or otherwise you're gonna kill me, right?' Claire looked at her sarcastically.

Jez rolled her eyes. 'Don't tempt me. Seriously, are you going to help?'

'No.'

Jez froze, looking down at the shorter girl. '*What?*'

'Jez – don't get mad, but I don't think I *can*. Not that way.' Claire was looking back up steadily, her small face serious and surprisingly determined. 'I mean how can I possibly just walk away, after hearing all that? If everything you said is true, how can I *forget?*'

'You can because you have to. We all do what we have to do.' Jez looked around the station. Another train should be coming any minute. She simply didn't have time to spend convincing a human to stay out of business that would kill her. To properly explain it to Claire would take days.

All she could do was ask for something she never would have imagined Claire could give her.

'Claire . . . there's no way I can convince you or *make* you do what I want. But I'm asking you—' She let out her breath and went on: 'I'm asking you to trust me. I'm asking you to walk away and at least try to forget this. And to believe that *I'm* trying the best I can to do the right thing.'

Claire kept looking at her steadily for a moment. Then, all at once, the dark eyes filled. They turned away, and Claire's throat moved once as she swallowed. Then, slowly, she nodded.

'OK,' she whispered. 'I mean – it's OK for now. I mean, I guess I can talk to you later about it.'

Jez let out her breath. 'That's right.'

Claire stood there for another second, then straightened her shoulders and turned away. But just as suddenly she turned back, looking tense and almost explosive. 'There's something I have to say to you.'

Jez glanced down the tracks. No train. 'OK.'

'It's – it's . . . that I'm sorry. I'm sorry I bugged you and tried to get Mum mad at you and everything. I was just –

I was jealous because they let you get away with anything, and . . .' She shook her head fiercely and then went on, shrugging grimly as if she hated to admit it. 'And, yeah, because you're so gorgeous and confident and everything. It made me feel bad and I wanted to hurt you. So. Anyway. There. I'm sorry.'

She started to walk away, wobbling a little.

'Claire.'

Claire paused, then turned around.

Jez spoke a little hesitantly around the obstruction in her throat. 'It's OK. And thank you.'

'Yeah.' Claire grinned and gave a little shrug. 'See ya later.' She turned around and started walking again.

See ya, Jez thought. She felt suddenly tired and strangely emotional. There was too much inside her: sadness and relief and worry and a new feeling for Claire. She crossed her arms and looked around the station, trying to relax, taking deep, even breaths.

And saw two werewolves coming straight for Claire.

CHAPTER
15

Jez recognized them immediately – not the individuals, but the type. They were 'wolves, and they were thugs. Somebody's hired muscle.

She didn't have her stick, but she didn't need it. She could feel a dangerous smile come to her lips; part anticipation and part sheer fury. Suddenly she wasn't tired, wasn't sore, wasn't anything but perfectly in tune with her body and dying to use it as a weapon.

She launched herself like a streak of red lightning, passing Claire easily and knocking the human girl flat before landing in front of the 'wolves. A guy and a girl. They snapped to attention in front of her, each dropping into a fighting stance.

Behind her, she could hear Claire say, '*Ow.*'

'Good morning and welcome to the Bay Area,' Jez told the 'wolves; then she snap-kicked the girl in the face.

The girl flew backward. She wasn't out of commission, but it had wrecked the joint attack they had been about to make. The guy knew this, but he was a 'wolf, so instead of waiting for his partner to recover, he growled and threw himself at Jez.

Oh, Goddess, this is too easy. As he drove a punch at her

face, Jez turned sideways and let his fist whistle past her. Then she threw her left arm around his left hip, holding him in what was almost an embrace. A deadly one, though. At the same instant she slammed her left hand up to his chin, striking with enough force to stun him.

He staggered in her arms, snarling. Bristly hairs erupted on his face.

'Sweet dreams, Fido,' Jez said. She hooked her left leg around his right just below the knee and brought him crashing to the platform. His head hit the concrete and he went limp.

Somewhere behind Jez, a sort of thin shrieking had begun. Claire. Jez ignored it, and ignored the two or three people scrambling for the stairs – avoiding the down escalator because it was right beside Jez. She was focussed on the female werewolf, who was back on her feet.

'Do yourself a favour and don't even try anything,' she said, grinning. 'You're way outclassed.'

The girl, who had reddish-brown hair and a feral expression, didn't answer. She simply showed her teeth and lunged for Jez.

With both hands reaching for Jez's face. You'd think they would *learn*, Jez thought. Especially after what just happened.

Even as she was thinking it, her body was making the right moves. She grabbed the girl's leading arm with both hands, then twisted, pulling her off balance. She took the girl down with a pull drop, flipping her to the platform. As soon as the girl was flat Jez locked the arm she still held and began to apply leverage against the elbow joint.

'Don't move or I'll break your elbow,' she said pleasantly. The girl was writhing in pain, spitting and struggling and hurting herself worse.

Absently, Jez noticed that Claire had stopped shrieking.

She glanced up to make sure her cousin was all right and saw that Claire was on her feet, staring openmouthed. Jez gave her a reassuring nod.

Then she looked back at the female 'wolf. Now that the fight was over she had the leisure to wonder what was going *on*. There were plenty of people who might want to kill her, but she couldn't think of any reason for them to target Claire. And they *had* been targeting her; Jez was sure of that.

This was no random thing. This was two 'wolves attacking a human right in public, in front of witnesses, as if they didn't care who saw them. This was something planned, something important.

She gave the girl's arm a little twist, and the girl snarled wildly, glaring at Jez with reddish eyes full of animal fury and hatred.

'OK, you know what I want,' Jez said. 'I need answers, and I don't have much time. What are you doing here? Who sent you? And why do you want *her*?' She jerked her head toward Claire.

The girl just glared harder. Jez applied more pressure.

'Look, I can *make* time for this if I need to. I can do this all day. After I break this elbow I'll do the other one. And then I'll break your ribs, and then your kneecaps—'

'Filthy halfbreed scum,' the werewolf snarled.

Jez's heart gave an odd lurch.

She tried to quiet it. Well, now, that was interesting. Somebody obviously knew her secret. And since they'd been going for Claire, they knew Claire was connected with her . . .

They knew about her family.

Jez saw white light. She threw sudden pressure against the 'wolf's elbow joint. The girl screamed, a sound more of anger than of pain.

'Who hired you?' Jez said softly, each word coming out like a chip of ice. 'Who sent you after my cousin?'

She stared into the reddish eyes, trying to reach into the girl's soul and yank an answer out of her.

'Nobody messes with my family,' she whispered. 'Whoever sent you is going to be sorry.'

She couldn't ever remember feeling so angry. And she was so focussed on the girl, so intent, that it wasn't until Claire screamed that she realized someone was approaching behind her.

'Jez, watch out!'

The yell woke Jez up. Without releasing her hold on the female 'wolf, she turned around – just in time to see a male vampire stalking her. He must have come up the down escalator.

And behind *him*, unbelievably, was Claire, running and getting ready for a flying tackle.

'Claire, don't!' Jez yelled. She struck the female 'wolf once, with deadly accuracy, on the side of the jaw to knock her out. Then she sprang toward the vampire.

But Claire was already grabbing him – a completely futile and foolish gesture. He whipped around and seized a handful of dark hair, and then he was holding Claire in a choke hold, putting her body between him and Jez.

'One more step and I'll break her neck,' he warned.

Jez skidded to a stop.

'You let go of my *cousin*,' she spat.

'No, I really think we need to talk first,' he said, the beginnings of an ugly grin on his face. 'You're the one who's going to give answers—'

Jez kicked him.

A roundhouse kick to his knees while he was busy talking. She didn't worry about keeping it nonlethal. She only cared about breaking his hold on Claire.

It worked. He lost his grip, stumbling sideways. Jez grabbed Claire and thrust her out of the way, shouting 'Run! The escalator's right there!'

But Claire didn't run. 'I want to help you!'

'Idiot!' Jez didn't have time to say that Claire *couldn't* help her; could only hurt her. The vampire had recovered and was moving toward her in fighting position.

He was big, probably over two hundred pounds. And he was a full vampire, which gave him the advantage of strength and speed. And he was smarter than the 'wolves; he wasn't just going to lunge. And Jez didn't have a weapon.

'Just keep behind me, OK?' she snarled under her breath to Claire.

The vampire grinned at that. He knew Jez was vulnerable. She was going to have to keep half her attention on protecting Claire.

And then, just as he was about to make an attack, Jez heard the smack of footsteps on concrete. Running footsteps, with a weird little hesitation between them, like somebody with a limp . . .

She flashed a look toward the stairs. Hugh had just rounded the top. He was out of breath and bleeding from cuts on his face. But as soon as he saw her and the vampire he waved his arms and yelled.

'Hey! Ugly Undead! Your friend missed me! You want to have a try?'

Hugh? Jez thought in disbelief. Fighting?

'Come on, hey; I'm here; I'm easy.' Hugh was hopping toward the vampire, who was also flashing looks at him, trying to assess this new danger while not taking his focus off Jez.

'You want to go a few rounds?' Hugh dropped into a boxer's pose, throwing punches at the air. 'Huh? You want to try for the title?' All the time he was speaking, he was dancing closer to the vampire, circling to get behind him.

Beautiful, Jez thought. All she needed was for the vampire to shift his attention for one second – just to glance behind him once – and she could kick his face in.

It didn't work that way. Something went wrong.

The vampire tried to glance behind him. Jez saw her chance and made the kick, a high kick that snapped his head back. But somehow instead of falling backward the vampire managed to blunder forward straight at her. She could easily have gotten away – except for Claire.

Claire had obediently kept behind her – even when behind her meant standing right by the BART tracks, on the yellow metal squares that marked the edge of the platform. Now, as the vampire stumbled forward and Jez began to slide out of the way, she heard Claire gasp, felt Claire clutch at her wildly.

She knew what had happened instantly. Claire had tried to run the wrong way and was teetering on the edge of the platform. More, she was taking Jez with her.

There was a distant rumble like thunder.

Jez knew she could save herself – by getting rid of Claire. She could use Claire's body as a springboard to propel herself away from the drop. That way, only one of them would die.

Instead, she tried to twist and throw Claire away from her, toward safety. It didn't work. They both lost their balance. Jez had the strange, surprised feeling one gets in the middle of a fall – where's the ground? – and then she hit it.

It was a bad fall because she was tangled with Claire. All Jez could do was try to keep Claire away from the third rail on the far side of the track. The impact winded both of them and Jez saw stars.

She could hear Hugh screaming her name.

The distant thunder had become a roaring, whizzing sound, carried through the tracks underneath Jez. Down here, she could feel a rattling that wasn't audible from above. It was a noise that filled her head and shook her body.

She knew absolutely, in that instant, that they were going to die.

Both of them. Crushed to pieces under the train. The white dragon would run right over them and not even know it.

There was simply no chance. Claire was clinging to her desperately, clawing Jez's arms hard enough to draw blood, and gasping in the breath for a scream. And even if Jez had been a full vampire, she couldn't have lifted Claire the four feet to the platform fast enough.

There was nothing to save them, no hope. No rescue. It was over.

All of this flashed through Jez's mind in the single instant it took her to look up and see the train bearing down on them. Its sleek white nose was only thirty feet away, and it was braking, but nowhere near fast enough, and this was it, the actual moment of her death, the last thoughts she would ever think, and the last thing she would ever see was white, white, white –

Blue.

It happened all at once, filling her vision. One second she could see clearly, the next the entire world was blue. Not just blue. Fiery, dazzling, lightning-shot blue. Like being inside some sort of science-fiction special effect. There was blue streaming and crackling and sizzling all around her, a cocoon of blue that enfolded her and shot past her and disappeared somewhere ahead.

I'm dead, Jez thought. So *this* is what it's like.

Completely different from what people say.

Then she realized that she could hear a faint shrieking sound beneath her. It was Claire. They were still holding on to each other.

We're both dead. Or we've fallen into some kind of space warp. The rest of the world is gone. There's just – this.

She had an impulse to touch the blue stuff, but she couldn't move because of Claire's grip on her arms. It might not have been safe anyway. Where it flowed over her, she could feel a sort of zinging and tingling as if all her blood were being excited. It smelled like the air after a storm.

And then it disappeared.

All at once. Not by stages. But it still took Jez several moments to see anything, because her eyes were blinded with dark yellow after-images. They burned and danced in front of her like a new kind of lightning, and she only gradually realized where she was.

On the train tracks. Exactly where she had been before. Except that now there was a huge, sleek BART train two feet in front of her.

She had to tilt her head to look up at its nose. It was gigantic from this angle, a monster of white, like the iceberg that sank the *Titanic*. And it was stopped dead, looking as if it had always been here, like some mountainous landmark. As if it had never moved an inch in its history.

People were yelling.

Shrieking and yowling and making all kinds of noise. It seemed to come from far away, but when Jez looked she could see them staring down at her. They were at the edge of the platform, waving their arms hysterically. As Jez stared back at them, a couple jumped down to the tracks.

Jez looked down at her cousin.

Claire was dragging in huge breaths, hyperventilating, her whole body shaking in spasms. She was staring at the train that loomed over them with eyes that showed white all around.

A loudspeaker was booming. One of the people who had jumped, a man in a security guard's uniform, was jabbering at Jez. She couldn't understand a word he was saying.

'Claire, we've got to go now.'

Her cousin just whooped in air, sobbing.

'Claire, we have to *go* now. Come on.' Jez's whole body felt light and strange, and when she tried to move she felt as if she were floating. But she *could* move. She stood up and pulled Claire with her.

She realized that somebody was calling her name.

It was the other person who had jumped to the tracks. It was Hugh. He was reaching for her. His grey eyes were as wide as Claire's, but not wide and hysterical. Wide and still. He was the only calm person in the crowd, beside Jez.

'Come on. Up this way,' he said.

He helped her boost Claire to the platform, and then Jez scrambled up and reached down to help him. When they were all up, Jez glanced around. She knew she was looking for something – yes. There. The werewolves she'd knocked out. It seemed a hundred years ago, but they were still lying there.

'The other guy got away,' Hugh said.

'Then we have to get out of here fast.' Jez heard her own voice, sounding quiet and faraway. But she was beginning to feel more attached to her body. Hugh was guiding Claire toward the escalator. Jez got on the other side of Claire, and they both helped keep her on her feet.

The security guy was behind them, yelling. Jez still

couldn't understand him and ignored him completely. When they reached the lower level, she and Hugh began to walk faster, pulling Claire along with them. They shoved Claire through the handicapped gate by the ticket window and vaulted over themselves.

From down here, Jez could see that the train was smoking all along its bottom. White smoke that sizzled up into the muggy air.

'We can't go on the street,' Hugh said. 'They've got cars out there.'

'The garage,' Jez said.

They both headed for it, a multistorey brick building that looked dark and cool inside. They were almost running with Claire, now, and they didn't stop until they were deep within the bowels of the garage, with emptiness echoing all around them.

Then Jez sagged against a brick pillar. Hugh bent over with his hands on his knees. Claire simply folded to the ground like a marionette with all its strings cut.

Jez let herself breathe for a few minutes, let her brain settle down, before slowly lowering herself beside her cousin.

They all looked as if they'd been in an accident. Hugh's shirt was ripped and there was drying blood all down one side of his face. Claire's hair was wildly dishevelled, and there were scrapes and small cuts on her face and arms. Jez herself had lost a lot of skin to the tracks, and her forearms were bleeding where Claire had scratched her.

But they were alive. Beyond all hope, they were alive.

Claire looked up just then to find Jez gazing at her. They sat for several moments simply staring into each other's eyes. Then Jez reached out to touch her cousin's cheek.

'It was you,' she whispered. 'All that time – and it was *you*.'

She looked up at Hugh and began to laugh.

He looked back, his face pale in the semidarkness. He shook his head and began to laugh, too, but shakily.

'Oh, Goddess,' he said. 'I thought you were dead, there, Jez. I thought I'd lost you.'

'Not while she's around, apparently,' Jez said, and laughed harder. She was slightly hysterical, but she didn't care.

Hugh's laughter sounded a little like crying. 'I saw that train – and there was no way it was going to stop in time. And then – that light. It just shot out – and the train hit it. It was like a physical thing. Like a giant cushion. The train hit it and it squashed and the train went slower and then it kept squashing—'

Jez stopped laughing. 'I wonder if the people on the train got hurt.'

'I don't know.' Hugh was sober now, too. 'They must've gotten thrown around. It stopped so fast. But it didn't *smash*. They're probably OK.'

'I just – from the inside, it looked like lightning—'

'From the outside, too. I didn't imagine it would look like that—'

'I didn't know it would be so *powerful*. And, think about it; she's untrained—'

There they were, an Old Soul and a vampire hunter who'd seen everything the streets had to offer, babbling like a couple of kids.

It was Claire who stopped them. She had been looking from one of them to the other, getting more and more agitated. Now she grabbed Jez's arm.

'What are you guys *talking* about?'

Jez turned to her. She glanced at Hugh, then spoke gently.

'We're talking about you, Claire. You're the Wild Power.'

CHAPTER 16

'I am *not*,' Claire said.

'Yeah, you are,' Jez said, still gently, as if humouring a child.

'I am *not*.'

'You don't even know what it is.' Jez looked at Hugh. 'You know what? I just realized something. The Wild Powers are all supposed to be "born in the year of the blind Maiden's vision," right?'

'Yeah . . .'

'Well, I was trying to figure that out all yesterday. And now, it just came to me, like *that*.' She snapped her fingers. 'I was thinking about visions like prophecies, you know? But I think what it meant was vision, like sight. Eyesight. Aradia only had her eyesight for a year – and *that's* the year. Seventeen years ago.'

Hugh looked at Claire. 'And she's—'

'Seventeen.'

'So what?' Claire yelled. 'So are you! So are lots of people!'

'So am I,' Hugh said with a wry smile. 'But not everybody can stop a train with blue fire.'

'I didn't stop anything,' Claire said with passionate

intensity. 'I don't know what a Wild Power is, but *I didn't do anything* back there. I was just lying there and I knew we were going to die—'

'And then the blue light came and the train stopped,' Jez said. 'You see?'

Claire shook her head. Hugh frowned and looked suddenly doubtful.

'But, Jez – what about the fire at the Marina? Claire wasn't there, was she?'

'No. But she was watching it live on TV. And she was very, very upset about it. I've still got the scars.'

Hugh drew in a slow breath. His eyes were unfocussed. 'And you think it works across that distance?'

'I don't know. I don't see why it shouldn't.' They were talking around Claire again, Jez gazing into the depths of the garage. 'I think maybe distance is irrelevant to it. I think what happens is that she sees something, and if she's upset enough about it, if she's desperate enough and there's no physical way to do anything, she just – sends out the Power.'

'It's completely unconscious, then,' Hugh said.

'And who knows, maybe she's done it before.' Jez straightened, excited. 'If it's happening far away, and she doesn't *see* the flash, and she doesn't feel anything . . .' She turned on Claire. 'You didn't feel anything when you stopped the train?'

'I didn't stop the train,' Claire said, slowly and with shaky patience. 'And I didn't do anything about that fire at the Marina, if that's what you're talking about.'

'Claire, why are you in such total denial about this?'

'Because it's not the truth. I *know* I didn't do anything, Jez. When you know, you know.'

'Actually, I don't blame her,' Hugh said. 'It's not a great job.'

Jez blinked, and then the truth swept over her. Her entire body went cold.

Oh, Goddess . . . *Claire*.

Claire's life as a normal person was over. She was going to have to leave everything, her family, her friends, and go into hiding. From this point on, she would be one of the four most important people in the world – the *only* of the four Wild Powers who was identified.

Constantly hunted. Constantly in danger. Sought after by everyone in the Night World, for a hundred different reasons.

And Claire had no experience. She was so innocent. How was she supposed to adjust to a life like that?

Jez shut her eyes. Her knees were so weak that she had to sit down.

'Oh, Claire . . . I'm sorry.'

Claire gulped, staring at her. There was fear in her dark eyes.

Hugh knelt. His expression was still and sad. 'I'm sorry, too,' he said, speaking directly to Claire. 'I don't blame you at all for not wanting this. But for right now, I think we'd better think about getting you someplace safe.'

Claire now had the look of somebody after an earthquake. How could this happen to me? Why wasn't I paying attention before it hit?

'I . . . have to go home,' she said. But she said it very slowly, looking at Jez in fear.

Jez shook her head. 'Claire – you can't. I—' She paused to gather herself, then spoke quietly and firmly. 'Home isn't safe anymore. There are going to be people looking for you – bad people.' She glanced at Hugh.

He nodded. 'A werewolf tried to run me down with a car, then jumped me. I think he must have followed me from the station. I knocked him out, but I didn't kill him.'

'And there's the vampire from the platform,' Jez said. 'He got away – did he see the flash?'

'He saw everything. We were both right there, looking down at you. After that, he took off running. I'm sure he's going back to report to whoever sent him.'

'And they'll be putting everything they have on the streets, looking for us.' Jez looked around the garage. 'We need transportation, Hugh.'

Hugh gave a tiny grin. 'Why do I have the feeling you don't mean a taxi?'

'If you've got a pocketknife, I can hotwire a car. But we have to make sure nobody's around. The last thing we need is the police.'

They both stood up, Jez reaching down absentmindedly to pull Claire to her feet.

Claire whispered, 'Wait. I'm not ready for this—'

Jez braced herself to be merciless. 'You're never going to be ready, Claire. Nobody is. But you have no idea what these people will do to you if they find you. You . . . just have no idea.'

She located a Mustang across the garage. 'That's a good one. Let's go.'

There was a loose brick in the wall near the car. Jez wrapped it in her jacket and broke the window.

It only took a moment to get the door open and another few seconds to start the car. And then everybody was inside and Jez was pulling smoothly out.

'Take Ygnacio Boulevard to the freeway,' Hugh said. 'We've got to head south. There's a safe house in Fremont.'

But they never made it out of the garage.

Jez saw the Volvo as she turned the first corner toward the exit. It had its brights on and it was heading right for them. She twisted the wheel, trying to manoeuvre, but a Mustang wasn't a motorcycle. She didn't have room. She couldn't slip out and get away.

The Volvo never even slowed down. And this time there was no blue light. There was a terrible crashing of metal on metal, and Jez fell into darkness.

Everything hurt.

Jez woke up slowly. For a long moment she had no idea where she was. Someplace – moving.

She was being jolted and jarred, and that wasn't good, because she seemed to be bruised all over. Now, how had that happened . . . ?

She remembered.

And sat up so fast that it made her head spin. She found herself looking around the dim interior of a van.

Dim because there were no real windows. The one in back had been covered from the outside with duct tape, and only a little light came through at the top and bottom. No light came from the front. The driver's compartment was closed off from the back by a metal wall.

There were no seats in back, nothing at all to work with. Only three figures lying motionless on the floor.

Claire. Hugh. And . . . Morgead.

Jez stared, crawling forward to look at each of them.

Claire looked all right. She had been in the back-seat with a seat belt on. Her face was very pale, but she didn't seem to be bleeding and she was breathing evenly.

Hugh looked worse. His right arm was twisted oddly under him. Jez touched it gently and determined that it was broken.

And I don't have anything to set it with. And I think something else is wrong with him – his breathing's raspy.

Finally she looked at Morgead.

He looked great. He wasn't scraped or bruised or cut

like the rest of them. The only injury she could find was a huge lump on his forehead.

Even as she brushed his hair back from it, he stirred.

His eyes opened and Jez found herself looking into dark emeralds.

'Jez!' He sat up, too fast. She pushed him back down. He struggled up again.

'Jez, what happened? Where are we?'

'I was hoping you might tell me that.'

He was looking around the van, catching up fast. Like any vampire, he didn't stay groggy long.

'I got hit. With wood. Somebody got me when I left my apartment.' He looked at her sharply. 'Are you OK?'

'Yeah. I got hit with a car. But it could be worse; it was almost a train.'

They were both looking around now, automatically in synch, searching for clues to their situation and ways to get out. They didn't have to discuss it. The first order of business was always escape.

'Do you have any idea who hit you?' Jez said, running her fingers over the back door. No handles, no way to get out.

'No. Pierce called to say he'd come up with something on the Wild Power. I was going to meet him when suddenly I got attacked from behind.' He was going over the metal barrier that separated them from the driver's cabin, but now he glanced at her. 'What do you mean, it was almost a train?'

'Nothing here. Nothing on the sides. This van is stripped.'

'Nothing here, either. What do you mean, a train?'

Jez wiggled around to face him. 'You really don't know?'

He stared at her for a moment. Either he was a fantastic

actor, or he was both innocent and outraged. 'You think *I* would do something to hurt you?'

Jez shrugged. 'It's happened in the past.'

He glared, seemed about to get into one of his Excited States. Then he shook his head. 'I have no idea what's going on. And I would not try to hurt you.'

'Then we're both in trouble.'

He leaned back against the metal wall. 'I believe you there.' He was silent for a moment, then said in an odd, deliberate tone, 'It's the Council, isn't it? They found out about Hunter's deal with us, and they're moving in.'

Jez opened her mouth, shut it. Opened it again.

'Probably,' she said.

She needed Morgead. Claire and Hugh weren't fighters. And whoever had them was a formidable enemy.

She didn't think it was the Council. The Council wouldn't use hired thugs; it would work through the Elders in San Francisco. And it would have no reason to kidnap Morgead; the deal with Hunter Redfern didn't really exist.

Whoever it really was had a good intelligence system, good enough to discover that Morgead knew something about the Wild Power. And had a lot of money, because it had imported a lot of muscle. And had a sense of strategy, because the kidnappings of Jez and Claire and Hugh and Morgead had been beautifully timed and nicely executed.

It might be some rogue vampire or werewolf chieftain who wanted to grab power. It might be some rival vampire gang in California. For all Jez knew, it might even be some insane faction of Circle Daybreak. The only thing that was certain was that she was going to have to fight them whenever this van got where it was going, and that she needed all the help she could get.

So it was important to lie to Morgead one last time, and hope that he would fight with her.

She had to get Claire away safely.

That was all that mattered. The world would survive without her and Morgead, and even without Hugh, although it would be a darker place. But it wouldn't survive without Claire.

'Whether it's the Council or not, we're going to have to fight them,' she said out loud. 'How's your energy-blast trick? The one you demonstrated when we were stick-fighting.'

He snorted. 'Not good. I used up all my Power fighting the guys who tackled me. It'll be a long time before I recharge.'

Jez's heart sank. 'Too bad,' she said unemotionally. 'Because those two aren't going to be able to do much.'

'Those humans? Who are they, by the way?' His voice was so carefully careless again.

Jez hesitated. If she said they were unimportant, he might not help her save them. But she couldn't tell the truth, either.

'That's Claire, and this is Hugh. They're – acquaintances. They've helped me in the past.'

'Humans?'

'Even humans can be useful sometimes.'

'I thought maybe one of them might be the Wild Power.'

'You thought if I found the Wild Power I wouldn't tell you?'

'It occurred to me.'

'You're so cynical, Morgead.'

'I prefer to call it observant,' he said. 'For instance, I can tell you something about your friend Hugh, there. I saw him in the city, just once, but I remember his face. He's a damned Daybreaker.'

161

Jez felt a tension in her chest, but she kept her face expressionless. 'So maybe I'm using him for something.'

'And maybe,' Morgead said, simply and pleasantly, 'you're using me.'

Jez lost her breath. She stared at him. His face was shadowed, but she could see its clean lines, the strong but delicate features, the darkness of his eyebrows and the tension in his jaw. And she knew, as he narrowed his eyes, that they were the colour of glacier ice.

'You know,' he said, 'there's still a connection between us. I can feel it, sort of like a cord between our minds. It pulls. You can't deny it, Jez. It's there whether you like it or not. And—' He considered, as if thinking of the best way to put this. 'It tells me things. Things about you.'

Oh, hell, Jez thought. It's over. I'm just going to have to protect Hugh and Claire myself. From him and whoever's got us.

Part of her was scared, but part was just furious, the familiar fury of needing to bash Morgead over the head. He was so certain of himself, so . . . smug.

'So what's it telling you now?' she said sarcastically before she could stop herself.

'That you're not telling the truth. That there's something you're keeping from me, something you've been keeping from me. And that it has to do with him.' He nodded toward Hugh.

He knew. The jerk knew and he was just playing with her. Jez could feel self-control slipping away.

'Something to do with why you want the Wild Power,' Morgead went on, a strange smile playing on his lips. 'And with where you've been for the past year, and with why you suddenly want to protect humans. And why you say "Goddess" when you're surprised. No vampire says that. It's a witch thing.'

Goddess, I'm going to kill him, Jez thought, clenching her teeth. 'Anything else?' she said evenly.

'And with why you're scared of me reading your thoughts.' He smirked. 'Told you I was observant.'

Jez lost it. 'Yeah, Morgead, you're brilliant. So are you smart enough to figure out what it all means? Or just to get suspicious?'

'It means—' He looked uncertain suddenly, as if he *hadn't* exactly figured out where all this was leading. He frowned. 'It means . . . that you're . . .' He looked at her. 'With Circle Daybreak.'

It came out as a statement, but a weak one. Almost a question. And he was staring at her with an I-don't-believe-it look.

'Very good,' Jez said nastily. 'Two points. No, one; it took you long enough.'

Morgead stared at her. Then he suddenly erupted out of his side of the van. Jez jumped forward, too, in a crouch that would let her move fluidly and protect Hugh and Claire.

But Morgead didn't attack. He just tried to grab her shoulders and shake her.

'You little *idiot*!' he yelled.

Jez was startled. 'What?'

'You're a *Daybreaker*?'

'I thought you had it all figured out.' What was wrong with him? Instead of looking betrayed and bloodthirsty he looked scared and angry. Like a mother whose kid has just run in front of a bus.

'I did – I guess – but I still can't *believe* it. Jez, why? Don't you know how stupid that is? Don't you realize what's going to happen to them?'

'Look, Morgead—'

'They're going to *lose*, Jez. It's not just going to be the

Council against them now. Everybody in the Night World is going to be gunning for them. They're going to get wiped out, and anybody who sides with them will be wiped out, too.'

His face was two inches from hers. Jez glared at him, refusing to give ground. 'I'm not just siding with them,' she hissed. 'I *am* one of them. I'm a damned Daybreaker.'

'You're a dead Daybreaker. I can't believe this. How am I supposed to protect you from the whole Night World?'

She stared at him. '*What?*'

He settled back, glaring, but not at her. He was looking around the van, avoiding her eyes. 'You heard me. I don't care who your friends are, Jez. I don't even care that you came back to use me. I'm just glad you came back. We're soulmates, and nothing can change that.' Then he shook his head furiously. 'Even if you won't admit it.'

'Morgead . . .' Suddenly the ache in Jez's chest was too much to stay inside. It was closing off her throat, making her eyes sting, trying to make her cry.

She had misjudged Morgead, too. She'd been so sure that he would hate her, that he could never forgive.

But of course, he didn't know the whole truth yet.

He probably thought that her being a Daybreaker was something she would grow out of. That it was just a matter of getting her to see the light and change sides again, and she would become the old Jez Redfern. He didn't realize that the old Jez Redfern had been an illusion.

'I'm sorry,' she said abruptly, helplessly. 'For all of this, Morgead – I'm sorry. It really wasn't fair to you for me to come back.'

He looked irritated. 'I told you; I'm glad you did. We can work things out – if you'll just stop being so *stubborn*. We'll get out of this—'

'Even if we do get out of it, nothing's going to change.' She looked up at him. She wasn't frightened of what he might do anymore. The only thing she was frightened of was seeing disgust in his eyes – but she still had to tell him. 'I can't be your soulmate, Morgead.'

He hardly seemed to be listening to her. 'Yes, you can. I told you, I don't care who your friends are. We'll keep you alive somehow. The only thing I don't understand is why you'd *want* to ally yourself with stupid humans, when you know they're going to lose.'

Jez looked at him. Morgead, the vampire's vampire, whose only interest was in seeing the Night World conquer humanity completely. Who was what she had been a year ago, and what she could never be again. Who thought of her as an ally, a descendent of one of the first families of the lamia.

Who thought he loved who he thought she was.

Jez kept looking at him steadily, and when she spoke, it was very quietly. And it was the truth.

'Because *I'm* a human,' she said.

CHAPTER
17

Morgead's entire body jerked once and then went absolutely still. As if he'd been turned to stone. The only thing alive about him was his eyes, which were staring at Jez with shock and burning disbelief.

Well, Jez told herself, with a grim humour that was almost like sobbing grief, I startled him, that's for sure. I finally managed to stun Morgead speechless.

It was only then that she realized some part of her had hoped that he already knew this, too. That he would be able to brush it off with exasperation, the way he had the fact that she was a Daybreaker.

But that hope was shattered now. It had been a stupid hope anyway. Being a Daybreaker was something that could change, a matter of confused attitude.

Being vermin was permanent.

'But that's – that's not—' Morgead seemed to be having trouble getting the words out. His eyes were large with horror and denial. 'That's not *possible*. You're a vampire.'

'Only half,' Jez said. She felt as if she were killing something – and she was. She was murdering any hope for what was between them.

Might as well stomp it good, she thought bitterly. She couldn't understand the wetness that was threatening to spill out of her eyes.

'The other half is human,' she said shortly, almost viciously. 'My mother was human. Claire is my cousin, and she's human. I've been living with my uncle Jim, my mother's brother, and his family. They're all human.'

Morgead shut his eyes. A moment of astonishing weakness for him, Jez thought coldly.

His voice was still a whisper. 'Vampires and humans can't have kids. You can't be half and half.'

'Oh, yeah, I can. My father broke the laws of the Night World. He fell in love with a human, and they got married, and here I am. And then, when I was three or so, some other vampires came and tried to kill us all.' In her mind Jez was seeing it again, the woman with red hair who looked like a medieval princess, begging for her child's life. The tall man trying to protect her. '*They* knew I was half human. They kept yelling "Kill the freak." So that's what I am, you see.' She turned eyes she knew were feverishly bright on him. 'A freak.'

He was shaking his head, gulping as if he were about to be sick. It made Jez hate him, and feel sorry for him at the same time. She scarcely noticed that hot tears were spilling down her cheeks.

'I'm vermin, Morgead. One of *them*. Prey. That's what I realized a year ago, when I left the gang. Up until then I had no idea, but that last night we hunted, I remembered the truth. And I knew that I had to go away and try to make up for all the things I'd done to humans.'

He put a hand up to press against his eyes.

'I didn't just become a Daybreaker. I became a vampire hunter. I track down vampires who like to kill, who enjoy

167

making humans suffer, and I stake them. You know why? Because they deserve to die.'

He was looking at her again, but as if he could hardly stand to. 'Jez—'

'It's weird. I don't know about our *connection*' – she smiled bitterly at him, to let him know she knew all that was over now – 'but I felt bad lying to you. I'm almost glad to finally tell you the truth. I kind of wanted to tell you a year ago when it happened, but I knew you'd kill me, and that made me a little hesitant.'

She was laughing now. She realized she was more than a little hysterical. But it didn't seem to matter. Nothing mattered while Morgead was looking at her with that sick disbelief in his eyes.

'So, anyway . . .' She stretched her muscles, still smiling at him, but ready to defend herself. 'Are you going to try and kill me now? Or is the engagement just off?'

He simply looked at her. It was as if his entire spirit had gone out of him. He didn't speak, and all at once Jez couldn't think of anything to say, either. The silence stretched and stretched, like a yawning chasm between them.

They were so far away from each other.

You knew all along it would come to this, Jez's mind told her mockingly. How can you presume to be upset? He's actually taking it better than you expected. He hasn't tried to tear your throat out yet.

At last Morgead said, in a flat and empty voice, 'That's why you wouldn't drink my blood.'

'I haven't had a blood meal for a year,' Jez said, feeling equally empty. 'I don't need to, if I don't use my Powers.'

He stared past her at the metal wall. 'Well, maybe you'd better drink some of your human friends',' he said tiredly. 'Because whoever has us—'

He broke off, suddenly alert. Jez knew what it was.

The van was slowing down, and the tires were crunching on gravel.

They were pulling into a driveway.

A long driveway, and a steep one. We're somewhere out in the country, Jez thought.

She didn't have time for any more banter with Morgead. Although she felt drained and numb, she was focussed on outside issues now.

'Look,' she said tensely as the van braked. 'I know you hate me now, but whoever has us hates us both. I'm not asking you to help me. I just want to get my cousin away – and I'm asking you not to stop me from doing that. Later, you can fight me or whatever. We can take care of that between the two of us. Just don't stop me from saving Claire.'

He just looked at her with dark and hollow eyes. He didn't agree or disagree. He didn't move when she positioned herself to erupt out of the van as soon as the back door was opened.

But, as it turned out, she could have saved her breath. Because when the door did open, letting in sunlight that blinded Jez, it was to reveal five vicious-looking thugs, completely blocking the entrance. Three of them had spears with deadly points levelled right at Jez. The other two had guns.

'If anybody tries to fight,' a voice from around the side of the van said, 'shoot the unconscious ones in the kneecaps.'

Jez sagged back. She didn't try to fight as they forced her out of the van.

Neither, strangely, did Morgead. There were more thugs standing around behind the van, enough to surround both Jez and Morgead with a forest of spears as they were led to the house.

It was a nice house, a small sturdy Queen Anne painted barn red. There were trees all around and no other buildings in sight.

We're out in the boondocks, Jez thought. Maybe Point Reyes Park. Somewhere remote, anyway, where nobody can hear us scream.

They were shepherded into the living room of the house, and Hugh and Claire were dumped unceremoniously on the floor.

And then they were all tied up.

Jez kept watching for an opportunity to attack. But one never came. All the time she and Morgead were being tied, two of the thugs pointed guns at Claire and Hugh. There was no way Jez could disarm them both before they got off a shot.

Worse, she was being rendered helpless by an expert. The cords were made of bast, the inner bark of trees. Equally effective against vampires and humans. When the guy tying her up was through, she had no use of her arms or legs.

Hugh woke up, gasping with pain, when they tied his injured arm. Claire woke up when the werewolf thug who'd finished winding cords around her slapped her.

Jez looked at that particular 'wolf carefully. She was too angry to glare at him. But she wanted to remember his face.

Then she looked back at Claire, who was staring around her in bewilderment.

'I – where are we? What's going on, Jez?'

Hugh was also looking around, but with much less confusion. His grey eyes were simply sad and full of pain.

'It's all right, Claire,' Jez said. 'Just keep quiet, OK? We're in a little trouble, but don't tell them anything.' She stared at her cousin, trying to will her to understand.

'A little trouble? I don't think so,' came a voice from the living room doorway.

It was the same voice that had given the order about shooting kneecaps. A light, cold voice, like an Arctic wind.

The speaker was a girl.

A very pretty girl, Jez thought irrelevantly. She had black hair that fell straight down her back like silk, and eyes that gleamed like topaz. Porcelain skin. A cruel smile. Lots of Power that surrounded her like a dark aura.

A vampire.

She looked perhaps a year older than Jez, but that didn't mean anything. She could be any age.

And those eyes, Jez thought. They're vaguely familiar. Like something I've seen in a picture . . .

'I should probably introduce myself,' the girl said, looking at her with cold mockery. 'I'm Lily Redfern.'

Jez felt her stomach plummet.

Hunter Redfern's daughter.

Well, that explained a lot.

She was working for her father, of course. And she was a powerful enemy herself over four hundred years old. There were rumours that last year she'd been working the human slave trade, and making a lot of money at it.

I should laugh, Jez thought. There I was telling Morgead that Hunter wanted to steal a march on the Council – and here he really did. Just not through me, of course. He's sent his only surviving child out to take care of us, to get Morgead to turn over the Wild Power.

And that's why so many thugs – he can afford to buy as many as he needs. And the smooth operation – Lily's a born strategist. Not to mention absolutely merciless and cold as ice.

She was right. We're not in a little trouble. We're in a whole lot.

Somebody, Jez thought with a strange, quiet certainty, is going to die here.

Lily was still talking. 'And now let me introduce my associates, who've done so much to make this all possible.' She gestured at someone hidden in the hall to come forward. 'This is Azarius. I think you've met.'

It was the vampire Jez had fought on the platform. He was tall, with dark skin and a look of authority.

'And this,' Lily said, smiling, 'is someone you've also met.' She gestured again, and a second figure appeared in the doorway.

It was Pierce Holt.

He was smiling faintly, his aristocratic face drawn in lines of genteel triumph. He waved one slender hand at them, his eyes as cold as Lily's.

Morgead gave an inarticulate roar and tried to lunge at him.

He only succeeded in falling on the floor, a struggling body in a cocoon of bast. Lily and Azarius both laughed. Pierce just looked scornful.

'You really didn't guess?' he said. 'You're so stupid, Morgead. Coming out this morning to meet me, so trusting, so naive – I thought you were smarter. I'm disappointed.'

'No, you're *dead*,' Morgead raged from the floor. He was staring at Pierce, black hair falling over his forehead and into green eyes that were blazing with rage. 'You are *dead* when this is over! You betrayed the gang. You're complete scum. You're—'

'Shut him up,' Lily said, and one of the thugs kicked Morgead in the head.

He must really be out of power, Jez thought, wincing. Or he'd have blasted Pierce then.

'I'm smart,' Pierce was saying. 'And I'm going to

172

survive. I knew something was fishy when *she'* – he nodded toward Jez without looking at her – 'said she had a deal with Hunter Redfern. It didn't sound right – and then the way she was *so* worried about that vermin kid. So I made a few calls, and I found out the truth.'

'You realize that your friend there is working with Circle Daybreak,' Lily interrupted. She was also looking at Morgead and ignoring Jez. 'She lied to you and tricked you. She was trying to get the Wild Power for them.'

Morgead snarled something inarticulate.

'And she's not just a Daybreaker,' Pierce said. Finally he looked at Jez, and it was with venomous spite. 'She's a mutant abomination. She's half vermin. She should have been drowned at birth.'

'*You* should have been drowned at birth,' Morgead said through locked teeth.

Lily had been watching in amusement, but now she waved one hand. 'OK, enough fun and games. Down to business.' Two of the thugs sat Morgead back up, and Lily walked to the middle of the room. She looked at each of them in turn, Jez last. 'I've only got one question for you,' she said in her cool, quiet voice. 'Which human is the Wild Power?'

Jez stared at her.

She doesn't know. She knows almost everything else, but not that. And if she can't find out . . .

Jez gave Hugh and Claire one long, intense look, telling them to keep silent. Then she looked back at Lily.

'I have no idea what you're talking about.'

Lily hit her.

It was a pretty good blow, but nothing to compare with what Jez got when she was in a fight. Jez laughed, a natural laugh of surprise and scorn.

Lily's hawklike golden eyes went icy.

'You think this is funny?' she said, still quietly. 'My father sent me to get the Wild Power, and that's just what I'm going to do. Even if it means tearing you and your vampire boyfriend to pieces, mutant.'

'Yeah, well, suppose I don't know? Did you ever think of that? Then I *can't* tell, no matter what you and your little . . .' Jez glanced at Pierce and Azarius. 'Your little hobgoblins do.'

Lily's porcelain skin was flushing with fury. It brought out faint scars on one side of her face that Jez hadn't noticed before, like mostly-healed burn marks. 'Look, you little freak—' Then she turned to the thugs. 'Teach her a lesson.'

Things were exciting for a while. Jez could hear Claire and Hugh yelling and Morgead snarling while the hobgoblins beat her up. She hardly felt the blows herself. She was in a place where they didn't matter.

When they finally got tired and stopped, Lily walked up to her again.

'Now,' she said sweetly, 'has your memory gotten any better.'

Jez looked at her from under a swelling eyelid. 'I can't tell you something I don't know.'

Lily opened her mouth, but before she could speak, a new voice cut in.

'She doesn't have to tell you,' Hugh said. 'I'll tell you. It's me.'

Lily swivelled slowly to look at him.

He was sitting up straight inside his cocoon of bonds, his face calm under the dried blood. His grey eyes were clear and straightforward. He didn't look afraid.

Oh, Hugh, Jez thought. Her heart was beating slow and hard and her eyes prickled.

Lily glanced at Azarius.

He shrugged. 'Sure, it could be. I told you, it could be either of them. They were both at the station when the flash came and the train stopped.'

'Hmm,' Lily said, a sound like a cat purring to dinner. She moved toward Hugh. He didn't look away from her, didn't flinch.

But beside him, Claire gave a convulsive wiggle.

She had been watching everything with a desperate, dazed expression. Jez was sure she didn't understand a quarter of what was going on. But now she suddenly lost the muddled look. Her dark eyes sparked and she looked like the Claire who'd taunted Jez a hundred times in the hallway back home.

'I don't know *what* you're talking about,' she said to Hugh. 'You know perfectly well it's me.' She turned to Lily. 'I'm the Wild Power.'

Lily's mouth tightened. She put her hands on her hips, looking from Hugh to Claire.

Then Jez heard the strangest sound of her life.

It was laughing – a wild and reckless laughing. There was an edge almost like crying to it, but also something that was exhilarated, daredevil, free.

'If you *really* want to know who it is,' Morgead said, 'it's *me*.'

Lily whirled to glare at him. Jez simply stared, dumbfounded.

She'd never seen him look so handsome – or so mocking. His smile was brilliant and flashing, his dark hair was falling all over his eyes, and his eyes were blazing green emeralds. He was tied up, but he was sitting with his head thrown back like a prince.

Something tore inside Jez.

She didn't understand why he would do it. He must know he wasn't saving her. The only people he might possibly save were Hugh and Claire. And why would he care about them?

Besides, it was a futile gesture. He didn't realize that he *couldn't* be the Wild Power, that he hadn't been around when the train stopped.

But – it was such a gallant gesture, too. Probably the most gallant thing Jez had ever seen.

She stared at him, feeling the wetness spill from her eyes again, wishing she were telepathic and could ask him why in the worlds he had done it.

Then his green eyes turned to her, and she heard his mental voice.

There's just a chance they'll let one of them go with a beating. Just maybe – as a warning to Circle Daybreak not to mess with Hunter anymore. Especially if I convince Lily I'll work with her.

Jez couldn't answer, but she shook her head very faintly, and looked at him in despair. She knew he could read that. Do you know what they'll do to *you*? Especially when they find out you're a fake?

She saw his faint answering smile. He knew.

What difference does it make? he said in her mind. *You and me – we're lost anyway. And without you, I don't care what happens.*

Jez couldn't show any reaction to that at all. Her vision was dimming, and her heart felt as if it were trying to claw itself out of her chest.

Oh, Morgead . . .

Lily was breathing hard, on the verge of losing control. 'If I have to kill all of you—'

'Wait,' Pierce said, his cool voice a striking contrast to Lily's strained one. 'There's a simple way to find out.' He pointed at Jez. 'Stake her.'

Lily glared at him. '*What?*'

'She's never going to tell you anything. She's

expendable. And there's something you have to understand about the Wild Power.' He moved smoothly to Lily's side. 'I think Morgead was right about one thing. I think the Wild Power isn't operating consciously at this point. It's only when the danger is greatest, when there's no physical way to escape, that the power comes out.'

Lily cast a sideways look at Hugh and Claire, who were sitting tensely, their eyes wide. 'You mean *they* may not know which it is?'

'Maybe not. Maybe it's completely automatic at this point. But there's one way to find out. They all seem – attached – to the halfbreed. Put her life in danger, and then see which of them can break free and try to save her.'

Lily's perfect lips slowly curved in a smile. 'I knew there was a reason I liked you,' she said.

Then she gestured at the thugs. 'Go on, do it.'

Everything was confused for a bit. Not because Jez was struggling. She wasn't. But Claire was screaming and Hugh and Morgead were shouting, and Lily was laughing. When the worst of the noise died down, Jez found herself on her back. Azarius was standing over her, and he was holding a hammer and stake.

'Isn't it interesting,' Lily was saying, 'that a stake through the heart is the one thing that takes care of humans and vampires equally efficiently?'

'And halfbreeds, too,' Pierce said. They were on either side of Azarius, looking down and laughing.

'Lily, listen. *Listen*,' Morgead said, his voice hoarse and desperate. 'You don't have to do this. I already told you, it's me. Just wait a minute and *talk* to me—'

'Don't even bother, human-lover,' Lily said without glancing at him. 'If you're the Wild Power, then save her.'

'Don't any of you do anything!' Jez yelled. 'Not *anything*, do you understand?'

She was yelling it mainly at Claire – or was she?

Suddenly Jez felt strangely uncertain.

Her heart was beating very quickly, and her mind was racing even faster. Fragments of thought were glittering through her consciousness, like bits of melody almost too faint to catch. It was as if all the prophecies she'd heard about the Wild Powers were echoing, ricocheting around her brain at insane speed. And there was something about them, something that was bothering her. Something that made her wonder . . .

Could it be that Claire *wasn't* the Wild Power? Jez had assumed she was – but was it possible that she'd been wrong?

Hugh had been on the platform, too, watching the train approach. Hugh had reason to be upset at having to watch Jez die. He cared about her. Jez knew that now. And Hugh was seventeen.

Could Hugh be the Wild Power?

He hadn't been in the Marina district – but he lived in the Bay Area; there was no reason he couldn't have been watching the fire just as she and Claire had.

But there was still something nagging at her. The prophecies . . . 'two eyes are watching' . . . 'Four of blue fire, power in their blood . . .'

Lily was speaking. Jez heard her as if from a great distance.

'Do it. Right beside the heart first.'

Azarius positioned the stake. He raised the hammer.

Morgead screamed, '*Jez!*'

Jez shouted, 'None of you do anything—'

And then the hammer came down and the universe exploded in red agony.

CHAPTER
18

Jez heard herself scream, but only faintly.

There was a roaring in her ears as if the BART train was coming at her again. And a pain that engulfed her whole body, sending agonized spasms through her limbs. It centred in her chest, though, where something white-hot was lodged inside her, crushing her lung and dislodging her internal organs and burning right beside her heart.

She'd been staked.

What she had done so often to others had been done to her.

She hadn't realized anything could hurt like this. She was glad none of her victims had lived long to keep suffering.

The wood of the stake was poisoning her heart, she knew. Even if it were removed, she would die. No vampire could survive contact between living wood and its undead heart.

Still, she would live for a little while – in unimaginable agony as the poison ate through her.

A voice was screaming in her mind. *JezJezJezJez* . . . Over and over, incoherently.

Morgead, she thought. And she hoped he wasn't feeling any of what she was feeling through the silver cord that connected them.

Hugh and Claire were sobbing. Jez wished they wouldn't. They had to stay calm; to think of a way to save themselves.

Because she couldn't help them anymore.

Over the sobbing she heard a shrill and angry voice. Lily.

'What is wrong with you?' Lily was saying. 'Don't you see what's happening to her? Don't you *want* to save her?'

Through the red haze that filled Jez's vision, she felt dim approval. They were doing what she'd told them. Whichever of them was the Wild Power was suppressing it.

Good. That was what mattered. Although she couldn't really remember why any longer . . .

Suddenly a face broke through the red haze. It was Lily, bending over her.

'Don't *you* understand?' Lily yelled. 'You can stop this right now. I'll have him kill you cleanly – all the pain will be over. All you have to do is tell me who it is.'

Jez smiled at her faintly. She couldn't breathe to answer, and she didn't want to try.

Would you believe that I don't know? she thought. No, I don't think you would . . .

The pain was getting less by itself. It was as if Jez was moving farther and farther away from it.

'How can you be so *stupid*?' Lily was screaming. Her face was twisted, and to Jez's vision, floating in a scarlet mist. She looked like a monster. Then she turned and seemed to be screaming at someone else. 'All right. Get the other vampire down here, too. Morgead.' She was looking at Jez again. 'We'll just have to stake your friends one after another until the Wild Power decides to reveal itself.'

No. *No* . . .

Suddenly everything was much clearer around Jez. She could see the room again, and she could feel her own body. There was still the roaring in her ears, but she could hear Claire's sobs over it.

No. Lily couldn't mean it. This couldn't be happening . . .

But it was. They were shoving Morgead down on the floor beside her, and Claire and Hugh beyond him. The thugs with spears were getting into position.

No. No. *This can't happen.*

Jez wanted to scream at them, to tell the Wild Power to do something, because everything was lost now anyway. But she didn't have air to scream. And she felt so adrift and confused anyway . . . Her universe had become disjointed. Her thoughts seemed to be unraveling at all once, past memories combining with flashing sensory impressions from the present, and with strange new ideas . . .

If it was involuntary, why didn't the Wild Power work magic more often? Unless there was some other requirement . . .

I can't let this happen.

The dampness of blood spreading around her heart . . .

Claire's nails digging into her arms.

'*When there's no physical way to escape* . . .'

Power in the blood.

Claire on the floor there. Screaming and screaming . . .

Something building inside her, hotter than the stake.

Morgead beside her whispering, 'Jez, I love you.'

Pierce with the stake over him. Morgead looking up unafraid . . .

Hotter than the heart of a star.

Hugh in the distance saying almost quietly, 'Goddess of Life, receive us; guide us to the other world . . .'

Hotter than the sun and colder and bluer than the moon, like fire that burned and froze and crackled like lightning all at once. Something that filled her with an energy that was past rage and past love and past all controlling and that she recognized in her soul even though she'd never consciously felt it before. It was swelling Jez to bursting, a pure and terrible flame that was never meant to be unleashed like this . . .

'Do it!' Lily shouted.

And Jez let it free.

It came roaring out from her in a silent explosion. Blue fire that streamed from her body and blasted in all directions, but especially up. It came out and out and out, engulfing everything, flowing from her in a neverending torrent. Like a solar flare that didn't stop.

It was all she could see. Blue flames, streaked with blue-white lightning that crackled almost soundlessly. Just like the fire that had cocooned her on the BART tracks.

Except that now she could tell where it was coming from, even if she couldn't direct it. She knew how to let it out, now, but once out it did what it wanted.

And it wasn't meant to be used this way. That was the only thing she knew clearly about it. She'd been letting it slip out when she was desperately upset – when she was worried for someone's life, and she knew that she couldn't do anything else to save them. That was forgivable, because it had been unconscious.

This wasn't. She was probably violating some law of the universe or something. The blue fire was only meant to be used in the last battle, when the darkness came and the Four were called to stand against it.

I suppose that means I should try to stop now, Jez thought.

She wasn't sure how to do it. She guessed that she needed to call it back, somehow, to draw it down into her body again.

Maybe if I sort of tug . . .

She did – something. A gathering-up with her mind. It was harder than letting the fire go had been, but it worked. She could feel it returning, flooding back inside her, as if she were sucking it in . . .

And then it was gone, and Jez could see the world again. Could see what it had done.

The house had disappeared.

Or most of it, anyway. There was about a foot and a half of ragged wall left all around, with charred insulation spilling out. Blue energy like electricity ran along the edges here and there, fizzing.

Other than that, no house. Not even chunks of wreckage lying around. There were fine bits of debris floating down, making the sunlight hazy, but that was all.

It got . . . vaporized, Jez thought, searching for the right word.

No Lily. No Azarius. No Pierce. And none of the ugly thugs.

Goddess, Jez thought. I didn't mean to do that. I only wanted to stop them from hurting Morgead and Claire and Hugh . . .

What about them? she thought in a sudden panic. She turned her head, painfully.

They were there. And alive. They were even stirring. The cords they'd been tied with were lying on the carpet, sizzling with that same blue energy.

It's so weird to have a carpet without a house to go with it, Jez thought fuzzily.

She was going away again. And that was too bad, but at least it didn't hurt anymore. The pain was gone completely, replaced by a warm and sleepy feeling – and the sensation of gently floating outward.

Her eyelids felt heavy.

'Jez? Jez!'

It was a husky whisper. Jez opened her eyes to see Morgead's face.

He was crying. Oh, dear, that was bad. Jez hadn't seen him cry since . . . when was it? Sometime when they'd been little kids . . .

Jez, can you hear me? Now he was talking in her mind.

Jez blinked again, and tried to think of something comforting to say to him.

'I feel warm,' she whispered.

'No, you don't!' He said it almost in a growl. Then he looked behind him, and Jez saw Hugh and Claire crawling up. They were all shining with golden light.

'You're so pretty,' she told them. 'Like angels.'

'This isn't the time for your weird humour!' Morgead shouted.

'Stop it! Don't yell at her!' That was Claire. Claire was crying, too, lovely tears that shone as they fell. She reached out and took Jez's hand, and that was nice, although Jez couldn't exactly feel it. She could see it.

'She's going to be all right,' Morgead was snarling. 'She's lost blood, but she'll be OK.'

Someone was stroking Jez's hair off her face. She felt that; it was pleasant. She frowned slowly at Morgead, because there was something important to tell him, and talking was difficult.

'Tell Hugh . . .' she whispered.

'Tell Hugh your freaking self! He's right here! And you're not going anywhere.'

Jez blinked with the difficulty changing focus. Yes, there was Hugh. He was the one stroking her hair.

'Hugh . . . the prophecy. I figured out what the two eyes watching were. They're the sun and the moon – get it? Two eyes . . . for somebody who belongs to both worlds.'

'The Day World and the Night World,' Hugh said softly. 'You got it, Jez. That was so smart.'

'And blood,' Jez whispered. ' "Power in the blood" – that's why I couldn't do it anytime I wanted. Blood has to flow before you can let out the power. The first two times Claire was scratching me. And this time . . .' Her voice died off, but it wasn't important. Everybody could see the blood this time, she knew.

Hugh's voice was thick. 'That was smart, too, Jez. You figured it out. And you saved us. You did everything just right.'

'No . . . because there's only going to be three Wild Powers now . . .'

'No, there *aren't*,' Morgead raged. 'Listen to me, Jez. There's no reason for you to die—'

Jez couldn't manage a smile anymore, or a sentence. But she whispered gently, 'Wood . . . poison.'

'No, it isn't! Not to humans. And you're half human, Jez. You're vampire enough to survive something that would kill a human, but you're human enough not to be poisoned by wood.'

Jez knew better. She couldn't see much anymore. Only Morgead, and he was getting indistinct. It wasn't that the world was dimming, though – it was getting brighter. Everything was golden and shining.

Four less one and darkness triumphs, Jez thought. I'm so sorry about that. I hope they can manage it somehow. It would be so sad for everything human to be lost. There's so much good in the world, and so much to love . . .

She couldn't even see Morgead now. Only gold. But she could hear. She could hear Claire whispering to her in a voice broken by tears, and feel wetness dropping on her face.

'I love you, Jez. You're the best cousin anybody could ever have.'

And Hugh. He was crying, too. 'Jez, I'm so proud to be your friend . . .'

And then, through the mist and the gold and the warmth and peace, came a voice that wasn't gentle at all. That was roaring in sheer outrage and fury.

'*DON'T YOU DARE DIE ON ME, JEZEBEL! DON'T YOU DARE! Or I'll follow you to the next world and KILL you.*'

Suddenly, in the pretty gold mist, she could see something else. The only thing in the universe that wasn't golden.

It was a silver cord.

'*You come back and you do it right now,*' Morgead bellowed in her ears and in her mind. '*Right now! Do you hear me?*'

The peace was shattered. Nothing seemed quite so warm and wonderful anymore, and she knew that once Morgead got into one of his Excited States, he wouldn't stop yelling until he got what he wanted.

And there was the cord right in front of her. It was strong, and she could feel that the other end was somewhere in Morgead's heart, and that he was trying to drag her back to him.

All right. Maybe if I just grab on . . .

Somehow, she was holding on to it, and bit by bit, pulling herself back. And then the golden light was fading and she was inside a body that hurt and Morgead was holding her and kissing her and crying all at the same time.

Claire's voice came from beyond him. 'She's breathing again! She's breathing!'

'I love you, you stupid human,' Morgead gasped against Jez's cheek. 'I can't live without you. Don't you know that?'

Jez whispered, 'I told you never to call me Jezebel.'

Then she fainted.

'Time for a nice bath,' the nurse said. 'And then we can have a visitor.'

Jez eyed her narrowly. The woman was kind, but she had some mania for sponge baths, and she was always putting strange-smelling ingredients in the water. Which was actually not that surprising since she was a witch.

'Skip the bath,' Jez said. 'Let the visitor in.'

'Now, now,' the witch said, shaking a finger and advancing with the sponge.

Jez sighed. Being a Wild Power in a Circle Daybreak sanctuary meant that she could have pretty much anything she wanted – except that everyone was still treating her like a little kid. Especially the nurses, who spoiled her and flattered her, but talked to her as if she were about three.

Still, she was glad to let the Circle take care of some things. Keeping her relatives safe, for instance. Although she was almost fully recovered, thanks to a strong constitution and a lot of healing spells from the witches, she wasn't up to that yet. Uncle Bracken and the entire Goddard family needed constant protection, since Hunter Redfern and the Night World Council were all undoubtedly after them by now.

The Circle had imported some experts from back East to take care of it. A rival vampire hunter, of all things, named Rashel something. Plus her soulmate, a vampire-turned-Daybreaker called Quinn.

At least they were competent. They'd gotten Jez's uncle Bracken, as well as the remnants of the gang out of San Francisco, a city that was going to be bad for their health for a while. Morgead was trying to get the gang to join Circle Daybreak for their own good, and he said that Raven, at least, was showing some interest. Val and Thistle were being stubborn, but that was hardly surprising. What was important was that they were alive.

Pierce, on the other hand, was simply gone. No one had seen a trace of him or Lily or any of her people since Jez blasted them. Apparently they had truly been vaporized, and Jez couldn't bring herself to feel *too* badly.

'All done!' the nurse said brightly, straightening Jez's pyjama top. Which was just as well because at that moment a black head came poking in the door.

'What is going *on* in here? You getting ready to go to the opera or something?'

Jez raised her eyebrows at Morgead. 'Maybe. Are you telling me I can't?'

He snorted and came in as the nurse went out. 'I wouldn't dare tell you that. You're the princess, right? You can have anything.'

'Right,' Jez said, with huge satisfaction. 'So how're Hugh and Claire?'

'Claire's fine; she fits right in with the witches here. I think she's trying to get them to put up a Web page. And Hugh's just his same stupid self. He's off saving chipmunks from toxic waste or something.'

'And how about the kid?'

'The kid,' Morgead said, 'is living it up. The Daybreakers are crazy about her; something about one of the oldest Old Souls ever found – I dunno. Anyway, they're trying to talk her mum into letting her live here. She says thanks for saving her life and she's drawing you a picture.'

Jez nodded, pleased. It would be nice if Iona came to live at the sanctuary; it meant Jez could see her a lot. Not that Jez planned to live here all the time herself – she and Morgead needed their freedom. They couldn't be penned in; they had to be able to come and go. She just hadn't gotten around to telling the Daybreakers that yet.

With the people she loved taken care of, she could turn her attention to other matters. 'Is that chocolate?'

'It's the only reason you like to see me, isn't it?' Morgead said, allowing her to take the box. He sat beside her, looking tragic.

'Nah,' Jez said with her mouth full. She swallowed. 'Everybody brings 'em.' Then she grinned. 'I like to see you for a different reason.'

He grinned wickedly back. 'I can't think what that could be.'

'Hmm . . . you're right . . . maybe there *is* no other reason.'

'Watch it, Jezebel,' he growled and leaned forward menacingly.

'Don't call me that, idiot.'

'You're the idiot, idiot.'

'And you're—' But Jez never got to finish, because he stopped her mouth with a kiss.

And then his arms were around her – so gently – and the silver cord was humming and everything was warm and there were only the two of them in the world.

> *One from the land of kings long forgotten;*
> *One from the hearth which still holds the spark;*
> *One from the Day World where two eyes are watching;*
> *One from the twilight to be one with the dark.*

BLACK
DAWN

For Michael Penny and Matthew Penny

CHAPTER

1

Maggie Neely woke up to the sound of her mother screaming.

She'd gone to bed as usual, with Jake the Great Dane sprawled heavily across her feet and the three cats jockeying for position around her head. Her cheek was resting on her open geometry book; there were homework papers scattered among the blankets, along with fragments of potato chips and an empty bag. She was wearing her jeans and a flowered pyjama top plus the only two socks she'd been able to find last night: one red velveteen anklet and one blue cotton slouch sock.

Those particular socks would eventually mean the difference between life and death for her, but at the moment Maggie had no idea of that.

She was simply startled and disorientated from being wakened suddenly. She'd never heard this kind of screaming before, and she wondered how she could be so certain it was her mother doing it.

Something . . . really bad is happening, Maggie realized slowly. The worst.

The clock on her nightstand said 2:11 A.M.

And then before she even realized she was moving, she

was lurching across her bedroom floor, with piles of dirty clothes and sports equipment trying to trip her up. She banged her shin on a wastebasket in the middle of the room and ploughed right on through. The hallway was dim, but the living room at the end was blazing with light and the screams were coming from there.

Jake trotted along beside her. When they got to the foyer by the living room he gave a half-growl, half-bark.

Maggie took in the whole scene in a glance. It was one of those moments when everything changes forever.

The front door was open, letting in the cold air of a November night in Washington. Maggie's father was wearing a short bathrobe and holding her mother, who was pulling and tearing at him as if she were trying to get away, screaming breathlessly all the while. And in the doorway four people were standing: two sheriffs, a National Park ranger, and Sylvia Weald.

Sylvia. Her brother Miles's girlfriend.

And knowledge hit her quick and hard as a hammer blow.

My brother is dead, Maggie thought.

CHAPTER
2

Beside her, Jake growled again, but Maggie only heard it distantly. No one else even looked toward them.

I can't believe how well I'm taking this, Maggie thought. Something's wrong with me. I'm not hysterical at all.

Her mind had gotten hold of the idea quite clearly, but there was no reaction in her body, no terrible feeling in her stomach. An instant later it swept over her, exactly what she'd been afraid of. A wash of adrenaline that made her skin tingle painfully and a horrible sensation of falling in her stomach. A numbness that started in her cheeks and spread to her lips and jaw.

Oh, please, she thought stupidly. Please let it not be true. Maybe he's just hurt. That would be all right. He had an accident and he's hurt – but not dead.

But if he were hurt her mother wouldn't be standing there screaming. She would be on her way to the hospital, and nobody could stop her. So that didn't work, and Maggie's mind, darting and wheeling like a frightened little animal, had to go back to *Please don't let this be true.*

Strangely, at that moment, it seemed as if there might be some way to make it not true. If she turned around and sneaked back to her bedroom before anyone saw her; if she got into bed and pulled the blankets over her head and shut her eyes . . .

But she couldn't leave her mother screaming like this.

Just then the screams died down a little. Her father was speaking in a voice that didn't sound at all like his voice. It was a sort of choked whisper. 'But why didn't you tell us you were going climbing? If you left on Halloween then it's been six days. We didn't even know our son was missing . . .'

'I'm sorry.' Sylvia was whispering, too. 'We didn't expect to be gone long. Miles's roommates knew we were going, but nobody else. It was just a spur-of-the-moment thing – we didn't have classes on Halloween and the weather was so nice and Miles said, hey, let's go out to Chimney Rock. And we just *went* . . .'

Hey, let's go. He used to say that kind of thing to me, Maggie thought with a strange, dazed twinge. But not since he met Sylvia.

The male sheriff was looking at Maggie's father. 'You weren't surprised that you hadn't heard from your son since last Friday?'

'No. He's gotten so independent since he moved out to go to college. One of his roommates called this afternoon to ask if Miles was here – but he didn't say that Miles had been gone for almost a week. I just thought he'd missed a class or something . . .' Maggie's father's voice trailed off.

The sheriff nodded. 'Apparently his roommates thought he'd taken a little unauthorized vacation,' he said. 'They got worried enough to call us tonight, but by then a ranger had already picked up Sylvia.'

Sylvia was crying. She was tall but willowy, fragile looking. Delicate. She had shimmering hair so pale it was almost silvery and clear eyes the exact colour of wood violets. Maggie, who was short and round faced, with fox-coloured hair and brown eyes, had always envied her.

But not now. Nobody could look at Sylvia now without feeling pity.

'It happened that first evening. We started up, but then the weather started turning bad and we turned around. We were moving pretty fast.' Sylvia stopped and pressed a fist against her mouth.

'It's kind of a risky time of year for climbing,' the female sheriff began gently, but Sylvia shook her head.

And she was right, Maggie thought. It wasn't that bad. Sure, it rained here most of the fall, but sometimes what the weather people called a high pressure cell settled in and the skies stayed blue for a month. All hikers knew that.

Besides, Miles wasn't scared of weather. He was only eighteen but he'd done lots of hard climbs in Washington's Olympic and Cascade ranges. He'd keep climbing all winter, getting alpine experience in snow and storms.

Sylvia was going on, her voice getting more jerky and breathless. 'Miles was . . . he'd had the flu a week before and he wasn't completely over it. But he seemed OK, strong. It happened when we were rappelling down. He was laughing and joking and everything . . . I never thought he might be tired enough to make a mistake . . .' Her voice wavered and turned into a ragged sob and the ranger put his arm around her.

Something inside Maggie froze. A mistake? Miles?

She was prepared to hear about a sudden avalanche or a piece of equipment failing. Even Sylvia falling and knocking Miles off. But Miles making a mistake?

Maggie stared at Sylvia, and suddenly something in the pitiful figure bothered her.

There was something odd about that delicately flushed

face and those tear-drenched violet eyes. It was all too perfect, too tragic, as if Sylvia were an Academy award-winning actress doing a famous scene – and enjoying it.

'I don't know *how* it happened,' Sylvia was whispering. 'The anchor was good. We should have had a back-up anchor, but we were in a hurry. And he must have . . . oh, God, there must have been something wrong with his harness. Maybe the buckle wasn't fastened right, or the carabiners might have been upside down . . .'

No.

Suddenly Maggie's feelings crystalized. It was as if everything came into focus at once.

That's impossible. That's *wrong*.

Miles was too good. Smart and strong and an amazing technical climber. Confident but careful. Maggie only hoped she'd be that good someday.

No way he'd buckle his harness wrong, or clip his 'biners upside down. No matter how sick he was. In fact, no way he'd go without a back-up anchor. *I'm* the one who tries to do things like that, and then he yells at me that if I'm not careful I'm going to have an adventure.

Miles doesn't.

So it meant Sylvia was lying.

The thought came to Maggie on a little wave of shock. It made her feel as if she were suddenly speeding backwards, or as if the room were receding from her very fast.

But *why*? Why would Sylvia make up such a terrible story? It didn't make any sense.

Sylvia had a hand half covering her eyes now.

'I looked for him, but . . . there was icefall . . . a crevasse . . .'

No body. She's saying there's *no body*.

With that, a new wave of heat swept over Maggie. And,

strangely, what made her certain of it was Sylvia's eyes.

Those violet eyes had been turned down for most of the time Sylvia had been talking, fixed on the Spanish tiles in the entry hall. But now, as Sylvia got to the last revelation, they had shifted toward Maggie. Toward Maggie's feet. They fixed there, slid away, and then came back and stayed.

It made Maggie glance down at her own feet.

My socks. She's staring at my socks.

One red and one blue – and she's noticing that. Like an actress who's said the same lines often enough that she doesn't even need to pay attention to them anymore.

All at once, hot anger was burning through Maggie's shock, filling her so there was no room for anything else. She stared hard at Sylvia, who seemed to be very far away but very bright. And in that same instant she knew for certain.

This girl is lying.

She must have done something – something terrible. And she can't show us Miles's body – or maybe there isn't a body because he's still alive.

Yes! Maggie felt suddenly lifted by hope. It *is* all a mistake. There's no reason for Miles to be dead. All we have to do is make Sylvia tell the truth.

But nobody else in the room knew. They were all listening as Sylvia went on with her story. They all believed.

'I didn't get out before the weather hit . . . I had to stay in the tent for three days. When I got out I was so weak, but I managed to signal to some climbers. They saved me, took care of me . . . By then it was too late to look for him. I knew there was no chance he'd made it through that storm . . .'

She broke down completely.

The ranger began talking about weather conditions and recovery efforts, and suddenly Maggie's mother was making strange gasping noises and sinking toward the floor.

'Mom!' Frightened, Maggie started toward her. Her father looked up and seemed to realize for the first time that she was there.

'Oh, Maggie. We've had some bad news.'

He's trying to take care of me. But he doesn't realize . . . I've got to tell him . . .

'Dad,' she said urgently. 'Listen. There's something—'

'Maggie,' her mother interrupted, stretching out a hand. She sounded rational, but there was something wild in her eyes. 'I'm so sorry, baby. Something awful has happened—'

And then she fainted. Suddenly Maggie's father was staggering under dead weight. And then the ranger and one of the sheriffs were brushing past Maggie. They were holding her mother up, and her mother's head was *lolling*, moving around on a boneless neck, and her mother's mouth and eyes were part open and part closed. A new kind of awful feeling came to Maggie, making her weak and giddy. She was afraid she would faint herself.

'Where can we—' the male officer began.

'There's the couch,' Maggie's father said hoarsely at the same time. There was no room for Maggie. She could only stand out of the way and dizzily watch them carry her mother.

As they did, Sylvia began murmuring. It took Maggie a moment to focus on the words. 'I'm so sorry. I'm so sorry. I wish there was something . . . I should go home now.'

'You stay right here,' the female officer said, looking toward Maggie's mother. 'You're in no condition to be walking anywhere. You'd be in the hospital now if you hadn't insisted on coming here first.'

'I don't need a hospital. I'm just so tired . . .'

The officer turned. 'Why don't you go sit in the car?' she said gently.

Sylvia nodded. She looked fragile and sad as she walked down the path toward the squad car. It was a beautiful exit, Maggie thought. You could practically hear the theme music swelling.

But Maggie was the only one with the chance to appreciate it. She was the only one watching as Sylvia reached the car . . . and paused.

And then turned away from it and continued on down the street.

And the end credits run, Maggie thought.

Then she thought, she's going to her apartment.

Maggie stood frozen, pulled in two directions.

She wanted to stay and help her mother. But something inside her was utterly furious and focused and it was screaming at her to follow Sylvia.

Instinct had always been Maggie's strong point.

She hung there for a moment, with her heart pounding so hard that it seemed to be coming out of her mouth. Then she ducked her head and clenched her fists.

It was a gesture the girls on her soccer team would have recognized. It meant that Steely Neely had made up her mind and was going to rush in where smarter people feared to tread. Look out, world; it's stomping time.

Maggie whirled and dashed back down the hall into her bedroom.

She slapped the light switch on and looked around as if she'd never seen the place before. What did she need – and why did she always keep it so messy? How could she *find* things?

She kicked and pulled at a pile of bath towels until a

pair of high-top tennis shoes emerged, then she jammed her feet in them. There was no time to change her pyjama top. She snatched a dark blue jacket off the floor and found herself, just for a moment, nose to nose with a photograph stuck into the frame of her mirror.

A picture of Miles, on the summit of Mount Rainier. He was grinning and giving the thumbs up sign. His hat was off and his auburn hair was shining in the sun like red gold. He looked handsome and a little wicked.

Scrawled in black marker across white snow was 'For the bossiest, nosiest, stubbornest, BEST little sister in the world. Love, Miles.'

With no idea *why* she was doing it, Maggie pulled the picture out of the mirror. She shoved it in her jacket pocket and ran back down the hall.

Everyone was gathered around the couch, now. Even Jake was nosing his way in. Maggie couldn't see her mother, but the lack of frantic activity told her that there wasn't any crisis going on. Everyone seemed quiet and restrained.

It'll just take a few minutes. It's better for me not to tell them anything until I'm sure. I'll probably be back before they even realize I'm gone.

With that jumble of excuses in her mind, she slipped out the front door to follow Sylvia.

CHAPTER
3

It was raining, of course. Not a terrible storm, just a steady spitting patter that Maggie hardly noticed. It plastered her hair down but it also concealed the noise of her steps.

And the low-lying clouds blocked out Mount Rainier. In clear weather the mountain loomed over the city like an avenging white angel.

I'm actually following somebody, Maggie thought. She could hardly believe it, but she was really moving down her own home street like a spy, skirting cars and ducking behind rhododendron bushes.

While all the time keeping her eyes on the slender figure in front of her.

That was what kept her going. She might have felt silly and almost embarrassed to be doing this – but not tonight. What had happened put her far beyond embarrassment, and if she started to relax inside and feel the faint pricklings of uncertainty, memory surged up again and swept everything else away.

The memory of Sylvia's voice. *The buckle might not have been fastened right.* And the memory of her mother's hand going limp as her body sagged.

I'll follow you no matter where you go, Maggie thought. And then . . .

She didn't know what then. She was trusting to instinct, letting it guide her. It was stronger and smarter than she was at the moment.

Sylvia's apartment was in the U district, the college area around the University of Washington. It was a long walk, and by the time they reached it, the rain was coming down harder. Maggie was glad to get out of it and follow Sylvia into the underground garage.

This is a dangerous place, she thought as she walked into the echoing darkness. But it was simply a note made by her mind, with no emotion attached. At the moment she felt as if she could punch a mugger hard enough to splatter him against the wall.

She kept a safe distance as Sylvia waited for the elevator, then headed for the stairs. Third floor. Maggie trotted up faster than the elevator could make it and arrived not even breathing hard. The door of the stairwell was half open and she watched from behind it as Sylvia walked to an apartment door and raised a hand to knock.

Before she could, the door opened. A boy who looked a little older than Maggie was holding it, letting a couple of laughing girls out. Music drifted to Maggie, and the smell of incense.

They're having a party in there.

That shouldn't be so shocking – it was Saturday night. Sylvia lived with three roommates; *they* were undoubtedly the ones having the party. But as the girls walked past Sylvia they smiled and nodded and Sylvia smiled and nodded back before walking calmly through the door.

Hardly the sort of thing you do when your boyfriend's just been killed, Maggie thought fiercely. And it doesn't exactly fit the 'tragic heroine' act, either.

Then she noticed something. When the boy holding the door let go, it had swung almost shut – but not quite.

Can I do it? Maybe. If I look confident. I'd have to walk right in as if I belonged, not hesitate.

And hope she doesn't notice. Then get behind her. See if she talks to anybody, what she says . . .

The laughing girls had caught the elevator. Maggie walked straight up to the door and, without pausing, she pushed it open and went inside.

Look confident, she thought, and she kept on going, instinctively moving toward a side wall. Her entry didn't seem to have caused a stir, and it was easier than she'd thought to walk in among these strangers. The apartment was very dark, for one thing. And the music was medium loud, and everybody seemed to be talking.

The only problem was that she couldn't see Sylvia. She put her back to the wall and waited for her eyes to adjust.

Not over there, not by the stereo. Probably in one of the bedrooms in back, changing.

It was as she moved toward the little hallway that led to the bedrooms that Maggie really noticed the strangeness. Something about this apartment, about this party . . . was off. Weird. It gave her the same feeling that Sylvia did.

Danger.

This place is dangerous.

Everybody there was so good-looking – or else ugly in a really fashionable way, as if they'd just stepped off MTV. But there was an air about them that reminded Maggie of the sharks at the Seattle Aquarium. A coldness that couldn't be seen, only sensed.

There is something so wrong here. Are they all drug dealers or something? Satanists? Some kind of junior mafia? They just feel so *evil* . . .

Maggie herself felt like a cat with all its fur standing on end.

When she heard a girl's voice coming from the first bedroom, she froze, hoping it was Sylvia.

'Really, the most secret place you've ever imagined.' It wasn't Sylvia. Maggie could just see the speaker through the crack in the door. She was pale and beautiful, with one long black braid, and she was leaning forward and lightly touching the back of a boy's hand.

'So exotic, so mysterious – it's a place from the past, you see. It's ancient, and everybody's forgotten about it, but it's still there. Of course, it's terribly dangerous – but not for *us* . . .'

Not relevant, Maggie's mind decided, and she stopped listening. Somebody's weird vacation plans; nothing to do with Sylvia or Miles.

She kept on edging down the hall. The door at the end was shut.

Sylvia's bedroom.

Well, she has to be in there; she isn't anywhere else.

With a surreptitious glance behind her, Maggie crept closer to the door. She leaned toward it until her cheek touched the cool white paint on the wood, all the while straining her eyes toward the living room in case somebody should turn her way. She held her breath and tried to look casual, but her heart was beating so loudly that she could only hear it and the music.

Certainly there was nobody talking behind the door. Maggie's hopes of eavesdropping faded.

All right, then, I'll go in. And there's no point in trying to be stealthy; she's going to *notice*.

So I'll just do it.

It helped that she was so keyed up. She didn't even need to brace herself; her body was at maximum tension already. Despite her sense that there was something menacing about this whole place, she wasn't frightened, or at least not in a way that *felt* like fear. It felt like rage instead, like being desperately ready for battle. She wanted to grab something and shake it to pieces.

She took hold of the knob and pushed the door open.

A new smell of incense hit her as the air rushed out. It was stronger than the living room smell, more earthy and musky, with an overlying sweetness that Maggie didn't like. The bedroom was even darker than the hall, but Maggie stepped inside. There was tension on the door somehow; as soon as she let go of it, it whispered shut behind her.

Sylvia was standing beside the desk.

She was alone, and she was still wearing the Gore-Tex climbing outfit she'd had on at Maggie's house. Her shimmering fine hair was starting to dry and lifting up like little angel feathers away from her forehead.

She was doing something with a brass incense burner, adding pinches of powder and what looked like herbs to it. That was where the sickeningly sweet smell was coming from.

Maggie had planned – as far as she'd planned anything at all – to rush right up and get in Sylvia's face. To startle her into some kind of confession. She was going to say, 'I need to talk to you.' But before she could get the first word out, Sylvia spoke without looking up.

'What a shame. You really should have stayed home with your parents, you know.' Her voice was cool and languorous, not hasty and certainly not regretful.

Maggie stopped in her tracks.

Now, what's *that* supposed to mean? Is it a threat? Fine. Whatever. I can threaten, too.

But she was taken by surprise, and she had to swallow

hard before speaking roughly. 'I don't know what you're talking about, but at least you've dropped the weepy-weepy act. You were really bad at it.'

'I thought I was very good,' Sylvia said and added a pinch of something to the incense burner. 'I'm sure the officers thought so, too.'

Once again, Maggie was startled. This wasn't going at all as she expected. Sylvia was so calm, so much at ease. So much in control of the situation.

Not anymore, Maggie thought.

She just *admitted* it was an act. All that chokey stuff while she was talking about Miles . . .

Fury uncoiled in Maggie's stomach like a snake.

She took three fast steps forward. 'You know why I'm here. I want to know what really happened to my brother.'

'I told you—'

'You told a bunch of lies! I don't know what the truth is. The only thing I *do* know is that Miles would never make a stupid mistake like not buckling his harness. Look, if *you* did something dumb, if he's lying out there hurt or something, and you were too scared to admit it, you'd better tell me right now.' It was the first time she'd put into words a reason for Sylvia to be lying.

Sylvia looked up.

Maggie was startled. In the light of the single candle by the incense burner, Sylvia's eyes were not violet but a more reddish colour, like amethyst. They were large and clear and the light seemed to play in them, quivering.

'Is that what you think happened?' Sylvia asked softly.

'I said, I don't *know* what happened!' Maggie felt dizzy suddenly, and fought it, glaring into Sylvia's strange eyes. 'Maybe you had a fight or something. Maybe you've got some other boyfriend. Maybe you weren't even out climbing on Halloween in the first place. All I know is that you lied and that there's no body to find. And I want to know the truth!'

Sylvia looked back steadily, the candlelight dancing in her purple eyes. 'You know what your brother told me about you?' she asked musingly. 'Two things. The first was that you never gave up. He said, 'Maggie's no rocket scientist, but once she gets hold of something she's just like a little bull terrier.' And the second was that you were a complete sucker for anybody in trouble. A real bleeding heart.'

She added a few fingernail-sized chips of smooth bark to the mixture that was smoking in the incense burner.

'Which is too bad,' she went on thoughtfully. 'Strong-willed and compassionate: that's a real recipe for disaster.'

Maggie had had it.

'What happened to Miles? What did you *do* to him?'

Sylvia laughed, a little secret laugh. 'I'm afraid you couldn't guess if you spent the rest of your short life trying.' She shook her head. 'It was too bad, actually. I liked him. We could have been good together.'

Maggie wanted to know one thing. 'Is he dead?'

'I told you, you'll never find out. Not even when you go where you're going.'

Maggie stared at her, trying to make sense of this. She couldn't. When she spoke it was in a level voice, staring into Sylvia's eyes.

'I don't know what your problem is – maybe you're crazy or something. But I'm telling you right now, if you've done anything to my brother, I am going to *kill* you.'

She'd never said anything like this before, but now it came out quite naturally, with force and conviction. She was so angry that all she could see was Sylvia's face. Her stomach was knotted and she actually felt a burning in her middle, as if there were a glowing fire there.

'Now,' she said, *'are you going to tell me what happened to him?'*

Sylvia sighed, spoke quietly. 'No.'

Before Maggie quite knew she was doing it, she had reached out and grabbed the front of Sylvia's green Gore-Tex jacket with both hands.

Something sparked in Sylvia's eyes. For a moment, she looked startled and interested and grudgingly respectful. Then she sighed again, smiling faintly.

'And now you're going to kill me?'

'Listen, you . . .' Maggie leaned in. She stopped.

'Listen to what?'

Maggie blinked. Her eyes were stinging suddenly. The smoke from the incense burner was rising directly into her face.

'You . . .'

I feel strange, Maggie thought.

Very strange. Dizzy. It seemed to come over her all at once. There was a pattern of flashing grey spreading across her vision. Her stomach heaved and she felt a wave of queasiness.

'Having a problem?' Sylvia's voice seemed to come from far away.

The incense.

It was rising right in her face. And now . . .

'What did you do to me?' Maggie gasped. She reeled backward, away from the smoke, but it was too late. Her knees were horribly rubbery. Her body seemed to be far away somehow, and the sparkling pattern blinded her completely.

She felt the back of her legs come up against a bed. Then they simply weren't supporting her anymore; she was slithering down, unable to catch herself with her useless arms. Her lips were numb.

'You know, for a moment there, I thought I might be in trouble,' Sylvia's voice was saying calmly. 'But I was wrong. The truth is that you're just an ordinary girl, after all. Weak and powerless – and ordinary. How could you even think about going up against me? Against my people?'

Am I dying? Maggie wondered. I'm losing myself. I can't see and I can't move . . .

'How could you come here and attack me? How could you think you had a chance at winning?' Even Sylvia's voice seemed to be getting more and more distant. 'You're pathetic. But now you'll find out what happens when you mess with real power. You'll learn . . .'

The voice was gone. There was only a rushing noise in an endless blackness.

Miles, Maggie thought. I'm sorry . . .

Then she stopped thinking at all.

CHAPTER
4

Maggie was dreaming. She knew she was dreaming, and that was strange enough, but what was even stranger was the fact that she knew it wasn't an ordinary dream.

This was something . . . that came from outside her, that was being . . . *sent*. Some deep part of her mind fumbled for the proper words, seething with frustration, even while the normal part of her was busy staring around her and being afraid.

Mist. Mist everywhere, white tendrils that snaked gracefully across her vision and coiled around her like genii that had just been let out of lamps. She had the feeling that there were dark shapes out in the mist; she seemed to see them looming out of the corner of her eye, but as soon as she turned they were obscured again.

Gooseflesh rose on Maggie's arms. It wasn't just the touch of the mist. There was a noise that made the hairs on the back of her neck tingle. It was just at the threshold of hearing, distorted by distance or something else, and it seemed to be calling over and over again, 'Who are you?'

Give me a *break*, Maggie thought. She shook her head hard to get rid of the prickly feeling on her neck. This is just way too . . . too *Gothic*. Do I always have corny dreams like this?

But the next moment something happened that sent a new chill washing over her, this time one of simple, everyday alarm. Something was coming through the mist, fast.

She turned, stiffening. And then, strangely, everything seemed to change at once.

The mist began to recede. She saw a figure, dark against it, nothing more than a silhouette at first. For just an instant she thought of Miles, but the thought was gone almost as quickly as it came. It was a boy, but a stranger, she could tell by the shape of him and the way he moved. He was breathing hard and calling in a desperate voice, 'Where are you? Where are you?'

So that was it. Not '*Who* are you,' Maggie thought.

'Where are you? Maggie! Where are you?'

The sound of her own name startled her. But even as she drew in a sharp breath, he turned and saw her.

And stopped short. The mist was almost gone now and she could see his face. His expression was one of wonder and relief and joy.

'Maggie,' he whispered.

Maggie stood rooted to the spot. She didn't know him. She was positive she had never seen him before. But he was staring at her as if . . . as if she were the most important thing in the universe to him, and he'd been searching for her for years until he'd almost given up hope. She was too astonished to move as he suddenly erupted from stillness. In three long steps he was in front of her, his hands closing on her shoulders.

Gently. Not possessively. But as if he had the absolute right to do this, and as if he needed to convince himself she was real.

'It worked. I got through,' he said.

He was the most striking person she'd ever seen. Dark hair, a little rough and tousled, with a tendency to wave. Smooth fair skin, elegant bones. A mouth that looked as if it normally might be proud and wilful, but right now was simply vulnerable.

And fearless, brilliant yellow eyes.

It was those eyes that held her, arresting and startling in an already distinctive face. No, she had never seen him before. She would have remembered.

He was a whole head taller than she was, and lithe and nicely muscled. But Maggie didn't have a feeling of being overpowered. There was so much tender anxiety in his face, and something near pleading in those fierce, black-lashed golden eyes.

'Listen, I know you don't understand, and I'm sorry. But it was so hard getting through – and there isn't much time.'

Dazed and bewildered, Maggie latched onto the last sentence almost mechanically. 'What do you mean – getting through?'

'Never mind. Maggie, you have to leave; do you understand that? As soon as you wake up, you get out of here.'

'Leave *where*?' Maggie was more confused than ever, not for lack of information, but because she was suddenly threatened by too much of it. She needed to remember – where had she gone to sleep? Something had happened, something involving Miles. She'd been worried about him . . .

'My brother,' she said with sudden urgency. 'I was looking for my brother. I need to find him.' Even though she couldn't remember exactly why.

The golden eyes clouded over. 'You can't think about him now. I'm sorry.'

'You know something a—'

'Maggie, the important thing is for you to get away safe. And to do that you have to go as soon as you wake up. I'm going to show you the way.'

He pointed through the mist, and suddenly Maggie could see a landscape, distant but clear, like a film being projected on a veil of smoke.

'There's a pass, just below the big overhanging rock. Do you see it?'

Maggie didn't understand why she *needed* to see it. She didn't recognize the landscape, although it might have been anywhere in the Olympics or the Cascade mountain range above the tree line.

'First you find the place where you see three peaks together, the same height and leaning toward each other. Do you see? And then you look down until you find the overhanging rock. It's shaped like a wave breaking. Do you see?'

His voice was so urgent and imperious that Maggie had to answer. 'I see. But—'

'Remember it. Find it. Go and never look back. If you get away all right, the rest doesn't matter.' His face was pale now, the features carved in ice. 'The whole world can fall into ruin, for all I care.'

And then, with the suddenness that characterized all his movements, he leaned forward and kissed her.

A nice kiss, on the cheek. She felt his warm, quick breath there, then his lips pressing lightly, and then a sudden quivering in them, as if he were overcome by some strong emotion. Passion, maybe, or excruciating sadness.

'I love you,' he whispered, his breath stirring the hair by her ear. 'I did love you. Always remember that.'

Maggie was dizzy with confusion. She didn't understand anything, and she should push this stranger away. But she didn't *want* to. However frightened she was, it wasn't of him. In fact, she had an irresistible feeling of peace and security in his arms. A feeling of belonging.

'Who are you?' she whispered.

But before he could answer, everything changed again.

The mist came back. Not slowly, but like fog rolling in, quick and silent, muffling everything. The warm, solid body against Maggie's suddenly seemed insubstantial, as if it were made of fog itself.

'Wait a minute—' She could hear her voice rising in panic, but deadened by the pearly cocoon around her.

And then . . . he was gone. Her arms were holding only emptiness. And all she could see was white.

CHAPTER
5

Maggie woke slowly.

And painfully.

I must be sick, she thought. It was the only explanation for the way she felt. Her body was heavy and achy, her head was throbbing, and her sinuses were completely stuffed up. She was breathing through her mouth, which was so dry and gluey that her tongue stuck to the roof of it.

I was having a dream, she thought. But even as she grasped at bits of it, it dissolved. Something about . . . fog? And a boy.

It seemed vaguely important for her to remember, but even the importance was hard to keep hold of. Besides, another, more practical consideration was overriding it. Thirst. She was dying of thirst.

I need a glass of water . . .

It took a tremendous effort to lift her head and open her eyes. But when she did, her brain cleared fast. She wasn't in her bedroom. She was in a small, dark, smelly room; a room that was moving jerkily, bouncing her painfully up and down and from side to side. There was a rhythmic noise coming from just outside that she felt she should be able to recognize.

Below her cheek and under her fingers was the roughness of unpainted wood. The ceiling and walls were made of the same silvery, weathered boards.

What kind of room is small and made of wood and . . .

Not a room, she thought suddenly. A *vehicle*. Some kind of wooden cart.

As soon as she realized it, she knew what the rhythmic sound was.

Horses' hoofs.

No, it can't be, she thought. It's too bizarre. I *am* sick; I'm probably hallucinating.

But it felt incredibly real for a hallucination. It felt exactly as if she were in a wooden cart being drawn by horses. Over rough ground. Which explained all the jostling.

So what was going *on*? What was she doing here?

Where did I go to sleep?

All at once adrenaline surged through her – and with it a flash of memory. Sylvia. The incense . . .

Miles.

Miles is dead . . . no. He's not. Sylvia said that but she was lying. And then she said I'd never find out what happened to him. And then she drugged me with that smoke.

It gave Maggie a faint feeling of satisfaction to have put this much together. Even if everything else was completely confusing, she had a solid memory to hang on to.

'You woke up,' a voice said. 'Finally. This kid says you've been asleep for a day and a half.'

Maggie pushed herself up by stages until she could see the speaker. It was a girl with untidy red hair, an angular, intense face, and flat, hard eyes. She seemed to be about Maggie's age. Beside her was a younger girl, maybe nine or ten. She was very pretty, slight, with short blonde hair under a red plaid baseball cap. She looked frightened.

'Who are you?' Maggie said indistinctly. Her tongue was thick – she was so *thirsty*. 'Where am I? What's going on?'

'Huh. You'll find out,' the red-haired girl said.

Maggie looked around. There was a fourth girl in the cart, curled up in the corner with her eyes shut.

Maggie felt stupid and slow, but she tried to gather herself.

'What do you mean I've been asleep for a day and a half?'

The red-haired girl shrugged. 'That's what *she* said. I wouldn't know. They just picked me up a few hours ago. I almost made it out of this place, but they caught me.'

Maggie stared at her. There was a fresh bruise on one of the girl's angular cheekbones and her lip was swollen.

'What – place?' she said slowly. When nobody answered, she went on, 'Look. I'm Maggie Neely. I don't know where this is or what I'm doing here, but the last thing I remember is a girl named Sylvia knocking me out. Sylvia Weald. Do you guys know her?'

The redhead just stared back with narrowed green eyes. The girl lying down didn't stir, and the blonde kid in the plaid cap cringed.

'Come on, somebody talk to me!'

'You really don't know what's going on?' the red-haired girl said.

'If I knew, I wouldn't be asking over and over!'

The girl eyed her a moment, then spoke with a kind of malicious pleasure. 'You've been sold into slavery. You're a slave now.'

Maggie laughed.

It was a short involuntary sound, and it hurt her aching

head. The blonde kid flinched again. Something in her expression made Maggie's grin fade away.

She felt a cold ripple up her spine.

'Come on,' she said. 'Give me a break. There aren't slaves anymore!'

'There are here.' The redhead smiled again, nastily. 'But I bet you don't know where you are, either.'

'In Washington State—' Even as she said it, Maggie felt her stomach tighten.

'Wrong. Or right, but it doesn't matter. Technically we may be in Washington, but where we really are is hell.'

Maggie was losing her self control. 'What are you *talking* about?'

'Take a look through that crack.'

There were lots of cracks in the cart; the pale light that filtered through them was the only illumination. Maggie knelt up and put her eye to a big one, blinking and squinting.

At first she couldn't see much. The cart was bouncing and it was hard to determine what she was looking at. All she knew was that there seemed to be no *colour*. Everything was either phosphorescent white or dead black.

Gradually she realized that the white was an overcast sky, and the black was a mountain. A *big* mountain, close enough to smack her face against. It reared up haughtily against the sky, its lower reaches covered with trees that seemed ebony instead of green and swimming with mist. Its top was completely wreathed in clouds; there was no way to judge how high it was.

And beside it was another mountain just like it. Maggie shifted, trying to get a wider view. There were mountains everywhere, in an impenetrable ring surrounding her.

They were . . . scary.

Maggie knew mountains, and loved them, but these were different from any she'd ever seen. So cold, and with that haunted mist creeping everywhere. The place seemed to be full of ghosts, materializing and then disappearing with an almost audible wail.

It was like another world.

Maggie sat down hard, then slowly turned back to look at the redheaded girl.

'Where is this?' she said, and her voice was almost a whisper.

To her surprise, the girl didn't laugh maliciously again. Instead she looked away, with eyes that seemed to focus on some distant and terrible memory, and she spoke in almost a whisper herself. 'It's the most secret place in the Night World.'

Maggie felt as if the mist outside had reached down the back of her pyjama top.

'The *what*?'

'The Night World. It's like an organization. For all of *them*, you know.' When Maggie just looked at her, she went on, 'Them. The ones that aren't human.'

This time what Maggie felt was a plunging in her stomach, and she honestly didn't know if it was because she was locked up in here with a loony, or if some part of her already accepted what the loony was saying. Either way, she was scared sick, and she couldn't say anything.

The girl with red hair flicked a glance at her, and the malicious pleasure came back. 'The vampires,' she said distinctly, 'and the shapeshifters and the witches—'

Oh, God, Maggie thought. *Sylvia*.

Sylvia is a witch.

She didn't know how she knew and probably part of

her didn't believe it anyway, but the word was thundering around inside her like an avalanche, gathering evidence as it fell. The incense, those strange purple eyes, the way Miles fell for her so fast and hardly ever called the family after he met her, and changed his whole personality, just as if he'd been under a spell, bewitched and helpless, and, oh, Miles, why didn't I *guess* . . .

I'm not smart, but I've always been a good judge of character. How could I screw up when it counted?

'They don't normally have places of their own,' the redheaded girl was going on; and the words were somehow finding their way to Maggie's ears despite the chaos going on inside her. 'Mostly they just live in *our* cities, pretending to be like us. But this valley is special; it's been here in the Cascades for centuries and humans have never found it. It's all surrounded by spells and fog – and those mountains. There's a pass through them, big enough for carts, but only the Night People can see it. It's called the Dark Kingdom.'

Oh, *terrific*, Maggie thought numbly. The name was strangely suited to what she'd seen outside. Yellow sunlight was almost impossible to imagine in this place. Those filmy wraiths of mist held it in a shimmering silvery-white spell.

'And you're trying to say that we're all . . . slaves now? But how did you guys get here?'

When the redhead didn't answer, she looked at the little blonde girl.

The girl shifted her slight body, gulped. Finally she spoke in a husky little voice.

'I'm P.J. Penobscot. I was – it happened to me on Halloween. I was trick-or-treating.' She looked down at herself and Maggie realized she was wearing a tan cable-knit sweater and a vest. 'I was a golfer. And I was only supposed to go on my own block because the weather was getting bad. But my friend Aaron and I went across the street and this car stopped in front of me . . .' She trailed off and swallowed hard.

Maggie reached over and squeezed her hand. 'I bet you were a great golfer.'

P.J. smiled wanly. 'Thanks.' Then her small face hardened and her eyes became distant. 'Aaron got away, but this man grabbed me. I tried to hit him with my golf club, but he took it away. He looked at me and then he put me in the car. He was strong.'

'He was a professional slave trader,' the red-haired girl said. 'Both the guys I've seen are pros. That's why they looked at her face – they take pretty slaves when they can get them.'

Maggie stared at her, then turned to P.J. 'And then what?'

'They put something over my face – I was still fighting and yelling and everything – and then I went to sleep for a while. I woke up in this warehouse place.' She breathed once and looked at her thin wrists. 'I was chained to a bed and I was all alone. I was alone for a while. And then, maybe it was the next day, they brought in *her*.' She nodded at the girl sleeping in the corner.

Maggie looked at the still form. It didn't move except when the cart shook it. 'Is she all right?'

'She's sick. They left her there for a long time, maybe four days, but she never really woke up. I think she's getting worse.' P.J.'s voice was quiet and detached. 'They came in to give us food, but that was all. And then yesterday they brought *you* in.'

Maggie blinked. 'To the warehouse.'

P.J. nodded solemnly. 'You were asleep, too. But I don't know what happened after that. They put the cloth over my face again. When I woke up I was in a van.'

'They use those for transport on the other side,' the red-haired girl said. 'To get up to the pass. Then they switch to a cart. The people in this valley have never seen a car.'

'So you mean I slept through all that?' Maggie asked P.J.

P.J. nodded again, and the redhead said, 'They probably gave you more of the drug. They try to keep everybody too doped up to fight.'

Maggie was chewing her lip. Something had occurred to her. Maybe Sylvia hadn't gone climbing with Miles at all. 'So, P.J., you never saw any other slaves besides that girl? You didn't see a boy?' She fished in her jacket pocket and pulled out the photo of Miles. 'A boy who looked like this?'

P.J. looked at the photograph gravely, then shook her head. 'I never saw him before. He looks like you.'

'He's my brother, Miles. He disappeared on Halloween, too. I thought maybe . . .' Maggie shook her head, then held the photograph toward the red-haired girl.

'Never seen him before,' the girl said shortly.

Maggie looked at her. For somebody who liked to talk about scary things, she didn't say much that was helpful. 'And what about you? How'd you get here?'

The girl snorted. 'I told you. I was getting *out* of the valley.' Her face tightened. 'And I almost made it through the pass, but they caught me and stuck me in here. I should have made them kill me instead.'

'Whoa,' Maggie said. She glanced at P.J., meaning that they shouldn't frighten her unnecessarily. 'It can't be *that* bad.'

To her surprise, the girl didn't sneer or get mad. 'It's worse,' she said, almost whispering again. 'Just leave it alone. You'll find out.'

Maggie felt the hair at the back of her neck stir. 'What are you saying?'

The girl turned, her green eyes burning darkly. 'The Night People have to eat,' she said. 'They can eat normal things, food and water. But the vampires have to drink blood and the shapeshifters have to eat flesh. Is that clear enough for you?'

Maggie sat frozen. She wasn't worried about scaring P.J. anymore. She was too scared herself.

'We're slave labour for them, but we're also a food supply. A food supply that lasts a long time, through lots of feedings,' the girl said brusquely.

Maggie ducked her head and clenched her fists. 'Well, then, obviously we've got to escape,' she said through her teeth.

The redhead gave a laugh so bitter that Maggie felt a chill down her spine.

She looked at P.J. 'Do *you* want to escape?'

'Leave her alone!' the redhead snapped. 'You don't understand what you're talking about. We're only humans; they're Night People. There's nothing we can do against them, *nothing*!'

'But—'

'Do you know what the Night People do to slaves who try to escape?'

And then the red-haired girl turned her back on Maggie. She did it with a lithe twist that left Maggie startled.

Did I hurt her feelings? Maggie thought stupidly.

The redhead glanced back over her shoulder, at the same time reaching around to grasp the bottom of her shirt in back.

Her expression was unreadable, but suddenly Maggie was nervous.

'What are you doing?'

The red-haired girl gave a strange little smile and pulled the shirt up, exposing her back.

Somebody had been playing noughts and crosses there.

The lines were cut into the flesh of her back, the scars shiny pink and only half healed. In the squares were Xs and Os, raggedy-looking and brighter red because for the most part they'd been burned in. A few looked cut, like the strategic position in the middle which would have been taken first. Somebody had won, three diagonal Xs, and had run a burn-line through the winning marks.

Maggie gasped. She kept on gasping. She started to hyperventilate, and then she started to faint.

The world seemed to recede from her, narrowing down to a one-dimensional point of light. But there wasn't room to actually fall over. As she slumped backward, she hit the wall of the cart. The world wobbled and came back, shiny at the edges.

'Oh, God,' Maggie said. 'Oh, *God*. They did this to you? How could they *do* that?'

'This is nothing,' the girl said. 'They did it when I escaped the first time. And now I escaped again – and I got caught again. This time they'll do something worse.' She let go of her top and it slid down to cover her back again.

Maggie tried to swallow, but her mouth was too dry. Before she knew she was moving, she found herself grabbing the girl's arms from behind.

'What's your name?'

'Who ca—'

'What's your name?'

The red-haired girl gave her a peculiar look over her shoulder. Then her arms lifted slightly under Maggie's hands as she shrugged.

'Jeanne.'

'Jeanne. It's got to stop,' Maggie said. 'We can't let them *do* things like that to people. And we've got to get away. If they're already going to punish you for escaping, what difference does it make if you try it again now? Don't you think?'

Maggie liked the way that sounded, calm and competent and logical. The swift decision for action didn't blot out the memory of what she'd just seen, but it made the whole situation more bearable. She'd witnessed an injustice and she was going to do something about it. That simple. Something so wicked had to be fixed, *now*.

She started to cry.

Jeanne turned around, gave her a long, assessing look. P.J. was crying, too, very quietly.

Maggie found her tears running out. They weren't doing any good. When she stopped, Jeanne was still watching her with narrowed eyes.

'So you're going to take on the whole Night World alone,' she said.

Maggie wiped her cheeks with her hands. 'No, just the ones here.'

Jeanne stared at her another moment, then straightened abruptly. 'OK,' she said, so suddenly that Maggie was startled. 'Let's do it. If we can figure out a way.'

Maggie looked toward the back of the cart. 'What about those doors?'

'Locked and chained on the outside. It's no good kicking them.'

From nowhere, an image came into Maggie's mind. Herself and Miles in a rowboat on Lake Chelan with their grandfather. Deliberately rocking it while their grandfather yelled and fumed.

'What if we all throw our weight from one side to the

other? If we could turn the cart over, maybe the doors would pop open. You know how armoured cars always seem to do that. Or maybe it would smash one of the walls enough that we could get out.'

'And maybe we'd go falling straight down a ravine,' Jeanne said acidly. 'It's a long way down to the valley, and this road is narrow.' But there was a certain unwilling respect in her eyes. 'I guess we could try it when we get to a meadow,' she said slowly. 'I know a place. I'm not saying it would work; it probably won't. But . . .'

'We have to try,' Maggie said. She was looking straight at Jeanne. For a moment there was something between them – a flash of understanding and agreement. A bond.

'Once we got out, we'd have to run,' Jeanne said, still slowly. 'They're sitting up *there*.' She pointed to the ceiling at the front of the cart, above Maggie's head. 'This thing is like a stagecoach, OK? There's a seat up there, and the two guys are on it. Professional slave traders are tough. They're not going to want us to get away.'

'They might get smashed up when we roll over,' Maggie said.

Jeanne shook her head sharply. 'Night People are strong. It takes a lot more than that to kill them. We'd have to just take off and head for the forest as fast as we could. Our only chance is to get lost in the trees – and hope they can't track us.'

'OK,' Maggie said. She looked at P.J. 'Do you think you could do that? Just run and keep running?'

P.J. gulped twice, sank her teeth into her top lip, and nodded. She twisted her baseball cap around so the visor faced the back.

'I can run,' she said.

Maggie gave her an approving nod. Then she looked at

the fourth girl, the one still curled up asleep. She leaned over to touch the girl's shoulder.

'Forget it,' Jeanne said shortly. 'We can't take her.'

Maggie looked up at her, shocked. 'What are you talking about? Why not?'

CHAPTER

6

'Because there's no point. She's as good as dead already.' Jeanne's expression was as hard and closed as it had been in the beginning.

'But—'

'Can't you see? She'd slow us down. There's no way she could run without help. And besides that, P.J. says she's blind.'

Blind. A new little shock went though Maggie. What would that be like, to be in this situation and sick and blind on top of it?

She tugged on the girl's shoulder gently, trying to see the averted face.

But she's beautiful.

The girl had smooth skin the colour of coffee with cream, delicate features, high cheekbones, perfect lips. Her black hair was pulled into a loose, glossy knot on her neck. Her eyes were shut, long eyelashes trembling as if she were dreaming.

It was more than just the physical features, though. There was a serenity about this girl's face, a gentleness and stillness that was . . . unique.

'Hey, there,' Maggie said softly. 'Can you hear me? I'm

Maggie. What's your name?'

The girl's eyelashes fluttered; her lips parted. To Maggie's surprise, she murmured something. Maggie had to lean down close to catch it.

'Arcadia?' she repeated. It was a strange name; she wasn't sure she'd heard right.

The girl seemed to nod, murmuring again.

She can hear me, Maggie thought. She can respond.

'OK. Can I call you Cady? Listen to me, Cady.' Maggie shook the girl's shoulder slightly. 'We're in a bad place but we're going to try to escape. If we help you out, do you think you can run?'

Again, the eyelashes fluttered. Then the eyes opened.

Doe eyes, Maggie thought, startled. They were extraordinarily large and clear, a warm brown with an inner radiance. And they might be blind, but Maggie had the oddest sensation that she had just been *seen* more clearly than ever before in her life.

'I'll try,' Cady murmured. She sounded dazed and in pain, but quietly rational. 'Sometimes I feel strong for a little while.' She pushed herself up. Maggie had to help her get into a sitting position.

She's tall. But she's pretty light . . . and I've got good muscles. I can support her.

'What are you *doing*?' Jeanne said in a voice that was not just harsh and impatient but horrified. 'Don't you see? You're only making it worse. You should just have let her sleep.'

Maggie glanced up. 'Look. I don't know what you're thinking, but we can't leave anybody with *them*. How would you like to be left behind if it was you?'

Jeanne's face changed. For a moment, she looked more like a savage animal than a girl. 'I'd understand,' she snarled. 'Because that's the way it has to be. It's the law of the jungle, here. Only strong people survive. The weak ones . . .' She shook her head. 'They're better off dead. And the faster you learn that, the more chance you'll have.'

Maggie felt a spurt of horror and anger – and fear. Because Jeanne clearly knew the most about this place, and Jeanne might be right. They might all get caught because of one weak person who wouldn't make it anyway . . .

She turned and looked at the lovely face again. Arcadia was Miles's age, eighteen or nineteen. And although she seemed to hear what Jeanne was saying, she'd turned her face that way, she didn't speak or argue. She didn't lose her still gentleness, either.

I can't leave her. What if Miles is alive but hurt somewhere, and somebody won't help him?

Maggie shot a glance at P.J. in her baseball cap. She was young – she might be able to take care of herself, but that was all.

'Look, this isn't your problem,' she finally said to Jeanne. 'You just help P.J. get away safe, OK? You take care of her, and I'll be responsible for Cady.'

'You'll be caught with Cady,' Jeanne said flatly.

'Don't worry about it.'

'I'm not. And I'm telling you right now; I'm not going to help you if you get in trouble.'

'I don't *want* you to,' Maggie said. She looked right into Jeanne's angry eyes. 'Really. I don't want to wreck your chances, OK? But I'm not going to leave her.'

Jeanne looked furious for another moment; then she shrugged. All the emotion drained from her face as if she were deliberately distancing herself. The bond she and Maggie had shared for that brief moment was severed.

She turned, looked through a crack behind her, then turned back.

'Fine,' she said in a dull, indifferent tone. 'Whatever you're going to do, you'd better get ready to do it now. Because the place is coming right up.'

'Ready?' Maggie said.

They were all standing – or crouching, actually, since there wasn't room to straighten up – with their backs against the walls of the cart. Jeanne and P.J. on one side, Maggie on the other, with Cady in the corner.

'When I say go, you guys jump over here. Then all of us throw ourselves back that way,' Maggie whispered.

Jeanne was peering out of the crack. 'OK, this is it,' she said. 'Now.'

Maggie said, '*Go!*'

She had been a little worried that P.J. would freeze. But the moment the word was out of Maggie's mouth, Jeanne launched herself across the cart, crashing heavily into her, and P.J. followed. The cart rocked surprisingly hard and Maggie heard the groan of wood.

'Back!' she yelled, and everybody lunged the other way. Maggie hit a solid wall and knew she would have bruises, but the cart rocked again.

'Come on!' she yelled, and realized that they were all already coming on, throwing themselves to the other side in perfect sync. It was as if some flocking instinct had taken over and they were all three moving as one, throwing their weight alternately back and forth.

And the cart was responding, grinding to a halt and lurching off balance. It was like one of those party tricks where five or six people each use only two fingers to lift someone on a chair. Their combined force was impressive.

But not enough to tip the cart over. It was surprisingly well-balanced. And at any minute, Maggie realized, the people driving it were going to jump out and put a stop to it.

'Everybody – come on! Really hard! *Really hard!*' She was yelling as if she were encouraging her soccer team. 'We've got to do it, *now*.'

She launched herself at the other side as the cart began to sway that way, jumping as high as she could, hitting the wall as it reached the farthest point of its rock. She could feel the other girls flinging themselves with her; she could hear Jeanne giving a primal yell as she crashed into the wood.

And then there was a splintering sound, amazingly loud, amazingly long. A sort of groaning and shrieking that came from the wood itself, and an even louder scream of panic that Maggie realized must have come from the horses. The whole world was teetering and unstable – and suddenly Maggie was falling.

She hadn't known that it would be this violent, or this confusing. She wasn't sure of what was happening, except that there was no floor anymore and that she was engulfed in a deafening chaos of crashing and screeching and sobbing and darkness. She was being rolled over and over, with arms and legs that belonged to other people hitting her. A knee caught her in the nose, and for a few moments all she could think of was the pain.

And then, very suddenly, everything was still.

I think I killed us all, Maggie thought.

But then she realized she was looking at daylight – pale and feeble, but a big swathe of it. The cart was completely upside down and the doors at the back were hanging loose.

It did pop open, she thought. Just like those armoured cars in the movies.

Outside, somebody was yelling. A man. Maggie had never heard such cold fury in a voice before. It cleared the last cobwebs out of her head.

'Come on! We've got to get out!'

Jeanne was already scrambling across the floor – which had previously been the ceiling – toward the hanging back doors.

'Are you OK? Come on, move, move!' Maggie yelled to P.J. 'Follow her!'

A scared white face turned toward her, and then the younger girl was obeying.

Cady was lying in a heap. Maggie didn't wait for conversation, but grabbed her under the arms and hauled her into the light.

Once outside, she caught a glimpse of P.J. running and Jeanne beckoning. Then she tried to make sense of the scene around her. She saw a line of trees, their tops hidden in cloudlike vapours, their edges blurred by mist.

Mist, she thought. I remember . . .

But the thought was cut short almost before it was started. She found herself running, pounding toward the forest, nearly carrying Arcadia in her panic. The flat area she was running through was a sub-alpine meadow, the kind she'd often seen on hikes. In spring it would be a glorious mass of blue lupines and pink Indian paintbrush. Now it was just a tangle of old grass that slowed her down and tried to trip her.

'There they go! Get them!' the rough shout came behind her.

Don't look, she told herself. Don't slow down.

But she was looking, twisting her head over her

shoulder. For the first time she saw what had happened to the cart.

It had fallen right off a narrow road and onto the sloping hillside below. They'd been lucky; only an outcrop of dark rock had stopped it from falling farther. Maggie was amazed to see how much damage there was – the cart looked like a splintered matchbox. Above, the horses seemed tangled in reins and shafts and fastenings; one of them was down and struggling frantically. Maggie felt a distant surge of remorse, she hoped its legs weren't broken.

There were also two men scrambling down the hillside. They were the ones shouting. And one was pointing straight at Maggie.

Run, Maggie thought. Stop looking now. *Run*.

She ran into the forest, dragging Cady with her. They had to find a place to hide – underbrush or something. Maybe they could climb a tree . . .

But one look at Cady and she realized how stupid *that* idea was. The smooth skin of the girl's face was clammy and luminous with sweat, her eyes were half shut, and her chest was heaving.

At least Jeanne and P.J. got away, Maggie thought.

Just then there was a crashing behind her, and a voice cursing. Maggie threw another glance back and found herself staring at a man's figure in the mist.

A scary man. The mist swirling behind him made him look eerie, supernatural, but it was more than that. He was *huge*, with shoulders as broad as a two-by-four, a massive chest, and heavily muscled arms. His waist was surprisingly narrow. His face was cruel.

'Gavin! I've got two of them!' he shouted.

Maggie didn't wait to hear more. She took off like a black-tailed deer.

And for a long time after that it was just a nightmare of running and being chased, stopping sometimes when she couldn't hold Cady up anymore, looking for places to hide. At one point, she and Cady were pressed together inside a hollow tree, trying desperately to get their breath back without making a sound, when their pursuers passed right by them. Maggie heard the crunch and squish of footsteps on ferns and started praying. She could feel Cady's heart beating hard, shaking them both, and she realized that Cady's lips were moving soundlessly.

Maybe she's praying, too, Maggie thought, and applied her eye to a crack in the tree.

There were two people there, horribly close, just a few feet away. One was the man she'd seen before and he was doing something bizarre, something that sent chills up her spine. He was turning his face this way and that with his eyes shut, his head twisting on a surprisingly long and supple neck.

As if he's *smelling* us out, Maggie thought, horrified.

Eyes still shut, the man said, 'Do you sense anything?'

'No. I can't feel them at all. And I can't see them, with these trees for cover.' It was a younger man who spoke, a boy really. He must be Gavin, Maggie thought. Gavin had dark blond hair, a thin nose, and a sharp chin. His voice was impatient.

'I can't feel them either,' the big man said flatly, refusing to be hurried. 'And that's strange. They can't have gotten too far away. They must be blocking us.'

'I don't care what they're doing,' Gavin said. 'We'd better get them back fast. It's not like they were ordinary slaves. If we don't deliver that maiden we're dead. *You're* dead, Bern.'

Maiden? Maggie thought. I guess in a place where they have slaves it's not weird to talk about maidens. But which girl does he mean? Not me; I'm not important.

'We'll get her back,' Bern was saying.

'We'd better,' Gavin said viciously. 'Or I'm going to tell *her* that it was your fault. We were supposed to make sure this didn't happen.'

'It hasn't happened yet,' Bern said. He turned on his heel and walked into the mist. Gavin stared after him for a moment, and then followed.

Maggie let out her breath. She realized that Cady's lips had stopped moving.

'Let's go,' she whispered, and took off in the opposite direction to the one the men had gone.

Then there was a time of endless running and pausing and listening and hiding. The forest was a terrible place. Around them was eerie twilight, made even spookier by the mist that lay in hollows and crept over fallen trees. Maggie felt as if she were in some awful fairy tale. The only good thing was that the dampness softened their footsteps, making it hard to track them.

But it was so quiet. No ravens, no grey jays. No deer. Just the mist and the trees, going on forever.

And then it ended.

Maggie and Cady suddenly burst out into another meadow. Maggie gave a frantic glance around, looking for shelter. Nothing. The mist was thinner here, she could see that there were no trees ahead, only an outcrop of rocks.

Maybe we should double back . . .

But the voices were shouting in the forest behind them.

Above the rocks was a barren ledge. It looked like the end of a path, winding the other way down the mountain.

If we could get there, we'd be safe, Maggie thought. We could be around the corner in a minute, and out of sight.

Dragging Cady, she headed for the rocks. They didn't

belong here; they were huge granite boulders deposited by some ancient glacier. Maggie clambered up the side of one easily, then leaned down.

'Give me your hand,' she said rapidly. 'There's a path up above us, but we've got to climb a little.'

Cady looked at her.

Or – not looked, Maggie supposed. But she turned her face toward Maggie, and once again Maggie had the odd feeling that those blind eyes could somehow see better than most people's.

'You should leave me,' Cady said.

'Don't be stupid,' Maggie said. 'Hurry up, give me your hand.'

Cady shook her head. 'You go,' she said quietly. She seemed completely rational, and absolutely exhausted. She hadn't lost the tranquility which had infused her from the beginning, but now it seemed mixed with a gentle resignation. Her fine-boned face was drawn with weariness. 'I'll just slow you down. And if I stay here, you'll have more time to get away.'

'I'm not going to leave you!' Maggie snapped. 'Come on!'

Arcadia remained for just a second, her face turned up to Maggie's, then her clear and luminous brown eyes filled. Her expression was one of inexpressible tenderness. Then she shook her head slightly and grabbed Maggie's hand – very accurately.

Maggie didn't waste time. She climbed as fast as she could, pulling Cady, rapping out breathless instructions. But the delay had cost them. She could hear the men getting nearer.

And when she reached the far end of the pile of boulders she saw something that sent shock waves through her system.

She was looking up a barren cliff face. There was no connection from the rocks to the ledge above. And below her, the hillside dropped off steeply, a hundred feet down into a gorge.

She'd led Cady right into a trap.

There was nowhere else to go.

CHAPTER
7

Maggie could have made it to the path above – if she'd been by herself. It was an easy climb, third level at most. But she wasn't alone. And there was no way to guide Arcadia up a cliff like that.

No time to double back to the forest, either.

They're going to get us, Maggie realized.

'Get down,' she whispered to Cady. There was a hollow at the base of the boulder pile. It would only hold one of them, but at least it was shelter.

Even as she shoved Cady down into it, she heard a shout from the edge of the forest.

Maggie pressed flat against the rock. It was slippery with moss and lichen and she felt as exposed as a lizard on a wall. All she could do was hang on and listen to the sounds of two men getting closer and closer.

And closer, until Maggie could hear harsh breathing on the other side of the boulders.

'It's a dead end—' Gavin's young voice began.

'No. They're here.' And that, of course, was Bern.

And then there was the most horrible sound in the world. The grunts of somebody climbing up rock.

We're caught.

Maggie looked around desperately for a weapon.

To her own amazement, she found one, lying there as if it had been left especially for her. A dried branch wedged in between the rocks above her. Maggie reached for it, her heart beating fast. It was heavier than it looked, the climate must be too wet here for anything to really dry out.

And the rocks are wet, too. Wet and slippery. And there's one good thing about this place – they'll have to come at us one at a time. Maybe I can push them off, one by one.

'Stay put,' she whispered to Cady, trying to make her breath last to the end of that short sentence. 'I've got an idea.'

Cady looked beyond exhaustion. Her beautiful face was strained, her arms and legs were shaken by a fine trembling, and she was breathing in silent shudders. Her hair had come loose in a dark curtain around her shoulders.

Maggie turned back, her heart beating in her throat and her fingertips, and watched the top of the boulders.

But when what she was watching for actually came, she felt a terrible jolt, as if it were completely unexpected. She couldn't believe that she was seeing the close-cropped top of a man's head, then the forehead, then the cruel face. Bern. He was climbing like a spider, pulling himself by his fingertips. His huge shoulders appeared, then his barrel chest.

And he was looking right at Maggie. His eyes met hers, and his lips curved in a smile.

Adrenaline washed over Maggie. She felt almost disengaged from her body, as if she might float away from it. But she didn't faint. She stayed motionless as the terror buzzed through her like electricity – and she tightened her grip on the stick.

Bern kept smiling, but his eyes were dark and expressionless. As she looked into them, Maggie had no sense of connecting to another mind like hers.

He's not human. He's . . . something else, a distant part of her mind said with absolute conviction.

And then one of his legs came up, bulging with muscle under the jeans, and then he was pulling himself to stand, looming over her, towering like a mountain.

Maggie braced herself, gripping the stick. 'Stay away from us.'

'You've caused me a lot of trouble already,' Bern said. 'Now I'm going to show you something.'

There was a little noise behind her. She glanced back in alarm and saw that it was Cady, trying to get up.

'Don't,' Maggie said sharply. Cady couldn't, anyway. After a moment of trying to pull herself out of the hollow, she slumped down again, eyes shut.

Maggie turned back to see Bern lunging at her.

She thrust the stick out. It was completely instinctive. She didn't go for his head or his mid-section; she jabbed at a fist-sized pit near his feet, turning the stick into a barrier to trip him.

It almost worked.

Bern's foot caught underneath it and his lunge became uncontrolled. Maggie saw him start to unbalance. But he wasn't the huge muscle-bound ape he looked like. In an instant he was recovering, throwing his weight sideways, jamming a foot to arrest his fall.

Maggie tried to get the stick unwedged, to use it again, but Bern was *fast*. He wrenched it out of her hand, leaving splinters in her palm. Then he threw it overhand, like a lance. Maggie heard it hit the ledge behind her with explosive force.

She tried to dodge, but it was already too late. Bern's

big hand flashed forward, and then he had her.

He was holding her by both arms, looming over her.

'You trying to mess with me?' he asked in disbelief. 'With *me*? Take a look at this.'

His eyes weren't cold and emotionless now. Anger was streaming from him like the strong, hot scent of an animal. And then . . .

He changed.

It was like nothing Maggie had ever seen. She was staring at his face, trying to look defiant, when the features seemed to ripple. The coarse dark hair on his head *moved*, waves of it spreading down his face like fungus growing across a log. Maggie's stomach lurched in horror and she was afraid she was going to be sick, but she couldn't stop looking.

His eyes got smaller, the brown irises flowing out to cover the white. His nose and mouth thrust forward and his chin collapsed. Two rounded ears uncurled like awful flowers on top of his head. And when Maggie was able to drag her eyes from his face, she saw that his body had re-formed into a shapeless, hulking lump. His broad shoulders were gone, his waist was gone, his long legs bulging with muscle were squat little appendages close to the ground.

He was still holding Maggie tightly, but not with hands. With coarse paws that had claws on the ends and that were unbelievably strong. He wasn't a person at all anymore, but something huge and vaguely person-shaped. He was a black bear, and his shiny little pig-eyes stared into hers with animal enjoyment. He had a musky feral smell that got into Maggie's throat and made her gag.

I just saw a shapeshifter shift shape, Maggie thought with an astonishment that seemed dim and faraway. She was sorry she'd doubted Jeanne.

And sorry she'd blown it for Cady – and Miles. Sylvia had been right. She was just an ordinary girl, only maybe extraordinarily stupid.

Down on the lower boulders, Gavin was laughing maliciously, watching as if this were a football game.

The bear opened his mouth, showing ivory-white teeth, darker at the roots, and lots of saliva. Maggie saw a string of it glisten on the hair of his jowl. She felt the paws flex on her arms, scooping her closer, and then—

Lightning hit.

That was what it looked like. A flash that blinded her, as bright as the sun, but blue. It crackled in front of her eyes, seeming to fork again and again, splitting and rejoining the main body of its energy. It seemed alive.

It was electrocuting the bear.

The animal had gone completely rigid, his head thrown back, his mouth open farther than Maggie would have believed possible. The energy had struck him just below what would have been the neck on a man.

Dimly, Maggie was aware of Gavin making a thin sound of terror. His mouth was open as wide as Bern's, his eyes were fixed on the lightning.

But it *wasn't* lightning. It didn't strike and stop. It kept on crackling into Bern, its form changing every second. Little electrical flickers darted through his bristling fur, crackling down his chest and belly and up around his muzzle. Maggie almost thought she could see blue flames in the cavern of his mouth.

Gavin gave a keening, inhuman scream and scrambled backward off the rocks, running.

Maggie didn't watch to see where he went. Her mind was suddenly consumed with one thought.

She had to make Bern let go of her.

She had no idea what was happening to him, but she

did know that he was being killed. And that when he was dead he was going to topple off the mountain and take her with him.

She could *smell* burning now, the stink of smoking flesh and fur, and she could actually see white wisps rising from his coat. He was being cooked from the inside out.

I have to do something *fast*.

She squirmed and kicked, trying to get out of the grip of the paws that seemed to clutch her reflexively. She pushed and shoved at him, trying to get him to loosen his hold just an inch. It didn't work. She felt as if she were being smothered by a bearskin rug, a horrible-smelling pelt that was catching on fire. Why the lightning wasn't killing her, too, she didn't know. All she knew was that she was being crushed by his size and his weight and that she was going to die.

And then she gave a violent heave and kicked as hard as she could at the animal's lower belly. She felt the shock of solid flesh as her shin connected. And, unbelievably, she felt him recoil, stumbling back, his huge forelegs releasing her.

Maggie fell to the rock, instinctively spread-eagling and grabbing for holds to keep from sliding down the mountain. Above her, the bear stood and quivered for another second, with that impossibly bright blue energy piercing him like a lance. Then, just as quickly as it had come, the lightning was gone. The bear swayed for a moment, then fell like a marionette with cut strings.

He toppled backwards off the cliff into thin air. Maggie caught a brief glimpse of him hitting rock and bouncing and falling again, and then she turned her face away.

Her closed lids were imprinted with a blazing confusion of yellow and black after-images. Her breath was coming so fast that she felt dizzy. Her arms and legs were weak.

What the *hell* was that?

The lightning had saved her life. But it was still the scariest thing she'd ever seen.

Some kind of magic. Pure magic. If I were doing a movie and I needed a special effect for magic, that's what I'd use.

She slowly lifted her head.

It had come from the direction of the ledge. When she looked that way, she saw the boy.

He was standing easily, doing something with his left arm – tying a handkerchief around a spot of blood at the wrist, it looked like. His face was turned partially away from her.

He's not much older than me, Maggie thought, startled. Or – is he? There was something about him, an assurance in the way he stood, a grim competence in his movements. It made him seem like an adult.

And he was dressed like somebody at a Renaissance Faire. Maggie had been to one in Oregon two summers ago, where everyone wore costumes from the Middle Ages and ate whole roast turkey legs and played jousting games. This boy was wearing boots and a plain dark cape and he could have walked right in and started sword fighting.

On the streets of Seattle Maggie would have taken one look at him and grinned herself silly. Here, she didn't have the slightest urge to smile.

The Dark Kingdom, she thought. Slaves and maidens and shapeshifters – and magic. He's probably a wizard. What have I gotten myself into?

Her heart was beating hard and her mouth was so dry that her tongue felt like sandpaper. But there was something stronger than fear inside her. Gratitude.

'*Thank you*,' she said.

He didn't even look up. 'For what?' He had a clipped, brusque voice.

'For saving us. I mean, you did that, didn't you?'

Now he did look up, to measure her with a cool, unsympathetic expression. 'Did what?' he said in those same unfriendly tones.

But Maggie was staring at him, stricken with sudden recognition that danced at the edges of her mind and then moved tantalizingly away.

I had a dream – didn't I? And there was somebody like you in it. He looked like you, but his expression was different. And he said . . . he said that something was important . . .

She couldn't remember! And the boy was still watching her, waiting impatiently.

'That . . . thing.' Maggie wiggled her fingers, trying to convey waves of energy. 'That thing that knocked him off the cliff. You did that.'

'The blue fire. Of course I did. Who else has the Power? But I didn't do it for you.' His voice was like a cold wind blowing at her.

Maggie blinked at him.

She had no idea what to say. Part of her wanted to question him, and another part suddenly wanted to slug him. A third part, maybe smarter than both the others, wanted to run the way Gavin had.

Curiosity won out. 'Well, why did you do it, then?' she asked.

The boy glanced down at the ledge he was standing on. 'He threw a stick at me. Wood. So I killed him.' He shrugged. 'Simple as that.'

He didn't throw it *at* you, Maggie thought, but the boy was going on.

'I couldn't care less what he was doing to you. You're

only a slave. He was only a shapeshifter with the brain of a bear. Neither of you matter.'

'Well, it doesn't matter why you did it. It still saved both of us—' She glanced at Arcadia for confirmation – and broke off sharply.

'Cady?' Maggie stared, then scrambled over the rocks toward the other girl.

Arcadia was still lying in the hollow, but her body was now limp. Her dark head sagged bonelessly on her slender neck. Her eyes were shut; the skin over her face was drawn tight.

'Cady! Can you hear me?'

For a horrible second she thought the older girl was dead. Then she saw the tiny rise and fall of her chest and heard the faint sound of breathing.

There was a roughness to the breathing that Maggie didn't like. And at this distance she could feel the heat that rose from Cady's skin.

She's got a high fever. All that running and climbing made her sicker. She needs help, fast.

Maggie looked back up at the boy.

He had finished with the handkerchief and was now taking the top off some kind of leather bag.

Suddenly Maggie's eyes focused. Not a leather bag; a canteen. He was tilting it up to drink.

Water.

All at once she was aware of her thirst again. It had been shoved to the back of her mind, a constant pain that could be forgotten while she was trying to escape from the slave traders. But now it was like a raging fire inside her. It was the most important thing in the world.

And Arcadia needed it even more than she did.

'Please,' she said. 'Can we have some of that? Could you drop it to me? I can catch it.'

He looked at her quickly, not startled but with cool annoyance. 'And how am I supposed to get it back?'

'I'll bring it to you. I can climb up.'

'You can't,' he said flatly.

'Watch me.'

She climbed up. It was as easy as she'd thought; plenty of good finger- and toeholds.

When she pulled herself up onto the ledge beside him, he shrugged, but there was reluctant respect in his eyes.

'You're quick,' he said. 'Here.' He held out the leather bag.

But Maggie was simply staring. This close, the feeling of familiarity was overwhelming.

It was *you* in my dream, she thought. Not just somebody like you.

She recognized everything about him. That supple, smoothly muscled body, and the way he had of standing as if he were filled with tightly leashed tension. That dark hair with the tiny waves springing out where it got unruly. That taut, grim face, those high cheekbones, that wilful mouth.

And especially the eyes. Those fearless, black-lashed yellow eyes that seemed to hold endless layers of clear brilliance. That were windows on the fiercely intelligent mind behind them.

The only difference was the expression. In the dream, he had been anxious and tender. Here, he seemed joyless and bitter . . . and cold. As if his entire being were coated with a very thin layer of ice.

But it was you, Maggie thought. Not just somebody like you, because I don't think there *is* anybody like you.

Still lost in her memories, she said, 'I'm Maggie Neely. What's your name?'

He looked taken aback. The golden eyes widened, then

narrowed. 'How dare you ask?' he rapped out. He sounded quite natural saying 'How dare you,' although Maggie didn't think she'd ever heard anybody say it outside of a movie.

'I had a dream about you,' Maggie said. 'At least – it wasn't *me* having the dream; it was more as if it was sent to me.' She was remembering details now. 'You kept telling me that I had to do something . . .'

'I don't give a damn about your dreams,' the boy said shortly. 'Now, do you want the water or not?'

Maggie remembered how thirsty she was. She reached out for the leather bag eagerly.

He held on to it, not releasing it to her. 'There's only enough for one,' he said, still brusque. 'Drink it here.'

Maggie blinked. The bag did feel disappointingly slack in her grip. She tugged at it a little and heard a faint slosh.

'Cady needs some, too. She's sick.'

'She's more than sick. She's almost gone. There's no point in wasting any on her.'

I can't believe I'm hearing this again, Maggie thought. He's just like Jeanne.

She tugged at the bag harder. 'If I want to share with her, that's my business, right? Why should it matter to you?'

'Because it's stupid. There's only enough for one.'

'Look—'

'You're not afraid of me, are you?' he said abruptly. The brilliant yellow eyes were fixed on her as if he could read her thoughts.

It was strange, but she *wasn't* afraid, not exactly. Or, she *was* afraid, but something inside her was making her go on in spite of her fear.

'Anyway, it's my water,' he said. 'And I say there's only enough for one. You were stupid to try and protect her before, when you could have gotten away. Now you have to forget about her.'

Maggie had the oddest feeling that she was being tested. But there was no time to figure out for what, or why.

'Fine. It's your water,' she said, making her voice just as clipped as his. 'And there's only enough for one.' She pulled at the bag harder, and this time he let go of it.

Maggie turned from him, looked down at the boulders where Cady was lying. She judged the distance carefully, noting the way one boulder formed a cradle.

Easy shot. It'll rebound and wedge in that crack, she thought. She extended her arm to drop the bag.

'Wait!' The voice was harsh and explosive – and even more harsh was the iron grip that clamped on her wrist.

'What do you think you're doing?' the boy said angrily, and Maggie found herself looking into fierce yellow eyes.

CHAPTER

8

'**W**hat are you doing?' he repeated ferociously. His grip was hurting her.

'I'm throwing the water bag down there,' Maggie said. But she was thinking, He's so strong. Stronger than anybody I've ever met. He could break my wrist without even trying.

'I know that! *Why*?'

'Because it's easier than carrying it down in my teeth,' Maggie said. But that wasn't the real reason, of course. The truth was that she needed to get temptation out of the way. She was so thirsty that it was a kind of madness, and she was afraid of what she would do if she held on to this cool, sloshing water bag much longer.

He was staring at her with those startling eyes, as if he were trying to pry his way into her brain. And Maggie had the odd feeling that he'd succeeded, at least far enough that he knew the real reason she was doing this.

'You are an idiot,' he said slowly, with cold wonder. 'You should listen to your body; it's telling you what it needs. You can't ignore thirst. You can't deny it.'

'Yes, you can,' Maggie said flatly. Her wrist was going numb. If this went on, she was going to drop the bag involuntarily, and in the wrong place.

'You can't,' he said, somehow making the words into an angry hiss. 'I should know.'

Then he showed her his teeth.

Maggie should have been prepared.

Jeanne had told her. Vampires and witches and shapeshifters, she'd said. And Sylvia was a witch, and Bern had been a shapeshifter.

This boy was a vampire.

The strange thing was that, unlike Bern, he didn't get uglier when he changed. His face seemed paler and finer, like something chiselled in ice. His golden eyes burned brighter, framed by lashes that looked even blacker in contrast. His pupils opened and seemed to hold a darkness that could swallow a person up.

But it was the mouth that had changed the most. It looked even more wilful, disdainful, and sullen – and it was drawn up into a sneer to display the fangs.

Impressive fangs. Long, translucent white, tapering into delicate points. Shaped like a cat's canines, with a sheen on them like jewels. Not yellowing tusks like Bern's, but delicate instruments of death.

What amazed Maggie was that although he looked completely different from anything she'd seen before, completely abnormal, he also looked completely natural. This was another kind of creature, just like a human or a bear, with as much right to live as either of them.

Which didn't mean she wasn't scared. But she was frightened in a new way, a way ready for action.

She was ready to fight, if fighting became necessary. She'd already changed that much since entering this valley: fear now made her not panicked but hyper alert.

If I have to defend myself I need both hands. And it's better not to let him see I'm scared.

'Maybe you can't ignore your kind of thirst,' she said, and was pleased that her voice didn't wobble. 'But I'm fine. Except that you're hurting my wrist. Can you please let go?'

For just an instant, the brilliant yellow eyes flared even brighter, and she wondered if he was going to attack her. But then his eyelids lowered, black lashes veiling the brightness. He let go of her wrist.

Maggie's arm sagged, and the leather bag dropped from her suddenly nerveless fingers. It landed safely at her feet. She rubbed her hand.

And didn't look up a moment later, when he said with a kind of quiet hostility, 'Aren't you afraid of me?'

'Yes.' It was true. And it wasn't just because he was a vampire or because he had a power that could send blue death twenty feet away. It was because of *him*, of the way he was. He was scary enough in and of himself.

'But what good is it, being afraid?' Maggie said, still rubbing her hand. 'If you're going to try to hurt me, I'll fight back. And so far, you haven't tried to hurt me. You've only helped me.'

'I told you, I didn't do it for *you*. And you'll never survive if you keep on being insane like this.'

'Insane like what?' Now she did look up, to see that his eyes were burning dark gold and his fangs were gone. His mouth simply looked scornful and aristocratic.

'Trusting people,' he said, as if it should have been obvious. 'Taking care of people. Don't you know that only the strong ones make it? Weak people are deadweight – and if you try to help them, they'll drag you down with them.'

Maggie had an answer for that. 'Cady isn't weak,' she said flatly. 'She's *sick*. She'll get better – if she gets the chance. And if we don't take care of each other, what's going to happen to all of us?'

He looked exasperated, and for a few minutes they stared at each other in mutual frustration.

Then Maggie bent and picked up the bag again. 'I'd better give it to her now. I'll bring your canteen back.'

'Wait.' His voice was abrupt and cold, unfriendly. But this time he didn't grab her.

'What?'

'Follow me.' He gave the order briefly and turned without pausing to see if she obeyed. It was clear that he *expected* people to obey him, without questions. 'Bring the bag,' he said, without looking over his shoulder.

Maggie hesitated an instant, glancing down at Cady. But the hollow was protected by the overhanging boulders; Cady would be all right there for a few minutes.

She followed the boy. The narrow path that wound around the mountain was rough and primitive, interrupted by bands of broken, razor-sharp slate. She had to pick her way carefully around them.

In front of her, the boy turned toward the rock suddenly and disappeared. When Maggie caught up, she saw the cave.

The entrance was small, hardly more than a crack, and even Maggie had to stoop and go in sideways. But inside it opened into a snug little enclosure that smelled of dampness and cool rock.

Almost no light filtered in from the outside world. Maggie blinked, trying to adjust to the near-darkness, when there was a sound like a match strike and a smell of sulphur. A tiny flame was born, and Maggie saw the boy lighting some kind of crude stone lamp that had been carved out of the cave wall itself. He glanced back at her and his eyes flashed gold.

But Maggie was gasping, looking around her. The light

of the little flame threw a mass of shifting, confusing shadows everywhere, but it also picked out threads of sparkling quartz in the rock. The small cave had become a place of enchantment.

And at the boy's feet was something that glittered silver. In the hush of the still air, Maggie could hear the liquid, bell-like sound of water dripping.

'It's a pool,' the boy said. 'Spring fed. The water's cold, but it's good.'

Water. Something like pure lust overcame Maggie. She took three steps forward, ignoring the boy completely, and then her legs collapsed. She cupped a hand in the pool, felt the coolness encompass it to the wrist, and brought it out as if she were holding liquid diamond in her palm.

She'd never tasted anything as good as that water. No Coke she'd drunk on the hottest day of summer could compare with it. It ran through her dry mouth and down her parched throat – and then it seemed to spread all through her, sparkling through her body, soothing and reviving her. A sort of crystal clearness entered her brain. She drank and drank in a state of pure bliss.

And then, when she was in the even more blissful state of being not thirsty anymore, she plunged the leather bag under the surface to fill it.

'What's that for?' But there was a certain resignation in the boy's voice.

'Cady. I have to get back to her.' Maggie sat back on her heels and looked at him. The light danced and flickered around him, glinting bronze off his dark hair, casting half his face in shadow.

'Thank you,' she said, quietly, but in a voice that shook slightly. 'I think you probably saved my life again.'

'You were really thirsty.'

'Yeah.' She stood up.

'But when you thought there wasn't enough water, you were going to give it to her.' He couldn't seem to get over the concept.

'Yeah.'

'Even if it meant you dying?'

'I didn't die,' Maggie pointed out. 'And I wasn't planning to. But, yeah, I guess, if there wasn't any other choice.' She saw him staring at her in utter bewilderment. 'I took *responsibility* for her,' she said, trying to explain. 'It's like when you take in a cat, or – or it's like being a queen or something. If you say you're going to be responsible for your subjects, you are. You owe them afterward.'

Something glimmered in his golden eyes, just for a moment. It could have been a dagger point of anger or just a spark of astonishment. There was a silence.

'It's not *that* weird, people taking care of each other,' Maggie said, looking at his shadowed face. 'Doesn't anybody do it here?'

He gave a short laugh. 'Hardly,' he said dryly. 'The nobles know how to take care of themselves. And the slaves have to fight each other to survive.' He added abruptly, 'All of which you should know. But of course you're not from here. You're from Outside.'

'I didn't know if you *knew* about Outside,' Maggie said.

'There isn't supposed to be any contact. There wasn't for about five hundred years. But when my – when the old king died, they opened the pass again and started bringing in slaves from the outside world. New blood.' He said it simply and matter-of-factly.

Mountain men, Maggie thought. For years there had been rumours about the Cascades, about men who lived in hidden places among the glaciers and preyed on climbers. Men or monsters. There were always hikers who claimed to have seen Bigfoot.

And maybe they had – or maybe they'd seen a shapeshifter like Bern.

'And you think that's OK,' she said out loud. 'Grabbing people from the outside world and dragging them in here to be slaves.'

'Not people. Humans. Humans are vermin; they're not intelligent.' He said it in that same dispassionate tone, looking right at her.

'Are you *crazy*?' Maggie's fists were clenched; her head was lowered. Stomping time. She glared up at him through narrowed lashes. 'You're talking to a human right now. Am I intelligent or not?'

'You're a slave without any manners,' he said curtly. 'And the law says I could kill you for the way you're talking to me.'

His voice was so cold, so arrogant . . . but Maggie was starting not to believe it.

That couldn't be all there was to him. Because he was the boy in her dream.

The gentle, compassionate boy who'd looked at her with a flame of love behind his yellow eyes, and who'd held her with such tender intensity, his heart beating against hers, his breath on her cheek. That boy had been real, and even if it didn't make any sense, Maggie was somehow certain of it. And no matter how cold and arrogant this one seemed, they had to be part of each other.

It didn't make her less afraid of this one, exactly. But it made her more determined to ignore her fear.

'In my dream,' she said deliberately, advancing a step on him, 'you cared about at least one human. You wanted to take care of me.'

'You shouldn't even be *allowed* to dream about me,' he said. His voice was as tense and grim as ever, but as

Maggie got closer to him, looking directly up into his face, he did something that amazed her. He fell back a step.

'Why not? Because I'm a slave? I'm a *person*.' She took another step forward, still looking at him challengingly. 'And I don't believe that you're as bad as you say you are. I think I saw what you were really like in my dream.'

'You're crazy,' he said. He didn't back up any farther; there was nowhere left to go. But his whole body was taut. 'Why should I want to take care of you?' he added in a cold and contemptuous voice. 'What's so special about you?'

It was a good question, and for a moment Maggie was shaken. Tears sprang to her eyes.

'I don't know,' she said honestly. 'I'm nobody special. There *isn't* any reason for you to care about me. But it doesn't matter. You saved my life when Bern was going to kill me, and you gave me water when you knew I needed it. You can talk all you want, but those are the facts. Maybe you just care about everybody, underneath. Or—'

She never finished the last sentence.

As she had been speaking to him, she was doing something she always did, that was instinctive to her when she felt some strong emotion. She had done it with P.J. and with Jeanne and with Cady.

She reached out toward him. And although she was only dimly aware that he was pulling his hands back to avoid her, she adjusted automatically, catching his wrists . . .

And that was when she lost her voice and what she was saying flew out of her head. Because something happened. Something that she couldn't explain, that was stranger than secret kingdoms or vampires or witchcraft.

It happened just as her fingers closed on his hands. It was the first time they had touched like that, bare skin to bare skin. When he had grabbed her wrist before, her jacket sleeve had been in between them.

It started as an almost painful jolt, a pulsating thrill that zigged up her arm and then swept through her body. Maggie gasped, but somehow she couldn't let go of his hand. Like someone being electrocuted, she was frozen in place.

The blue fire, she thought wildly. He's doing the same thing to me that he did to Bern.

But the next instant she knew that he wasn't. This wasn't the savage energy that had killed Bern, and it wasn't anything the boy was doing to her. It was something being done to both of them, by some incredibly powerful source outside either of them.

And it was trying . . . to open a channel. That was the only was Maggie could describe it. It was blazing a path open in her mind, and connecting it to his.

She felt as if she had turned around and unexpectedly found herself facing another person's soul. A soul that was hanging there, without protection, already in helpless communication with hers.

It was by far the most intense thing that had ever happened to her. Maggie gasped again, seeing stars, and then her legs melted and she fell forward.

He caught her, but he couldn't stand up either. Maggie knew that as well as she knew what was going on in her own body. He sank to his knees, holding her.

What are you doing to me?

It was a thought, but it wasn't Maggie's. It was his.

I don't know . . . I'm not doing it . . . I don't understand! Maggie had no idea how to send her thoughts to another person. But she didn't need to, it was simply happening. A pure line of communication had been opened between them. It was a fierce and terrible thing, a bit like being fused together by a bolt of lightning, but it was also so wonderful that Maggie's entire skin was prickling and her mind was hushed with awe.

She felt as if she'd been lifted into some new and wonderful place that most people never even saw. The air around her seemed to quiver with invisible wings.

This is how people are supposed to be, she thought. *Joined like this. Open to each other. With nothing hidden and no stupid walls between them.*

A thought came back at her, sharp and quick as a hammer strike. *No!*

It was so cold, so full of rejection, that for a moment Maggie was taken aback. But then she sensed what else was behind it.

Anger . . . and fear. He was afraid of this, and of her. He felt invaded. Exposed.

Well, I do, too, Maggie said mentally. It wasn't that she wasn't afraid. It was that her fear was irrelevant. The force that held them was so much more powerful than either of them, so immeasurably ancient, that fear was natural but not important. The same light shone through each of them, stripping away their shields, making them transparent to each other.

It's all right for you. Because you don't have anything to be ashamed of! The thought flashed by so quickly that Maggie wasn't even sure she had heard it.

What do you mean? she thought. *Wait . . . Delos.*

That was his name. Delos Redfern. She knew it now, as unquestionably as she knew the names of her own family. She realized, too, as a matter of minor importance, an afterthought, that he was a prince. A vampire prince who'd been born to rule this secret kingdom, as the Redfern family had ruled it for centuries.

The old king was your father, she said to him. *And he*

died three years ago, when you were fourteen. You've been ruling ever since.

He was pulling away from her mentally, trying to break the contact between them. *It's none of your business,* he snarled.

Please wait, Maggie said. But as she chased after him mentally, trying to catch him, to help him, something shocking and new happened, like a second bolt of lightning.

CHAPTER 9

She was in his mind. It was all around her, like a strange and perilous world. A terribly frightening world, but one that was full of stark beauty.

Everything was angles, as if she'd fallen into the heart of a giant crystal. Everything glittered, cold and clear and sharp. There were flashes of colour as light shimmered and reflected, but for the most part it was dazzling transparency in every direction. Like the fractured ice of a glacier.

Really dangerous, Maggie thought. The spikes of crystal around her had edges like swords. The place looked as if it had never known warmth or soft colour.

And you live *here?* she thought to Delos.

Go away. Delos's answering thought came to her on a wave of cold wind. *Get out!*

No, Maggie said. *You can't scare me. I've climbed glaciers before*. It was then that she realized what this place reminded her of. A summit. The bare and icy top of a mountain where no plants – and certainly no people – could survive.

But didn't anything *good ever happen to you?* she wondered. *Didn't you ever have a friend . . . or a pet . . . or something?*

No friends, he said shortly. *No pets. Get out of here before I hurt you.*

Maggie didn't answer, because even as he said it things were changing around her. It was as if the glinting surfaces of the nearby crystals were suddenly reflecting scenes, perfect little pictures with people moving in them. As soon as Maggie looked at one, it swelled up and seemed to surround her.

They were his memories. She was seeing bits of his childhood.

She saw a child who had been treated as a weapon from the time he was born. It was all about some prophecy. She saw men and women gathered around a little boy, four years old, whose black-lashed golden eyes were wide and frightened.

'No question about it,' the oldest man was saying. Delos's teacher, Maggie realized, the knowledge flowing to her because Delos knew it, and she was in Delos's mind.

'This child is one of the Wild Powers,' the teacher said, and his voice was full of awe – and fear. His trembling hands smoothed out a brittle piece of scroll. As soon as Maggie saw it she knew that the scroll was terribly old and had been kept in the Dark Kingdom for centuries, preserved here even when it was lost to the outside world.

'Four Wild Powers,' the old man said, 'who will be needed at the millennium to save the world – or to destroy it. The prophecy tells where they will come from.' And he read:

'One from the land of kings long forgotten;
One from the hearth which still holds the spark;
One from the Day World where two eyes are
    watching;
One from the twilight to be one with the dark.'

The child Delos looked around the circle of grim faces, hearing the words but not understanding them.

' "The land of kings, long forgotten," ' a woman was saying. 'That must be the Dark Kingdom.'

'Besides, we've seen what he can do,' a big man said roughly. 'He's a Wild Power, all right. The blue fire is in his blood. He's learned to use it too early, though; he can't control it. See?'

He grabbed a small arm – the left one – and held it up. It was twisted somehow, the fingers clawed and stiff, immobile.

The little boy tried to pull his hand away, but he was too weak. The adults ignored him.

'The king wants us to find spells to hold the power in,' the woman said. 'Or he'll damage himself permanently.'

'Not to mention damaging us,' the rough man said, and laughed harshly.

The little boy sat stiff and motionless as they handled him like a doll. His golden eyes were dry and his small jaw was clenched with the effort not to give in to tears.

That's awful, Maggie said indignantly, aiming her thought at the Delos of the present. *It's a terrible way to grow up. Wasn't there anybody who cared about you? Your father?*

Go away, he said. *I don't need your sympathy.*

And your arm, Maggie said, ignoring the cold emptiness of his thought. *Is that what happens to it when you use the blue fire?*

He didn't answer, not in a thought directed at her. But another memory flashed in the facets of a crystal, and Maggie found herself drawn into it.

She saw a five-year-old Delos with his arm wrapped in what looked like splints or a brace. As she looked at it, she knew it wasn't just a brace. It was made of spells and wards to confine the blue fire.

'This is it,' the woman who had spoken before was saying to the circle of men. 'We can control him completely.'

'Are you sure? You witches are careless sometimes. You're sure he can't use it at all now?' The man who said it was tall, with a chilly, austere face – and yellow eyes like Delos's.

Your father, Maggie said wonderingly to Delos. *And his name was . . . Tormentil? But . . .* She couldn't go on, but she was thinking that he didn't look much like a loving father. He seemed just like the others.

'Until I remove the wards, he can't use it at all. I'm sure, majesty.' The woman said the last word in an everyday tone, but Maggie felt a little shock. Hearing somebody get called majesty – it made him *more* of a king, somehow.

'The longer they're left on, the weaker he'll be,' the woman continued. 'And *he* can't take them off himself. But I can, at any time—'

'And then he'll still be useful as a weapon?'

'Yes. But blood has to run before he can use the blue fire.'

The king said brusquely, 'Show me.'

The woman murmured a few words and stripped the brace off the boy's arm. She took a knife from her belt and with a quick, casual motion, like Maggie's grandmother gutting a salmon, opened a gash on his wrist.

Five-year-old Delos didn't flinch or make a sound. His golden eyes were fixed on his father's face as blood dripped onto the floor.

'I don't think this is a good idea,' the old teacher said. 'The blue fire isn't meant to be used like this, and it damages his arm every time he does it—'

'Now,' the king interrupted, ignoring him and speaking

to the child for the first time. 'Show me how strong you are, son. Turn the blue fire on . . .' He glanced up deliberately at the teacher. 'Let's say – him.'

'Majesty!' The old man gasped, backing against the wall.

The golden eyes were wide and afraid.

'Do it!' the king said sharply, and when the little boy shook his head mutely, he closed his hand on one small shoulder. Maggie could see his fingers tighten painfully. 'Do what I tell you. Now!'

Delos turned his wide golden eyes on the old man, who was now shrinking and babbling, his trembling hands held up as if to ward off a blow.

The king changed his grip, lifted the boy's arm.

'Now, brat! *Now!*'

Blue fire erupted. It poured in a continuous stream like the water from a high-power fire hose. It struck the old man and spread-eagled him against the wall, his eyes and mouth open with horror. And then there *was* no old man. There was only a shadowy silhouette made of ashes.

'Interesting,' the king said, dropping the boy's arm. His anger had disappeared as quickly as it had come. 'Actually, I thought there would be more power. I thought it might take out the wall.'

'Give him time.' The woman's voice was slightly thick, and she was swallowing over and over.

'Well, no matter what, he'll be useful.' The king turned to look at the others in the room. 'Remember, all of you. A time of darkness is coming. The end of the millennium means the end of the world. But whatever happens outside, this kingdom is going to survive.'

Throughout all of this, the little boy sat and stared at the place where the old man had been. His eyes were wide, the pupils huge and fixed. His face was white, but without expression.

Maggie struggled to breathe.

That's – that's the most terrible thing I've ever seen. She could hardly get the words of her thought out. *They made you kill your teacher –* he *made you do it. Your father.* She didn't know what to say. She turned blindly, trying to find Delos himself in this strange landscape, trying to talk to him directly. She wanted to look at him, to hold him. To comfort him. *I'm so sorry. I'm so sorry you had to grow up like that.*

Don't be stupid, he said. *I grew up to be strong. That's what counts.*

You grew up without anyone loving you, Maggie said.

He sent a thought like ice. *Love is for weak people. It's a delusion. And it can be deadly.*

Maggie didn't know how to answer. She wanted to shake him. *All that stuff about the end of the millennium and the end of the world – what did that mean?*

Exactly what it sounded like, Delos said briefly. *The prophecies are coming true. The world of humans is about to end in blood and darkness. And then the Night People are going to rule again.*

And that's why they turned a five-year-old into a lethal weapon? Maggie wondered. The thought wasn't for Delos, but she could feel that he heard it.

I am what I was meant to be, he said. *And I don't want to be anything else.*

Are you sure? Maggie looked around. Although she couldn't have described what she was doing, she knew what it was. She was looking for something . . . something to prove to him . . .

A scene flashed in the crystal.

The boy Delos was eight. He stood in front of a pile of

boulders, rocks the size of small cars. His father stood behind him.

'Now!'

As soon as the king spoke, the boy lifted his arm. Blue fire flashed. A boulder exploded, disintegrating into atoms.

'Again!'

Another rock shattered.

'More power! You're not trying. You're useless!'

The entire pile of boulders exploded. The blue fire kept streaming, taking out a stand of trees behind the boulders and crashing into the side of a mountain. It chewed through the rock, melting shale and granite like a flamethrower burning a wooden door.

The king smiled cruelly and slapped his son on the back.

'That's better.'

No. That's horrible, Maggie told Delos. *That's* wrong. *This is what it should be like.*

And she sent to him images of her own family. Not that the Neelys were anything special. They were like anybody. They had fights, some of them pretty bad. But there were lots of good times, too, and that was what she showed him. She showed him her life . . . herself.

Laughing as her father frantically blew on a flaming marshmallow on some long-past camping trip. Smelling turpentine and watching magical colours unfold on canvas as her mother painted. Perching dangerously on the handlebars of a bike while Miles pedalled behind her, then shrieking all the way down a hill. Waking up to a rough warm tongue licking her face, opening one eye to see Jake the Great Dane panting happily. Blowing out candles at a birthday party. Ambushing Miles from her doorway with a heavy-duty water rifle . . .

Who is that? Delos asked. He had been thawing; Maggie could feel it. There were so many things in the memories that were strange to him: yellow sunshine, modern houses, bicycles, machinery – but she could feel interest and wonder stir in him at the people.

Until now, when she was showing him a sixteen-year-old Miles, a Miles who looked pretty much like the Miles of today.

That's Miles. He's my brother. He's eighteen and he just started college. Maggie paused, trying to feel what Delos was thinking. *He's the reason I'm here. He got involved with this girl called Sylvia – I think she's a witch. And then he disappeared. I went to see Sylvia, and the next thing I know I'm waking up in a slave-trader's cart. In a place I never knew existed.*

Delos said, *I see.*

Delos, do you know him? Have you seen him before? Maggie tried to keep the question calm. She would have thought she could see anything that Delos was thinking, that it would all be reflected in the crystals around her, that there was nothing he could hide. But now suddenly she wasn't sure.

It's best for you to leave that alone, Delos said.

I can't, Maggie snapped back. *He's my brother! If he's in trouble I have to find him – I have to help him. That's what I've been trying to explain to you. We help each other.*

Delos said, *Why?*

Because we do. Because that's what people are supposed to do. And even you know that, somewhere down deep. You were trying to help me in my dream—

She could feel him pull away. *Your dreams are just your fantasies.*

Maggie said flatly, *No. Not this one. I had it before I met you.*

She could remember more of it now. Here in his mind the details were coming to her, all the things that had been unclear before. And there was only one thing to do.

She showed it to Delos.

The mist, the figure appearing, calling her name. The wonder and joy in his face when he caught sight of her. The way his hands closed on her shoulders, so gently, and the look of inexpressible tenderness in his eyes.

And then – I remember! Maggie said. *You told me to look for a pass, underneath a rock that looked like a wave about to break. You told me to get away from here, to escape. And then . . .*

She remembered what had happened then, and faltered.

And then he had kissed her.

She could feel it again, his breath a soft warmth on her cheek, and then the touch of his lips, just as soft. There had been so much in that kiss, so much of himself revealed. It had been almost shy in its gentleness, but charged with a terrible passion, as if he had known it was the last kiss they would ever share.

It was . . . so sad, Maggie said, faltering again. Not from embarrassment, but because she was suddenly filled with an intensity of emotion that frightened her. *I don't know what it meant, but it was so sad . . .*

Then, belatedly, she realized what was happening with Delos.

He was agitated. Violently agitated. The crystal world around Maggie was trembling with denial and fury – and fear.

That wasn't me. I'm not like that, he said in a voice that was like a sword made of ice.

It was, she said, not harshly but quietly. *I don't understand it, but it really was you. I don't understand any of this. But there's a connection between us. Look what's happening to us right now. Is this normal? Do you people always fall into each others' minds?*

Get out! The words were a shout that echoed around Maggie from every surface. She could feel his anger; it was huge, violent, like a primal storm. And she could feel the terror that was underneath it, and hear the word that he was thinking and didn't want to think, that he was trying to bury and run away from.

Soulmates. That was the word. Maggie could sense what it meant. Two people connected, bound to each other forever, soul to soul, in a way that even death couldn't break. Two souls that were destined for each other.

It's a lie, Delos said fiercely. *I don't believe in souls. I don't love anyone. And I don't have any feelings!*

And then the world broke apart.

That was what it felt like. Suddenly, all around Maggie, the crystals were shattering and fracturing. Pieces were falling with the musical sound of ice. Nothing was stable, everything was turning to chaos.

And then, so abruptly that she lost her breath, she was out of his mind.

She was sitting on the ground in a small cave lit only by a dancing, flickering flame. Shadows wavered on the walls and ceiling. She was in her own body, and Delos was holding her in his arms.

But even as she realized it, he pulled away and stood up. Even in the dimness she could see that his face was pale, his eyes fixed.

As she got to her feet, she could see something else, too. It was strange, but their minds were still connected, even though he'd thrown her out of his world.

And what she saw . . . was herself. Herself through his eyes.

She saw someone who wasn't at all the frail blonde princess type, not a bit languid and perfect and artificial. She saw a sturdy, rosy-brown girl with a straight gaze. A girl with autumn-coloured hair, warm and vivid and real, and sorrel-coloured eyes. It was the eyes that caught her attention: there was a clarity and honesty in them, a depth and spaciousness that made mere prettiness seem cheap.

Maggie caught her breath. Do *I* look like that? she wondered dizzily. I can't. I'd have noticed in the mirror.

But it was how he saw her. In his eyes, she was the only vibrant, living thing in a cold world of black and white. And she could feel the connection between them tightening, drawing him toward her even as he tried to pull farther away.

'No.' His voice was a bare whisper in the cave. 'I'm not bound to you. I don't love you.'

'Delos—'

'I don't love anyone. I don't have feelings.'

Maggie shook her head wordlessly. She didn't have to speak, anyway. All the time he was telling her how much he didn't love her, he was moving closer to her, fighting it every inch.

'You mean nothing to me,' he raged through clenched teeth. 'Nothing!'

And then his face was inches away from hers, and she could see the flame burning in his golden eyes.

'Nothing,' he whispered, and then his lips touched hers.

CHAPTER
10

But at the instant which would have made it a kiss, Delos pulled away. Maggie felt the brush of his warm lips and then cold air as he jerked back.

'No,' he said. 'No.' She could see the clash of fear and anger in his eyes, and she could see it suddenly resolve itself as the pain grew unbearable. He shuddered once, and then all the turmoil vanished, as if it were being swept aside by a giant hand. It left only icy determination in its wake.

'That's not going to help,' Maggie said. 'I don't even understand why you *want* to be this way, but you can't just squash everything down—'

'Listen,' he said in a clipped, taut voice. 'You said that in your dream I told you to go away. Well, I'm telling you the same thing now. Go away and don't ever come back. I never want to see your face again.'

'Oh, fine.' Maggie was trembling herself with frustration. She'd had it; she'd finally reached the limit of her patience with him. There was so much bitterness in his face, so much pain, but it was clear he wasn't going to let anyone help.

'I mean it. And you don't know how much of a

concession it is. I'm letting you go. You're not just an escaped slave, you're an escaped slave who knows about the pass in the mountains. The penalty for that is death.'

'So kill me,' Maggie said. It was a stupid thing to say and she knew it. He was dangerous – and the master of that blue fire. He could do it at the turn of an eyelash. But she was feeling stupid and reckless. Her fists were clenched.

'I'm telling you to leave,' he said. 'And I'll tell you something else. You wanted to know what happened to your brother.'

Maggie went still. There was something different about him suddenly. He looked like somebody about to strike a blow. His body was tense and his eyes were burning gold like twin flames.

'Well, here it is,' he said. 'Your brother is dead. I killed him.'

It *was* a blow. Maggie felt as if she'd been hit. Shock spread through her body and left her tingling with adrenalin. At the same time she felt strangely weak, as if her legs didn't want to hold her up any longer.

But she didn't believe it. She couldn't believe it, not just like that.

She opened her mouth and dragged in a breath to speak – and froze.

Somewhere outside the cave a voice was calling. Maggie couldn't make out the words, but it was a girl's voice. And it was close . . . and coming closer.

Delos's head whipped around to look at the entrance of the cave. Then, before Maggie could say anything, he was moving.

He took one step to the wall and blew out the flame of the little stone lamp. Instantly, the cave was plunged into darkness. Maggie hadn't realized how little light came from the entrance crack – almost none at all.

No, she thought. Less light is coming through than before. It's getting *dark*.

Oh, God, she thought. Cady.

I just walked off and left her there. What's wrong with me? I forgot all about her – I didn't even think . . .

'Where are you going?' Delos whispered harshly.

Maggie paused in mid rush and looked at him wildly. Or looked *toward* him, actually, because now she couldn't see anything but darkness against paler darkness.

'To Cady,' she said, distracted and frantic, clutching the water bag she'd grabbed. 'I left her down there. Anything could have happened by now.'

'You can't go outside,' he said. 'That's the hunting party I came with. If they catch you I won't be able to help—'

'I don't care!' Maggie's words tumbled over his. 'A minute ago you never wanted to see me again. Oh, God, I *left* her. How could I do that?'

'It hasn't been that long,' he hissed impatiently. 'An hour or so.' Vaguely, Maggie realized that he must be right. It seemed like a hundred years since she had climbed up to his ledge, but actually everything had happened quickly after that.

'I still have to go,' she said, a little more calmly. 'She's sick. And maybe Gavin came back.' A wave of fear surged through her at the thought.

'If they catch you, you'll wish you were dead,' he said distinctly. Before Maggie could answer, he was going on, his voice as brusque as ever. 'Stay here. Don't come out until everybody's gone.'

She felt the movement of air and the brush of cloth as he passed in front of her. The light from the entrance crack was cut off briefly, and then she saw him silhouetted for an instant against grey sky.

Then she was alone.

Maggie stood tensely for a moment, listening. The sound of her own breathing was too loud. She crept quietly to the entrance and crouched.

And felt a jolt. She could hear footsteps crunching on the broken slate outside. *Right* outside. Then a shadow seemed to fall across the crack and she heard a voice.

'Delos! What are you doing up here?'

It was a light, pleasant voice, the voice of a girl only a little older than Maggie. Not a woman yet. And it was both concerned and casual, addressing Delos with a familiarity that was startling.

But that wasn't what gave her the *big* jolt. It was that she recognized the voice. She knew it and she hated it.

It was Sylvia.

She's here, Maggie thought. And from the way she's talking she's been here before – enough to get to know Delos. Or maybe she was born here, and she's just started coming Outside.

Whatever the truth, it somehow made Maggie certain that Miles had been brought here, too. But then – what? What had happened to him after that? Had he done something that meant he had to disappear? Or had it been Sylvia's plan from the beginning?

Could Delos have really . . . ?

I don't believe it, Maggie thought fiercely, but there was a pit of sick fear in her stomach.

Outside, Sylvia was chatting on in a musical voice. 'We didn't even know you'd left the group – but then we saw the blue fire. We thought you might be in trouble—'

'Me?' Delos laughed briefly.

'Well, we thought there might *be* trouble,' Sylvia amended. Her own laugh was like wind chimes.

'I'm fine. I used the fire for practice.'

'Delos.' Sylvia's voice was gently reproving now, in a way that was almost flirtatious. 'You know you shouldn't do that. You'll only do more damage to your arm – it's never going to get better if you keep using it.'

'I know.' Delos's brusque tone was a sharp contrast to Sylvia's teasing. 'But that's my business.'

'I only want what's best for you—'

'Let's go. I'm sure the rest of the party is waiting for us.'

He doesn't like her, Maggie thought. All her whinnying and prancing doesn't fool him. But I wonder what she is to him?

What she really wanted at that moment was to dash out and confront Sylvia. Grab her and shake her until she coughed up some answers.

But she'd already tried that once – and it had gotten her thrown into slavery. She gritted her teeth and edged closer to the entrance crack. It was dangerous and she knew it, but she wanted to see Sylvia.

When she did, it was another shock. Sylvia always wore slinky tops and fashionable jeans, but the outfit she had on now was completely medieval. More, she looked comfortable in it, as if these strange clothes were natural to her – and flattering.

She was wearing a sea-green tunic that had long sleeves and fell to the ground. Over that was another tunic, a shade paler, this one sleeveless and tied with a belt embroidered in green and silver. Her hair was loose in a fine shimmering mass, and she had a falcon on her wrist.

A real falcon. With a little leather hood on its head and leather ties with bells on its feet. Maggie stared at it, fascinated despite herself.

That whole fragile act Sylvia puts on, she thought. But you have to be *strong* to hold up a big bird like that.

'Oh, we don't have to rush back just yet,' Sylvia was

saying, moving closer to Delos. 'Now that I'm here, we could go a little farther. This looks like a nice path; we could explore it.'

Cady, Maggie thought. If they go to the end of the path, they'll see her. *Sylvia* will see her.

She had just decided to jump out of the cave when Delos spoke.

'I'm tired,' he said in his flat, cold way. 'We're going back now.'

'Oh, you're tired,' Sylvia said, and her smile was almost sly. 'You see. I told you not to use your powers so much.'

'Yes,' Delos said, even more shortly. 'I remember.'

Before he could say anything else, Sylvia went on. 'I forgot to mention, a funny thing happened. A guy named Gavin dropped in on the hunting party a little while ago.'

Gavin.

Maggie's stomach plummeted.

He got away. And he saw everything.

And he must have moved *fast*, she thought absently. To hook around and get to a hunting party on the other side of this ledge – in time for Sylvia to come find Delos.

'You probably don't know him,' Sylvia was saying. 'But I do. He's the slave trader I use to get girls from Outside. He's normally pretty good, but today he was all upset. He said a group of slaves got loose on the mountain, and somehow his partner Bern got killed.'

You . . . *witch*, Maggie thought. She couldn't think of a swear word strong enough.

Sylvia knew. There was no doubt about it. If Gavin was her flunky, and if he'd told her that Bern was dead, he must have told her the rest. That Bern had been killed by Prince Delos himself, fried with blue fire, and that there were two slave girls in front of Delos at the time.

She knew all along, Maggie thought, and she was just

trying to trap Delos. But why isn't she afraid of him? He's the prince, after all. His father's dead; he's in charge. So how come she *dares* to set up her little traps?

'We were all concerned,' Sylvia was going on, tilting her silvery head to one side. 'All the nobles, and especially your great-grandfather. Loose slaves can mean trouble.'

'How sweet of you to worry,' Delos said. From what Maggie could see of his face, it was expressionless and his voice was dry and level. 'But you shouldn't have. I used the fire for practice – on the other slave trader. Also on two slaves. They interrupted me when I wanted quiet.'

Maggie sat in helpless admiration.

He did it. He outsmarted her. Now there's nothing she can say. And there's no way to prove that he didn't kill us. Gavin ran; he couldn't have seen anything after that.

He saved us. Delos saved Cady and me both – again.

'I see.' Sylvia bowed her head, looking sweet and placating, if not quite convinced. 'Well, of course you had every right to do that. So the slaves are dead.'

'Yes. And since they were only slaves, why are we standing here talking about them? Is there something about them I don't know?'

'No, no. Of course not,' Sylvia said quickly. 'You're right; we've wasted enough time. Let's go back.'

In her mind, Maggie heard Gavin's voice. *'It's not like they were ordinary slaves. If we don't deliver that maiden we're dead.'*

So she's lying again, Maggie thought. What a surprise. But who's the maiden? And why's she so important?

For that matter, she thought, who's this great-grandfather of Delos's? When Sylvia mentioned him it sounded almost like a threat. But if he's a great-grandfather he's got to be ancient. How are Sylvia and some old geezer teamed up?

It was an interesting question, but there was no time to think about it now. Sylvia and Delos were turning away from the cave, Sylvia murmuring about having to take a look at Delos's arm when they got back. In another moment they'd passed out of Maggie's line of sight and she heard the crunching noise of feet on slate.

Maggie waited until the last footstep faded, then she held her breath and waited for a count of thirty. It was all she could stand. She ducked through the entrance crack and stood in the open air.

It was fully dark now. She was very nearly blind. But she could sense the vast emptiness of the valley in front of her, and the solidity of the mountain at her back.

And she should have felt relieved, to be outside and not caught – but instead she felt strangely stifled. It took her a moment to realize why.

There was no sound at all. No footsteps, no voices, and no animals, either. And that was what felt eerie. It might be too cold at night for mosquitoes and gnats and flies, but there should have been *some* animal life to be heard. Birds heading into the trees to rest, bats heading out. Deer feeding. Bucks charging around – it was autumn, after all.

There was nothing. Maggie had the unnerving feeling that she was alone in a strange lifeless world swathed in cotton, cut off from everything real.

Don't stick around and think about it, she told herself sternly. Find Cady. Now!

Gritting her teeth, she thrust the water bag into her jacket and started back. By keeping close to the mountain's bulk on her left and feeling ahead with her foot before each step, she could find her way in the dark.

When she reached the ledge, her stomach tightened in dismay.

Terrific. Going down in pitch darkness – there's going to

be no way to see the footholds. Oh, well, I'll feel for them. The worst that can happen is I fall a hundred feet straight down.

'Cady,' she whispered. She was afraid to talk too loudly; the hunting party might be anywhere and sound could carry surprisingly well on a mountain slope.

'Cady? Are you OK?'

Her heart thumped slowly five times before she heard something below. Not a voice, just a stirring, like cloth on rock, and then a sigh.

Relief flooded through Maggie in a wave that was almost painful. Cady hadn't died or been abducted because Maggie had left her. 'Stay there,' she whispered as loudly as she dared. 'I'm coming down. I've brought water.'

It wasn't as hard going down as she'd expected. Maybe because she was still high on adrenalin, running in survival mode. Her feet seemed to find the toeholds of their own accord and in a few minutes she was on the boulders.

'Cady.' Her fingers found warmth and cloth. It moved and she heard another little sigh. 'Cady, are you OK? I can't see you.'

And then the darkness seemed to lighten, and Maggie realized that she *could* see the shape she was touching, dimly but distinctly. She glanced up and went still.

The moon was out. In a sky that was otherwise covered with clouds, there was a small opening, a clear spot. The moon shone down through it like a supernatural white face, nearly full.

'Maggie.' The voice was a soft breath, almost a whisper, but it seemed to blow peace and calm into Maggie's heart. 'Thanks for letting me rest. I feel stronger now.'

Maggie looked down. Silver light touched the curves of Cady's cheek and lips. The blind girl looked like some ancient Egyptian princess, her dark hair loose in crimped waves around her shoulders, her wide, heavy-lashed eyes reflecting the moon. Her face was as serene as ever.

'I'm sorry it took so long. I got some water,' Maggie said. She helped Cady sit up and put the water bag to her lips.

She doesn't look as feverish, she thought as Cady was drinking. Maybe she can walk. But where? Where can we *go*?

They would never make it to the pass. And even if they did, what then? They'd be high on a mountain – some mountain – in the dark and cold of a November night.

'We need to get you to a doctor,' she said.

Cady stopped drinking and gave the bag back. 'I don't think there's anything like that here. There might be some healing woman down there in the castle – but . . .' She stopped and shook her head. 'It's not worth it.'

'What do you mean, it's not worth it? And, hey, you're really feeling better, aren't you?' Maggie added, pleased. It was the first time Cady had gotten out more than a few words. She sounded very weak, but rational, and surprisingly knowledgeable.

'It's not worth it because it's too much of a risk. *I'm* too much of a risk. You have to leave me here, Maggie. Go down and get to shelter yourself.'

'Not this again!' Maggie waved a hand. She really couldn't deal with this argument anymore. 'If I left you up here, you'd die. It's going to get freezing cold. So I'm not going to leave you. And if there's a healing woman down at the castle, then we're going to the castle. Wherever the castle is.'

'It's the place all the Night People are,' Arcadia said, unexpectedly grim. 'The slaves, too. Everybody who lives here is inside the castle gates; it's really like a little town.

And it's exactly the place you shouldn't go.'

Maggie blinked. 'How come you know so much? Are you an escaped slave like Jeanne?'

'No. I heard about it a year or so ago from someone who had been here. I was coming here for a reason – it was just bad luck that I got caught by the slave traders on my way in.'

Maggie wanted to ask her more about it, but a nagging voice inside her said that this wasn't the time. It was already getting very cold. They couldn't be caught on the mountainside overnight.

'That road the cart was on – does it go all the way to the castle? Do you know?'

Cady hesitated. She turned her face toward the valley, and Maggie had the strange sense that she was looking out.

'I think so,' she said, at last. 'It would make sense that it does, anyway – there's only one place to go in the valley.'

'Then we've got to find it again.' Maggie knew that wouldn't be easy. They'd run a long way from Bern and Gavin. But she knew the general direction. 'Look, even if we don't get to the castle, we should find the road so we know where we are. And if we have to spend the night on the mountain, it's much better to be in the forest. It'll be warmer.'

'That's true. But—'

Maggie didn't give her a chance to go on. 'Can you stand up? I'll help, put your arm around my neck . . .'

It was tricky, getting Cady out of the nest of boulders. She and Maggie both had to crawl most of the way. And although Cady never complained, Maggie could see how tired it made her.

'Come on,' Maggie said. 'You're doing great.' And she

thought, with narrowed eyes and set teeth, If it comes to that, I'll *carry* her.

Too many people had told her to leave this girl. Maggie had never felt quite this stubborn before.

But it wasn't easy. Once into the woods, the canopy of branches cut off the moonlight. In only minutes, Cady was leaning heavily on Maggie, stumbling and trembling. Maggie herself was stumbling, tripping over roots, slipping on club moss and liverwort.

Strangely, Cady seemed to have a better sense of direction than she did, and in the beginning she kept murmuring, 'This way, I think.' But after a while she stopped talking, and some time after that, she stopped even responding to Maggie's questions.

At last, she stopped dead and swayed on her feet.

'Cady—'

It was no good. The taller girl shivered once, then went limp. It was all Maggie could do to break her fall.

And then she was sitting alone in a small clearing, with the spicy aroma of red cedar around her, and an unconscious girl in her lap. Maggie held still and listened to the silence.

Which was broken suddenly by the crunch of footsteps.

Footsteps coming toward her.

It might be a deer. But there was something hesitant and stealthy about it. Crunch, pause; crunch pause. The back of Maggie's neck prickled.

She held her breath and reached out, feeling for a rock or a stick – *some* weapon. Cady was heavy in her lap.

Something stirred in the salal bushes between two trees. Maggie strained her eyes, every muscle tense.

'Who's there?'

CHAPTER
11

The bushes stirred again. Maggie's searching fingers found only acorns and liquorice fern, so she made a fist instead, sliding out from underneath Cady and holding herself ready.

A form emerged from the underbrush. Maggie stared so hard she saw grey dots but she couldn't tell anything about it.

There was a long, tense moment, and then a voice came to her.

'I told you you'd never make it.'

Maggie almost fainted with relief.

At the same moment the moon came out from behind a cloud. It shone down into the clearing and over the slender figure standing with a hand on one hip. The pale silvery light turned red hair almost black, but the angular face and narrowed sceptical eyes were unmistakable. Not to mention the sour expression.

Maggie let out a long, shuddering breath. 'Jeanne!'

'You didn't get very far, did you? The road's just over there. What happened? Did she drop dead on you?'

It was amazing how good that irritable, acerbic voice sounded to Maggie. She laughed shakily. 'No, Cady's not dead. *Bern's* dead – you know, the big slave trader guy. But—'

'You're joking.' Jeanne's voice sharpened with respect and she moved forward. 'You killed him?'

'No. It was – look, I'll explain later. First, can you help me get her to somewhere more protected? It's really getting freezing out here, and she's completely out.'

Jeanne leaned down, looking at Arcadia. 'I told you before I wasn't going to help you if you got in trouble.'

'I know,' Maggie said. 'Can you sort of pick her up from that side? If we both get an arm under her shoulders she might be able to walk a little.'

'Bull,' Jeanne said shortly. 'We'd better chair-carry her. Link hands and we can get her up.'

Maggie clasped a cold, slender hand with calluses and a surprisingly firm grip. She heaved weight, and then they were carrying the unconscious girl.

'You're strong,' she grunted.

'Yeah, well, that's one of the side benefits of being a slave. The road's this way.'

It was awkward, slow work, but Maggie was strong, too, and Jeanne seemed to be able to guide them around the worst of the underbrush. And it was so good just to be with another human being who was healthy and clear headed and didn't want to kill her, that Maggie felt almost lighthearted.

'What about P.J.? Is she OK?'

'She's fine. She's in a place I know – it's not much, but it's shelter. That's where we're going.'

'You took care of her,' Maggie said. She shook her head in the darkness and laughed.

'What are you snickering about?' Jeanne paused and they spent a few minutes manoeuvering around a fallen log covered with spongy moss.

'Nothing,' Maggie said. 'It's just – you're pretty nice, aren't you? Underneath.'

'I look out for myself first. That's the rule around here. And don't you forget it,' Jeanne said in a threatening mutter. Then she cursed as her foot sank into a swampy bit of ground.

'OK,' Maggie said. But she could still feel a wry and wondering smile tugging up the corner of her mouth.

Neither of them had much breath for talking after that. Maggie was in a sort of daze of tiredness that wasn't completely unpleasant. Her mind wandered.

Delos . . . she had never met anyone so confusing. Her entire body reacted just at the thought of him, with frustration and anger and a longing that she didn't understand. It was a physical pang.

But then *everything* was so confusing. Things had happened so fast since last night that she'd never had time to get her mental balance. Delos and the incredible thing that had happened between them was only one part of the whole mess.

He said he'd killed Miles . . .

But that couldn't be true. Miles couldn't be dead. And Delos wasn't capable of anything like that . . .

Was he?

She found that she didn't want to think about that. It was like a huge dark cloud that she didn't want to enter.

Wherever Jeanne was taking her, it was a long, cold trek. And a painful one. After about fifteen minutes Maggie's arms began to feel as if they were being pulled out of the sockets, and a hot spot of pain flared at the back of her neck. Her sweat was clammy running down her back and her feet were numb.

But she wouldn't give up, and Jeanne didn't either. Somehow they kept going. They had travelled for maybe about forty-five minutes, with breaks, when Jeanne said, 'Here it is.'

A clearing opened in front of them, and moonlight shone on a crude little shack made of weathered wood. It leaned dangerously to one side and several boards were missing, but it had a ceiling and walls. It was shelter. To Maggie, it looked beautiful.

'Runaway slaves built it,' Jeanne said breathlessly as they took the last few steps to the cabin. 'The Night People hunted them down, of course, but they didn't find this place. All the slaves at the castle know about it.' Then she called in a slightly louder tone, 'It's me! Open the door!'

A long pause, and then there was the sound of a wooden bolt sliding and the door opened. Maggie could see the pale blob of a small face. P.J. Penobscot, with her red plaid baseball cap still on backward and her slight body tense, was blinking sleepy, frightened eyes.

Then she focused and her face changed.

'Maggie! You're OK!' She flung herself at Maggie like a small javelin.

'Ow – hey!' Maggie swayed and Cady's limp body dipped perilously.

'I'm glad to see you, too,' Maggie said. To her own surprise, she found herself blinking back tears. 'But I've got to put this girl down or I'm going to drop her.'

'Back here,' Jeanne said. The back of the cabin was piled with straw. She and Maggie eased Arcadia down onto it and then P.J. hugged Maggie again.

'You got us out. We got away,' P.J. said, her sharp little chin digging into Maggie's shoulder.

Maggie squeezed her. 'Well, we all got us out, and Jeanne helped get you away. But I'm glad everybody made it.'

'Is she . . . all right?' P.J. pulled back and looked down at Arcadia.

'I don't know.' Cady's forehead felt hot under Maggie's hand, and her breathing was regular but with a rough, wheezy undertone Maggie didn't like.

'Here's a cover,' Jeanne said, dragging up a piece of heavy, incredibly coarse material. It seemed as big as a sail and so rigid it hardly sagged or folded. 'If we all get under it, we can keep warm.'

They put Cady in the middle, Maggie and P.J. on one side of her and Jeanne on the other. The cover was more than big enough to spread over them.

And the hay smelled nice. It was prickly, but Maggie's long sleeves and jeans protected her. There was a strange comfort in P.J.'s slight body cuddled up next to her – like a kitten, Maggie thought. And it was so blessedly good to *not* be moving, to not be carrying anyone, but just to sit still and relax her sore muscles.

'There was a little food stashed here,' Jeanne said, digging under the hay and pulling out a small packet. 'Dried meat strips and oatcakes with salal berries. We'd better save some for tomorrow, though.'

Maggie tore into the dried meat hungrily. It didn't taste like beef jerky; it was tougher and gamier, but right at the moment it seemed delicious. She tried to get Cady to eat some, but it was no use. Cady just turned her head away.

She and Jeanne and P.J. finished the meal off with a drink of water, and then they lay back on the bed of hay.

Maggie felt almost happy. The gnawing in her stomach was gone, her muscles were loosening up, and she could feel a warm heaviness settling over her.

'You were going . . . to tell me about Bern . . .' Jeanne said from the other side of Cady. The words trailed off into a giant yawn.

'Yeah.' Maggie's brain was fuzzy and her eyes wouldn't stay open. 'Tomorrow . . .'

And then, lying on a pile of hay in a tiny shack in a strange kingdom, with three girls who had been strangers to her before this afternoon and who now seemed a little like sisters, she was fast asleep.

Maggie woke up with her nose cold and her feet too hot. Pale light was coming in all the cracks in the boards of the cabin. For one instant she stared at the rough weathered-silver boards and the hay on the floor and wondered where she was. Then she remembered everything.

'Cady.' She sat up and looked at the girl beside her.

Cady didn't look well. Her face had the waxy inner glow of somebody with a fever, and there were little tendrils of dark hair curled damply on her forehead. But at Maggie's voice her eyelashes fluttered, then her eyes opened.

'Maggie?'

'How are you feeling? Want some water?' She helped Cady drink from the leather bag.

'I'm all right. Thanks to you, I think. You brought me here, didn't you?' Cady's face turned as if she were looking around the room with her wide, unfocused eyes. She spoke in short sentences, as if she were conserving her strength, but her voice was more gentle than weak. 'And Jeanne, too. Thank you both.'

She must have heard us talking last night, Maggie thought. Jeanne was sitting up, straw in her red hair, her green eyes narrow and alert instantly. P.J. was stirring and making grumpy noises.

'Morning,' Maggie said. 'Is everybody OK?'

'Yeah,' P.J. said in a small, husky voice. There was a loud rumble from her stomach. 'I guess I'm still a little hungry,' she admitted.

'There're a couple oatcakes left,' Jeanne said. 'And one strip of meat. We might as well finish it off.'

They made Cady eat the meat, although she tried to refuse it. Then they divided the oatcakes solemnly into four parts and ate them, chewing doggedly on dry, flaky mouthfuls.

'We're going to need more water, too,' Maggie said, after they'd each had a drink. The leather bag was almost empty. 'But I think the first thing is to figure out what we're going to do now. What our plan is.'

'The first thing,' Jeanne said, 'is to tell us what happened to Bern.'

'Oh.' Maggie blinked, but she could see why Jeanne would want to know. 'Well, he's definitely dead.' She sketched in what had happened after she and Cady had started running through the woods. How Gavin and Bern had chased them and had finally driven them into a corner on the boulder pile. How Bern had climbed up and changed . . .

'He was a shapeshifter, you know,' she said.

Jeanne nodded, unsurprised. 'Bern means bear. They usually have names that mean what they are. But you're saying you tried to fight *that* guy off with a stick? You're dumber than I thought.' Still, her green eyes were gleaming with something like wry admiration, and P.J. was listening with awe.

'And then – there was this lightning,' Maggie said. 'And it killed Bern and Gavin ran away.' She realized, even as she said it, that she didn't want to tell everything that had happened with Delos. She didn't think Jeanne would understand. So she left out the way their minds had linked when they touched, and the way she'd seen his memories – and the fact that she'd dreamed about him before ever coming to this valley.

'Then I filled the water bag and we heard Sylvia coming and he went out to make sure she didn't find me or Cady,' she finished. She realized that they were all staring at her. Cady's face was thoughtful and serene as always, P.J. was scared but interested in the story – but Jeanne was riveted with disbelief and horror.

'You're saying *Prince Delos* saved your life? With the blue fire? You're saying he didn't turn you over to the hunting party?' She said it as if she were talking about Dracula.

'It's the truth.' Good thing I didn't tell her about the kiss, Maggie thought.

'It's impossible. Delos hates everybody. He's the most dangerous of all of them.'

'Yeah, that's what he kept telling me.' Maggie shook her head. The way Jeanne was looking at her made her uncomfortable, as if she were defending someone irredeemably evil. 'He also said at one point that he killed my brother,' she said slowly. 'But I didn't know whether to believe it . . .'

'Believe it.' Jeanne's nostrils were flared and her lip curled as if she were looking at something disgusting. 'He's the head of this whole place and everything that goes on here. There's nothing he wouldn't do. I can't believe he let you go.' She considered for a moment, then said grimly, 'Unless he's got something special in mind. Letting you go and then hunting you down later. It's the kind of thing he'd enjoy.'

Maggie had a strange feeling of void in her stomach that had nothing to do with hunger. She tried to speak calmly. 'I don't think so. I think – he just didn't care if I got away.'

'You're fooling yourself. You don't understand about

these people because you haven't been here. *None* of you have been here.' Jeanne looked at P.J., who was watching with wide blue eyes, and at Cady, who was listening silently, her head slightly bowed. 'The Night People are *monsters*. And the ones here in the Dark Kingdom are the worst of all. Some of them have been alive for hundreds of years, some of them were here when Delos's grandfather founded the place. They've been holed up in this valley all that time . . . and *all they do is hunt*. It's their only sport. It's all they care about. It's all they *do*.'

Maggie's skin was prickling. Part of her didn't want to pursue this subject any further. But she had to know.

'Last night I noticed something weird,' she said. 'I was standing outside and listening, but I couldn't hear any animal sounds anywhere. None at all.'

'They've wiped them out. All the animals in the wild are gone.'

P.J.'s thin little hand clutched at Maggie's arm nervously. 'But then what do they hunt?'

'Animals they breed and release. I've been a slave here for three years, and at first I only saw them breeding local animals – cougars and black bears and wolverines and stuff. But in the last couple of years they've started bringing in exotics. Leopards and tigers and things.'

Maggie let out her breath and patted P.J.'s hand. 'But not humans.'

'Don't make me laugh. Of course humans – but only when they can get an excuse. The laws say the vampires can't hunt slaves to death because they're too precious – pretty soon the food supply would be gone. But if slaves get loose, they at least get to hunt them down and bring them back to the castle. And if a slave has to be executed, they do a death hunt.'

'I see.' The void in Maggie's stomach had become a yawning chasm. 'But—'

'If he let you go, it was so he could come back and hunt you,' Jeanne said flatly. 'I'm telling you, he's *bad*. It was three years ago that the old king died and Delos took over, OK? And it was three years ago that they started bringing new slaves in. Not just grabbing people off the mountain if they got too close, but actually going down and kidnapping girls off the streets. That's why I'm *here*. That's why P.J.'s here.'

Beside Maggie, P.J. shivered. Maggie put an arm around her and felt the slight body shaking against hers. She gulped, her other hand clenching into a fist. 'Hey, kiddo. You've been really brave so far, so just hang on, OK? Things are going to work out.'

She could feel Jeanne's sarcastic eyes on her from beyond Cady, daring her to explain exactly *how* things were going to work out. She ignored them.

'Was it the same for you, Cady?' she asked. She was glad to get off the subject of Delos, and she was remembering the strange thing Cady had said last night. *I was coming here for a reason . . .*

'No. They got me on the mountain.' But the way Cady spoke alarmed Maggie. It was slowly and with obvious effort, the voice of someone who had to use all their strength just to concentrate.

Maggie forgot all about Delos and the slave trade and put a hand to Cady's forehead. 'Oh, God,' she said. 'You're burning up. You're totally on fire.'

Cady blinked slowly. 'Yes, it's the poison,' she said in a foggy voice. 'They injected me with something when they caught me, but I had a bad reaction to it. My system can't take it.'

Adrenalin flicked through Maggie. 'And you're getting

worse.' When Cady nodded reluctantly, she said, 'Right. Then there's no choice. We have to get to the castle because that's where the healing women are, right? If anybody can help, they can, right?'

'Wait a minute,' Jeanne said. 'We can't go down to the castle. We'd be walking right into their arms. And we can't get out of the valley. I found the pass before, but that was by accident. I couldn't find it again—'

'I could,' Maggie said. When Jeanne stared at her, she said, 'Never mind how. I just can. But going that way means climbing down a mountain on the other side and Cady can't make it. And I don't think she'll make it if we leave her alone here and go look for help.'

Jeanne's narrow green eyes were on her again, and Maggie knew what they were saying. *So we've got to give up on her. It's the only thing that makes sense.* But Maggie bulldozed on in determination. '*You* can take P.J. to the pass – I can tell you how to get there – and I'll take Cady to the castle. How about that? If you can tell me how to get to *it.*'

'It stinks,' Jeanne said flatly. 'Even if you make it to the castle with her hanging on you, you won't know how to get in. And if you *do* get in, you'll be committing suicide—'

She broke off, and everyone started. For an instant Maggie didn't understand why – all she knew was that she had a sudden feeling of alarm and alertness. Then she realized that Cady had turned suddenly toward the door. It was the quick, instinctive gesture of a cat who has heard something dangerous, and it triggered fear in the girls who were learning to live by their own instincts.

And now that Maggie sat frozen, she could hear it, too, faraway but distinct. The sound of people calling, yelling back and forth. And another sound, one that she'd only heard in movies, but that she recognized instantly. Hounds baying.

'It's them,' Jeanne whispered into the dead silence of the shack. 'I told you. They're hunting us.'

'With *dogs*?' Maggie said, shock tingling through her body.

'It's all over,' Jeanne said. 'We're dead.'

CHAPTER
12

'**N**o, we're not!' Maggie said. She kicked the heavy cover off and jumped up, grabbing Cady's arm. 'Come on!'

'Where?' Jeanne said.

'The castle,' Maggie said. 'But we've got to stick together.' She grabbed P.J.'s arm with her other hand.

'*The castle?*'

Maggie pinned Jeanne with a look. 'It's the only thing that makes sense. They'll be expecting us to try to find the pass, right? They'll find us if we stay here. The only place they *won't* expect us to go is the castle.'

'You,' Jeanne said, 'are completely crazy—'

'Come on!'

'But you just might be right.' Jeanne grabbed Cady from the other side as Maggie started for the door.

'You stay right behind us,' Maggie hissed at P.J.

The landscape in front of her looked different than it had last night. The mist formed a silver net over the trees, and although there was no sun, the clouds had a cool pearly glow.

It was beautiful. Still alien, still disquieting, but beautiful.

And in the valley below was a castle.

Maggie stopped involuntarily as she caught sight of it. It rose out of the mist like an island, black and shiny and solid. With towers at the edges. And a wall around it with a saw-toothed top, just like the castles in pictures.

It looks so real, Maggie thought stupidly.

'Don't stand there! What are you waiting for?' Jeanne snapped, dragging at Cady.

Maggie tore her eyes away and made her legs work. They headed at a good pace straight for the thickest trees below the shack.

'If it's dogs, we should try to find a stream or something, right?' she said to Jeanne. 'To cut off our scent.'

'I know a stream,' Jeanne said, speaking in short bursts as they made their way through dew-wet ferns and saxifrages. 'I lived out here a while the first time I escaped. When I was looking for the pass. But they're not just dogs.'

Maggie helped Cady scramble over the tentacle-like roots of a hemlock tree. 'What's that supposed to mean?'

'It means they're shapeshifters, like Bern and Gavin. So they don't just track us by scent. They also feel our life energy.'

Maggie thought about Bern turning his face this way and that, saying, *Do you sense anything?* And Gavin saying, *No. I can't feel them at all.*

'Great,' Maggie muttered. She glanced back and saw P.J. following doggedly, her face taut with concentration.

It was a strange sort of chase. Maggie and her group were trying to keep as quiet as possible, which was made easier by the dampness of the rainforest around them. Although there were four of them moving at once, the only sound from close up was the soft pant of quick breathing and the occasional short gasp of direction from Jeanne.

They slipped and plunged and stumbled between the huge dark trunks that stood like columns in the mist. Cedar boughs drooped from above, making it twilight where Maggie was trying to pick her way around moss-covered logs. There was a cool green smell like incense everywhere.

But however still the world was around them, there was always the sound of the hounds baying in the distance. Always behind them, always getting closer.

They crossed an icy, knee-deep stream, but Maggie didn't have much hope that it would throw the pursuit off. Cady began to lag seriously after that. She seemed dazed and only semi-conscious, following instructions as if she were sleepwalking, and only answering questions with a fuzzy murmur. Maggie was worried about P.J., too. They were all weak with hunger and shaky with stress.

But it wasn't until they were almost at the castle that the hunt caught up with them.

They had somehow finished the long, demanding trek down the mountain. Maggie was burning with pride for P.J. and Cady. And then, all at once, the baying of the hounds came, terribly close and getting louder fast.

At the same moment, Jeanne stopped and cursed, staring ahead.

'What?' Maggie was panting heavily. 'You see them?'

Jeanne pointed. 'I see the *road*. I'm an idiot. They're coming right down it, much faster than we can go through the underbrush. I didn't realize we were headed for it.'

P.J. leaned against Maggie, her slight chest heaving, her plaid baseball hat askew.

'What are we going to do?' she said. 'Are they going to catch us?'

'No!' Maggie set her jaw grimly. 'We'll have to go back fast—'

At that moment, faintly but distinctly, Cady said, 'The tree.'

Her eyes were half shut, her head was bowed, and she still looked as if she were in a trance. But for some reason Maggie felt she ought to listen to her.

'Hey, wait, look at this.' They were standing at the foot of a huge Douglas fir. Its lowest branches were much too high to climb in the regular way, but a maple had fallen against it and remained wedged, branches interlocked with the giant, forming a steep but climbable ramp. 'We can go up.'

'You're *crazy*,' Jeanne said again. 'We can't possibly hide here; they're going to go right by us. And besides, how does she even *know* there's a tree here?'

Maggie looked at Arcadia. It was a good question, but Cady wasn't answering. She seemed to be in a trance again.

'I don't know. But we can't just stand around and wait for them to come.' The truth was that her instincts were all standing up and screaming at her, and they said to trust. 'Let's try it, OK? Come on, P.J., can you climb that tree?'

Four minutes later they were all up. We're hiding in a Christmas tree, Maggie thought as she looked out between sprays of flat aromatic needles. From this height she could see the road, which was just two wheel tracks with grass growing down the middle.

Just then the hunt arrived.

The dogs came first, dogs as big as Jake the Great Dane, but leaner. Maggie could see their ribs clearly defined under their short, dusty tan coats. Right behind them were people on horses.

Sylvia was at the front of the group.

She was wearing what looked like a gown split for

riding, in a cool shade of glacier green. Trotting beside her stirrup was Gavin, the blond slave trader who'd chased Maggie and Cady yesterday and had run to tattle when Delos killed Bern with the blue fire.

Yeah, they're buddy-buddy all right, Maggie thought. But she didn't have time to dwell on it. Coming up fast behind Sylvia were two other people who each gave her a jolt, and she didn't know which shock was worse.

One was Delos. He was riding a beautiful horse, so dark brown it was almost black, but with reddish highlights. He sat straight and easy in the saddle, looking every inch the elegant young prince. The only discordant note was the heavy brace on his left arm.

Maggie stared at him, her heart numb.

He *was* after them. It was just as Jeanne had said. He was hunting them down with dogs. And he'd probably told Sylvia that he hadn't really killed two of the slaves.

Almost inaudibly, Jeanne breathed, 'You see?'

Maggie couldn't look at her.

Then she saw another rider below and froze in bewilderment.

It was Delos's father.

He looked exactly the way he had in Delos's memories. A tall man, with blood-red hair and a cold, handsome face. Maggie couldn't see his eyes at this distance, but she knew that they were a fierce and brilliant yellow.

The old king. But he was *dead*. Maggie was too agitated to be cautious.

'Who is that? The red-haired man,' she murmured urgently to Jeanne.

Jeanne answered almost without a sound. 'Hunter Redfern.'

'It's not the king?'

Jeanne shook her head minutely. Then, when Maggie

kept staring at her, she breathed. 'He's Delos's great-grandfather. He just came. I'll tell you about it later.'

Maggie nodded. And the next instant it was swept out of her head as P.J.'s hand clutched at her and she felt a wave of adrenaline.

The party below was stopping.

The hounds turned and circled first, forming a hesitant clump not twenty feet down the road. When the people pulled up their horses they were almost directly below Maggie's tree.

'What is it?' the tall man said, the one Jeanne had called Hunter Redfern.

And then one of the hounds changed. Maggie caught the movement out of the corner of her eye and looked quickly, or she would have missed it.

The lean, wiry animal reared up, like a dog trying to look over a fence. But when it reached its full height it didn't wobble or go back down. It steadied, and its entire dusty-tan body rippled.

Then, as if it were the most natural thing in the world, its shoulders went back and its arms thickened. Its spine straightened and it seemed to gain more height. Its tail pulled in and disappeared. And its hound face melted and re-formed, the ears and muzzle shrinking, the chin growing. In maybe twenty seconds the dog had become a boy, a boy who still wore patches of tan fur here and there, but definitely human-looking.

And he's got pants on, Maggie thought distractedly, even though her heart was pounding in her throat. I wonder how they manage that?

The boy turned his head toward the riders. Maggie could see the ribs in his bare chest move with his breathing.

'Something's wrong here,' he said. 'I can't follow their life force anymore.'

Hunter Redfern looked around. 'Are they blocking it?'

Gavin spoke up from beside Sylvia's stirrup. 'Bern said they were blocking it yesterday.'

'Isn't that impossible?' Delos's cool voice came from the very back of the group, where he was expertly holding his nervous, dancing horse in check. 'If they're only humans?'

Hunter didn't move or blink an eye, but Maggie saw a glance pass between Sylvia and Gavin. She herself twisted her head slightly, just enough to look at the other girls in the tree.

She wanted to see if Jeanne understood what they were talking about, but it was Cady who caught her eye. Cady's eyes were shut, her head leaning against the dark furrowed trunk of the tree. Her lips were moving, although Maggie couldn't hear any sound.

And Jeanne was watching her with narrowed eyes and an expression of grim suspicion.

'Human vermin are full of surprises,' Hunter Redfern was saying easily down below. 'It doesn't matter. We'll get them eventually.'

'They may be heading for the castle,' Sylvia said. 'We'd better put extra guards at the gate.'

Maggie noticed how Delos stiffened at that.

And so did Hunter Redfern, even though he was looking the other way. He said calmly, 'What do you think of that, Prince Delos?'

Delos didn't move for an instant. Then he said, 'Yes. Do it.' But he said it to a lean, bearded man beside him, who bowed his head in a quick jerk.

And he did something that made Maggie's heart go cold.

He looked up at her.

The other people in his party, including the hounds,

were looking up and down the road, or sideways into the forest at their own level. Delos was the only one who'd been sitting quietly, looking straight ahead. But now he tilted his chin and turned an expressionless face toward the cluster of branches where Maggie was sitting.

And met her gaze directly.

She saw the blaze of his yellow eyes, even at this distance. He was looking coolly and steadily – at her.

Maggie jerked back and barely caught herself from falling. Her heart was pounding so hard it was choking her. But she didn't seem to be able to do anything but cling to her branch.

We're dead, she thought dizzily, pinned into immobility by those golden eyes. He's stronger than the rest of them; he's a Wild Power. And he could sense us all along.

Now all they have to do is surround the tree. We can try to fight, but we don't have weapons. They'll beat us in no time . . .

Go away. The voice gave her a new shock. It was clear and unemotional – and it was in Maggie's head.

Delos? she thought, staring into that burning gaze. *You can—?*

His expression didn't change. *I told you before, but you wouldn't listen. What do I have to do to make you understand?*

Maggie's heart picked up more speed. *Delos, listen to me. I don't want—*

I'm warning you, he said, and his mental voice was like ice. *Don't come to the castle. If you do, I won't protect you again.*

Maggie felt cold to her bones, too numb to even form words to answer him.

I mean it, he said. *Stay away from the castle if you want to stay alive.*

Then he turned away and Maggie felt the contact between them broken off cleanly. Where his presence had been she could feel emptiness.

'Let's go,' he said in a short, hard voice, and spurred his horse forward.

And then they were all moving, heading on down the path, leaving Maggie trying to keep her trembling from shaking the tree.

When the last horse was out of sight, P.J. let out her breath, sagging. 'I thought they had us,' she whispered.

Maggie swallowed. 'Me, too. But Cady was right. They went on by.' She turned. 'Just what was that stuff about us blocking them?'

Cady was still leaning her head against the tree trunk, and her eyes were still closed. But she seemed almost asleep now – and her lips weren't moving.

Jeanne's eyes followed Maggie's. They were still narrowed, and her mouth was still tight with something like grim humour. But she didn't say anything. After a moment she quirked an eyebrow and shrugged minutely. 'Who knows?'

You know, Maggie thought. At least more than you're telling me. But there was something else bothering her, so she said, 'OK, then, what about that guy who looks like Delos's father? Hunter Redfern.'

'He's a bigwig in the Night World,' Jeanne said. 'Maybe the biggest. It was his son who founded this place back in the fourteen hundreds.'

Maggie blinked. 'In the *whats*?'

Jeanne's eyes glowed briefly, sardonically. 'In the fourteen hundreds,' she said with exaggerated patience. 'They're vampires, all right? Actually, they're lamia, which is the kind of vampire that can have kids, but that's not the point. The point is they're immortal, except for accidents.'

'That guy has been alive more than five hundred

years,' Maggie said slowly, looking down the path where Hunter Redfern had disappeared.

'Yeah. And, yeah, everybody says how much he looks like the old king. Or the other way around, you know.'

Delos sure thinks he looks like him, Maggie thought. She'd seen the way Hunter handled Delos, guiding him as expertly as Delos had guided his horse. Delos was *used* to obeying somebody who looked and sounded just like Hunter Redfern.

Then she frowned. 'But, how come *he* isn't king?'

'Oh . . .' Jeanne sighed and ducked under a spray of fir needles that was tangled in her hair. She looked impatient and uneasy. 'He's from the Outside, OK? He's only been here a couple of weeks. All the slaves say that he didn't even know about this place before that.'

'He didn't know . . .'

'Look. This is the way I heard it from the old slaves, OK? Hunter Redfern had a son named Chervil when he was really young. And when Chervil was, like, our age, they had some big argument and got estranged. And then Chervil ran off with his friends, and that left Hunter Redfern without an heir. And Hunter Redfern never knew that where the kid went was *here*.' Jeanne gestured around the valley. 'To start his own little kingdom of Night People. But then somehow Hunter found out, so he came to visit. And that's why he's here.'

She finished and stretched her shoulders, looking down the tree-ramp speculatively. P.J. sat quietly, glancing from Jeanne to Maggie. Cady just breathed.

Maggie chewed her lip, not satisfied yet. 'He's here just to visit? That's all?'

'I'm a slave. You think I asked him personally?'

'I think you *know*.'

Jeanne stared at her a moment, then glanced at P.J. Her

look was almost sullen, but Maggie understood.

'Jeanne, she's been through hell already. Whatever it is, she can take it. Right, kiddo?'

P.J. twisted her plaid cap in a complete circle and settled it more firmly on her head. 'Right,' she said flatly.

'So tell us,' Maggie said. 'What's Hunter Redfern doing here?'

CHAPTER
13

'I think,' Jeanne said, 'that he's here to get Delos to close the Dark Kingdom out. Shut up the castle and come join him Outside. And, incidentally, of course, kill all the slaves.'

Maggie stared. 'Kill them all?'

'Well, it makes sense. Nobody would need them anymore.'

'And that's why you were escaping now,' Maggie said slowly.

Jeanne gave her a quick, startled glance. 'You're really not as stupid as you seem at first sight, you know?'

'Gee, thanks.' Maggie shifted on her branch. A minute ago she'd been thinking how good it would feel to get away from the twigs poking her. Now she suddenly wanted to stay here forever, hiding. She had a *very* bad feeling.

'So why,' she said, forming her thoughts slowly, 'does Hunter Redfern want to do this right now?'

'What do *you* think? Really, Maggie, what do you know about all this?'

Four Wild Powers, Maggie thought, hearing Delos's old teacher's voice in her mind. *Who will be needed at the millennium, to save the world – or to destroy it.*

'I know that something's happening at the millennium, and that Delos is a Wild Power, and that the Wild Powers are supposed to do something—'

'Save the world,' Jeanne said in a clipped voice. 'Except that that's not what the Night People want. They figure there's going to be some huge catastrophe that'll wipe out most of the humans – and then *they* can take over. And that's why Hunter Redfern's here. He wants the Wild Powers on his side instead of on the humans'. He wants them to help destroy the human world instead of saving it. And it looks like he's just about convinced Delos.'

Maggie let out a shaky breath and leaned her head against a branch. It was just like what Delos had told her – except that Jeanne was an uninterested party. She still wanted not to believe it, but she had a terrible sinking feeling. In fact, she had a strange feeling of *weight*, as if something awful was trying to settle on her shoulders.

'The millennium really means the end of the world,' she said.

'Yeah. Our world, anyway.'

Maggie glanced at P.J., who was swinging her thin legs over the edge of a branch. 'You still OK?'

P.J. nodded. She looked frightened, but not unbearably so. She kept her eyes on Maggie's face trustingly.

'And do *you* still want to go to the castle?' Jeanne said, watching Maggie just as closely. 'Hunter Redfern is a very bad guy to mess with. And I hate to tell you, but your friend Prince Delos is out for our blood just like the rest of them.'

'No, I don't still *want* to go,' Maggie said briefly. Her head went down and she gave Jeanne a brooding look under her eyelashes. 'But I have to, anyway. I've got even more reasons now.'

'Such as?'

Maggie held up a finger. 'One, I've got to get help for Cady.' She glanced at the motionless figure clinging trance-like to the fir's trunk, then held up another finger. 'Two, I have to find out what happened to my brother.' Another finger. 'And, three, I have to get those slaves free before Hunter Redfern has them all killed.'

'You have to *what*?' Jeanne said in a muffled shriek. She almost fell out of the tree.

'I kind of thought you'd react that way. Don't worry about it. You don't have to get involved.'

'I was wrong before. You *are* as dumb as you look. And you are totally freaking crazy.'

Yeah, I know, Maggie thought grimly. It's probably just as well I didn't mention the fourth reason.

Which was that she had to keep Delos from aiding and abetting the end of the world. That was the responsibility that had settled on her, and she had no idea why it was hers except that she'd been inside his mind. She *knew* him. She couldn't just walk away.

If anybody could talk to him about it and convince him not to do it, she could. She had absolutely no doubt about that. So it was her job to try.

And if he was really as evil as Jeanne seemed to think – if it was true that he'd killed Miles . . . well, then she had a different job.

She had to do whatever was necessary to stop him. Distant and impossible as it seemed, she would have to kill him if that was what it took.

'Come on,' she said to the other girls. 'Cady, do you think you can climb down now? And, Jeanne, do you know a way into the castle?'

The moat stank.

Maggie had been glad to find Jeanne knew a way into

the castle. That was before she discovered that it involved swimming through stagnant water and climbing up what Jeanne called a garderobe but what was all too obviously the shaft of an old latrine.

'Just kill me, somebody,' Maggie whispered halfway up. She was soaking wet and daubed with unthinkable slime. She couldn't remember ever being quite this dirty.

The next moment she forgot about it in her worry about Cady. Cady had managed the swim, still doing everything she was told as if she were in a trance. But now she was getting shaky. Maggie wondered seriously whether this sort of activity was helpful to somebody who'd been poisoned.

When they were finally at the top of the shaft, Maggie looked around and saw a small room that seemed to be built directly into the castle wall. Everything was made of dark stone, with a cold and echoing feel to it.

'Don't make any noise,' Jeanne whispered. She bent close to Maggie, who was helping support Cady. 'We need to go down a passage and through the kitchen, OK? It's all right if slaves see us, but we have to watch out for *them*.'

'We've got to get Cady to a healing woman—'

'I know! That's where I'm trying to take you.' Jeanne clamped a hand on P.J.'s shoulder and steered her into a corridor.

More stone. More echoes. Maggie tried to walk without her shoes squishing or smacking. She was dimly impressed with the castle itself – it was grand and cold and so huge that she felt like an insect making her way through the passage.

After what seemed like an endless walk, they emerged in a small entryway partitioned off by wooden screens. Maggie could hear activity behind the screens and as Jeanne led them stealthily forward, she caught a glimpse of people moving on the other side. They were spreading white tablecloths over long wooden tables in a room that seemed bigger than Maggie's entire house.

Another doorway. Another passage. And finally the kitchen, which was full of bustling people. They were stirring huge iron cauldrons and turning meat on spits. The smell of a dozen different kinds of food hit Maggie and made her feel faint. She was so hungry that her knees wobbled and she had to swallow hard.

But even more than hungry, she was scared. They were in plain sight of dozens of people.

'Slaves,' Jeanne said shortly. 'They won't tell on us. Grab a sack to wrap around you and come on. And, P.J., take off that ridiculous hat.'

Slaves, Maggie thought, staring. They were all dressed identically, in loose-fitting pants and tops that were like short tunics. Jeanne was wearing the same thing – it had looked enough like clothes from Outside that Maggie hadn't really focused on it before. What struck her now was that everybody looked so . . . un-ironed. There were no sharp creases. And no real colour. All the clothes were an indeterminate shade of beige-brown, and all the faces seemed just as dull and faded. They were like drones.

What would it be like to live that way? she wondered as she threw a rough sack around her shoulders to hide the dark blue of her jacket. Without any choice in what you do, and any hope for the future?

It would be terrible, she decided. And it might just drive you crazy.

I wonder if any of them ever . . . snap?

But she couldn't look around anymore. Jeanne was hustling through a doorway into the open air. There was a kind of garden here just outside the kitchen, with scraggly fruit trees and what looked like herbs. Then there was a courtyard and finally a row of huts nestled against the high black wall that surrounded the castle.

'This is the really dangerous part,' Jeanne whispered harshly. 'It's the back, but if one of *them* looks out and sees us, we're in trouble. Keep your head down – and walk like this. Like a slave.' She led them at a shuffling run toward a hut.

This place *is* like a city, Maggie thought. A city inside a wall, with the castle in the middle.

They reached the shack. Jeanne pulled the door open and bustled them inside. Then she shut the door again and sagged.

'I think we actually made it.' She sounded surprised.

Maggie was looking around. The tiny room was dim, but she could see crude furniture and piles of what looked like laundry. 'This is it? We're safe?'

'Nowhere is safe,' Jeanne said sharply. 'But we can get some slave clothes for you here, and we can rest. And I'll go get the healing woman,' she added as Maggie opened her mouth.

While she was gone, Maggie turned to Cady and P.J. They were both shivering. She made Cady lie down and had P.J. help her go through one of the piles of laundry.

'Get your wet things off,' Maggie said. She pulled off her own hightops and shrugged out of her sodden jacket. Then she knelt to get Cady's shoes off. The blind girl was lying motionless on a thin pallet, and didn't respond to Maggie's touch. Maggie was worried about her.

Behind her, the door opened and Jeanne came in with two people. One was a gaunt and handsome woman, with dark hair pulled untidily back and an apron over her tunic and pants. The other was a young girl who looked frightened.

'This is Laundress.' The way Jeanne said it, it was

clearly a proper name. 'She's a healer, and the girl's her helper.'

Relief washed through Maggie. 'This is Cady,' she said. And then, since nobody moved and Cady couldn't speak for herself, she went on, 'She's from Outside, and she was poisoned by the slave traders. I'm not sure how long ago that was – at least a couple of days. She's been running a high fever and most of the time she's just sort of sleepwalking—'

'What is this?' The gaunt woman took a step toward Cady, but her expression was anything but welcoming. Then she turned on Jeanne angrily. 'How could you bring this – thing – in here?'

Maggie froze where she was by Cady's feet. 'What are you talking about? She's sick—'

'She's one of them!' The woman's eyes were burning darkly at Jeanne. 'And don't tell me you didn't notice. It's perfectly plain!'

'*What's* perfectly plain?' Maggie's fists were clenched. 'Jeanne, what's she talking about?'

The woman's burning eyes turned on her. 'This girl is a witch.'

Maggie went still.

Part of her was amazed and disbelieving. A witch? Like Sylvia? A Night Person?

Cady wasn't at all like that. She wasn't evil. She was *normal*, a nice, ordinary, gentle girl. She *couldn't* be anything supernatural . . .

But another part of Maggie wasn't even startled. It was saying that at some deep level she had known all along.

Her mind was bringing up pictures. Cady in the hollow tree, when she and Maggie were hiding from Bern and Gavin. Cady's lips moving – and Gavin saying *I can't feel them at all.*

The hound today had said the same thing. *I can't follow their life force anymore.*

She was blocking them from sensing us, Maggie thought. And she was the one who told us to climb the tree. She's blind, but she can see things.

It's true.

She turned slowly to look at the girl lying on the pallet.

Cady was almost perfectly still, her breathing barely lifting her chest. Her hair was coiled around her head like damp snakes, her face was smudged and dirty, her lashes spiky on her cheeks. But somehow she hadn't lost any of her serene beauty. It remained untouched, whatever happened to her body.

I don't care, Maggie thought. She may be a witch, but she's not like Sylvia. I *know* she's not evil.

She turned back to Laundress, and spoke carefully and deliberately.

'Look, I understand that you don't like witches. But this girl has been with us for two days, and all she's done is help us. And, I mean, look at her!' Maggie lost her reasonable tone. 'They were bringing her here as a slave! She wasn't getting any special treatment. She's not on their side!'

'Too bad for her,' Laundress said. Her voice was flat and . . . plain. The voice of a woman who saw things in black and white and didn't like arguments.

And who knew how to back up her beliefs. One big gaunt hand went beneath her apron, into a hidden pocket. When it came out again, it was gripping a kitchen knife.

'Wait a minute,' Jeanne said.

Laundress didn't look at her. 'Friends of witches are no friends of ours,' she said in her plain, heavy way. 'And that includes you.'

With one motion, Jeanne wheeled away from her and into a fighting stance. 'You're right. I knew what she was. I hated her, too, at first. But it's like Maggie told you. She's not going to hurt us!'

'I'm not going to miss a chance to kill one of *them*,' Laundress said. 'And if you try to stop me, you'll be sorry.'

Maggie's heart was pounding. She looked back and forth from the tall woman, who was holding the knife menacingly, to Jeanne, who was crouched with her teeth bared and her eyes narrowed. They were ready to fight.

Maggie found herself in the middle of the room, in a triangle formed by Cady and Jeanne and the knife. She was too angry to be frightened.

'You *put that down*,' she said to Laundress fiercely, forgetting that she was speaking to an adult. 'You're not going to do anything with that. How can you even try?'

Vaguely, she noticed movement behind the woman. The frightened young girl who hadn't said anything so far was stepping forward. She was staring at Maggie, pointing at Maggie. Her eyes and mouth were wide open, but her voice was an indrawn breath.

'The Deliverer!'

Maggie hardly heard the gasped words. She was rushing on. 'If you people don't stick together, what kind of chance do you have? How can you ever get free—'

'*It's her!*' This time the girl shrieked it, and nobody could help but hear. She clutched at Laundress's arm wildly. 'You heard what she said, Laundress. She's come to free us.'

'What are you talking a—?' Jeanne broke off, looking at Maggie with her eyebrows drawn together. Suddenly the eyebrows flew up and she straightened slightly from her crouch. 'Hmm.'

Maggie stared back. Then she followed all their eyes

and looked down at herself in bewilderment.

For the first time since she'd arrived in the Dark Kingdom she wasn't wearing her jacket and her shoes. She was wearing exactly what she'd been wearing when her mother's screams woke her three days before – her flowered pyjama top, wrinkled jeans, and mismatched socks.

' "She will come clothed in flowers, shod in blue and scarlet," ' the girl was saying. She was still pointing at Maggie, but now it was with something like reverence. ' "And she will speak of freedom." You heard her, Laundress! It's *her*. She's the one!'

The knife trembled slightly. Maggie stared at the red knuckles of the hand holding it, then looked up at Laundress's face.

The blotchy features were grim and sceptical – but there was an odd gleam of half-stifled hope in the eyes. 'Is she the one?' she said harshly to Jeanne. 'Is this idiot Soaker right? Did she say she's come to deliver us?'

Jeanne opened her mouth, then shut it again. She looked helplessly at Maggie.

And, unexpectedly, P.J. spoke up. 'She told us she had to get the slaves free before Hunter Redfern had them all killed,' she said in her light, strong child's voice. She was standing straight, her slender body drawn to its fullest height. Her blonde hair shone pale above her small earnest face. Her words had the unmistakable ring of truth.

Something flashed in Jeanne's eyes. Her lip quirked, then she bit it. 'She sure did. And I told her she was crazy.'

'And in the beginning, when Jeanne showed her what they do to escaped slaves here, Maggie said it had to stop.' P.J.'s voice was still clear and confident. 'She said she couldn't let them *do* things like that to people.'

'She said *we* couldn't let them do things like that,' Jeanne corrected. 'And she was crazy again. There's no way to stop them.'

Laundress stared at her for a moment, then turned her burning gaze on Maggie. Her eyes were so fierce that Maggie was afraid she was going to attack. Then, all at once, she thrust the knife back in her pocket.

'Blasphemer!' she said harshly to Jeanne. 'Don't talk about the Deliverer that way! Do you want to take away our only hope?'

Jeanne raised an eyebrow. '*You* were the one about to take it away,' she pointed out.

Laundress glared at her. Then she turned to Maggie and a change came over her gaunt features. It wasn't much; they still remained as severe and grim as ever, but there was something like a bleak smile twisting her mouth.

'If you are the Deliverer,' she said, 'you've got your work cut out for you.'

'Just everybody hang on one second,' Maggie said.

Her head was whirling. She understood what was going on – sort of. These people believed she was some legendary figure come to save them. Because of a prophecy – they seemed to have a lot of prophecies around here.

But she couldn't really be their Deliverer. She *knew* that. She was just an ordinary girl. And hadn't anybody else ever worn a flowered top in this place?

Well, maybe not. Not a slave anyway. Maggie looked at Laundress's clothes again with new eyes. If they all wore this sort of thing, hand sewn and plain as a burlap sack, maybe a machine-made top with bright colours and a little wilted lace *would* look like something from a legend.

And I bet nobody wears red and blue socks, she thought and almost smiled. Especially at once.

She remembered how Sylvia had looked at them. Normally she would have been terribly embarrassed by that, perfect Sylvia looking at her imperfections. But the socks had been what started her on this whole journey by convincing her that Sylvia was lying. And just now they'd saved her life. If Laundress had attacked Jeanne or Cady, Maggie would have had to fight her.

But I'm still not the Deliverer, she thought. I have to explain that to them . . .

'And since she's the Deliverer, you're going to help us, right?' Jeanne was saying. 'You're going to heal Cady and feed us and hide us and everything? And help Maggie find out what happened to her brother?'

Maggie blinked, then grimaced. She could see Jeanne looking at her meaningfully. She shut her mouth.

'I'll help you any way I can,' Laundress said. 'But you'd better do your part. Do you have a plan, Deliverer?'

Maggie rubbed her forehead. Things were happening very fast – but even if she wasn't the Deliverer, she *had* come to help the slaves get free. Maybe it didn't matter what they called her.

She looked at Cady again, then at Jeanne, and at P.J., who was staring at her with shining confidence in her young eyes. Then she looked at the girl named Soaker, who was wearing the same expression.

Finally she looked into the gaunt, hard-bitten face of Laundress. There was no easy confidence here, but there was that half-stifled look of hope deep in the burning gaze.

'I don't have a plan yet,' she said. 'But I'll come up with one. And I don't know if I can really help you people. But I'll try.'

CHAPTER
14

Maggie woke up slowly and almost luxuriously. She wasn't freezing. She wasn't aching or weak with hunger. And she had an unreasonable feeling of safety.

Then she sat up and the safe feeling disappeared.

She was in Laundress's hut of earth bricks. Jeanne and P.J. were there, but Cady had been taken to another hut to be treated. Laundress had stayed all night with her, and Maggie had no idea if she was getting better or not. The frightened girl called Soaker brought them breakfast, but could only say that Cady was still asleep.

Breakfast was the same as dinner last night had been: a sort of thick oatmeal sweetened with huckleberries. Maggie ate it gratefully. It was good – at least to somebody as hungry as she was.

'We're lucky to have it,' Jeanne said, stretching. She and P.J. were sitting opposite Maggie on the bare earth of the floor, eating with their fingers. They all were wearing the coarse, scratchy tunics and loose leggings of slaves, and Maggie kept going into spasms of twitching when the material made her itch somewhere she couldn't reach. Maggie's clothes, including her precious socks, were hidden at the back of the hut.

'They don't grow much grain or vegetable stuff,' Jeanne was saying. 'And of course slaves don't get to eat any meat. Only the vampires and the shapeshifters get to eat blood or flesh.'

P.J. shivered, hunching up her thin shoulders. 'When you say it like that, it makes me not *want* to eat it.'

Jeanne gave a sharp-toothed grin. 'They're afraid it would make the slaves too strong. Everything here's designed for that. Maybe you noticed, there's not much in the slave quarters made of wood.'

Maggie blinked. She *had* noticed that vaguely, at the back of her mind. The huts were made of bricks, with hard-packed dirt floors. And there were no wooden tools like rakes or brooms lying around.

'But what do they burn?' she asked, looking at the small stone hearth built right on the floor of the hut. There was a hole in the roof above to let smoke out.

'Charcoaled wood, cut in little pieces. They make it out in the forest in charcoal pits, and it's strictly regulated. Everybody only gets so much. If they find a slave with extra wood, they execute 'em.'

'Because wood kills vampires,' Maggie said.

Jeanne nodded. 'And silver kills shapeshifters. Slaves are forbidden to have silver, too – not that any of them are likely to get hold of any.'

P.J. was looking out the small window of the hut. There was no glass in it, and last night it had been stuffed with sacking against the cold air. 'If slaves can't eat meat, what are those?' she asked.

Maggie leaned to look. Outside two big calves were tethered to iron pickets. There were also a dozen trussed-up chickens and a pig in a pen made of rope.

'Those are for Night People,' Jeanne said. 'The shapeshifters and witches eat regular food, and so do the vampires, when they want to. It looks like they're going to have a feast, they don't bring the animals here until they're ready to slaughter.'

P.J.'s face was troubled. 'I feel sorry for them,' she said softly.

'Yeah, well, there are worse things than being hit over the head,' Jeanne said. 'See those cages just beyond the pig? That's where the exotics are – the tigers and things they bring in to hunt. *That's* a bad way to die.'

Maggie felt ice down her spine. 'Let's hope we never have to find out—' she was beginning, when a flash of movement outside caught her eye.

'Get down!' she said sharply, and ducked out of the line of sight of the window. Then, very carefully, with her body tense, she edged up to the open square again and peered out.

'What is it?' Jeanne hissed. P.J. just cowered on the floor, breathing quickly.

Maggie whispered, 'Sylvia.'

Two figures had appeared, walking through the back courtyard and talking as they went. Sylvia and Gavin. Sylvia's gown today was misty leaf green, and her hair rippled in shimmering waves over her shoulders. She looked beautiful and graceful and fragile.

'Are they coming here?' Jeanne breathed.

Maggie shook a hand – held low to the ground – toward her to be quiet. She was afraid of the same thing. If the Night People began a systematic search of the huts, they were lost.

But instead, Sylvia turned toward the cages that held the exotics. She seemed to be looking at the animals, occasionally turning to make a remark to Gavin.

'Now, what's she up to?' a voice murmured by Maggie's ear. Jeanne had crept up beside her.

'I don't know. Nothing good,' Maggie whispered.

'They must be planning a hunt,' Jeanne said grimly. 'That's bad. I heard they were going to do a big one when Delos came to an agreement with Hunter Redfern.'

Maggie drew in her breath. Had things gone that far already? It meant she didn't have much time left.

Outside, she could see Sylvia shaking her head, then moving on to the pens and tethers holding the domestic animals.

'Get back,' Maggie whispered, ducking down. But Sylvia never looked at the hut. She made some remark while looking at the calves and smiling. Then she and Gavin turned and strolled back through the kitchen garden.

Maggie watched until they were out of sight, chewing her lip. Then she looked at Jeanne.

'I think we'd better go see Laundress.'

The hut Jeanne led her to was a little bigger than the others and had what Maggie knew by now was an amazing luxury: two rooms. Cady was in the tiny room – hardly bigger than an alcove – in back.

And she was looking better. Maggie saw it immediately. The clammy, feverish look was gone and so were the blue-black shadows under her eyes. Her breathing was deep and regular and her lashes lay heavy and still on her smooth cheeks.

'Is she going to be all right?' Maggie asked Laundress eagerly.

The gaunt woman was sponging Cady's cheeks with a cloth. Maggie was surprised at how tender the big red-knuckled hands could be.

'She'll live as long as any of us,' Laundress said grimly, and Jeanne gave a wry snort. Even Maggie felt her lip twitch. She was beginning to like this woman. In fact, if

Jeanne and Laundress were examples, the slaves here had a courage and a black humour that she couldn't help but admire.

'I had a daughter,' Laundress said. 'She was about this one's age, but she had that one's colouring.' She nodded slightly at P.J., who clutched at the baseball cap stashed inside her tunic and smiled.

Maggie hesitated, then asked. 'What happened to her?'

'One of the nobles saw her and liked her,' Laundress said. She wrung out the cloth and put it down, then stood briskly. When she saw Maggie still looking at her, she added, as if she were talking about the weather, 'He was a shapeshifter, a wolf named Autolykos. He bit her and passed his curse on to her, but then he got tired of her. One night he made her run and hunted her down.'

Maggie's knees felt weak. She couldn't think of anything to say that wouldn't be colossally stupid, so she didn't say anything.

P.J. did. 'I'm sorry,' she said in a husky little voice, and she put her small hand in Laundress's rough one.

Laundress touched the top of the shaggy blonde head as if she were touching an angel.

'Um, can I talk to her? Cady?' Maggie asked, blinking fast and clearing her throat.

Laundress looked at her sharply. 'No. You won't be able to wake her up. I had to give her strong medicine to fight off what *they'd* given her. You know how the potion works.'

Maggie shook her head. 'What potion?'

'They gave her calamus and bloodwort – and other things. It was a truth potion.'

'You mean they wanted to get information out of her?'

Laundress only dignified that with a bare nod for an answer.

'But I wonder why?' Maggie looked at Jeanne, who shrugged.

'She's a witch from Outside. Maybe they thought she knew something.'

Maggie considered another minute, then gave it up. She would just have to ask Cady when Cady was awake.

'There was another reason I wanted to see you,' she said to Laundress, who was now briskly cleaning up the room. 'Actually, a couple of reasons. I wanted to ask you about this.'

She reached inside her slave tunic and pulled out the photo of Miles that she'd taken from her jacket last night.

'Have you seen him?'

Laundress took the picture between a callused thumb and forefinger and looked at it warily. 'Wonderfully small painting,' she said.

'It's called a photograph. It's not exactly painted.' Maggie was watching the woman's face, afraid to hope.

There was no sign of recognition. 'He's related to you,' Laundress said, holding the photo to Maggie.

'He's my brother. From Outside, you know? And his girlfriend was Sylvia Weald. He disappeared last week.'

'Witch Sylvia!' a cracked, shaky voice said.

Maggie looked up fast. There was an old woman in the doorway, a tiny, wizened creature with thin white hair and a face exactly like one of the dried-apple dolls Maggie had seen at fairs.

'This is Old Mender,' Jeanne said. 'She sews up torn clothes, you know? And she's the other healing woman.'

'So this is the Deliverer,' the cracked voice said, and the woman shuffled closer, peering at Maggie. 'She looks like an ordinary girl, until you see the eyes.'

Maggie blinked. 'Oh, thanks,' she said. Secretly she thought that Old Mender herself looked more like a witch than anyone she'd ever seen in her life. But there was bright intelligence in the old woman's birdlike gaze and her little smile was sweet.

'Witch Sylvia came to the castle a week ago,' she told Maggie, her head on one side. 'She didn't have any boy with her, but she was talking about a boy. My grand-nephew Currier heard her. She was telling Prince Delos how she'd chosen a human for a plaything, and she'd tried to bring him to the castle for Samhain. But the boy did something – turned on her somehow. And so she had to punish him, and that had delayed her.'

Maggie's heart was beating in her ears. 'Punish him,' she began, and then she said, 'What's Samhain?'

'Halloween,' Jeanne said. 'The witches here normally have a big celebration at midnight.'

Halloween. All right. Maggie's mind was whirring desperately, ticking over this new information. So now she knew for certain that Sylvia *had* gone hiking on Halloween with Miles, just as she'd told the sheriffs and rangers. Or maybe they'd been driving, if Jeanne's story about a mysterious pass that only Night People could see was true. But anyway they'd been coming here, to the Dark Kingdom. And something had delayed them. Miles had done something that made Sylvia terribly angry and changed her mind about taking him to the castle.

And made her ... punish him. In some way that Maggie wasn't supposed to be able to guess.

Maybe she just killed him after all, Maggie thought, with an awful sinking in her stomach. She could have shoved him off a cliff easily. Whatever she did, he never made it here, right?

'So there isn't any human boy in the dungeon or anything?' she asked, looking at Laundress and then

Mender. But she knew the answer before they shook their heads.

Nobody recognizes him. He can't be here.

Maggie felt her shoulders slump. But although she was discouraged and heartsick, she wasn't defeated. What she felt instead was a hard little burning like a coal in her chest. She wanted more than ever to grab Sylvia and shake the truth out of her.

At the very least, if nothing else, I'm going to find out how he died. Because that's important.

Funny how it didn't seem impossible anymore that Miles *was* dead. Maggie had learned a lot since coming to this valley. People got hurt and died and had other awful things happen to them, and that was that. The ones left alive had to find some way of going on.

But not of forgetting.

'You said you had two reasons for coming to see me,' Laundress prompted. She was standing with her big hands on her hips, her gaunt body erect and looking just slightly impatient. 'Have you come up with a plan, Deliverer?'

'Well, sort of. Not exactly a *plan* so much as – well, I guess it's a plan.' Maggie floundered, trying to explain herself. The truth was that she'd come up with the most basic plan of all.

To go see Delos.

That was it. The simplest, most direct solution. She was going to get him alone and talk to him. Use the weird connection between them if she had to. Pound some sort of understanding into his thick head.

And put her life on the line to back up her words.

Jeanne thought the slaves were going to be killed when Hunter Redfern and Delos made their deal. Maggie was a slave now. If the other slaves were killed, Maggie would be with them.

And you're betting that he'll *care*, a nasty little voice in her brain whispered. But you don't really know that. He keeps threatening to kill you himself. He specifically warned you not to come to the castle.

Well, anyway, we're going to find out, Maggie told the little voice. And if I can't convince him, I'll have to do something more violent.

'I need to get into the castle,' she said to Laundress. 'Not just into the kitchen, you know, but the other rooms – wherever I might be able to find Prince Delos alone.'

'Alone? You won't find him alone anywhere but his bedchamber.'

'Well, then, I have to go there.'

Laundress was watching her narrowly. 'Is it assassination you've got in mind? Because I know someone who has a piece of wood.'

'It . . .' Maggie stopped and took a breath. 'I really hope it isn't going to come to that. But maybe I'd better take the wood, just in case.'

And you'd better hope for a miracle, the nasty voice in her mind said. Because how else are you going to overpower him?

Jeanne was rubbing her forehead. When she spoke, Maggie knew she'd been thinking along the same lines. 'Look, dummy, are you sure this is a good idea? I mean, he's—'

'A Night Person,' Maggie supplied.

'And you're—'

'Just an ordinary human.'

'She's the Deliverer,' P.J. said stoutly, and Maggie paused to smile at her.

Then she turned back to Jeanne. 'I don't know if it's a good idea, but it's my only idea. And I know it's dangerous, but I have to do it.' She looked awkwardly at

Laundress and Old Mender. 'The truth is that it's not just about you people here. If what Jeanne told you about Hunter Redfern is right, then the whole human world is in trouble.'

'Oh, the prophecies,' Old Mender said, and cackled.

'You know them, too?'

'We slaves hear everything.' Old Mender smiled and nodded. 'Especially when it concerns our own prince. I remember when he was little, I was the Queen's seamstress then, before she died. His mother knew the prophecies, and she said,

"In blue fire, the final darkness is banished.
In blood, the final price is paid." '

Blood, Maggie thought. She knew that blood had to run before Delos could use the blue fire, but this sounded as if it were talking about something darker. Whose blood? she wondered.

'And the final darkness is the end of the world, right?' she said. 'So you can see how important it is for me to change Delos's mind. Not just for the slaves, but for all humans.' She looked at Jeanne as she spoke. Laundress and Old Mender didn't know anything about the world Outside, but Jeanne did.

Jeanne gave a sort of grudging nod, to say that, yeah, putting off the end of the world was important. 'OK, so we have to try it. We'd better find out which slaves are allowed in his room, and then we can go up and hide. The big chambers have wardrobes, right?' She was looking at Old Mender, who nodded. 'We can stay in one of those—'

'That's a good idea,' Maggie interrupted. 'Everything but the "we". You can't go with me this time. This is something I have to do alone.'

Jeanne gave an indignant wriggle of her shoulders. Her red hair seemed to stand up in protest and her eyes were sparking. 'That's ridiculous. I can help. There's no reason—'

'There is, too, a reason,' Maggie said. 'It's too dangerous. Whoever goes there might get killed today. If you stay here, you may at least have a few more days.' When Jeanne opened her mouth to protest, she went on, 'Days to try and figure out a new plan, OK? Which will probably be just as dangerous. And, besides, I'd like somebody to watch over P.J. and Cady for as long as possible.' She gave P.J. a smile, and P.J. lifted her head resolutely, obviously trying to stop her chin from quivering.

'I really do need to do it alone,' Maggie said gently, turning back to Jeanne. Somewhere in her own mind, she was standing back, astonished. Who would have ever thought, when she first met Jeanne in the cart, that she would end up having to talk her out of trying to get killed with Maggie?

Jeanne blew air out pursed lips, her eyes narrowed. Finally she nodded.

'Fine, fine. You go conquer the vampire and I'll stay and arrange the revolution.'

'I bet you will,' Maggie said dryly. For a moment their eyes met, and it was like that first time, when an unspoken bond had formed between them.

'*Try* to take care of yourself. You're not exactly the smartest, you know,' Jeanne said. Her voice was a little rough and her eyes were oddly shiny.

'I know,' Maggie said.

The next moment Jeanne sniffed and cheered up. 'I just thought of who's allowed up into the bedrooms in the morning,' she said. 'You can help her, and she'll lead you to Delos's room.'

Maggie looked at her suspiciously. 'Why are you so happy about it? Who is it?'

'Oh, you'll like her. She's called Chamber-pot Emptier.'

CHAPTER
15

Maggie shuffled behind Chamber-pot Emptier, heading back toward the castle. She was carrying piles of folded linen sheets given to her by Laundress, and she was doing her best to look like a slave. Laundress had smudged her face artistically with dirt to disguise her. She had also sifted a handful of dust into Maggie's hair to dull the auburn into a lifeless brown, and when Maggie bowed her head over the sheets, the hair further obscured her features. The only problem was that she was constantly afraid she was going to sneeze.

'Those are the wild animals,' Chamber-pot Emptier whispered over her shoulder. She was a big-boned girl with gentle eyes that reminded Maggie of the calves tethered by Laundress's hut. It had taken Laundress a while to make her understand what they wanted of her, but now she seemed to feel obligated to give Maggie a tour.

'They're brought in from Outside,' she said. 'And they're dangerous.'

Maggie looked sideways at the wicker cages where Sylvia and Gavin had walked earlier. From one a brown-grey wolf stared back at her with a frighteningly sad and steady gaze. In another a sleek black panther was pacing, and it snarled as they went by. There was something curled up in the back of a third that might have been a tiger – it was big, and it had stripes.

'Wow,' she said. 'I wouldn't want to chase that.'

Chamber-pot Emptier seemed pleased. 'And here's the castle. It's called Black Dawn.'

'It is?' Maggie said, distracted away from the animals.

'That's what my grandpa called it, anyway. He lived and died in the courtyard without ever going in.' Chamber-pot Emptier thought a moment and added, 'The old people say that you used to be able to see the sun in the sky – not just behind the clouds, you know. And when the sun came up in the morning it shone on the castle. But maybe that's just a story.'

Yeah, maybe it was just a story that you could see the sun in the sky, Maggie thought grimly. Every time she thought this place couldn't surprise her anymore, she discovered she was wrong.

But the castle itself was impressive . . . awe inspiring. It was the only thing in view that wasn't dusty brown or pallid grey. Its walls were shiny and black, almost mirror-like in places, and Maggie didn't have to be told that it wasn't built of any ordinary human stone. How they had gotten it to this valley was a mystery.

Delos lives here, she thought as Emptier led her up a stone staircase, past the ground floor which was just cellars and storage rooms. In this beautiful, frightening, impressive place. Not only lives in it, but commands it. It's all his.

She got just a glimpse of the great hall, where she'd seen slaves setting a long table yesterday. Chamber-pot Emptier led her up another floor and into a series of winding corridors that seemed to go on for miles.

It was dim in this internal labyrinth. The windows were

high and narrow and hardly let any of the pale daylight in.
On the walls there were candles in brackets and flares in
iron rings, but they only seemed to add wavering,
confusing shadows to the twilight.

'His bedroom's up here,' Emptier murmured finally.
Maggie followed her closely. She was just thinking that
they had made it all the way without even being
challenged, when a voice sounded from a side corridor.

'Where are you going? Who's this?'

It was a guard, Maggie saw, peering from under her
hair. A real medieval guard, with, of all things, a lance.
There was another one in the opposite corridor just like
him. She was fascinated in the middle of her terror.

But Chamber-pot Emptier of the not-so-quick wits
reacted beautifully. She took time to curtsey, then she said
slowly and stolidly, 'It's Folder from the laundry, sir.
Laundress sent her with the sheets and I was told she
could help me. There's more work because of the guests,
you know.'

'It's Chamber Maid's work to spread sheets,' the guard
said irritably.

Chamber-pot Emptier curtsied again and said just as
slowly, 'Yes, sir, but there's more work because of the
guests, you see—'

'Fine, fine,' the guard broke in impatiently. 'Why don't
you go and do it, instead of talking about it?' He seemed
to think that was funny, and he turned and elbowed the
other guard in the ribs.

Chamber-pot Emptier curtseyed a third time and
walked on, not hurrying. Maggie tried to copy the curtsey,
with her face buried in the sheets.

There was another endless corridor, then a doorway,
and then Emptier said, 'We're here. And there's
nobody around.'

Maggie lifted her face from the sheets. 'You're absolutely wonderful, you know that? You deserve an Academy Award.'

'A what?'

'Never mind. But you were great.'

'I only told the truth,' the girl said placidly, but there was a smile lurking in the depths of her gentle cow-like eyes. 'There is more work when guests come. We never had them before three years ago.'

Maggie nodded. 'I know. Look, I guess you'd better go now. And um – Emptier?' She couldn't bring herself to say the entire name. 'I really hope you don't get in trouble because of this.'

Chamber-pot Emptier nodded back, then went to reach under the bed and retrieve a ceramic container. She walked out again holding it carefully.

Maggie looked around the room, which was very big and very bare. It was somewhat better lit than the corridors, having several bowl-shaped oil lamps on stands. The bed was the only real piece of furniture in it. It was huge, with a heavy wooden frame and carved bedposts. Piled on top of it were quilts and what looked like fur coverlets, and hanging all around it were linen curtains.

I'm probably supposed to take all that stuff off and put the clean sheets on, Maggie thought. She didn't.

The rest of the furniture seemed to be large chests made of exotic-looking wood, and a few benches and stools. Nothing that offered a hiding place. But on one side there was a curtained doorway.

Maggie went through it and found a small anteroom – the wardrobe Jeanne had mentioned. It was much bigger than she'd expected, and seemed to be more of a storeroom than a closet.

OK. So I'll just sit down.

There were two stools beside a figure that vaguely resembled a dressmaker's dummy. Maggie dropped her sheets on a chest and pulled one of the stools close to the doorway. Through the space between the linen curtains she could see almost the entire bedchamber.

Perfect, she thought. All I have to do is wait until he comes in alone. And then –

She stiffened. She could hear voices from somewhere beyond the vast bedroom. No, she could hear *a* voice, a musical girlish voice.

Oh, please, she thought. Not *her*. Don't let him come in with her. I'll have to jump out and hit her with something; I won't be able to stop myself . . .

But when two figures came in the room, she had no desire to jump out.

It was Sylvia, all right, but she wasn't with Delos. She was with Hunter Redfern.

Maggie felt ice down her spine. Now, what were these two doing in Delos's bedroom? Whatever it was, if they caught her, she was dead meat. She held herself absolutely still, but she couldn't tear herself away from the curtain.

'He's out riding, and he won't be back for another half hour,' Sylvia was saying. She was wearing a dark holly-green gown and carrying a basket. 'And I've sent all the servants away.'

'Even so,' Hunter Redfern said. He gently moved the heavy wooden door until it was almost shut. Not all the way, but enough to screen the bedchamber from anyone outside.

'You really think he's spying on our rooms?' Sylvia turned in a swirl of skirts to look at the tall man.

'He's bright – much smarter than you give him credit for. And these old castles have spy-holes and listening tubes built in; I remember. It's a stupid prince who doesn't make use of them.'

He remembers, Maggie thought, for a moment too full of wonder to be scared. He remembers the days when castles were built, he means. He's really been alive that long.

She studied the handsome face under the blood-red hair, the aristocratic cheekbones, the mobile mouth – and the quick flashing eyes. This was the sort of man who could fascinate people, she decided. Like Delos, there was a sort of leashed tension about him, a reserve of power and intelligence that made an ordinary person feel awed. He was a leader, a commander.

And a hunter, Maggie thought. All these people are hunters, but he's *the* Hunter, the epitome of what they are. His name says it all.

But Sylvia was talking again. 'What is it that he's not supposed to know?'

'I've had a message from Outside. Don't ask how, I have my ways.'

'You have your little bats,' Sylvia said demurely. 'I've seen them.'

There was a pause, then Hunter said, 'You'd better watch yourself, girl. That mouth's going to get you in trouble.'

Sylvia had her face turned away from him, but Maggie saw her swallow. 'I'm sorry. I didn't know it was a secret. But what's happened?'

'The biggest news in your short life.' Hunter Redfern laughed once and added with apparent good humour restored, 'And maybe in mine. The witches have seceded from the Night World.'

Maggie blinked. It sounded impressive the way he said it – but more impressive was the way Sylvia froze and then whirled breathlessly.

'*What?*'

'It's happened. They've been threatening for a month, but most people didn't believe they'd really do it.'

Sylvia put a hand to her middle, pressed flat against her stomach as if to hold something in. Then she sat on the fur-covered bed.

'They've left the Council,' she said. She wasn't looking at Hunter Redfern.

'They've left the Council and everything else.'

'All of them?'

Hunter Redfern's fine red eyebrows went up. 'What did you expect? Oh, a few of the blackest practitioners from Circle Midnight are arguing, but most of them agree with the liberals in Circle Twilight. They want to save the humans. Avert the coming darkness.' He said it exactly the way Maggie had heard lumberjacks say, 'Save the spotted owls. Ha!'

'So it's really beginning,' Sylvia murmured. She was still looking at the stone floor. 'I mean, there's no going back, now, is there? The Night World is split forever.'

'And the millennium is upon us,' Hunter said, almost cheerfully. He looked young and . . . personable, Maggie thought. Somebody you'd vote for.

'Which brings me to the question,' he said smoothly, looking at Sylvia, 'of when you're going to find her.'

What, her? Maggie's stomach tightened.

Sylvia's face was equally tight. She looked up and said levelly, 'I told you I'd find her and I will.'

'But *when*? You do understand how important this is?'

'Of course I understand!' Sylvia flared up. Her chest was heaving. 'That's why I was trying to send her to you in the first place—'

Hunter was talking as if he didn't hear her. 'If it gets

out that Aradia, the Maiden of all the witches, is here in the valley—'

'I know!'

'And that you *had* her and let her slip through your fingers—'

'I was trying to bring her to *you*. I thought *that* was important,' Sylvia said. She was bristling and distraught. Which was exactly what Hunter wanted her to be, Maggie thought dazedly. He really knows how to play people.

But the analysis was faraway, in the shallowest part of her mind. Most of her consciousness was simply stricken into paralyzed amazement.

Aradia.

The Maiden of all the witches.

So it wasn't Arcadia at all, Maggie thought. She might have mentioned *that*, after I've been calling her Cady for days. But then she hasn't been conscious much, and when she was we had more urgent things to talk about.

Aradia. Aradia. That's really pretty.

The name had started an odd resonance in her mind, maybe bringing up some long-forgotten mythology lesson. Aradia was a goddess, she thought. Of . . . um, sylvan glades or something. The woods. Like Diana.

And what Maiden of all the witches was, she had no idea, but it was obviously something important. And not evil, either. From what Hunter was saying, it was clear that witches weren't like other Night People.

She was the maiden Bern and Gavin were talking about, Maggie realized. The one they were supposed to deliver. So Sylvia was bringing her to Hunter Redfern. But Cady herself told me – I mean, *Aradia* told me – that she was already coming to this valley for a reason.

Before she could even properly phrase the question, her mind had the answer.

Delos.

In a coincidence that lifted the hair on Maggie's arms, Sylvia said, 'She won't get to Delos.'

'She'd better not,' Hunter said. 'Maybe you don't realize how persuasive she can be. An ambassador from all the witches, coming to plead her case . . . she just might sway him. He has a despicable soft spot – a conscience, you might call it. And we know he's been in contact with the human girl who escaped with her. Who knows what messages the little vermin was carrying from her?'

No messages, Maggie thought grimly. Not with this vermin anyway. But I would have carried them if I'd known.

'Gavin said Aradia was still unconscious from the truth potion – that she was practically dead,' Sylvia said. 'I don't think she could have given any messages. I'd swear that Delos doesn't know she's in the valley at all.'

Hunter was still brooding. 'The witches have one Wild Power on their side already.'

'But they won't get another,' Sylvia said doggedly. 'I've got people looking for her. All the nobles are on our side. They won't let her get to Delos.'

'She should have been killed in the beginning,' Hunter mused. 'But maybe *you* have a soft spot for her, like you do for that human boy.'

Behind the linen curtains, Maggie stiffened.

Like you *do*. Not like you *did*. And who else could the human boy be?

She gritted her teeth, listening so hard she could hear the blood in her ears, willing them to talk about Miles.

But Hunter was going on in his smooth voice, 'Or maybe you still have some loyalty to the witches.'

Sylvia's pale face flushed. 'I do not! I'm finished with them, and you know it! I may be a spellcaster, but I'm not a witch anymore.'

'It's good to see you haven't forgotten what they've done to you,' Hunter said. 'After all, you could have been a Hearth-Woman, taken your rightful place on the witch Council.'

'Yes . . .'

'Like your grandmother and her mother before her. *They* were Harmans, and so was your father. What a pity the name isn't passed through the male line. You ended up being just a Weald.'

'I *was* a Harman,' Sylvia said with muted ferocity. She was staring at the floor again, and she seemed to be speaking to herself rather than to Hunter. 'I *was*. But I had to stand there and watch my cousins be accepted instead of me. I had to watch *half humans* be accepted – be welcomed. They took my place – just because they were descended through the female line.'

Hunter shook his head. 'A very sad tradition.'

Sylvia's breath came raggedly for another minute or so, then she looked up slowly at the tall man in the centre of the room. 'You don't have to worry about my loyalty,' she said quietly. 'I want a place in the new order after the millennium. I'm through with the witches.'

Hunter smiled.

'I know it,' he said, lightly and approvingly, and then he started pacing the room. He got what he wanted out of her, Maggie thought.

Almost casually, he added, 'Just be sure that Delos's power is kept in check until everything's decided.'

Sylvia bent and lifted the basket, which Maggie had forgotten about.

'The new binding spells will hold,' she said. 'I brought special ingredients from one of the oldest Midnight witches. And he won't suspect anything.'

'And nobody but you can take them off?'

'Nobody but me,' Sylvia said firmly. 'Not even the Crone of all the witches. Or the Maiden, for that matter.'

'Good girl,' Hunter said, and smiled again. 'I have every confidence in you. After all, you have lamia blood in you to balance the witch taint. You're my own eighth-great-granddaughter.'

Maggie wanted to punch him.

She was confused and frightened and indignant and furious, all at once. As far as she could tell, Hunter Redfern seemed to be manipulating everybody. And Delos, Delos the prince and Wild Power, was just another of his puppets.

I wonder what they plan to do if he *won't* join their new order? she thought bleakly.

After a few minutes, Hunter turned in his pacing and walked by the door. He paused briefly as if listening, then glanced at Sylvia.

'You don't know how happy it makes me just to think about it,' he said, in a voice that wasn't strained, or overly cheerful, or too loud, or anything that rang false. 'To finally have a true heir. A male heir of my own line, and untainted by witch blood. I would never have married that witch Maeve Harman if I had known my son was still alive. And not only alive, but out having sons! The only true Redferns left in the world, you might say.'

Maggie, with her teeth set in her lower lip, didn't need to guess who was on the other side of the door. She watched tensely.

And Delos came in, right on cue.

CHAPTER
16

'I'm sorry. Was I interrupting something?' he said,

Maggie had to struggle not to draw in her breath sharply.

It was always a little bit of a shock seeing him. And even in a room with Hunter Redfern and the pale and dazzling Sylvia, he stood out. Like a cold wind blowing through the door, he seemed to bring coiled energy in with him, to slap everyone awake with the chilly smell of snow.

And of course he was gorgeous, too.

And not awed by Hunter, Maggie thought. He faced his great-grandfather with those fearless yellow eyes level, and a measuring look on his fine-boned face.

'Nothing at all,' Hunter Redfern said amiably. 'We were waiting for you. And planning the celebrations.'

'Celebrations?'

'To honour our agreement. I'm so pleased that we've come to an understanding at last. Aren't you?'

'Of course,' Delos said, pulling off his gloves without any change in expression. 'When we do come to an understanding, I'll be very pleased.'

Maggie had to bite her lip on a snicker. At that

moment, looking at Hunter's facile smile and Sylvia's pinned-on simper, she had never liked Delos's dour, cold grimness better.

Idiot, she told herself. When did you ever like it at all? The guy's an icicle.

But there was something clean and sharp-edged about his iciness, and she couldn't help admiring the way he faced Hunter. There was a little aching knot in her chest as she watched him standing there, tense and elegant, with his dark hair tousled from riding.

Which wasn't to say she wasn't scared. That aura of power Delos carried along with him was very real. He had sensed her before, even with Aradia blocking the signs of her life-force. And now here he was, maybe twelve feet away, with only a piece of linen between them.

There was nothing Maggie could do but sit as still as possible.

'Sylvia has taken the liberty of beginning the preparations,' Hunter said. 'I hope you don't mind. I think we can work out any little details that are left before tomorrow, don't you?'

Suddenly Delos looked tired. He tossed his gloves on the bed and nodded, conceding a point. 'Yes.'

'Essentially,' Hunter Redfern said, 'we are agreed.'

This time Delos just nodded without speaking.

'I can't wait to show you off to the world outside,' Hunter said, and this time Maggie thought the note of pride and eagerness in his voice was sincere. 'My great-grandson. And to think that a year ago I didn't know of your existence.' He crossed to slap Delos on the back. It was a gesture so much like the old king's that Maggie's eyes widened.

'I'm going to make some preparations of my own,' he said. 'I think the last hunt before you leave should be special, don't you?'

He was smiling as he left.

Delos stared moodily at the fur coverlet.

'Well,' Sylvia said, sounding almost chirpy. 'How's the arm?'

Delos glanced down at it. He was still wearing the complicated brace thing Maggie had seen him in yesterday.

'It's all right.'

'Hurts?'

'A little.'

Sylvia sighed and shook her head. 'That's because you used it for practice. I did warn you, you know.'

'Can you make it better or not?' Delos said brusquely.

Sylvia was already opening the basket. 'I told you, it'll take time. But it should improve with each treatment – as long as you don't use it.'

She was fiddling with the brace, doing things that Maggie couldn't see. And Maggie's heart was beating hard with anger and an unreasonable protectiveness.

I can't let her do that to Delos – but how can I stop her? There's no way. If she sees me, it's all over . . .

'There,' Sylvia said. 'That should hold you for a while.'

Maggie ground her teeth.

But at least maybe she'll *go* now, she thought. It feels like about a century I've been sitting in here listening to her. And this stool isn't getting any more comfortable.

'Now,' Sylvia said briskly, tidying. 'Just let me put your gloves away—'

Oh, *no*, Maggie thought, horrified. On the shelf beside her was a pile of gloves.

'No,' Delos said, so quickly it was almost an echo. 'I need them.'

'Don't be silly. You're not going out again—'

'I'll take them.' Delos had wonderful reflexes. He put

himself between Sylvia and the wardrobe, and an instant later he was holding on to the gloves, almost tugging them from her hands.

Sylvia looked up at him wonderingly for a long moment. Maggie could see her face, the creamy skin delicately flushed, and her eyes, the colour of tear-drenched violets. She could see the shimmer of her pale blonde hair as Sylvia shook her head slightly.

Delos stared down at her implacably.

Then Sylvia shrugged her fragile shoulders and let go of the gloves.

'I'll go see to the feast,' she said lightly and smiled. She picked up her basket and moved gracefully to the door.

Delos watched her go.

Maggie simply sat, speechless and paralyzed. When Delos followed Sylvia and closed the door firmly behind her, she made herself get slowly off the stool. She backed away from the curtains slightly, but she could still see a strip of the bedroom.

Delos walked unerringly straight to the wardrobe.

'You can come out now,' he said, his voice flat and hard.

Maggie shut her eyes.

Great. Well, I should have known.

But he hadn't let Sylvia come in and discover her, and he hadn't simply turned her over to his guards. Those were very good signs, she told herself stoutly. In fact, maybe she wasn't going to have to persuade him of anything at all; maybe he was already going to be reasonable.

'Or do I have to come in?' Delos said dangerously.

Or maybe not, Maggie thought.

She felt a sudden idiotic desire to get the dust out of her hair. She shook her head a few times, brushing at it, then gave up.

Terribly conscious of her smudged face and slave

clothing, she parted the linen hangings and walked out.

'I warned you,' Delos said.

He was facing her squarely, his jaw set and his mouth as grim as she had ever seen it. His eyes were hooded, a dull and eerie gold in the shadows. He looked every inch the dark and mysterious vampire prince.

And here I am, Maggie thought. Looking like . . . well, like vermin, I bet. Like something fished out of the gutter. Not much of a representative for humanity.

She had never cared about clothes or hairstyles or things like that, but just now she wished that she could at least look presentable. Since the fate of the world might just depend on her.

Even so, there was something in the air between Delos and herself. A sort of quivering aliveness that quickened the blood in Maggie's veins. That stirred something in her chest, and started her heart pounding with an odd mixture of fear and hope.

She faced Delos just as squarely as he was facing her.

'I know some things that I think you need to know,' she said quietly.

He ignored that. 'I told you what would happen if you came here. I told you I wouldn't protect you again.'

'I remember. But you *did* protect me again. And I thank you – but I really think I'd better tell you what's going on. Sylvia is the suspicious type, and if she's gone to Hunter Redfern to say that you don't want people looking in your closet—'

'Don't you *understand*?' he said with such sudden violence that Maggie's throat closed, choking off her words. She stared at him. 'You're so close to dying, but you don't seem to care. Are you too stupid to grasp it, or do you just have a death wish?'

The thumping in Maggie's chest now was definitely fear.

'I do understand,' she began slowly, when she could get her voice to work.

'No, you *don't*,' he said. 'But I'll make you.'

All at once his eyes were blazing. Not just their normal brilliant yellow, but a dazzling and unnatural gold that seemed to hold its own light.

Even though Maggie had seen it before, it was still a shock to watch his features change. His face going paler, even more beautiful and clearly defined, chiselled in ice. His pupils widening like a predator's, holding a darkness that a human could drown in. And that proud and wilful mouth twisting in anger.

It all happened in a second or so. And then he was advancing on her, with dark fire in his eyes, and his lips pulling back from his teeth.

Maggie stared at the fangs, helplessly horrified all over again. They were even sharper than she remembered them looking. They indented his lower lip on either side, even with his mouth partly open. And, yes, they were definitely scary.

'This is what I am,' Delos said, speaking easily around the fangs. 'A hunting animal. Part of a world of darkness that you couldn't survive for a minute in. I've told you over and over to stay away from it, but you won't listen. You turn up *in my own castle*, and you just won't believe your danger. So now I'm going to show you.'

Maggie took a step backward. She wasn't in a good position; the wall was behind her and the huge bed was on her left. Delos was between her and the door. And she had already seen how fast his reflexes were.

Her legs felt unsteady; her pulse was beating erratically. Her breath was coming fast.

He doesn't really mean it – he won't really do it. He isn't serious . . .

But for all her mind's desperate chanting, panic was beginning to riot inside her. The instincts of forgotten ancestors, long buried, were surfacing. Some ancient part of her remembered being chased by hunting animals, being prey.

She backed up until she came in contact with the tapestry-hung wall behind her. And then there was nowhere else to go.

'Now,' Delos said and closed the distance between them with the grace of a tiger.

He was right in front of her. Maggie couldn't help looking up at him, looking directly into that alien and beautiful face. She could smell a scent like autumn leaves and fresh snow, but she could feel the heat from his body.

He's nothing dead or undead, some very distant part of her mind thought. He's ruthless, he's been raised to be a weapon, but he's definitely alive – maybe the most alive thing I've ever seen.

When he moved, there was nowhere she could go to avoid him. His hands closed on her shoulders like implacable bands of steel. And then he was pulling her forward, not roughly but not gently either, pulling her until her body rested lightly against his. And he was looking down at her with golden eyes that burned like twin flames.

Looking at my throat, Maggie thought. She could feel the pulse beating there, and with her chin tilted up to look at him and her upper body arched away from him, she knew he could see it. His eyes were fixed on it with a different kind of hunger than she had ever seen in a human face.

For just one instant the panic overwhelmed her, flooding up blackly to engulf everything else. She couldn't think; she was nothing but a terrified mass of instinct, and all she wanted to do was to *run*, to get away.

Then, slowly at first, the panic receded. It simply poured off her, draining away. She felt as if she were rising from deep water into air clear as crystal.

She looked straight into the golden eyes above her and said, 'Go ahead.'

She had the pleasure of seeing the golden eyes look startled. 'What?'

'Go ahead,' Maggie said distinctly. 'It doesn't matter. You're stronger than me; we both know that. But whatever you do, you can't make me your prey. You don't have that power. You can't control me.'

Delos hissed in fury, a reptilian sound. 'You are so—'

'You wanted me scared; I'm scared. But, then, I was scared before. And it doesn't matter. There's something more important than me at stake here. Prove whatever you've got to prove and then I'll tell you about it.'

'So completely stupid,' Delos raged. But Maggie had the odd feeling that his anger was more against himself than her. 'You don't think I'll hurt you,' he said.

'You're wrong there.'

'I *will* hurt you. I'll show you—'

'You can kill me,' Maggie said clearly. 'But that's all you can do. I told you, you can't control me. And you can't change what's between us.'

He was very, very angry now. The fathomless pupils of his eyes were like black holes, and Maggie suddenly remembered that he wasn't just a vampire, or just a weapon, but some doomsday creature with powers meant for the end of the world.

He hovered over her with his fangs showing.

'I *will* hurt you,' he said. 'Watch me hurt you.'

He bent to her angrily, and she could see his intent in his eyes. He meant to frighten and disillusion . . .

. . . and he kissed her mouth like raindrops falling on cool water.

Maggie clung to him desperately and kissed back. Where they touched they dissolved into each other.

Then she felt him tremble in her arms and they were both lost.

It was like the first time when their minds had joined. Maggie felt a pulsing thrill that enveloped her entire body. She could feel the pure line of communication open between them, she could feel herself lifted into that wonderful still place where only the two of them existed and nothing else mattered.

Dimly, she knew that her physical self was falling forward, that they were both falling, still clasped in each other's arms. But in the hushed place of crystalline beauty where she *really* was, they were facing each other in a white light.

It was like being inside his mind again, but this time he was there opposite her, gazing at her directly. He didn't look like a doomsday weapon anymore, or even like a vampire. His black-lashed golden eyes were large, like a solemn child's. There was a terrible wistfulness in his face.

He swallowed, and then she heard his mental voice. It was just the barest breath of sound. *I don't want this—*

Yes, you do, she interrupted, indignant. The normal barriers that existed between two people had melted; she knew what he was feeling, and she didn't like being lied to.

—to end, he finished.

Oh.

Maggie's eyes filled with sudden hot tears.

She did what was instinctive to her. She reached out to him. And then they were embracing in their minds, just as their physical bodies embraced, and there was that feeling of invisible wings all around them.

Maggie could catch fragments of his thoughts, not just the surface ones, but things so deep she wasn't sure he even knew he was thinking them. *So lonely . . . always been lonely. Meant to be that way. Always alone . . .*

No, you're not, she told him, trying to communicate it to the deepest part of him. *I won't let you be alone. And we were meant to be like this; can't you feel it?*

What she could feel was his powerful longing. But he couldn't be convinced all at once.

She heard something like *Destiny . . .* And she saw images of his past. His father. His teachers. The nobles. Even the slaves who had heard the prophecies. They all believed he had only one purpose, and it had to do with the end of the world.

You can change your destiny, she said. *You don't have to go along with it. I don't know what's going to happen with the world, but you don't have to be what they say. You have the power to fight them!*

For one heartbeat the image of his father seemed to loom closer, tall and terrible, a father seen through the eyes of childhood. Then the features blurred, changing just enough to become Hunter Redfern with the same cruel and accusing light in his yellow eyes.

And then the picture was swept away by a tidal wave of anger from Delos.

I am not a weapon.

I know that, Maggie told him.

I can choose what I am from now on. I can choose what path to follow.

Yes, Maggie said.

Delos said simply, *I choose to go with you.*

His anger was gone. Just briefly, she got the flicker of

another image from him, as she had once before seeing herself through his eyes.

He didn't see her as a slave girl with dusty hair and a smudged face and coarse sacking for clothes. He saw her as the girl with autumn-coloured hair and endlessly deep sorrel eyes – the kind of eyes that never wavered, but looked straight into his soul. He saw her as warm and real and vibrant, melting the black ice of his heart and setting him free.

And then this image was gone, too, and they were simply holding on to each other, lapped in peace.

They stayed like that for a while, their spirits flowing in and out of each other. Delos didn't seem inclined to move.

And Maggie wanted it to last, too. She wanted to stay here for a long time, exploring all the deepest and most secret places of the mind that was now open to her. To touch him in ways he'd never been touched before, this person who, beyond all logic, was the other half of her. Who belonged to her. Who was her soulmate.

But there was something nagging at her consciousness. She couldn't ignore it, and when she finally allowed herself to look at it, she remembered everything.

And she was swept with a wave of alarm so strong it snapped her right out of Delos's mind.

She could feel the shock of separation reverberate in him as she sat up, aware of her own body again. They were still linked enough that it hurt her just as it hurt him. But she was too frightened to care.

'Delos,' she said urgently. 'We've got to do something. There's going to be trouble.'

He blinked at her, as if he were coming from very far away. 'It will be all right,' he said.

'No. It won't. You don't understand.'

He sighed, very nearly his old exasperated snort. 'If it's

Hunter Redfern you're worried about—'

'It's him – and Sylvia. Delos, I heard them talking when I was in the wardrobe. You don't know what they've got planned.'

'It doesn't matter what they've got planned. I can take care of them.' He straightened a little, looked down at his left arm.

'*No, you can't,*' Maggie said fiercely. 'And that's the problem. Sylvia put a spell on you, a binding spell, she called it. You can't use your power.'

CHAPTER
17

He stared at her for an instant, his golden eyes wide.

'Don't you believe me?'

'I wouldn't put it past Sylvia to try,' he said. 'But I don't think she's strong enough.'

'She said she got special ingredients. And she said that nobody else could take the spell off.' When he still looked doubtful, although a bit more grim, Maggie added, 'Why don't you try it?'

He reached down with long, strong fingers to pull at the fastenings of his brace. It came off easily, and Maggie's eyebrows went up. She blinked.

He extended his arm, pointing it at the wall, and drew a dagger from his belt.

Maggie had forgotten about the blood part. She bit the inside of her cheek and didn't say anything as he opened a small cut on his wrist. Blood welled up red, then flowed in a trickle.

'Just a little blast,' Delos said, and looked calmly at the wall.

Nothing happened.

He frowned, his golden eyes flaring dangerously. Maggie could see the concentration in his face. He spread his fingers.

Still nothing happened.

Maggie let out her breath. I guess spells are invisible, she thought. The brace was just for show.

Delos was looking at his arm as if it didn't belong to him.

'We're in trouble,' Maggie said, trying not to make it sound like *I told you so*. 'While they thought they were alone in here, they were talking about all kinds of things. All Hunter cares about is getting you to help him destroy the humans. But there's been some big split in the Night World, and the witches have seceded from it.'

Delos went very still, and his eyes were distant. 'That means war. Open war between witches and vampires.'

'Probably,' Maggie said, waving a hand vaguely. 'But, listen, Delos, the witches sent somebody here, an ambassador, to talk to you. To try to get you on their side. Hunter said they've got one of the Wild Powers on their side already – the witches, I mean. Are you getting this?'

'Of course,' Delos said. But now his voice was oddly distant, too. He was looking at something Maggie couldn't see. 'But one out of four doesn't matter. Two out of four, three out of four – it's not good enough.'

'What are you talking about?' Maggie didn't wait for him to answer. 'But, look. I know the girl who came to talk to you. It's the girl I was with on the rocks, the other one you saved from Bern. She's Aradia, and she's Maiden of all the witches. And, Delos, they're looking for her right now. They want to kill her to stop her from getting to you. And she's my *friend*.'

'That's too bad.'

'We've got to *stop* them,' Maggie said, exasperated.

'We can't.'

That brought Maggie up short. She stared at him.

'What are you talking about?'

'I'm saying we can't stop them. They're too strong. Maggie, listen to me,' he said calmly and clearly, when she began an incoherent protest.

That's the first time he's said my name out loud, she thought dizzily, and then she focussed on his words.

'It's not just the spell they've put on me. And it's not just that they control the castle. Oh, yes, they do,' he said with a bitter laugh, cutting her off again. 'You haven't been here very long; you don't understand. The nobles here are centuries old, most of them. They don't like being ruled by a precocious child with uncanny powers. As soon as Hunter showed up, they transferred their loyalty to him.'

'But—'

'He's everything they admire. The perfect vampire, the ultimate predator. He's ruthless and bloodthirsty and he wants to give them the whole world as their hunting grounds. Do you really think any of them can resist that? After years of hunting mindless, bewildered animals that have to be rationed out one at a time? With maybe the odd creaky slave for a special treat? Do you think any of them won't follow him willingly?'

Maggie was silent. There was nothing she could say.

He was right, and it was scary.

'And that isn't all,' he continued remorselessly. 'Do you want to hear a prophecy?'

'Not really,' Maggie said. She'd heard more than enough of those for one lifetime.

He ignored her. 'My old teacher used to tell me this,' he said.

' "Four to stand between the light and the shadow,
Four of blue fire, power in their blood.

Born in the year of the blind Maiden's vision;
Four less one and darkness triumphs." '

'Uh huh,' Maggie said. To her it sounded like just more of
the same thing. The only interesting thing about it was
that it mentioned the blind Maiden. That had to be Aradia,
didn't it? She was one famous witch.

'What's "born in the year of the blind Maiden's
vision?" ' she asked.

'It means all the Wild Powers are the same age, born
seventeen years ago,' Delos said impatiently. 'But that's
not the point. The point is the last line, "Four less one and
darkness triumphs." That means that the darkness is going
to win, Maggie.'

'What do you mean?'

'It's inevitable. There's no way that the humans and the
witches can get all four Wild Powers on their side. And if
there's even one less than four, the darkness is going to
win. All the vampires need to do is kill one of the Wild
Powers, and it's all over. Don't you see?'

Maggie stared at him. She did see what he was saying,
and it was even scarier than what he'd said before. 'But
that doesn't mean we can just give up,' she said, trying to
puzzle out his expression. 'If we do that, it *will* be all over.
We can't just surrender and *let* them win.'

'Of course not,' he said harshly. 'We have to join them.'

There was a long silence. Maggie realized that her
mouth had fallen open.

'. . . *what?*'

'We have to be on the winning side, and that's the
vampire side.' He looked at her with yellow eyes that
seemed as remote and deathly calm as a panther's. 'I'm
sorry about your friends, but there's no chance for them.
And the only chance for you is to become a vampire.'

Maggie's brain suddenly surged into overdrive.

All at once, she saw exactly what he was saying. And fury gave her energy. He was lightning-fast, but she jumped up and out of the way before he could close his hands on her.

'*Are you out of your mind?*'

'No.'

'You're going to *kill* me?'

'I'm going to save your life, the only way I can.' He stood up, following her with that same eerie calm.

I can't believe this. I . . . really . . . can't . . . believe this, Maggie thought.

She circled around the bed, then stopped. It was pointless; he was going to get her eventually.

She looked into his face one more time, and saw that he was completely serious. She dropped her arms and relaxed her shoulders, trying to slow her breathing, meeting his eyes directly.

'Delos, this isn't just about me, and it's not just about my friends. It's about all the slaves here, and all the humans on the Outside. Turning me into a vampire isn't going to help them.'

'I'm sorry,' he said again. 'But you're all that really matters.'

'No, I'm *not*,' Maggie said, and this time the hot tears didn't stop at her eyes, but overflowed and rolled down her cheeks. She shook them off angrily, and took one last deep breath.

'I won't let you,' she said.

'You can't stop me.'

'I can fight. I can make you kill me before you turn me into a vampire. If you want to try it that way, come and take your best shot.'

Delos's yellow eyes bored into hers – and then

suddenly shifted and dropped. He stepped back, his face cold.

'Fine,' he said. 'If you won't cooperate, I'll put you in the dungeon until you see what's best for you.'

Maggie felt her mouth drop open again.

'You wouldn't,' she said.

'Watch me.'

The dungeon, like everything else in the castle, was heart-stoppingly authentic.

It had something that Maggie had read about in books but hadn't seen in the rooms above: rushes and straw on the floor. It also had stone bench carved directly into the stone wall and a narrow, barred window-slit about fifteen feet above Maggie's head. And that was all it had.

Once Maggie had poked into the straw enough to discover that she didn't really *want* to know what was down there and shaken the iron bars that made up the door and examined the stone slabs in the wall and stood on the bench to try to climb to the window, there was nothing else to do. She sat on the bench and felt the true enormity of the situation trickle in on her.

She was really stuck here. Delos was really serious. And the world, the actual, real world out there, could be affected as a consequence.

It wasn't that she didn't understand his motivation. She had been in his mind; she'd felt the strength of his protectiveness for her. And she wanted to protect him, too.

But it wasn't possible to forget about everyone else. Her parents, her friends, her teachers, the paper girl. If she let Delos give up, what happened to them?

Even the people in the Dark Kingdom. Laundress and Old Mender and Soaker and Chamber-pot Emptier and all the other slaves. She *cared* about them. She admired their gritty determination to go on living, whatever the circumstances – and their courage in risking their lives to help her.

That's what Delos doesn't understand, she thought. He doesn't see them as people, so he can't care about them. All his life he's only cared about himself, and now about me. He can't look beyond that.

If only she could think of a way to *make* him see – but she couldn't. As the hours passed and the silence began to wear on her, she kept trying.

No inspiration came. And finally the light outside her cell began to fade and the cold started to settle in.

She was half asleep, huddled on her chilly bench, when she heard the rattle of a key in a door. She jumped up and went to peer through the bars, hoping to see Delos.

The door at the end of the narrow stone corridor opened and someone came in with a flare. But it wasn't Delos. It was a guard, and behind him was another guard, and this one had a prisoner.

'Jeanne!' Maggie said in dismay.

And then her heart plummeted further.

A third guard was half marching, half supporting Aradia. Maggie looked at them wordlessly.

It wasn't like Jeanne not to fight, she thought, as the guards opened the cell door and shoved the other girls in.

The door clanged shut again, and the guards marched back out without speaking. Almost as an after-thought, one of them stuck a flare in an iron ring to give the prisoners some light.

And then they were gone.

Jeanne picked herself up off the floor, and then helped Aradia get up. 'They've got P.J. upstairs,' she said to Maggie, who was still staring. 'They said they wouldn't hurt her if we went quietly.'

Maggie opened her mouth, shut it again, and tried to swallow her heart, which was in her throat. At last she managed to speak.

'Delos said that?'

'Delos and Hunter Redfern and that witch. They're all very chummy.'

Maggie sat down on the cold bench.

'I'm sorry,' she said.

'Why? Because you're too stupidly trusting?' Jeanne said. 'You're not responsible for him.'

'I think she means because she's his soulmate,' Aradia said softly.

Jeanne stared at her as if she'd started speaking a foreign language. Maggie stared, too, feeling her eyes getting wider trying to study the beautiful features in the semi-darkness.

She felt oddly shy of this girl whom she'd called Cady and who had turned out to be something she could never have imagined.

'How did you know that?' she asked, trying not to sound tongue-tied. 'Can you just – tell?'

A smile curved the perfect lips in the shadows. 'I could tell before,' Aradia said gently, backing up quite accurately to sit on the bench. 'When you came back from seeing him the first time, but I was too foggy to really focus on anything then. I've seen a lot of it in the last few years, though. People finding their soulmates, I mean.'

'You're better, aren't you?' Maggie said. 'You sound lots more – awake.' It wasn't just that. Aradia had always had a quiet dignity, but now there was an authority and confidence about her that was new.

'The healing women helped me. I'm still weak,

though,' Aradia said softly, looking around the cell. 'I can't use any of my powers – not that breaking through walls is among them, anyway.'

Maggie let her breath out. 'Oh, well. I'm glad you're awake, anyway.' She added, feeling shy again, 'Um, I know your real name, now. Sorry about the misunderstanding before.'

Aradia put a hand – again perfectly accurately – on Maggie's. 'Listen, my dear friend,' she said, startling Maggie with both the word and the intensity of her voice, 'nobody has ever helped me more than you did, or with less reason. If you'd been one of my people, and you'd known who I was, it would have been amazing enough. But from a human, who didn't know anything about me . . .' She stopped and shook her head. 'I don't know if we'll even live through tonight,' she said. 'But if we do, and if there's ever anything the witches can do for you, all you have to do is ask.'

Maggie blinked hard. 'Thanks,' she whispered. 'I mean – you know. I couldn't just leave you.'

'I do know,' Aradia said. 'And that's the amazing thing.' She squeezed Maggie's hand. 'Whatever happens. I'll never forget you. And neither will the other witches, if I have anything to say about it.'

Maggie gulped. She didn't want to get started crying. She was afraid she wouldn't be able to stop.

Fortunately Jeanne was looking back and forth between them like someone at a tennis match. 'What's all this sappy stuff?' she demanded. 'What are you guys *talking* about?'

Maggie told her. Not just about Aradia being Maiden of the witches, but about everything she'd learned from listening to Hunter Redfern and Sylvia.

'So the witches have left the Night World,' Aradia said

quietly, when she was finished. 'They were about ready to when I left.'

'You were coming here to talk to Delos,' Maggie said.

Aradia nodded. 'We heard that Hunter had gotten some lead about the next Wild Power. And we knew he wasn't going to take any chances on letting Circle Daybreak get hold of this one.'

Jeanne was rubbing her forehead. 'What's Circle Daybreak?'

'It's the last circle of witches – but it isn't just witches. It's for humans, too, and for shapeshifters and vampires who want to live in peace with humans. And now it's for everybody who opposes the darkness.' She thought a moment and added, 'I used to belong to Circle Twilight, the . . . not-so-wicked witches.' She smiled, then it faded. 'But now there are really only two sides to choose from. It's the Daylight or the Darkness, and that's all.'

'Delos really isn't on the side of the Darkness,' Maggie said, feeling the ache in her chest tighten. 'He's just – confused. He'd join you if he didn't think it meant me getting killed.'

Aradia squeezed her hand again. 'I believe you,' she said gently.

'So, you're some kind of bigwig of the witches, huh?' Jeanne said.

Aradia turned toward her and laughed. 'I'm their Maiden, the representative of the young witches. If I live long enough, I'll be their Mother one day, and then their Crone.'

'What fun. But with all that, you still can't think of any way to get us out of here?'

Aradia sobered. 'I can't. I'm sorry. If – this isn't much use, but if I can do anything, it's only to give a prophecy.'

Maggie made an involuntary noise in her throat.

'It came while I was asleep in the healer's hut,' Aradia said apologetically. 'And it was just a thought, a concept. That if there was to be any help in this valley, it was through appealing to people's true hearts.'

Jeanne made a much louder and ruder noise than Maggie's.

'There is one more thing,' Aradia said, turning her wide unfocused eyes toward Maggie and speaking as gently as ever. 'I should have mentioned this earlier. I can tell you about your brother.'

CHAPTER

18

Maggie stared at her wildly.

'You . . . what?'

'I *should* have told you earlier,' Aradia said. 'But I didn't realize he was your brother until my mind became clearer. You're a lot alike, but I couldn't think properly to put it together.' She added, quickly and with terrible gentleness, 'But, Maggie, I don't want to get your hopes up. I don't think there's much chance he's all right.'

Maggie went still. 'Tell me.'

'He actually saved me before you ever did. I was coming to this valley, but I wasn't alone – there were several other witches with me. We didn't know where the pass was exactly, we'd only managed to get incomplete information from our spies in Hunter Redfern's household.'

Maggie controlled her breathing and nodded.

'It was Samhain evening – Halloween. We were wandering around in the general area of the pass, trying to find a spell that would reveal it. All we did was set off an avalanche.'

Maggie stopped breathing entirely. 'An avalanche?'

'It didn't hurt your brother. He was on the road, the

place we should have been, if we'd only known. But it did kill the others in my party.'

'Oh,' Maggie whispered. 'Oh, I'm sorry . . .'

'I wasn't seriously hurt, but I was completely dazed. I could feel that the others were dead, but I wasn't sure where *I* was anymore. And that was when I heard your brother shouting. He and Sylvia had heard the avalanche, of course, and they came to see if anyone was caught in it.'

'Miles would always stop to help people,' Maggie said, still almost in a whisper. 'Even if they only needed batteries or socks or things.'

'I can't tell you how grateful I was to hear him. He saved my life, I'm sure, I would have wandered around dazed until I froze. And I was so happy to recognize that the girl with him was a witch . . .' She grimaced.

'Huh,' Jeanne said, but not unsympathetically. 'I bet that didn't last.'

'She recognized me, too, immediately,' Aradia said. 'She knew what she had. A hostage to bargain with all the other witches. And to buy credit with Hunter Redfern. And of course, she knew that she could stop me from seeing Delos.'

'All she cares about is power,' Maggie said quietly. 'I heard her talking – it's all about her, and how the witches have given her a bad deal because she's not a Harman or something.'

Aradia smiled very faintly. 'I'm not a Harman by name, either. But all true witches are daughters of Hellewise Hearth-Woman – if they would just realize it.' She shook her head slightly. 'Sylvia was so excited about finding me that she couldn't resist explaining it all to your brother. And he . . . wasn't happy.'

'No,' Maggie said, burning with such fierce pride that

for a moment the cold cell seemed warm to her.

'She'd only told him before that she was taking him to some secret place where legends were still alive. But now she told him the truth about the Dark Kingdom, and how she wanted him to be a part of it. She told him that it could be theirs – their own private haven – after Delos left with Hunter Redfern. He could become a vampire or shapeshifter, whichever he liked better. They would both be part of the Night World, and they could rule here without any interference.'

Maggie lifted her hands helplessly, waving them in agitation because she couldn't find words. How stupid could Sylvia be? Didn't she know Miles at all?

'Miles wouldn't care about any of that,' she finally got out in a choked voice.

'He didn't. He told her so. And I knew right away that he was in trouble with her.' Aradia sighed. 'But there was nothing I could do. Sylvia played it very cool until they got me down the mountain. She pretended all she cared about was getting me to a doctor and telling the rangers about my friends. But once we were in her apartment, everything changed.'

'I remember her apartment,' Maggie said slowly. 'The people there were weird.'

'They were Night People,' Aradia said. 'And Sylvia's friends. As soon as we were inside she told them what to do. I was trying to explain to Miles, to see if we both could get away, but there were too many of them. He put himself in between me and them, Maggie. He said they'd have to kill him before getting to me.'

Maggie's chest felt not so much tight now as swollen, like a drum barrel full of water. She could feel her heart thudding slowly inside, and the way it echoed all through her.

She steadied her voice and said, 'Did they kill him?'

'No. Not then. And maybe not ever – but that's the part that I don't know. All I know is that they knocked him out, and then the two slave traders arrived. Bern and Gavin. Sylvia had sent for them.'

And they must have come fresh from kidnapping P.J., Maggie thought. What wonderful guys.

'They knocked *me* out. And then Sylvia bound me with spells and practised with her truth potions on me. She didn't get much information, because I didn't *have* much information. There was no army of witches coming to invade the Dark Kingdom – right now, I wish there were. And she already knew that I was coming to see Delos.'

Aradia sighed again and finished quickly. 'The truth potion poisoned me, so that for days afterwards I was delirious. I couldn't really understand what was going on around me – I just faded in and out. I knew that I was being kept in a warehouse until the weather cleared enough to take me to the valley. And I knew that Miles had already been disposed of – Sylvia mentioned that before she left me in the warehouse. But I didn't know what she had done with him – and I still don't.'

Maggie swallowed. Her heart was still thumping in that slow, heavy way. 'What I don't understand is why she had to set up a whole scenario to explain where he went. She let some rangers find her on the mountain, and she said that he fell down a crevasse. But if he was dead, why not just let him disappear?'

'I think I know the answer to that, at least,' Aradia said. 'When Miles was fighting them off he said that his roommates knew he'd gone climbing with her. He said that if he didn't come back, they'd remember that.'

Yes. It made sense. Everything made sense – except

that Maggie still didn't know what had become of him.

There was a long silence.

'Well, he was brave,' Jeanne said finally, and with unexpected seriousness. 'If he did die, he went out the right way. We just ought to hope we can do the same.'

Maggie glanced at her, trying to read the angular features in the darkness. There was no trace of mockery or sarcasm that she could see.

Well, Cady's changed into Aradia, Maiden of all the witches, and I've changed into the Deliverer – not that I've been much good at it, she thought. But I think maybe you've changed the most after all, Jeanne—

'You know, I don't even know your last name,' she said to Jeanne, so abruptly and so much off the subject that Jeanne reared back a little.

'Uh – McCartney. It was – it *is* – McCartney.' She added, 'I was fourteen when they got me. I was at the mall playing Fist of Death at the arcade. And I went to go to the bathroom, and it was down this long empty corridor, and the next thing I knew I was waking up in a slave trader's cart. And now you know everything,' she said.

Maggie put out a hand in the dimness, 'Hi, Jeanne McCartney.' She felt the cold grip of slender, callused fingers, and she shook Jeanne's hand. And then she just held on to it, and to Aradia's soft warm fingers on the other side. The three of them sat together in the dark cell, slave, human, and witch Maiden – except that we're really all just girls, Maggie thought.

'You didn't tell me one thing,' Maggie said suddenly. 'What'd they call you when you started working here? What was your job?'

Jeanne snorted. 'Second Assistant Stable Sweeper. And now you know *everything*.'

* * *

Maggie didn't think she could possibly sleep in a place like this, but after the three of them had sat quietly for a long time she found herself dozing. And when the rattle of the dungeon door startled her, she realized that she'd been asleep.

She had no idea what time it was – the flare was burning low. She could feel Aradia and Jeanne come awake beside her.

'Dinner?' Jeanne muttered.

'I just hope it's not P.J.—' Maggie began, and then broke off as firm, determined steps sounded on the stone floor of the corridor.

She recognized the stride and she stood up to meet Delos.

He stood outside the cell, the dying torchlight flickering on his dark hair, catching occasional sparks off his golden eyes. He was alone.

And he didn't waste time getting to the point.

'I came to see if you've decided to be reasonable,' he said.

'I've been reasonable from the beginning,' Maggie said quietly and completely seriously. She was searching his face and the slight link she felt between their minds at this distance, hoping to find some change in him. But although she felt turmoil that was almost anguish, she also felt the steel of his resolve.

I won't let you be killed. Nothing else matters.

Maggie felt her shoulders sag.

She turned slightly. Aradia and Jeanne were still sitting on the bench, Aradia motionless, Jeanne coiled and wary. But she could tell that they both felt this was her fight.

And they're right. If I can't do it, nobody can . . . But how?

'They're people,' she said, gesturing toward the other

girls, but watching Delos's face. 'I don't know how to get you to see that. They matter, too.'

He hardly glanced back at them. 'In the time of darkness that is coming,' he said, as carefully as if reciting a lesson, 'only the Night People will survive. The ancient forces of magic are rising. They've been asleep for ten thousand years, but they're waking up again.'

A low voice, not belligerent, but not afraid either, came from the back of the cell. 'Some of us believe that humans can learn to live with magic.'

'Some of you are idiots and fools and are going to die,' Delos said, without even looking.

He stared at Maggie. She stared back at him. They were willing each other as hard as possible to understand.

And I think he's got a stronger will, Maggie thought, as she broke the locked gaze and looked away, thumping the heel of a clenched fist against her forehead.

No. That's not right. I'm Steely Neely and I never give up.

If I tell him that some things are worth dying for . . .

But I don't think *he's* afraid to die. He's just afraid for me. And he just won't listen if I say that *I'd* rather die than see some things happen. But that's the truth. There are some things that you just can't allow to happen, whatever the cost. There are some things that have just got to be stopped.

She froze, and the cell seemed to disappear around her.

She was seeing, in her mind's eye, an equally dark and uncomfortable little cart. And her own voice was saying, *Jeanne. It's got to stop.*

Feeling very light-headed, she turned toward the bench. 'Jeanne? Come over here.'

Jeanne straightened and walked up doubtfully. She looked into Maggie's face.

Maggie looked at her and then at Delos.

'Now you show him,' she said in a voice that was like her own voice, but older and much grimmer, 'what his Night People do to slaves who try to escape. Like you showed me.'

Jeanne's expression was inscrutable. She went on staring at Maggie for a moment, then she raised her eyebrows and turned around.

She was wearing the same slave tunic she had been wearing for the last four days. She lifted it up in the same way and showed Delos her back.

He took one look and reeled back as if she'd hit him.

Maggie was braced, but even so the backlash of his shock and horror nearly swamped her. She grabbed on to the iron bars of the cell and waited it out, teeth gritted while her vision went from black to red to something like a normal grey.

'*Who did this?*' Delos managed finally, in a voice like ground glass. He was dead white, except for his eyes, which looked black in contrast. '*Who?*'

Jeanne dropped her tunic. 'I thought you didn't care about vermin.' And she walked away without answering him, leaving him speechless.

Maggie watched her sit down, then turned back.

'Some things have got to be stopped,' she said to Delos. 'Do you see what I mean? Some things you just can't let go on.'

And then she waited.

I knew he didn't know that kind of thing was happening, she thought, feeling vaguely glad in a very tired, sad, and distant way. But it's good to see it proved.

The silence stretched endlessly.

Delos was still staring at Jeanne. He had run a hand through his hair at some point; it was dishevelled and falling over his forehead. The skin of his face seemed to be stretched very tight and his eyes were burning gold.

He looked as if he'd completely lost his bearings, and he didn't know what to trust anymore.

And then he looked at Maggie.

She was still standing there, waiting and watching. Their eyes met and she realized suddenly that she'd never seen him so vulnerable – or so open.

But if there was one thing Prince Delos had, it was resolution. After another moment of helplessness, she saw him straighten his shoulders and draw himself up.

And, as usual, he got directly to the point.

'You're right,' he said simply. 'And I was wrong. There are some things that have got to be stopped.'

Maggie leaned against the bars and smiled.

'I'll get the key,' he said, and then went on, briskly planning. 'I want the three of you out of the castle, at least, before I confront Hunter.'

'You can't do it alone,' Maggie began. She should have known he'd immediately start arranging everybody's life again. 'Especially not with your power blocked—'

'There's no reason for you to be in any more danger than you have to be,' he said. 'I'll send you off with some of my people who can be trusted—'

'I'm afraid that won't be possible,' a voice said from the corridor.

It gave Maggie a horrible jolt. They were all tired, and all caught up in the moment, and none of them had seen the figure until it was almost behind Delos.

Hunter Redfern was standing there smiling. Sylvia was behind him. And behind *them*, crowded together, were armed guards.

'We've had to dispose of the few idiots who insisted on remaining loyal to you,' Hunter said amiably. His eyes were shining like the purest gold. 'The castle is now under our control. But do go on with your plans, it's very sweet to hear you trying to save each other.'

'And it's no use trying to pretend,' Sylvia added spitefully. 'We heard everything. We knew you couldn't be trusted, so we let you come down here on purpose, to see what you'd say.'

For someone who'd known Delos a while, she didn't understand him very well, Maggie thought. Maggie could have told her that pretending was the last thing that would occur to Delos. Instead he did what Maggie knew he would; he launched himself at Hunter Redfern's throat.

Delos was young and strong and very angry, but it was no contest. After Sylvia had squeaked and withdrawn, the guards all came to help Hunter. After that it was over quickly.

'Put him in with his friends,' Hunter said, brushing off his sleeves. 'It's a real pity to see my only surviving heir come to this,' he added, once Delos had been kicked and thrown into the cell. For a moment there was that note of genuine feeling in his voice that Maggie had heard before. Then the golden eyes went cold and more bitter than ever. 'I think tomorrow morning we'll have a very special hunt,' he said. 'And then there will be only three Wild Powers to worry about.'

This time, when the guards left, they took all the flares with them.

'I'm sorry,' Maggie whispered, trying to inspect Delos's bruises by touch alone. 'Delos, I'm sorry . . . I didn't know . . .'

'It doesn't matter,' he said, holding her hands. 'It would have happened eventually anyway.'

'For a vampire, you didn't put up much of a fight,' Jeanne's voice came from the back of the cell.

Maggie frowned, but Delos turned toward her and spoke without defensiveness. 'That witch bound more than just the blue fire when she put this spell on my arm,' he said. 'She took all my vampire powers. I'm essentially a human until she removes it.'

'Aradia?' Maggie said. 'Can you do anything? I mean, I know only Sylvia is supposed to be able to take the spell off, but . . .'

Aradia knelt beside them, graceful in the darkness. She touched Delos's arm gently, then sighed.

'I'm sorry,' she said. 'Even if I were at full power, there's nothing I could do.'

Maggie let out her breath.

'That's the only thing I regret,' Delos said. 'That I can't save you.'

'You have to stop thinking about that,' Maggie whispered.

She was filled with a strange resignation. It wasn't that she was giving up. But she was very tired, physically and emotionally, and there was nothing she could do right now . . .

And maybe nothing ever, she thought dimly. She felt something steadying her and realized it was Delos's arm. She leaned against him, glad of his warmth and solidity in the darkness. There was a tremendous comfort in just being held by him.

Sometimes just having fought is important, she thought. Even if you don't win.

Her eyelids were terribly heavy. It felt absolutely wonderful to close them, just for a moment . . .

She only woke up once during the night, and that was because of Delos. She could sense something in him – something in his mind. He seemed to be asleep, but very far away, and very agitated.

Was he calling my name? she wondered. I thought I heard that . . .

He was thrashing and muttering, now. Maggie leaned close and caught a few words.

'I love you . . . I did love you . . . always remember that . . .'

'Delos!' She shook him. 'Delos, what are you doing?'

He came awake with a start.

'Nothing.'

But she knew. She remembered those words – she'd heard them before she had actually met Delos on the mountain.

'It was my dream. You were . . . going back in time somehow, weren't you? And giving me that dream I had, warning me to get away from this valley.' She frowned. 'But how can you? I thought you couldn't use your powers.'

'I don't think this took vampire powers,' he said, sounding almost guilty. 'It was more – I think it was just the bond between us. The soulmate thing. I don't even know how I did it. I just – went to sleep and started dreaming about the you of the past. It was as if I was searching for you – and then I found you. I made the connection. I don't know if it's ever been done before, that kind of time travel.'

Maggie shook her head. 'But you already know it didn't work. The dream didn't change anything. I didn't leave as soon as I woke up in the cart, because I'm here. And if I *had* left, I would never have met you, and then you wouldn't have sent the dream . . .'

'I know,' he said, and his voice was tired and a bit forlorn. He sounded very young, just then. 'But it was worth a try.'

CHAPTER
19

'The hunt of your lives,' Hunter Redfern said. He was standing handsome and erect, smiling easily. The nobles were gathered around him, and Maggie even saw some familiar faces in the crowd.

That rough man from Delos's memories, the one who grabbed his arm, she thought dreamily. And the woman who put the first binding spell on him.

They were crowded in the courtyard, their faces eager. The first pale light was just touching the sky, not that the sun was visible, of course. But it was enough to turn the clouds pearly and cast an eerie, almost greenish luminescence over the scene below.

'Two humans, a witch, and a renegade prince,' Hunter proclaimed. He was enjoying himself hugely, Maggie could tell. 'You'll never have another chance at prey like this.'

Maggie gripped Delos's hand tightly.

She was frightened but at the same time strangely proud. If the nobles around Hunter were expecting their prey to cower or beg, they were going to be disappointed.

They were alone, the four of them, in a little empty space in the square. Maggie and Aradia and Jeanne in their slave clothes, Delos in his leggings and shirtsleeves. A little wind blew and stirred Maggie's hair, but otherwise they were prefectly still.

Aradia, of course, was always dignified. Just now her face was grave and sad, but there was no sign of anger or fear in it. She stood at her full height, her huge clear eyes turned toward the crowd, as if they were all welcome guests that she had invited.

Jeanne was more rumpled. Her red hair was dishevelled and her tunic was wrinkled, but there was a grim smile on her angular face and a wild battle light in her green eyes. She was one prey that was going to fight, Maggie knew.

Maggie herself was doing her best to live up to the others. She stood as tall as she could, knowing she would never be as impressive as Aradia, or as devil-may-care as Jeanne, but trying at least to look as if dying came easy to her.

Delos was magnificent.

In his shirtsleeves, he was more of a prince than Hunter Redfern would ever be. He looked at the crowd of nobles who had all promised to be loyal to him and were now thirsting for his blood – and he didn't get mad.

He tried to talk to them.

'Watch what happens here,' he said, his voice carrying easily across the square. 'And don't forget it. Are you really going to follow a man who can do this to his own great-grandson? How long is it going to be before he turns on *you*? Before you find yourselves in front of a pack of hunting animals?'

'Shut him up,' Hunter said. He tried to say it jovially, but Maggie could hear the fury underneath.

And the command didn't seem to make much sense. Maggie could see the nobles looking at each other – who was supposed to shut him up, and how?

'*There are some things that have to be stopped,*' Delos said. 'And this man is one of them. I admit it, I was willing to go along with him, but that was because I was blind and stupid. I know better now – and I knew better before he turned against me. You all know me. Would I be standing here, willing to give up my life for no reason?'

There was the tiniest stirring among the nobles.

Maggie looked at them hopefully – and then her heart sank.

They simply weren't used to thinking for themselves, or maybe they were used to thinking only *of* themselves. But she could tell there wasn't material for a rebellion here.

And the slaves weren't going to be of any help, either. The guards had weapons, they didn't. They were frightened, they were unhappy, but this kind of hunt was something they'd seen before. They knew that it couldn't be stopped.

'This girl came to us peacefully, trying to keep the alliance between witches and vampire,' Delos was saying, his hand on Aradia's shoulder. 'And in return we tried to kill her. I'm telling you right now, that by spilling her innocent blood, you're all committing a crime that will come back to haunt you.'

Another little stirring – among women, Maggie thought. Witches, maybe?

'Shut him *up*,' Hunter said, almost bellowing it.

And this time he seemed to be saying it to a specific person. Maggie followed his gaze and saw Sylvia near them.

'Some beasts have to be muzzled before they can be hunted,' Hunter said, looking straight at Sylvia. 'So take care of it now. The hunt is about to begin.'

Sylvia stepped closer to Delos, a little uneasily. He

stared back at her levelly, as if daring her to wonder what he'd do when she got nearer.

'Guards!' Hunter Redfern said, sounding tired.

The guards moved in. They had two different kinds of lances, a distant part of Maggie's mind noted. One tipped with metal – that must be for humans and witches – and one tipped with wood.

For vampires, she thought. If Delos wasn't careful, he might get skewered in the heart before the hunt even began.

'Now shut his lying mouth,' Hunter Redfern said.

Sylvia took her basket off her arm.

'In the new order after the millennium, we'll have hunts like this every day,' Hunter Redfern was saying, trying to undo the damage that his great-grandson had done. 'Each of us will have a city of humans to hunt. A city of throats to cut, a city of flesh to eat.'

Sylvia was fishing in her basket, not afraid to stand close to the vampire prince since he was surrounded by a forest of lances.

'Sylvia,' Aradia said quietly.

Sylvia looked up, startled. Maggie saw her eyes, the colour of violets.

'Each of us will be a prince—' Hunter Redfern was saying.

'Sylvia Weald,' Aradia said.

Sylvia looked down. 'Don't talk to me,' she whispered. 'You're not – I'm not one of you anymore.'

'All you have to do is follow me,' Hunter was saying.

'Sylvia Weald,' Aradia said. 'You were born a witch. Your name means the greenwood, the sacred grove. You are a daughter of Hellewise, and you will be until you die. You are my sister.'

'I am not,' Sylvia spat.

'You can't help it. Nothing can break the bond. In your deepest heart you know that. And as Maiden of all the witches, and in the name of Hellewise Hearth-Woman, I adjure you: *remove your spell from this boy.*'

It was the strangest thing – but it didn't seem to be Aradia who said it. Oh, it was Aradia's voice, all right, Maggie thought, and it was Aradia standing there. But at that moment she seemed to be fused with another form – a sort of shining aura all around her. Someone who was part of her, but more than she was.

It looked, Maggie thought dizzily, like a tall woman with hair as pale as Sylvia's and large brown eyes.

Sylvia gasped out, 'Hellewise . . .' Her own violet eyes were huge and frightened.

Then she just stood frozen.

Hunter was ranting on. Maggie could hear him vaguely, but all she could see was Sylvia, the shudders that ran through Sylvia's frame, the heaving of Sylvia's chest.

Appeal to their true hearts, Maggie thought.

'Sylvia,' she said. 'I believe in you.'

The violet eyes turned toward her, amazed.

'I don't care what you did to Miles,' Maggie said. 'I know you're confused, I know you were unhappy. But now you have a chance to make up for it. You can do something – something *important* here. Something that will change the world.'

'Rivers of blood,' Hunter was raving. 'And no one to stop us. We won't stop with enslaving the humans. The witches are our enemies now. Think of the power you'll feel when you drink their lives!'

'If you let this Wild Power be killed, *you'll* be responsible for the darkness coming,' Maggie said. 'Only you. Because you're the only one who can stop it *right now.*'

Sylvia put a trembling hand to her cheek. She looked as if she were about to faint.

'Do you really want to go down in history as the one who destroyed the world?' Maggie said.

'As Maiden of all the witches . . .' Aradia said.

And another, deeper voice seemed to follow on hers like an echo, *As Mother of all the witches . . .*

'And in the name of Hellewise . . .'

And in the name of my children . . .

'As you are a Hearth-Woman . . .'

As you are my own daughter, a true Hearth-Woman . . .

'*I adjure you!*' Aradia said, and her voice rang out in double tones so clearly that it actually stopped Hunter in mid-tirade.

It stopped everyone. For an instant there was absolutely no sound in the courtyard. Everyone was looking around to see where the voice had come from.

Sylvia was simply staring at Aradia.

Then the violet eyes shut and her entire body shivered in a sigh.

When she spoke it was on the barest whisper of breath, and only someone as close as Maggie was could have heard her.

'As a daughter of Hellewise, I obey.'

And then she was reaching for Delos's arm, and Delos was reaching toward her. And Hunter was shouting wildly, but Maggie couldn't make out the words. She couldn't make out Sylvia's words, either, but she saw her lips move, and she saw the slender pale fingers clasp Delos's wrist.

And saw the lance coming just before it pierced Sylvia's heart.

Then, as if everything came into focus at once, she realized what Hunter had been shouting in a voice so distorted it was barely recognizable.

'Kill her! Kill her!'

And that's just what they'd done, Maggie thought, her mind oddly clear, even as a wave of horror and pity seemed to engulf her body. The lance went right through Sylvia. It knocked her backward, away from Delos, and blood spurted all over the front of Sylvia's beautiful green dress.

And Sylvia looked toward Hunter Redfern and smiled. This time Maggie could read the words on her lips.

'Too late.'

Delos turned. There was red blood on his white shirt – his own, Maggie realized. He'd tried to get in the way of the guard's killing Sylvia. But now he had eyes only for his great-grandfather.

'It stops *here*!'

She had seen the blue fire before, but never like this. The blast was like a nuclear explosion. It struck where Hunter Redfern was standing with his most loyal nobles around him, and then it shot up into the sky in a pillar of electric blue. And it went on and on, from sky to earth and back again, as if the sun were falling in front of the castle.

CHAPTER
20

Maggie held Sylvia gently. Or at least, she knelt by her and tried to hold her as best she could without disturbing the piece of broken spear that was still lodged in Sylvia's body.

It was all over. Where Hunter Redfern and his most trusted nobles had been, there was a large scorched crater in the earth. Maggie vaguely recalled seeing a few people running for the hills – Gavin the slave trader had been among them. But Hunter hadn't been one of them. He had been at ground zero when the blue fire struck, and now there wasn't even a wisp of red hair to show that he had existed.

Except for Delos, there weren't any Night People left in the courtyard at all.

The slaves were just barely peeking out again from their huts.

'It's all right,' Jeanne was yelling. 'Yeah, you heard me – *it's all right*! Delos isn't dangerous. Not to us, anyway. Come on, you, get out of there – what are you doing hiding behind that pig?'

'She's good at this,' a grim voice murmured.

Maggie looked up and saw a tall, gaunt figure, with a

very small girl clasped to her side.

'Laundress!' she said. 'Oh, and P.J. – I'm so glad you're all right. But, Laundress, please . . .'

The healing woman knelt. But even as she did, a look passed between her and Sylvia. Sylvia's face was a strange, chalky colour, with shadows that looked like bruises under her eyes. There was a little blood at the corner of her mouth.

'It's no good,' she said thickly.

'She's right,' Laundress said bluntly. 'There's nothing you can do to help this one, Deliverer, and nothing I can do, either.'

'I'm not anybody's Deliverer,' Maggie said. Tears prickled behind her eyes.

'You could have fooled me,' Laundress said, and got up again. 'I see you sitting here, and I see all the slaves over there, free. You came and it happened – the prophecies were fulfilled. If you didn't do it, it's a strange coincidence.'

The look in her dark eyes, although as unsentimental as ever, made Maggie's cheeks burn suddenly. She looked back down at Sylvia.

'But she's the one who saved us,' she said, hardly aware that she was speaking out loud. 'She deserves some kind of dignity . . .'

'She's not the only one who saved us,' a voice said quietly, and Maggie looked up gratefully at Delos.

'No, you did, too.'

'That's not what I meant,' he said, and knelt where Laundress had. One of his hands touched Maggie's shoulder lightly, but the other one went to Sylvia's.

'There's only one thing I can do to help you,' he said. 'Do you want it?'

'To become a vampire?' Sylvia's head moved slightly in

a negative. 'No. And since there's wood next to my heart right now, I don't think it would work anyway.'

Maggie gulped and looked at the spear, which had cracked in the confusion when the guards ran. 'We could take it out—'

'I wouldn't live through it. Give up for once, will you?' Sylvia's head moved slightly again in disgust. Maggie had to admire her; even dying, she still had the strength to be nasty. Witches were tough.

'Listen,' Sylvia said, staring at her. 'There's something I want to tell you.' She drew a painful breath. 'About your brother.'

Maggie swallowed, braced to hear the terrible details. 'Yes.'

'It really bugged me, you know? I would put on my nicest clothes, do my hair, we would go out . . . and then he'd talk about *you*.'

Maggie blinked, utterly non-plussed. This wasn't at all what she had expected. 'He would?'

'About *his sister*. How brave she was. How smart she was. How stubborn she was.'

Maggie kept blinking. She'd heard Miles accuse her of lots of things, but never of being smart. She felt her eyelids prickle again and her throat swell painfully.

'He couldn't stand to hear a bad word about you,' Sylvia was saying. Her purple-shadowed eyes narrowed suddenly, the colour of bittersweet night-shade. 'And I hated you for that. But him . . . I liked him.'

Her voice was getting much weaker. Aradia knelt on her other side and touched the shimmering silvery hair.

'You don't have long,' she said quietly, as if giving a warning.

Sylvia's eyes blinked once, as if to say she understood. Then she turned her eyes on Maggie.

'I told Delos I killed him,' she whispered. 'But . . . I lied.'

Maggie felt her eyes fly open. Then all at once her heart was beating so hard that it shook her entire body.

'You *didn't* kill him? He's alive?'

'I wanted to punish him . . . but I wanted him near me, too . . .'

A wave of dizziness broke over Maggie. She bent over Sylvia, trying not to clutch at the slender shoulders. All she could see was Sylvia's pale face.

'Please tell me what you did,' she whispered with passionate intensity. 'Please tell me.'

'I had him . . . changed.' The musical voice was only a distant murmur now. 'Made him a shapeshifter . . . and added a spell. So he wouldn't be human again until I wanted . . .'

'What kind of spell?' Aradia prompted quietly.

Sylvia made a sound like the most faraway of sighs. 'Not anything that *you* need to deal with, Maiden . . . Just take the leather band off his leg. He'll always be a shapeshifter . . . but he won't be lost to you . . .'

Suddenly her voice swelled up a little stronger, and Maggie realized that the bruised eyes were looking at her with something like Sylvia's old malice.

'You're so smart . . . I'm sure you can figure out which animal . . .'

After that a strange sound came out of her throat, one that Maggie had never heard before. Somehow she knew without being told that it meant Sylvia was dying – right then.

The body in the green dress arched up once and went still. Sylvia's head fell back. Her eyes, the colour of tear-drenched violets, were open, staring up at the sky, but they seemed oddly flat.

Aradia put a slender dark hand on the pale forehead.

'Goddess of Life, receive this daughter of Hellewise,' she said in her soft, ageless voice. 'Guide her to the other world.' She added, in a whisper, 'She takes with her the blessing of all the witches.'

Maggie looked up almost fearfully to see if the shining figure who had surrounded Aradia like an aura would come back. But all she saw was Aradia's beautiful face, with its smooth skin the colour of coffee with cream and its compassionate blind gaze.

Then Aradia gently moved her hand down to shut Sylvia's eyes.

Maggie clenched her teeth, but it was no use. She gasped once, and then somehow she was in the middle of sobbing violently, unable to stop it. But Delos's arms were around her, and she buried her face in his neck, and that helped. When she got control of herself a few minutes later, she realized that in his arms she felt almost what she had in her dream, that inexpressible sense of peace and security. Of belonging, utterly.

As long as her soulmate was alive, and they were together, she would be all right.

Then she noticed that P.J. was pressed up against her, too, and she let go of Delos to put one arm around the small shaking body.

'You OK, kiddo?' she whispered.

P.J. sniffed. 'Yeah. I am, now. It's been pretty scary, but I'm glad it's over.'

'And you know,' Jeanne said, looking down at Sylvia with her hands on her hips, 'that's how I want to go. Taking my own way out . . . and totally pissing everybody off at the end.'

Maggie glanced up, startled, and choked. Then she gurgled. Then she shook her head, and knew that her crying spell was over. 'I don't even know why I'm like this about her. She wasn't a nice person. I wanted to kill her myself.'

'She was a person,' Delos said.

Which, Maggie decided, was about the best summing-up anybody could provide.

She realized that Jeanne and Laundress and Delos were looking at her intently, and that Aradia's face was turned her way.

'Well?' Jeanne said. '*Do* you know? Which animal your brother is?'

'Oh,' Maggie said. 'I think so.'

She looked at Delos. 'Do you happen to know what the name Gavin means? For a shapeshifter? Does it mean falcon?'

His black-lashed golden eyes met hers. 'Hawk or falcon. Yes.'

Warm pleasure filled Maggie.

'Then I know,' she said simply. She stood up, and Delos came with her as if he belonged by her. 'How can we find the falcon she had with her that first day we met? When you were out with the hunting party?'

'It should be in the mews,' Delos said.

A fascinated crowd gathered behind them as they went. Maggie recognized Old Mender, smiling and cackling, and Soaker, not looking frightened anymore, and Chamber-pot Emptier . . .

'We really need to get you guys some new names,' she muttered. 'Can you just pick one or something?'

The big girl with the moon face and the gentle eyes smiled at her shyly. 'I heard of a noble named Hortense once . . .'

'That's good,' Maggie said, after just the slightest pause. 'Yeah, that's great. I mean, comparatively.'

They reached the mews, which was a dark little room near the stable, with perches all over the walls. The falcons were upset and distracted, and the air was full of flapping wings. They all looked alike to Maggie.

'It would be a new bird,' Delos said. 'I think maybe that one. Is the falconer here?'

While everyone milled around looking for him, Jeanne edged close to Maggie.

'What I want to know is how you know. How did you even know Gavin was a shapeshifter at all?'

'I didn't – but it was sort of logical. After all, Bern was one. They both seemed to have the same kind of senses. And Aradia said that Sylvia took care of Miles down at her apartment, and Bern and Gavin were both there. So it seemed natural that maybe she made one of them pass the curse along to Miles.'

'But why did you figure Gavin was a *falcon*?'

'I don't know,' Maggie said slowly. 'I just – well, he looked a little bit like one. Sort of thin and golden. But it was more things that happened – he got away from Delos and over to the hunting party too fast to have gone by ground. I didn't really think about it much then, but it must have stuck at the back of my mind.'

Jeanne gave her a narrow sideways glance. 'Still doesn't sound like enough.'

'No, but mostly, it was that *Miles* just had to be a falcon. It had to be something small – Sylvia would hardly be carrying a pig or a tiger or a bear around with her up the mountain. And I saw her with a falcon that first day. It was something she *could* keep near her, something that she could control. Something that was an – accessory. It just all made sense.'

Jeanne made a sound like *hmph*. 'I still don't think you're a rocket scientist. I think you lucked out.'

Maggie turned as the crowd brought a little man with a lean, shrewd face to her – Falconer. 'Well, we don't know yet,' she murmured fervently. 'But I sure hope so.'

The little man held up a bird. 'This is the new one. Lady Sylvia said never to take the green band off his leg, but I've got a knife. Would you like to do it?'

Maggie held her breath. She tried to keep her hand steady as she carefully cut through the emerald green leather band, but her fingers trembled.

The leather tie fell free – and for a moment her heart stood still, because nothing happened.

And then she saw it. The rippling change as the bird's wings outstretched and thickened and the feathers merged and swam . . . and then Falconer was moving back, and a human form was taking shape . . .

And then Miles was standing there, with his auburn hair shining red gold and his handsome, wicked smile.

He gave her the thumbs-up sign.

'Hey, I knew you would rescue me. What are little sisters for?' he said, and then Maggie was in his arms.

It seemed a long time later that all the hugging and crying and explaining was done. The slaves – the *ex*-slaves, Maggie corrected herself – had begun to gather and organize themselves and make plans. Delos and Aradia had sent various messengers out of the valley.

There were still things to be settled – months' and years' worth of things. And Maggie knew that life would never be the same for her again. She would never be a normal schoolgirl.

Her brother was a shapeshifter – well, at least it was a form he could enjoy, she thought wryly. He was already talking to Jeanne about a new way of getting to the summits of mountains – with wings.

Her soulmate was a Wild Power. Aradia had already told her what that meant. It meant that they would have to be protected by the witches and Circle Daybreak until the time of darkness came and Delos was needed, so that the Night World didn't kill them. And even if they survived until the final battle . . . it was going to be a tough one.

Plus, she herself had changed forever. She felt she owed something to the people of the valley, who were still calling her the Deliverer. She would have to try to help them adjust to the Outside world. Her fate would be intertwined with theirs all her life.

But just now, everybody was talking about getting some food.

'Come into the castle – all of you,' Delos said simply.

He took Maggie's arm and started toward it. Just then P.J. pointed to the sky, and there was an awed murmur from the crowd.

'The sun!'

It was true. Maggie looked up and was dazzled. In the smooth, pearly sky of the Dark Kingdom, in exactly the place where the blue fire had flashed from the earth, there was a little clearing in the clouds. The sun was shining through, chasing away the mist, turning the trees in the surrounding hills emerald green.

And glinting off the sleek black walls of the castle like a mirror.

A place of enchantment, Maggie thought, looking around in wonder. It really is beautiful here.

Then she looked at the boy beside her. At his dark hair – just now extremely tousled – and his smooth fair skin, and his elegant bones. At the mouth which was still a bit proud and wilful, but was mostly vulnerable.

And at those fearless, brilliant yellow eyes which

looked back at her as if she were the most important thing in the universe.

'I suppose that all prophecies come true by accident,' she said slowly and thoughtfully. 'From just ordinary people trying and lucking out.'

'There is *nothing* ordinary about you,' Delos said, and kissed her.

> *One from the land of kings long forgotten;*
> *One from the hearth which still holds the spark;*
> *One from the Day World where two eyes are watching;*
> *One from the twilight to be one with the dark.*

WITCHLIGHT

For Zachary and Anna Bokulic

CHAPTER

1

The mall was so peaceful. There was no hint of the terrible thing that was about to happen.

It looked like any other shopping mall in North Carolina on a Sunday afternoon in December. Modern. Brightly decorated. Crowded with customers who knew there were only ten shopping days until Christmas. Warm, despite the chilly grey skies outside. Safe.

Not the kind of place where a monster would appear.

Keller walked past a display of 'Santa Claus Through the Ages' with all her senses alert and open. And that meant a lot of senses. The glimpses she caught of herself in darkened store windows showed a high-school-aged girl in a sleek jumpsuit, with straight black hair that fell past her hips and cool grey eyes. But she knew that anybody who watched her closely was likely to see something else – a sort of prowling grace in the way she walked and an inner glow when the grey eyes focussed on anything.

Raksha Keller didn't look quite human. Which was hardly surprising, because she wasn't. She was a shapeshifter, and if people looking at her got the impression of a half-tamed panther on the loose, they were getting it exactly right.

'OK, everybody.' Keller touched the brooch on her collar, then pressed a finger to the nearly invisible receiver in her ear, trying to tune out the Christmas music that filled the mall. 'Report in.'

'Winnie here.' The voice that spoke through the receiver was light, almost lilting, but professional. 'I'm over by Sears. Haven't seen anything yet. Maybe she's not here.'

'Maybe,' Keller said shortly into the brooch – which wasn't a brooch at all but an extremely expensive transmission device. 'But she's supposed to love shopping, and her parents said she was headed this way. It's the best lead we've got. Keep looking.'

'Nissa here.' This voice was cooler and softer, emotionless. 'I'm in the parking lot, driving by the Bingham Street entrance. Nothing to report – wait.' A pause, then the ghostly voice came back with a new tension: 'Keller, we've got trouble. A black limo just pulled up outside Brody's. They know she's here.'

Keller's stomach tightened, but she kept her voice level. 'You're sure it's them?'

'I'm sure. They're getting out – a couple of vampires and . . . something else. A young guy, just a boy really. Maybe a shapeshifter. I don't know for sure; he isn't like anything I've seen before.' The voice was troubled, and that troubled Keller. Nissa Johnson was a vampire with a brain like the Library of Congress. Something *she* didn't recognize?

'Should I park and come help you?' Nissa asked.

'No,' Keller said sharply. 'Stay with the car; we're going to need it for a fast getaway. Winnie and I will take care of it. Right, Winnie?'

'Oh, right, Boss. In fact, I can take 'em all on myself; you just watch.'

'*You* watch your mouth, girl.' But Keller had to fight the grim smile that was tugging at her lips. Winfrith Arlin was Nissa's opposite – a witch and inclined to be emotional. Her odd sense of humour had lightened some black moments.

'Both of you stay alert,' Keller said, completely serious now. 'You know what's at stake.'

'Right, Boss.' This time, both voices were subdued.

They did know.

The world.

The girl they were looking for could save the world – or destroy it. Not that she knew that . . . yet. Her name was Iliana Harman, and she had grown up as a human child. She didn't realize that she had the blood of witches in her and that she was one of the four Wild Powers destined to fight against the time of darkness that was coming.

She's about to get quite a surprise when we tell her, Keller thought.

That was assuming that Keller's team got to her before the bad guys did. But they would. They had to. There was a reason they'd been chosen to come here, when every agent of Circle Daybreak in North America would have been glad to do this job.

They were the best. It was that simple.

They were an odd team – vampire, witch, and shapeshifter – but they were unbeatable. And Keller was only seventeen, but she already had a reputation for never losing.

And I'm not about to blow that now, she thought. 'This is it, kiddies,' she said. 'No more talking until we ID the girl. Good luck.' Their transmissions were scrambled, of course, but there was no point in taking chances. The bad guys were extremely well organized.

Doesn't matter. We'll still win, Keller thought, and she

paused in her walking long enough *really* to expand her senses.

It was like stepping into a different world. They were senses that a human couldn't even imagine. Infrared. She saw body heat. Smell. Humans didn't have any sense of smell, not really. Keller could distinguish Coke from Pepsi from across a room. Touch. As a panther, Keller had exquisitely sensitive hairs all over her body, especially on her face. Even in human form, she could feel things with ten times the intensity of a real human. She could feel her way in total darkness by the air pressure on her skin.

Hearing. She could hear both higher and lower pitches than a human, and she could pinpoint an individual cough in a crowd. Sight. She had night vision like – well, like a cat's.

Not to mention more than five hundred muscles that she could move voluntarily.

And just now, all her resources were attuned to finding one teenage girl in this swarming mall. Her eyes roved over faces; her ears pricked at the sound of every young voice; her nose sorted through thousands of smells for the one that would match the T-shirt she'd taken from Iliana's room.

Then, just as she froze, catching a whiff of something familiar, the receiver in her ear came to life.

'Keller – I spotted her! Hallmark, second floor. But they're here, too.'

They'd found her first.

Keller cursed soundlessly. Aloud, she said, 'Nissa, bring the car around to the west side of the mall. Winnie, don't do anything. I'm coming.'

The nearest escalator was at the end of the mall. But from the map in her hand, she could see that Hallmark was directly above her on the upper level. And she couldn't waste time.

Keller gathered her legs under her and jumped.

One leap, straight up. She ignored the gasps – and a few shrieks – of the people around her as she sprang. At the top of her jump, she caught the railing that fenced off the upper-level walkway. She hung for a second by her hands, then pulled herself up smoothly.

More people were staring. Keller ignored them. They got out of her way as she headed for the Hallmark store.

Winnie was standing with her back to the display window of the store beside it. She was short, with a froth of strawberry curls and a pixie face. Keller edged up to her, careful to keep out of the line of sight of the Hallmark.

'What's up?'

'There's three of them,' Winnie murmured in a barely audible voice. 'Just like Nissa said. I saw them go in – and then I saw her. They've got her surrounded, but so far they're just talking to her.' She glanced sideways at Keller with dancing green eyes. 'Only three – we can take them easy.'

'Yeah, and that's what worries me. Why would they only send three?'

Winnie shrugged slightly. 'Maybe they're like us – the best.'

Keller only acknowledged that with a flicker of her eyebrows. She was edging forward centimetre by centimetre, trying to get a glimpse of the interior of the Hallmark shop between the stockings and stuffed animals in the display window.

There. Two guys in dark clothing almost like uniforms – vampire thugs. Another guy Keller could see only as a partial silhouette through a rack of Christmas ornaments.

And her. Iliana. The girl everybody wanted.

She was beautiful, almost impossibly so. Keller had seen a picture, and it had been beautiful, but now she saw that it hadn't come within miles of conveying the real girl. She had the silvery-fair hair and violet eyes that showed her Harman blood. She also had an extraordinary delicacy of features and grace of movement that made her as pretty to watch as a white kitten on the grass. Although Keller knew she was seventeen, she seemed slight and childlike. Almost fairylike. And right now, she was listening with wide, trusting eyes to whatever the silhouette guy was saying.

To Keller's fury, she couldn't make it out. He must be whispering.

'It's really her,' Winnie breathed from beside Keller, awed. 'The Witch Child. She looks just like the legends said, just like I imagined.' Her voice turned indignant. 'I can't stand to watch *them* talk to her. It's like – blasphemy.'

'Keep your hair on,' Keller murmured, still searching with her eyes. 'You witches get so emotional about your legends.'

'Well, we should. She's not just a Wild Power, she's a pure soul.' Winfrith's voice was softly awed. 'She must be so wise, so gentle, so farsighted. I can't wait to talk to her.' Her voice sharpened. 'And those thugs shouldn't be *allowed* to talk to her. Come on, Keller, we can take them fast. Let's go.'

'Winnie, don't—'

It was too late. Winnie was already moving, heading straight into the shop without any attempt at concealment.

Keller cursed again. But she didn't have any choice now. 'Nissa, stand by. Things are going to get exciting,' she snapped, touching her brooch, and then she followed.

Winnie was walking directly toward the little group of

three guys and Iliana as Keller reached the door. The guys were looking up, instantly alert. Keller saw their faces and gathered herself for a leap.

But it never happened. Before she could get all her muscles ready, the silhouette guy turned – and everything changed.

Time went into slow motion. Keller saw his face clearly, as if she'd had a year to study it. He wasn't bad-looking – quite handsome, actually. He didn't look much older than she was, and he had clean, nicely moulded features. He had a small, compact body with what looked like hard muscles under his clothes. His hair was black, shaggy but shiny, almost like fur. It fell over his forehead in an odd way, a way that looked deliberately disarrayed and was at odds with the neatness of the rest of him.

And he had eyes of obsidian.

Totally opaque.

Shiny silver-black, with nothing clear or transparent about them. They revealed nothing; they simply threw light back at anyone who looked into them. They were the eyes of a monster, and every one of Keller's five hundred voluntary muscles froze in fear.

She didn't need to hear the roar that was far below the pitch that human ears could pick up. She didn't need to see the swirl of dark energy that flared like a red-tinged black aura around him. She knew already, instinctively, and she tried to get the breath to yell a warning to Winnie.

There was no time.

She could only watch as the boy's face turned toward Winnie and power exploded out of him.

He did it so casually. Keller could tell that it was only a flick of his mind, like a horse slapping its tail at a fly. But the dark power slammed into Winnie and sent her flying through the air, arms and legs outstretched, until she hit a wall covered with display plates and clocks. The crash was tremendous.

Winnie! Keller almost yelled it out loud.

Winnie fell behind the cash register counter, out of Keller's line of sight. Keller couldn't tell if she were alive or not. The cashier who had been standing behind the counter went running and screaming toward the back of the shop. The customers scattered, some following the cashier, some dashing for the exit.

Keller hung in the doorway a second longer as they streamed out around her. Then she reeled away to stand with her back against the window of the next shop, breathing hard. There were coils of ice in her guts.

A dragon.

He was a *dragon*.

CHAPTER

2

They'd gotten a dragon.

Keller's heart was pounding.

Somehow, somewhere, the people of the Night World had found one and awakened him. And they'd paid him – bribed him – to join their side. Keller didn't even want to imagine what the price might have been. Bile rose in her throat, and she swallowed hard.

Dragons were the oldest and most powerful of the shapeshifters, and the most evil. They had all gone to sleep thirty thousand years ago – or, rather, they had been put to sleep by the witches. Keller didn't know exactly how it had been done, but all the old legends said the world had been better off since.

And now one was back.

But he might not be fully awake yet. From the glimpse she'd had, his body was still cold, not much heat radiating from it. He'd be sluggish, not mentally alert.

It was the chance of a lifetime.

Keller's decision was made in that instant. There was no time to think about it – and no need. The inhabitants of the Night World wanted to destroy the human world. And there were plenty of them to do it, vampires and dark witches and ghouls. But *this* was something in another league altogether. With a dragon on their side, the Night World would easily crush Circle Daybreak and all other forces that wanted to save the humans from the end of the world that was coming. It would be no contest.

And as for that little girl in there, Iliana the Witch Child, the Wild Power meant to help save humankind – she would get swatted like a bug if she didn't obey the dragon.

Keller couldn't let that happen.

Even as Keller was thinking it, she was changing. It was strange to do it in a public place, in front of people. It went against all her most deeply ingrained training. But she didn't have time to dwell on that.

It felt good. It always did. Painful in a nice way, like the feeling of having a tight bandage removed. A release.

Her body was changing. For a moment, she didn't feel like anything – she almost had no body. She was fluid, a being of pure energy, with no more fixed form than a candle flame. She was utterly . . . free.

And then her shoulders were pulling in, and her arms were becoming more sinewy. Her fingers were retracting, but in their place long, curved claws were extending. Her legs were twisting, the joints changing. And from the sensitive place at the end of her spine, the place that always felt unfinished when she was in human form, something long and flexible was springing. It lashed behind her with fierce joy.

Her jumpsuit was gone. The reason was simple: she wore only clothes made out of the hair of other shapeshifters. Even her boots were made of the hide of a dead shifter. Now both were being replaced by her own fur, thick black velvet with darker black rosettes. She felt complete and whole in it.

Her arms – now her front legs – dropped to the ground, her paws hitting with a soft but heavy thump. Her face prickled with sensitivity; there were long, slender whiskers extending from her cheeks. Her tufted ears twitched alertly.

A rasping growl rose in her chest, trying to escape from her throat. She held it back – that was easy and instinctive. A panther was by nature the best stalker in the world.

The next thing she did was instinctive, too. She took a moment to gauge the distance from herself to the black-haired boy. She took a step or two forward, her shoulders low. And then she jumped.

Swift. Supple. Silent. Her body was in motion. It was a high, bounding leap designed to take a victim without an instant of warning. She landed on the dark boy's back, clinging with razor claws.

Her jaws clamped on the back of his neck. It was the way panthers killed, by biting through the spine.

The boy yelled in rage and pain, grabbing at her as her weight knocked him to the ground. It didn't do any good. Her claws were too deep in his flesh to be shaken off, and her jaws were tightening with bone-crushing pressure. A little blood spilled into her mouth, and she licked it up automatically with a rough, pointed tongue.

More yelling. She was dimly aware that the vampires were attacking her, trying to wrench her away, and that the security guards were yelling. She ignored it all. Nothing mattered but taking the life under her claws.

She heard a sudden rumble from the body beneath her. It was lower in pitch than anything human ears could pick up, but to Keller it was both soft and frighteningly loud.

Then the world exploded in agony.

The dragon had caught hold of her fur just above the

right shoulder. Dark energy was crackling into her, searing her. It was the same black power he'd used against Winnie, except that now he had direct contact.

The pain was scalding, nauseating. Every nerve ending in Keller's body seemed to be on fire, and her shoulder was a solid red blaze. It made her muscles convulse involuntarily and spread a metallic taste through her mouth, but it didn't make her let go. She held on grimly, letting the waves of energy roll through her, trying to detach her mind from the pain.

What was frightening was not just the power but the sense of the dragon's mind beneath it. Keller could feel a terrible coldness. A core of mindless hatred and evil that seemed to reach back into the mists of time. This creature was old. And although Keller couldn't tell what he wanted with the present age, she knew what he was focussed on right now.

Killing her. That was all he cared about.

And of course he was going to succeed. Keller had known that from the beginning.

But not before I kill you, she thought.

She had to hurry, though. There almost certainly were other Night People in the mall. These guys could call for reinforcements, and they would probably get them.

You can't . . . make me . . . let go, she thought.

She was fighting to close her jaws. He was much tougher than a normal human. Panther jaws could crush the skull of a young buffalo. And right now, she could hear muscle crunching, but still she couldn't finish him.

Hang on . . . hang on . . .

Black pain . . . blinding . . .

She was losing consciousness.

For Winnie, she thought.

Sudden strength filled her. The pain didn't matter

anymore. She tossed her head, trying to break his neck, wrenching it back and forth.

The body underneath her convulsed violently. She could feel the little lapsing in it, the weakening that meant death was close. Keller felt a surge of fierce joy.

And then she was aware of something else. Someone was pulling her off the dragon. Not in the fumbling way the thugs had. This person was doing it skilfully, touching pressure points to make her claws retract, even getting a finger into her mouth, under the short front teeth between the lethal canines.

No! Keller thought. From her panther throat came a short, choking snarl. She lashed out with her back legs, trying to rip the person's guts out.

No. The voice didn't come in through Keller's ears. It was in her mind. A boy's voice. And it wasn't afraid, despite the fact that she was now scrabbling weakly, still trying to turn his stomach to spaghetti. It was concerned and anxious but not afraid. *Please – you have to let go.*

Even as he said it, he was pushing more pressure points. Keller was already weak. Now, all at once, she saw stars. She felt her hold on the dragon loosen.

And then she was being jerked backward, and she was falling. A hundred and ten pounds of black panther was landing on whoever had yanked her free.

Dizzy . . .

Her vision was blurred, and her body felt like rubber. She hardly had enough strength to twist her head toward the boy who had pulled her away.

Who was he? *Who?*

Her eyes met blazing green-gold ones.

Almost the eyes of a leopard. It gave Keller a jolt. But the rest of the boy was different. Dark gold hair over a rather pale and strained face with perfectly sculpted features. Human, of course. And those eyes seemed to be blazing with worry and intensity rather than animal ferocity.

Not many people could look at an angry panther like that.

She heard his mental voice again. *Are you all right?*

And then, for just an instant, something happened. It was as if some barrier had been punctured. Keller felt not just his voice but his *worry* inside her head. She could feel . . . him.

His name . . . Galen. And he's someone born to command, she thought. He understands animals. Another shapeshifter?

But I can't feel what animal he turns into. And there's no bloodthirstiness at all . . .

She didn't understand it, and her panther brain wasn't in the mood to try. It was grounded in the here and now, and all it wanted was to finish what she had started.

She wrenched her eyes away from Galen and looked at the dragon.

Yes, he was still alive but badly wounded. A little snarl worked out of Keller's throat. The vampire thugs were still alive, too; one was picking up the injured dragon and hauling him away.

'Come on!' he was shouting in a voice sharp with panic. 'Before that cat recovers—'

'But the girl!' the second vampire said. 'We don't have the girl.' He looked around. Iliana was standing by a display of porcelain figures, looking just as pale and graceful as any of them. She had both hands at her throat and seemed to be in shock.

The second vampire started toward her.

No, Keller thought. But she couldn't get her legs

to move. She could only lie helplessly and stare with burning eyes.

'No!' a voice beside her said, out loud this time. Galen was jumping up. He got between the vampire and Iliana.

The vampire grinned, a particularly nasty grin. 'You don't look like a fighter to me, pretty boy.'

It wasn't exactly true, Keller thought. Galen wasn't pretty; he was beautiful. With that gold hair and his colouring, he looked like a prince from a storybook. A rather young and inexperienced prince. He stood his ground, his expression grim and determined.

'I won't let you get to her,' he said steadily.

Who the hell is this guy? Keller thought.

Iliana, pale and wide-eyed, glanced up at him, too. And then Keller saw her . . . melt. Her drawn features softened; her lips parted. Her eyes seemed to quiver with light. She had been cowering away from the vampire, but now her body relaxed just a little.

He certainly *looked* more like a champion defender than Keller had. He was clean, for one thing. Keller's fur was matted with her own blood and the dragon's. More, she couldn't help the little raspy snarls of rage and despair she was making, showing dripping teeth in a red-stained muzzle.

Too bad he was about to be slaughtered.

He *wasn't* a fighter. Keller had seen the inside of his mind, and she knew he didn't have the tiger instinct. The vampire was going to massacre him.

The vampire started forward.

And a voice from the front of the store said, 'Hold it right there.'

CHAPTER
3

Keller turned her head quickly.

Nissa was standing there, cool and imperturbable as always, one hand on her hip. Her short mink-coloured hair wasn't even ruffled; her eyes, just a shade or two darker, were steady. And she was holding an ironwood fighting stick with a very sharp point.

Keller growled faintly in relief. You couldn't ask Nissa to be creative – her mind didn't work that way. But on any question of logic, she was unbeatable, and she had nerves of ice. More important right now, she was a superb fighter.

'If you want to play, why don't you try me?' she suggested, and whipped the fighting stick around expertly a few times. It whistled in the air, traced a complicated figure, and ended up casually across her shoulder. Then she slowly extended the point toward the vampire's throat.

'Yeah, and don't leave me out.' This voice was husky and shaky but still grim. It came from behind the counter. Winnie was pulling herself up. She coughed once, then stood straight, facing the vampire. Energy, orange and pulsating, flared between her cupped hands. Witch power.

You're alive, Keller thought. She couldn't suppress the flash of relief.

The vampire looked from one girl to the other. Then he glanced at Keller, who was lying on her side, feebly trying to make her legs work. Her tail lashed furiously.

'Come *on*!' the other vampire shouted. He was staggering under the weight of the dragon, heading for the door. 'Let's get Azhdeha out of here. He's the most important thing.'

The first vampire hesitated one instant, then whirled and plunged after his friend. Together, they hustled the dragon out into the mall.

Then they were gone.

Keller gave one final gasping snarl and felt herself change. This time, it felt more like a snail falling out of a shell. Her claws dissolved, her tail withered, and she slumped into her human body.

'Boss! Are you OK?' Winnie came toward her, a little unsteadily.

Keller raised her head, black hair falling on either side to the floor. She pushed herself up with her arms and looked around, taking stock.

The shop was quiet. It was also a wreck. Winnie's impact with the wall had knocked off most of the decorative plates and clocks there. Keller's fight with the dragon had trashed a lot of the shelves. There were shattered Christmas ornaments everywhere, little glittering fragments of scarlet and holly green and royal purple. It was like being in a giant kaleidoscope.

And outside, chaos was gathering. The entire fight had only taken about five minutes, but all the time it had been going on, people had been running away from the shop and screaming. Keller had noticed them; she had simply filed them away in her mind as unimportant. There had been nothing she could do about them.

Now, there were security officers closing in, and someone had undoubtedly called the police.

She pushed with her arms again and managed to stand up.

'Nissa.' It hurt her throat to speak. 'Where's the car?'

'Right down *there*.' Nissa pointed at the floor. 'Directly below us, parked outside the Mrs Fields cookie store.'

'OK. Let's get Iliana out.' Keller looked at the young girl with the shimmering hair who as yet hadn't spoken a single word. 'Can you walk?'

Iliana stared at her. She didn't say anything. Stunned and frightened, Keller guessed. Well, a lot had happened in the last few minutes.

'I know this all seems bizarre to you, and you're probably wondering who we are. I'll explain everything. But right now, *we have to get out of here*. OK?'

Iliana shrank a little, trembling.

Not exactly a hero, Keller thought. *Or* quick on the uptake. Then she decided she was being unfair. This girl was the Witch Child; she undoubtedly had hidden strengths.

'Come on,' Galen said to Iliana gently. 'She's right; it isn't safe here.'

Iliana looked up at him earnestly. She seemed about to agree. Then she gave a little shiver, shut her eyes, and fainted.

Galen caught her as she fell.

Keller stared.

'She's too pure to deal with this kind of stuff,' Winnie said defensively. 'Violence and all. It's not the same as being *chicken*.'

It was at that exact moment that Keller could pinpoint her first real doubts about the new Wild Power.

Galen looked down at the girl who lay in his arms like a broken lily. He looked at Keller.

'I—'

'You take her; we'll surround you and cover you,' Keller said, cutting him off. She knew her hair was in complete disarray, a wild cyclone of black around her. Her sleek jumpsuit was torn and stained, and she was clutching her right shoulder, which still throbbed in agony. But she must have looked fairly commanding, because Galen didn't say another word, just nodded and started toward the door.

Nissa led the way in front of him. Winnie and Keller fell in behind. They were ready to fight, but when the security guards with walkie-talkies saw Nissa whirling her stick, they backed away. The ordinary people, curious onlookers attracted by all the noise, not only backed away but ran. Lots of them screamed.

'Go,' Keller said. 'Fast. Go.'

They made it to Mrs Fields without anybody trying to stop them.

A girl with a red apron flattened herself against a wall as they thrust their way behind the counter and into the sanctum full of industrial-sized ovens in the back. A gangly boy dropped a tray with a clang, and lumps of raw cookie dough scattered on the floor.

And then they were bursting through the back entrance, and there was the car, a white limousine illegally parked at the curb. Nissa whipped out a key chain and pressed a button, and Keller heard the click of doors unlocking.

'Inside!' she said to Galen. He got in. Winnie ran around the car to get in the other side. Nissa slid into the driver's seat. Keller ducked in last and snapped, 'Go!' even as she slammed the door.

Nissa floored it.

The limousine shot forward like a dolphin – just as a security truck sped up from the rear. A police car appeared dead in front of them.

Nissa was an excellent driver. The limo swerved with a squeal of tyres and peeled out of another of the parking lot's exits. A second police car swung toward them as Nissa dodged traffic. This one had lights and sirens on. Nissa gunned the engine, and the limo surged forward again. A freeway on-ramp was ahead.

'Hang on,' Nissa said briefly.

They were passing the on-ramp – they were past it. No, they weren't. At the last possible second, the limo screamed into a ninety-degree turn. Everyone inside was thrown around. Keller clenched her teeth as her wounded arm hit the window. Then they were shooting up the on-ramp and onto the freeway.

With a little patter, cat's paws of rain appeared on the windshield. Keller, leaning forward to look over Nissa's shoulder, was happy. With icy rain and the low, grey fog, they probably wouldn't be chased by helicopter. The big limousine roared past the few other cars on the road and Winnie sat looking out the rear window, murmuring a spell to confuse and delay any pursuit.

'We lost them,' Nissa said. Keller sat back and let out her breath. For the first time since she'd entered the mall, she allowed herself to relax minutely.

We did it.

At the same moment, Winnie turned. She pounded the backseat with a small, hard fist. 'We did it! Keller – we got the Wild Power! We . . .' Her voice trailed off as she saw Keller's face. 'And, uh . . . I guess I disobeyed orders.' Her pounding was self-conscious now; she ducked her strawberry-blond head. 'Um, I'm sorry, Boss.'

'You'd better be,' Keller said. She held Winnie's gaze a moment, then said, 'You could have gotten yourself killed, witch – and for absolutely no good reason.'

Winnie grimaced. 'I know. I lost it. I'm sorry.' But she smiled timidly at Keller afterward. Keller's team knew how to read her.

'Sorry, too, Boss,' Nissa said from the front seat. She slanted a glance at Keller from her mink-coloured eyes. 'I wasn't supposed to leave the car.'

'But you thought we might need a little help,' Keller said. She nodded, meeting Nissa's eyes in the mirror. 'I'm glad you did.'

The faintest flush of pleasure coloured Nissa's cheeks.

Galen cleared his throat.

'Um, for the record, I'm sorry, too. I didn't mean to charge in like that in the middle of your operation.'

Keller looked at him.

He was smiling slightly, hesitantly, the way Winnie had. A nice smile. The corner of his mouth naturally quirked upward, giving him a hint of mischief in all but the most serious moments. His green-gold eyes were apologetic but hopeful.

'Yeah, who are you, guy?' Winnie was looking him up and down, her dark lashes twinkling. 'Did Circle Daybreak send you? I thought we were on this mission alone.'

'You were. I belong to Circle Daybreak, but they didn't send me. I just – well, I was outside the shop, and I couldn't just stand there . . .' His voice died. The smile died, too. 'You're really mad, aren't you?' he said to Keller.

'Mad?' She took a slow breath. '*I'm furious.*'

He blinked. 'I don't—'

'You stopped me. I could have killed him!'

His gold-green eyes opened in shock and something like remembered pain. 'He was killing *you*.'

'I know that,' Keller snarled. 'It doesn't matter what happens to me. What matters is that now he's free. Don't you understand what he is?'

Winfrith was looking sober. '*I* don't know. But he hit me with something powerful. Pure energy like what I use, but about a hundred times stronger.'

'He's a dragon,' Keller said. She saw Nissa's shoulders stiffen, but Winnie just shook her head, bewildered. 'A kind of shapeshifter that hasn't been around for about thirty thousand years.'

'He can turn into a *dragon*?'

Keller didn't smile. 'No, of course not. Don't be silly. I don't know what he can do – but a dragon is what he *is*. Inside.' Winnie suddenly looked queasy as this hit home. Keller turned back to Galen.

'And that's what you let loose on the world. It was the only chance to kill him – nobody will be able to take him by surprise like that again. Which means that everything he does after this is going to be your fault.'

Galen shut his eyes, looking dizzy. 'I'm sorry. But when I saw you – I couldn't let you die . . .'

'I'm expendable. I don't know who you are, but I'm willing to bet *you're* expendable. The only one here who *isn't* expendable is her.' Keller jerked a thumb at Iliana, who lay in a pool of pale silver-gold hair on the seat beside Galen. 'And if you think that dragon isn't going to come back and try to get her again, you're crazy. I'd have died happy knowing that I'd gotten rid of him.'

Galen's eyes were open again, and Keller saw a flicker in them at the 'don't know who you are'. But at the end, he said quietly, 'I'm expendable. And I'm sorry. I didn't think—'

'That's right! You didn't! And now the whole world is going to suffer.'

Galen shut up and sat back.

And Keller felt odd. She wasn't sorry for slapping him down, she told herself. He deserved it.

But his face was so pale now, and his expression was so bleak. As if he'd not only understood everything she'd said but expanded on it in his own mind. And the look of hurt in his eyes was almost insupportable.

Good, Keller told herself. But then she remembered the moment she'd spent inside his mind. It had been a sunlit place, warm and open, without dark corners or shadowed crevasses. Now that would be gone forever. There was going to be a huge black fissure in it, full of horror and shame. A mark he would carry for the rest of his life.

Well, welcome to the real world, Keller thought, and her throat tightened and hurt. She stared out the window angrily.

'See, it's really important that we keep Iliana safe,' Winfrith was saying quietly to Galen. He didn't ask why, and Keller had noticed before that he hadn't asked why Iliana wasn't expendable. But Winnie went on telling him anyway. 'She's a Wild Power. You know about those?'

'Who doesn't these days?' He said it almost in a whisper.

'Well, most *humans*, for one thing. But she's not just a Wild Power, she's the Witch Child. Somebody we witches have been expecting for centuries. The prophecies say she's going to unite the shapeshifters and the witches. She's going to marry the son of the First House of the shapeshifters. And then the two races will be united, and all the shapeshifters will join Circle Daybreak, and we'll be able to hold off the end of the world at the millennium.' Winnie finished out of breath. Then she cocked her strawberry-blonde head. 'You don't seem surprised. Who *are* you, guy? You didn't really say before.'

'Me?' He was still looking into the distance. 'I'm nobody, compared to you people.' Then he gave a little wry smile that didn't reach his eyes. 'I'm expendable.'

Nissa caught Keller's eye in the rearview mirror, looking concerned. Keller just shrugged. Sure, Winnie was telling this expendable guy a lot. But it didn't matter. He wasn't on the enemy side; and anyway, the enemy knew everything Winnie was saying. They had identified Iliana as the third Wild Power; the dragon proved that. They wouldn't have sent him if they hadn't been sure.

But still, it was time to get rid of this interfering boy. They certainly couldn't take him to the safe house where they were taking Iliana.

'Nobody tailing us?' Keller said.

Nissa shook her head. 'We lost them all miles ago.'

'You're sure?'

'Dead certain.'

'OK. Take any exit, and we'll drop him off.' She turned to Galen. 'I hope you can find your way home.'

'I want to go with you.'

'Sorry. We have important things to do.' Keller didn't need to add, *And you're not part of them*.

'Look.' Galen took a deep breath. His pale face was strained and exhausted, as if he'd somehow lost three days' sleep since he'd gotten into the limo. And there was something close to desperation in his eyes. 'I need to go with you. I need to help, to try and make up for what I did. I need to make it *right*.'

'You can't.' Keller said it even more brusquely than she meant to. 'You're not trained, and you're not involved in this. You're no good.'

He gave her a look. It didn't disagree with anything

she'd said, but somehow, for just an instant, it made her feel small. His greeny-gold eyes were just the opposite of the dragon's opaque ones. Keller could see for miles in them, endless light-filled fathoms, and it was all despair. A sorrow so great that it shook her.

She knew it must be costing him a lot to show her that, to hold himself so open and vulnerable. But he kept looking at her steadily.

'You don't understand,' he said quietly. 'I *have* to help you. I have to try, at least. I know I'm not in your class as a fighter. But I . . .' He hesitated. 'I didn't want to say this—'

At that moment, Iliana groaned and sat up.

Or tried to. She didn't make it all the way. She put a hand to her head and started to fall off the seat.

Galen steadied her, putting an arm around her to keep her propped up.

'Are you all right?' Keller asked. She leaned forward, trying to get a look at the girl's face. Winnie was leaning forward, too, her expression eager.

'How're you feeling? You're not really hurt, are you? You just fainted from the shock.'

Iliana looked around the limousine. She seemed utterly confused and disoriented.

Keller was struck again by the girl's unearthly beauty. This close, she looked like a flower, or maybe a girl made from flowers. She had peach-blossom skin and hazy iris-coloured eyes. Her hair was like corn silk, fine and shimmering even in this dim light. Her hands were small and graceful, fingers half curled like flower petals.

'It's such an honour to meet you,' Winnie said, and her voice turned formal as she uttered the traditional greeting of the witches. 'Unity, Daughter of Hellewise. I'm Winfrith Arlin.' She dimpled. 'But it's really "Arm-of-Lightning".

My family's an old one, almost as old as yours.'

Iliana stared at her. Then she stared at the back of Nissa's mink-coloured head. Then her eyes slid to Keller. Then she sucked in a deep breath and started screaming.

CHAPTER 4

Winnie's jaw dropped.

'You–you – *keep away from me*!' Iliana said, and then she got another breath and started shrieking again. She had good lungs, Keller thought. The shrieks were not only loud, they were piercing and pitched high enough to shatter glass. Keller's sensitive eardrums felt as if somebody were driving ice picks through them.

'All of you!' Iliana said. She was holding out both hands to fend them off. 'Just let me go! I want to go home!'

Winnie's face cleared a little. 'Yeah, I'll bet you do. But, you see, that place is dangerous. We're going to take you somewhere safe—'

'You kidnapped me! Oh, God, I've been *kidnapped*. My parents aren't rich. What do you *want*?'

Winnie looked at Keller for help.

Keller was watching their prize Wild Power grimly. She was getting a bad feeling about this girl.

'It's nothing like that.' She kept her voice quiet and level, trying to cut through the hysteria.

'You – don't you even talk to me!' Iliana waved a hand at Keller desperately. 'I *saw*. You changed. You were a monster! There was blood all over – you *killed* that man.'

She buried her face in her hands and began to sob.

'No, she didn't.' Winnie tried to put a hand on the girl's shoulder. 'And anyway, he attacked me first.'

'He did not. He didn't touch you.' The words were muffled and jerky.

'He didn't *touch* me, no, but—' Winnie broke off, looking puzzled. She tried again. 'Not with his *hands*, but—'

In the front seat, Nissa shook her head slightly, amused. 'Boss—'

'I'm way ahead of you,' Keller said grimly. This was going to be difficult. Iliana didn't even know that the dragon was the bad guy. All she had seen was a boy trying to talk with her, a girl inexplicably flying against a wall, and a panther that attacked unprovoked.

Keller's head hurt.

'I want to go *home*,' Iliana repeated. All at once, with surprising speed, she lunged for the door handle. It took Keller's animal reflexes to block her, and the movement sent another pang through her injured shoulder.

Strangely, as it happened, pain seemed to flicker across Galen's face. He reached out and gently pulled Iliana back.

'Please don't,' he said. 'I know this is all really strange, but you've got it backwards. That guy who was talking to you – *he* was going to kill you. And Keller saved you. Now they want to take you somewhere safe and explain everything.'

Iliana raised her head and looked at him. She looked for a long time. Finally, she said, still almost whispering, 'You're all right. I can tell.'

Can she? Keller wondered. Does she see something in his eyes? Or does she just see that he's a handsome blond guy with long lashes?

'So you'll go with her?' Galen asked.

Iliana gulped, sniffed, and finally nodded. 'Only if

you go, too. And only for a little while. After that, I want
to go home.'

Winfrith's face cleared – at least slightly. Keller stopped
guarding the door, but she wasn't happy.

'Straight to the safe house, Boss?' Nissa asked, swinging
the car back toward the freeway.

Keller nodded grimly. She glanced at Galen. 'You win.'
She didn't have to say the rest. The girl would only go if
he went. Which made him a member of the team.

For the present.

He smiled, very faintly. There was nothing smug in it,
but Keller looked again.

Nothing was going the way she'd planned. And Winnie
might still have faith in her Witch Child, but Keller's
doubts had crystallized.

We are all, she thought, *in very big trouble*.

And there was a dragon that might start looking for them
at any minute. How fast did dragons recover, anyway?

Big trouble, Keller thought.

The safe house was a nondescript brick bungalow. Circle
Daybreak owned it, and nobody in the Night World knew
about it.

That was the theory, anyway. The truth was that no
place was safe. As soon as they had hidden the limo in an
ivy-covered carport in back and Keller had made a phone
call to Circle Daybreak headquarters, she told Winnie to
set up wards around the house.

'They won't be all that strong,' Winnie said. 'But they'll
warn us if something tries to get in.' She bustled around,
doing witch things to the doors and windows.

Nissa stopped Keller on her own trip of inspection.
'We'd better look at your arm.'

'It's all right.'

'You can barely move it.'

'I'll manage. Go look at Winnie; she hit that wall pretty hard.'

'Winnie's OK; I already checked her. And, Keller, just because you're the team leader doesn't mean you have to be invulnerable. It's all right to accept help sometimes.'

'We don't have time to waste on *me*!' Keller went back to the living room.

She'd left Iliana in the care of Galen. She hadn't actually *told* him that, but she'd left them alone together, and now she found he'd gotten a root beer from the refrigerator and some tissues from the bathroom. Iliana was sitting huddled on the couch, holding the drink and blotting her eyes. She jumped at every noise.

'OK, now I'm going to try to explain,' Keller said, pulling up an ottoman. Winnie and Nissa quietly took seats behind her. 'I guess the first thing I should tell you about is the Night World. You don't know what that is, do you?'

Iliana shook her head.

'Most humans don't. It's an organization, the biggest underground organization in the world. It's made up of vampires and shapeshifters and witches – well, not witches now. Only a few of the darkest witches from Circle Midnight are still part of it. The rest of them have seceded.'

'Vampires . . .' Iliana whispered.

'Like Nissa,' Keller said. Nissa smiled, a rare full smile that showed sharp teeth. 'And Winnie is a witch. And you saw what I am. But we're all part of Circle Daybreak, which is an organization for everybody who wants to try to live together in peace.'

'Most of the Night People hate humans,' Winnie said. 'Their only laws are that you can't tell humans about the

Night World and that you can't fall in love with them.'

'But even humans can join Circle Daybreak,' Keller said.

'And that's why you want me?' Iliana looked bewildered.

'Well, not exactly.' Keller ran a hand over her forehead. 'Look, the main thing you need to know about Circle Daybreak is what it's trying to do right now. What it's trying to keep from happening.' Keller paused, but there was no easy way to say it. 'The end of the world.'

'The end of the *world*?'

Keller didn't smile, didn't blink, just waited it out while Iliana sputtered, gasped, and looked at Galen for some kind of sanity. When she finally ran down, Keller went on.

'The millennium is coming. When it gets here, a time of darkness is going to begin. The vampires *want* it to happen; they want the darkness to wipe out the human race. They figure that then they'll be in charge.'

'The end of the world,' Iliana said.

'Yes. I can show you the evidence if you want. There are all sorts of things happening right now that prove it. The world is falling into disorder, and pretty soon it's going to fall apart. But the reason we need you is because of the prophecies.'

'I want to go home.'

I bet you do, Keller thought. For a moment, she felt complete sympathy for the girl. 'Like this.' She quoted:

'Four to stand between the light and the shadow,
Four of blue fire, power in their blood.
Born in the year of the blind Maiden's vision;
Four less one and darkness triumphs.'

'I really don't know what you're *talking about*—'

'Four Wild Powers,' Keller went on relentlessly. 'Four people with a special gift, something nobody else has. Each one of them born seventeen years ago. If Circle Daybreak can get all four of them to work together – and *only* if Circle Daybreak can get them to work together – then we can hold off the darkness.'

Iliana was shaking her head, edging away even from Galen. Behind Keller, Winnie and Nissa stood up, closing in. They faced her in a solid block, unified.

'I'm sorry,' Keller said. 'You can't escape it. You're part of it. You're a Wild Power.'

'And you should be happy,' Winnie burst out, unable to contain herself any longer. 'You're going to help save the world. You know that thing I did back in the Hallmark shop? With the orange fire?' She cupped her hands. 'Well, you're full of *blue* fire. And that's so much stronger – nobody even knows what it can do.'

Iliana put out her hands. 'I'm sorry. I *really* am. But you guys are nuts, and you've got the wrong person. I mean, I don't know, maybe you're not completely nuts. The things that happened back at that store . . .' She stopped and gulped. 'But I don't have anything to do with it.' She shut her eyes, as if that would bring the real world into focus. 'I'm not any Wild Power,' she said more firmly. 'I'm just a human kid—'

'Actually, no,' Nissa said.

'You're a lost witch,' Winnie cut in. 'You're a *Harman*. A Hearth-Woman. That's the most famous family of witches; they're like – they're royalty. And you're the most famous of all of them. You're the Witch Child. We've been waiting for you.'

Keller shifted. 'Winnie, maybe we don't need to tell her all of this right now.'

But Winnie was racing on. 'You're the one who's going

to unite the shapeshifters and the witches. You're going to marry a prince of the shapeshifters, and then we're all going to be like this.' She held up two intertwined fingers.

Iliana stared at her. 'I'm only seventeen. I'm not marrying *anybody*.'

'Well, you can do a promise ceremony; that's binding. The witches would accept it, and I think the shapeshifters would.' She glanced at Keller for confirmation.

Keller pinched the bridge of her nose. 'I'm just a grunt; I can't speak for the 'shifters.'

Winnie was already turning back to Iliana, her curls shaking with earnestness. 'Really, you know,' she said, 'it's incredibly important. Right now, the Night World is split. Vampires on one side, witches on the other. And the shapeshifters – well, they could go either way. And *that's* what could determine the battle.'

'Look—'

'The witches and the shapeshifters haven't been allies for thirty thousand—'

'*I don't care!*'

Full-blown hysteria.

It was about as scary as a six-week-old kitten hissing, but it was the best raving Iliana could manage. Both her small fists were clenched, and her face and throat were flushed.

'I don't care about the shapeshifters *or* the witches. I'm just a normal kid with a normal life, and I want to go *home*! I don't know anything about fighting. Even if I believed all this stuff, I couldn't help you. I hate PE; I'm totally uncoordinated. I get sick when I see blood. And—' She looked around and made an inarticulate sound of exasperation. 'And *I lost my purse*.'

Keller stood up. 'Forget your purse.'

'It had my mum's credit card in it. She's going to *kill me* if I come home without that. I just – where's my purse?'

'Look, you little idiot,' Keller said. 'Worry about your mother, not about her credit card.'

Iliana backed up a step. Even in the middle of a hysterical fit, she was beautiful beyond words. Strands of angel-fine hair stuck to her flushed, wet cheeks. Her eyes were dark as twilight, shadowed by heavy lashes – and they wouldn't quite meet Keller's.

'I don't know what you mean.'

'Yes, you do. Where's your mum going to be when the end of the world comes? Is a credit card going to save her then?'

Iliana was in a corner now. Keller could hear both Nissa and Winnie making warning noises. She knew herself that this was the wrong way to get someone on their side. But patience wasn't one of Keller's great virtues. Neither was keeping her temper.

'Let's see,' Galen said, and his voice was like cool water flowing through the room. 'Maybe we could take a little break—'

'I don't need advice from you,' Keller snapped. 'And if this little idiot is too stupid to understand that she can't turn her back on this, we have to show her.'

'I'm not an idiot!'

'Then you're just a big baby? Scared?'

Iliana sputtered again. But there was unexpected fire in her violet eyes as she did it. She was looking right at Keller now, and for a moment Keller thought that there might be a breakthrough.

Then she heard a noise.

Her ears picked it up before either Winnie's or Nissa's. A car on the street outside.

'Company,' Keller said. She noticed that Galen had stiffened. Had he heard it?

Winnie was moving to stand behind the door; Nissa slipped as quietly as a shadow to the window. It was dark outside now, and vampire eyes were good at night.

'Blue car,' Nissa said softly. 'Looks like them inside.'

'Who?' Iliana said.

Keller gestured at her to be quiet. 'Winnie?'

'I have to wait until they cross the wards.' A pause, then she broke into a smile. 'It's her!'

'Who?' Iliana said. 'I thought nobody was supposed to know we were here.'

Good thinking. Logical, Keller thought. 'This is someone I called. Someone who came all the way from Nevada and has been waiting to see you.' She went to the door.

It took a few minutes for the people in the car to get out – they moved slowly. Keller could hear the crunch of footsteps and the sound of a cane. She opened the door.

There was no light outside; the figures approaching were in shadow until they actually reached the threshold.

The woman who stepped in was old. So old that anyone's first thought on first seeing her was *How can she still be alive?* Her skin was creased into what seemed like hundreds of translucent folds. Her hair was pure white and almost as fine as Iliana's, but there wasn't much of it. Her already tiny figure was stooped almost double. She walked with a cane in one hand and the other tucked into the arm of a nondescript young man.

But the eyes that met Keller's were anything but senile. They were bright and almost steely, grey with just the faintest touch of lavender.

'The Goddess's bright blessings on you all,' she said, and smiled around the room.

It was Winnie who answered. 'We're honoured by your presence – Grandma Harman.'

In the background, Iliana demanded plaintively for the third time, 'Who?'

'She's your great-great-aunt,' Winnie said, her voice quiet with awe. 'And the oldest of the Harmans. She's the Crone of all the Witches.'

Iliana muttered something that might have been, 'She looks like it.'

Keller stepped in before Winnie could attack her. She introduced everyone. Grandma Harman's keen eyes flickered when Galen's turn came, but she merely nodded.

'This is my apprentice and driver, Toby,' she told them. 'He goes everywhere with me, so you can speak freely in front of him.'

Toby helped her to the couch, and everyone else sat, too – except Iliana, who stubbornly stayed in her corner.

'How much have you told her?' Grandma Harman asked.

'Almost everything,' Keller said.

'And?'

'She – isn't quite certain.'

'I *am* certain,' Iliana piped up. 'I want to go home.'

Grandma Harman extended a knobby hand toward her. 'Come here, child. I want to take a look at my great-great-niece.'

'I'm not your great-great-niece,' Iliana said. But with those steely-but-soft eyes fixed on her, she took one step forward.

'Of course you are; you just don't know it. Do you realize, you're the image of my mother when she was your age? And I'll bet your great-grandmother looked like her, too.' Grandma Harman patted the couch beside her. 'Come here. I'm not going to hurt you. My name is Edgith, and your great-grandmother was my little sister, Elspeth.'

Iliana blinked slowly. 'Great-grandmother Elspeth?'

'It was almost ninety years ago that I last saw her. It was just before the First World War. She and our baby brother, Emmeth, were separated from the rest of the family. We all thought they were dead, but they were being raised in England. They grew up and had children there, and eventually some of those children came to America. Without ever suspecting their real heritage, of course. It's taken us a long time to track down their descendants.'

Iliana had taken another involuntary step. She seemed fascinated by what the old woman was saying. 'Mum always talked about Great-grandmother Elspeth. She was supposed to be so beautiful that a prince fell in love with her.'

'Beauty has always run in our family,' Grandma Harman said carelessly. 'Beauty beyond comparison, ever since the days of Hellewise Hearth-Woman, our foremother. But that isn't the important thing about being a Harman.'

'It isn't?' Iliana said doubtfully.

'No.' The old woman banged her cane. 'The important thing, child, is the art. Witchcraft. You are a witch, Iliana; it's in your blood. It always will be. And you're the gift of the Harmans in this last fight. Now, listen carefully.' Staring at the far wall, she recited slowly and deliberately:

'One from the land of kings long forgotten;
One from the hearth which still holds the spark;
One from the Day World where two eyes are
   watching;
One from the twilight to be one with the dark.'

Even when she had finished, the words seemed to hang in the air of the room. No one spoke.

Iliana's eyes had changed. She seemed to be looking inside herself, at something only she could see. It was as if deeply buried memories were stirring.

'That's right,' Grandma Harman said softly. 'You can feel the truth of what I'm telling you. It's all there, the instinct, the art, if you just let it come out. Even the courage is there.'

Suddenly, the old woman's voice was ringing. 'You're the spark in the poem, Iliana. The hope of the witches. Now, what do you say? Are you going to help us beat the darkness or not?'

CHAPTER
5

Everything hung in the balance, and for a moment Keller thought that they had won. Iliana's face looked different, older and more clearly defined. For all her flower-petal prettiness, she had a strong little chin.

But she didn't say anything, and her eyes were still hazy.

'Toby,' Grandma Harman said abruptly. 'Put in the disc.'

Her apprentice went to the DVD player. Keller stared at the disc in his hand, her heart picking up speed.

A disc. Could that be what she thought it was?

'What you're about to see is – well, let's just say it's very secret,' Grandma Harman said to Iliana as the apprentice fiddled with the controls. 'So secret that there's only one recording of it, and that stays locked up in Circle Daybreak headquarters at all times. I'm the only person I trust to carry it around. All right, Toby, play it.'

Iliana looked at the TV apprehensively. 'What is it?'

The old woman smiled at her. 'Something the enemy would really like to see. It's a record of the other Wild Powers – in action.'

The first scene on the disc was live news coverage of a

fire. A little girl was trapped in a second-storey apartment, and the flames were getting closer and closer. Suddenly, the recording went into slow motion, and a blue flash lit the screen. When the flash died away, the fire was out.

'The blue fire,' Grandma Harman said. 'The first Wild Power we found did that, smothered those ordinary flames with a single thought. That's just one example of what it can do.'

The next scene was of a dark-haired young man. This one was obviously deliberately filmed; the boy was looking directly into the camera. He took a knife from his belt and very coolly made a cut on his left wrist. Blood welled up in the wound and dripped to the ground.

'The second Wild Power,' Grandma Harman said. 'A vampire prince.'

The boy turned and held out the arm that was bleeding. The camera focussed on a large boulder about thirty feet away. And then the tape went into slow motion again, and Keller could actually *see* the blue fire shoot out from his hand.

It started as a burst, but what followed was a steady stream. It was so bright that the camera couldn't deal with it; it bleached out the rest of the picture. But when it hit the rock, there was no doubt about what happened.

The two-ton boulder exploded into gravel.

When the dust settled, there was only a charred crater in the ground. The dark-haired boy looked back at the camera, then shrugged and targeted another boulder. He wasn't even sweating.

Keller's breath came out involuntarily. Her heart was pounding, and she knew her eyes were glittering. She saw Galen glance sideways at her but ignored him.

Power like *that*, she thought. I never really imagined it. If I had that power, the things I could do with it . . .

Before she could help herself, she had turned to Iliana.

'Don't you see? That's what you'll bring to our side if you choose to fight with us. That's what's going to give us a *chance* against them. You have to do it, don't you understand?'

It was the wrong thing to say. Iliana's reaction to the DVD had been completely different from Keller's own. She was staring at the TV as if she were watching open-heart surgery. *Unsuccessful* open-heart surgery.

'I don't . . . I can't do anything like that!'

'Iliana—'

'And I don't want to! No. Look.' A veil seemed to have dropped down behind Iliana's beautiful eyes. She was facing Keller, but Keller wondered if she actually saw anything. She spoke rapidly, almost frantically.

'You said you had to talk to me, so I listened. I even watched your – your special effects stuff.' She waved a hand at the screen where the boy was blowing up more boulders. 'But now it's over, and I'm going home. This is all – I don't know. It's all too *weird* for me! I'm telling you, I can't *do* that kind of thing. You're looking at the wrong person.'

'We looked at all your cousins first,' Grandma Harman said. 'Thea and Blaise. Gillian, who was a lost witch like yourself. Even poor Sylvia, who was seduced over to the enemy side. But it was none of them. Then we found you.' She leaned forward, trying to hold Iliana with her eyes. 'You have to accept it, child. It's a great responsibility and a great burden, but no one else can do it for you. Come and take your place with us.'

Iliana wasn't listening.

It was as simple as that. Keller could almost see the words bouncing off her. And her eyes . . .

Not a veil, Keller thought. A *wall* had dropped down. It

had slammed into place, and Iliana was hiding behind it.

'If I don't get home soon, my mother's going to go crazy. I just ran out for a few minutes to get some gold stretchy ribbon – you know, the kind that has like a rubber band inside? It seems like I'm always looking for that. We have some from last year, but it's already tied, and it won't fit on the presents I'm doing.'

Keller stared at her, then cast a glance heavenward. She could see the others staring, too. Winnie's mouth was hanging open. Nissa's eyebrows were in her hair. Galen looked dismayed.

Grandma Harman said, 'If you won't accept your responsibilities as a Wild Power, will you at least do your duty as the Witch Child? The winter solstice is next Saturday. On that night, there's going to be a meeting of the shapeshifters and the witches. If we can show them a promise ceremony between you and the son of the First House of the shapeshifters, the shapeshifters will join us.'

Keller half expected Iliana to explode. And in the deepest recesses of her own heart, she wouldn't really have blamed her. She could understand Iliana losing it and saying, *What do you think you're doing, waltzing in and trying to hitch me up to some guy I've never met? Asking me to fight is one thing, but ordering me to marry – giving me away like some object – that's another.*

But Iliana didn't say anything like that. She said, 'And I've still got so many present to wrap, and I'm not anywhere near done shopping. Plus, this week at school is going to be completely crazy. And Saturday, that's the night Jaime and Brett Ashton-Hughes are having their birthday party. I can't miss that.'

Keller lost it.

'What is wrong with you? Are you deaf or just stupid?'

Iliana talked right over her. 'They're twins, you know.

And I think Brett kind of likes me. Their family is really rich, and they live in this big house, and they only invite a few people to their parties. All the girls have crushes on him. Brett, I mean.'

'No,' Keller answered her own question. 'You're just the most selfish, spoiled little brat I've ever met!'

'Keller,' Nissa said quietly. 'It's no good. The harder you push her, the more she goes into denial.'

Keller let out her breath. She knew that it was true, but she had never been more frustrated in her life.

Grandma Harman's face suddenly looked very old and very tired. 'Child, we can't force you to do anything. But you have to realize that we're not the only ones who want you. The other side knows about you, too. They won't give up, and they *will* use force.'

'And they've got a lot of force.' Keller turned to the old woman. 'I need to tell you about that. I didn't want to say it on the phone, but they already tried to get Iliana once today. We had to fight them at the mall.' She took a deep breath. 'And they had a dragon.'

Grandma Harman's head jerked up. Those steely lavender-grey eyes fixed on Keller. 'Tell me.'

Keller told everything. As she did, Grandma Harman's face seemed to get older and older, sinking into haggard lines of worry and sadness. But all she said at the end was, 'I see. We'll have to try to find out how they got him, and what exactly his powers are. I don't think there's anybody alive today who's an expert on – those creatures.'

'They called him Azhdeha.'

'Hmm – sounds Persian.'

'It is,' Galen said. 'It's one of the old names for the constellation Draco. It means "man-eating serpent".'

Keller looked at him in surprise. He had been sitting quietly all this time, listening without interrupting. Now he was leaning forward, his gold-green eyes intense.

'The shapeshifters have some old scrolls about dragons. I think you should ask for them. They might give some idea about what powers they have and how to fight them. I saw the scrolls once, but I didn't really study them; I don't think anybody has.'

He'd seen the ancient scrolls? Then he *was* a shapeshifter, after all. But why hadn't she been able to sense an animal form for him?

'Galen—' Keller began, but Grandma Harman was speaking.

'It's a good idea. When I get them, I'll send copies to you and Keller. He's one of your people, after all, and you may be able to help figure out how to fight him.'

Keller wanted to say indignantly that he wasn't any connection to her, but of course it wasn't true. The dragons had ruled the shapeshifters, once. Their blood still ran in the First House, the Drache family that ruled the shapeshifters today. Whatever that monster was, he *was* one of her people.

'So it's decided. Keller, you and your team will take Iliana home. I'll go back to Circle Daybreak and try to find out more about dragons. Unless . . .' She looked at Iliana. 'Unless this discussion has changed your mind.'

Iliana, unbelievably, was still prattling, having a conversation about presents with nobody in particular. It was clear that her mind hadn't changed. What wasn't clear to Keller was whether she *had* a mind.

But Keller had other things to worry about.

'I'm sorry – but you're not serious, are you? About taking her home?'

'Perfectly serious,' Grandma Harman said.

'But we *can't*.'

'We can, and we have to. You three girls will be her

bodyguards – and her friends. I'm hoping that you can persuade her to accept her responsibility by Saturday night at midnight, when the shapeshifters and the witches convene. But if not . . .' Grandma Harman bowed her head slightly, leaning on her cane. She was looking at Iliana. 'If not,' she said in a barely audible voice, 'you'll just have to protect her for as long as you can.'

Keller was choking. 'I don't see how we can protect her at all. With all respect, ma'am, it's an insane idea. They have to know where her house is by now. Even if we stick beside her twenty-four hours a day – and I don't see how we can even do *that*, with her family around—'

The white head came up, and there was even a faint curve to the old woman's lips. 'I'll take care of that. I'll have a talk with her mother – young Anna, Elspeth's granddaughter. I'll introduce myself and explain that her daughter's "long-lost cousins" have come to visit for Christmas.'

And undoubtedly do something witchy to Anna's mind, Keller thought. Yeah, after that they'd be accepted, although none of them looked a bit like Iliana's cousins.

'And then *I* will put up wards around that house.' There was a flash like silver lightning in Grandma Harman's eyes as she said it. 'Wards that will hold against anything from the outside. As long as nobody inside disturbs them, you'll be safe.' She cocked an eyebrow at Keller. 'Satisfied?'

'I'm sorry – no. It's still too dangerous.'

'Then what would you suggest we do?'

'Kidnap her,' Keller said instantly. She could hear Iliana stop babbling in the background; she wasn't gaining any Brownie points there. She bulldozed on grimly. 'Look, I'm just a grunt; I obey orders. But I think that she's too important for us to just let her run around loose where *they* might get hold of her. I think we should take her to a Circle Daybreak enclave like the ones where the other Wild Powers are. Where we can protect her from the enemy.'

Grandma Harman looked her in the eye. 'If we do that,' she said mildly, 'then we *are* the enemy.'

There was a pause. Keller said, 'With all respect, ma'am—'

'I don't want your respect. I want your obedience. The leaders of Circle Daybreak made a firm decision when this whole thing started. If we can't convince a Wild Power by reasoning, we will not resort to force. So your orders are to take your team and stay with this child and protect her as long as you can.'

'Excuse me.' It was Galen. The others had been sitting and watching silently. Nissa and Winnie were too smart to get involved in an exchange like this, but Keller could see that they were both unhappy.

'What is it?' Grandma Harman asked.

'If you don't mind, I'd like to go with them. I could be another "cousin". It would make four of us to watch over her – better odds.'

Keller thought she might have an apoplexy.

She was so mad, she couldn't even get words out. While she was choking uselessly, Galen was going on. His face still looked pale and strained, like a young soldier coming back from battle, but his dark gold hair was shining, and his eyes were steady. His whole attitude was one of earnest pleading.

'I'm not a fighter, but maybe I can learn. After all, that's what we're asking Iliana to do, isn't it? Can we ask anything of her that we're not ready to do ourselves?'

Grandma Harman, who had been frowning, now looked him up and down appraisingly. 'You have a fine young mind,' she said. 'Like your father's. He and your mother were both strong warriors, as well.'

Galen's eyes darkened. 'I'd hoped I wouldn't have to be one. But it looks like we can't always choose.'

Keller didn't know what they were talking about or why the Crone of all the Witches knew the parents of this guy she'd met in a mall. But she'd finally gotten the obstruction out of her throat.

'No way!' she said explosively. She was on her feet now, too, black hair flying as she looked from Grandma Harman to Galen. 'I mean it. There is *no way* I am taking this boy back with us. And you may be the leader of the witches, ma'am, but, no offence intended, I don't think you have the authority to make me. I'd have to hear it from the leaders of Circle Daybreak themselves, from Thierry Descouedres or Lady Hannah. Or from the First House of the shapeshifters.'

Grandma Harman gave an odd snort. Keller ignored it. 'It's not just that he's not a fighter. He's not *involved* in this. He doesn't have any part in it.'

Grandma Harman looked at Galen, not entirely approvingly. 'It seems you've been keeping secrets. Are you going to tell her, or shall I?'

'I—' Galen turned from her to Keller. 'Listen. I'm sorry – I should have mentioned it before.' His eyes were embarrassed and apologetic. 'It just – there just didn't seem to be a right time.' He winced. 'I wasn't in that mall today accidentally. I came by to look for Iliana. I wanted to see her, maybe get to know her a little.'

Keller stared at him, not breathing. 'Why?'

'Because . . .' He winced again. 'I'm Galen Drache . . . of the First House of the shapeshifters.'

Keller blinked while the room revolved briefly.

I should have known. I should have *realized*. That's why

he seemed like a shapeshifter, but I couldn't get any animal sense from him.

Children of the First House weren't born connected to any particular animal. They had power over all animals, and they were allowed to choose when they became adults which one they would shift into.

It also explained how he'd known which pressure points to use to get her off the dragon. And his telepathy – children of the First House could connect to any animal mind.

When the room settled back into place, Keller realized that she was still standing there, and Galen was still looking at her. His eyes were almost beseeching.

'I should have explained,' he said.

'Well, of course, it was your choice,' Keller said stiffly. There was an unusual amount of blood in her cheeks; she could feel it burning. She went on, 'And, naturally, I'm sorry if anything I've said has given offence.'

'Keller, please don't be formal.'

'Let's see, I haven't greeted you properly, or given you my obedience.' Keller took his hand, which was well made, long-fingered, and cold. She brought it to her forehead. 'Welcome, Drache, son of the First House of the shapeshifters. I'm yours to command, naturally.'

There was a silence. Keller dropped Galen's hand. Galen looked miserable.

'You're *really* mad now, aren't you?' he observed.

'I wish you every happiness with your new bride,' Keller said through her teeth.

She couldn't figure out exactly *why* she was so mad. Sure, she'd been made a fool of, and now she was going to have to take responsibility for an untrained boy who couldn't even shapeshift into a mouse. But it was more than that.

He's going to marry that whiny little flower in the corner, a voice in Keller's head whispered. He *has* to marry her, or at least go through a promise ceremony that's just as binding as marriage. If he doesn't, the shapeshifters will never join with the witches. They've said so, and they'll never back down. And if they don't join with the witches . . . everything you've ever worked for is finished.

And your job is to persuade the flower to do her duty, the voice continued brightly. That means you've got to convince her to marry him. Instead of eating her.

Keller's temper flared. *I don't want to eat her*, she snapped back at the voice. *And I don't care who this idiot marries. It's none of my business.*

She realized that the room was still silent, and everyone was watching Iliana and Galen. Iliana had stopped prattling. She was looking at Galen with huge violet eyes. He was looking back, strained and serious.

Then he turned to Keller again. 'I'd still like to help, if you'll let me come.'

'I told you, I'm yours to command,' Keller said shortly. 'It's your decision. I'd like to mention that it just makes things a little harder on my team. Now we're going to have to look out for you as well as her. Because, you see, you're *not* expendable after all.'

'I don't want you to look out for me,' he said soberly. 'I'm not important.'

Keller wanted to say, Don't be an idiot. No you, no promise ceremony, no treaty. It's as simple as that. We've *got* to protect you. But she'd already said more than enough.

Toby was retrieving the DVD from the DVD player. Grandma Harman was making getting-ready-to-rise motions with her cane. 'I think we've stayed here long enough,' she said to Keller.

Keller nodded stiffly. 'Would you like to come in the limo? Or would you rather follow us to her house?'

Grandma Harman opened her mouth to answer, but she never got the chance. Keller's ears caught the sound of movement outside just before the living room window shattered.

CHAPTER
6

It was a full-force invasion. Even before the echoes of breaking glass had died, figures in black uniforms were swarming through the window.

Dark ninjas, Keller thought. An elite group made up of vampires and shapeshifters, the Night World experts at sneaking and killing.

Keller's mind, which had been roiling in clouds of stifled anger, was suddenly crystal clear.

'Nissa, take her!' she shouted. It was all she needed to say. Nissa grabbed Iliana. It didn't matter that Iliana was screaming breathlessly and too shocked to want to go anywhere. Nissa was a vampire and stronger than a human Olympic weight lifter. She simply picked Iliana up and ran with her toward the back door.

Without being told, Winfrith followed close behind, orange energy already sizzling between her palms. Keller knew she would provide good cover – Winnie was a fighting witch. She made full use of the new powers that all the Night People were developing as the millennium got closer. As one of the ninjas lunged after them, she let loose with a blast of poppy-coloured energy that knocked him sideways.

'Now you!' Keller shouted to Galen, trying to hustle him into the hallway without turning from the ninjas. She hadn't changed and didn't want to if she could avoid it. Changing took time, left you vulnerable for the few seconds that you were between forms. Right now seconds counted.

Galen got a few steps down the hall, then stopped. 'Grandma Harman!'

I knew it, Keller thought. He's a liability.

The old woman was still in the living room, standing with her feet braced apart, cane ready. Her apprentice, Toby, was in front of her, working up some witch incantation and tossing energy. They were right in the flow of the ninjas.

Which was as it ought to be. Keller's mind had clicked through the possibilities right at the beginning and had come to the only reasonable conclusion.

'We have to leave her!'

Galen turned to her, his face lit by the multicoloured energy that was flying around them. '*What?*'

'She's too slow! We have to protect you and Iliana. Get moving!'

His features were etched in shock. 'You're joking. Just wait here – *I'll* bring her.'

'No! Galen—'

He was already running back.

Keller cursed.

'Go on!' she yelled to Nissa and Winnie, who were at the entrance to the kitchen, where the back door was. 'Take the limo if you can get to it. Don't wait for us!'

Then she turned and plunged into the living room.

Galen was trying to shield Grandma Harman from the worst of the energy being exchanged. Keller gritted her teeth. This group of ninjas was only the first wave. They were here to breach the wards and make an opening for whatever was going to follow.

Which could be a dragon.

The ninjas hadn't finished their job, though. Most of the wards were holding, and the one that had fallen was on a small window. The dark figures could only squirm in one at a time. The house shook as whoever was outside slammed power at it, trying to break a bigger entrance.

Faintly, Keller heard an engine rev up outside. She hoped it was the limo.

Galen was pulling at Grandma Harman. Toby was grappling hand-to-hand with a ninja.

Keller batted a couple of the sneaks out of her way. She wasn't trying to kill them, just put them out of commission. She had almost reached Galen.

And then she heard the rumbling.

Only her panther ears could have picked it up. Just as the first time when she'd heard it, it was so deep that it seemed both soft and frighteningly loud. It shook her to her bones.

In a flash, she knew what was coming.

And there was no time to think about what to do.

Galen seemed to have sensed it, too. Keller saw him looking at the roof just above the door. Then he turned toward Grandma Harman, shouting.

After that, everything happened at once. Galen knocked the old woman down and fell on top of her. At the same time, Keller sprang and landed on top of both of them.

She was changing even as she did it. Changing and spreading herself out, trying to make herself as wide and flat as possible. A panther rug to cover them.

The brick wall exploded just as the window had, only louder.

Shattered with Power, Keller thought. The dragon had recovered . . . fast.

And then it was raining bricks. One hit Keller in the leg, and she lashed her tail in fury. Another struck her back, and she felt a deep pain. Then one got her in the head, and she saw white light. She could hear Galen shouting under her. It seemed to be her name.

Then nothing.

Something wet touched her face. Keller hissed automatically, pawing at it in annoyance.

'Lemme 'lone.'

'Boss, wake up. Come on, it's morning already.'

Keller opened heavy eyes.

She was dreaming. She had to be. Either that, or the afterlife was full of teenage girls. Winnie was bending over her with a dripping washcloth, and Nissa was peering critically over her shoulder. Behind Nissa was Iliana's anxious little heart-shaped face, her hair falling like two shimmering curtains of silvery-starlight gold on either side.

Keller blinked. 'I was sure I was dead.'

'Well, you got close,' Winnie said cheerfully. 'Me and Toby and Grandma Harman have been working on you most of the night. You're going to be kind of stiff, but I guess your skull was too thick to crack.'

Keller sat up and was rewarded with a stabbing pain in her temples. 'What happened? Where's Galen?'

'Well, golly gee, Boss, I didn't know you cared—'

'Stop fooling around, Winnie! Where's the guy who's got to be alive if the shapeshifters are going to join Circle Daybreak?'

Winnie sobered. Nissa said calmly, 'He's fine, Keller. This is Iliana's house. Everybody's OK. We got you guys out—'

Keller frowned, struck by a new worry. 'You did? Why? I told you to take the girl and go.'

Nissa raised an eyebrow wryly. 'Yes, well, but the girl didn't want to go. She made us stop and turn back for you.'

'For Galen,' Keller said. She looked at Iliana, who was wearing a pink nightgown with puffy sleeves and looked about seven. She tried to make her voice patient. 'It was good to think of him, but you should have followed the plan.'

'Anyway, it worked out,' Nissa said. 'Apparently, the dragon blew the house down on top of you, but then he walked right over you trying to get to us.'

'Yeah. I was kind of hoping he wouldn't realize Galen was there,' Keller said. 'Or wouldn't realize he was important.'

'Well, when he found we'd already gotten away in the limo, he and his buddies took after us in cars,' Winnie said. 'But Nissa lost them. And then Iliana . . . insisted, and so we circled back. And there you were. Galen and Toby were digging you out. We helped them and brought you here.'

'What about Grandma Harman?'

'She came out of it without a scratch. She's tougher than she looks,' Winnie said.

'She talked to Iliana's mum last night,' Nissa added. 'She fixed everything up so we can stay here. You're supposed to be a distant cousin, and the rest of us are your friends. We're from Canada. We graduated last year, and we're touring the U.S. by bus. We ran into Iliana last night, and that's why she was late. It's all covered, nice and neat.'

'It's all ludicrous,' Keller said. She looked at Iliana. 'And it's time to stop. Haven't you seen enough yet?

That's twice you've been attacked by a monster. Do you really want to try your luck for a third time?'

It was a mistake. Iliana's face had been sweet and anxious, but now Keller could see the walls slam down. The violet eyes hazed over and sparked at the same time.

'*Nobody* attacked me until you guys came!' Iliana flared. 'In fact, nobody's attacked *me* so far at all. I think it's you people they're after – or maybe Galen. I keep telling you that I'm not the one you're looking for.'

This was the time for diplomacy, but Keller was too exasperated to think. 'You don't really believe that. Unless you *practise* being stupid—'

'Stop calling me stupid!' The last word was a piercing shriek. At the same time, Iliana threw something at Keller. She batted it out of the air automatically before it could hit.

'I'm not stupid! And I'm not your Witch Child or whatever you call it! I'm just a normal kid, and I like my life. And if I can't live my life, then I don't want to – to do *anything*.' She whirled around and stalked out, her nightgown billowing.

Keller stared at the missile she'd caught. It was a stuffed lamb with outrageously long eyelashes and a pink ribbon tied around its white neck.

Nissa folded her arms. 'Well, you sure handled that one, Boss.'

'Give me a break.' Keller tossed the lamb onto the window seat. 'And just how did she *make* you two turn around and come back for us, by the way?'

Winnie pursed her lips. 'You heard it. Volume control. She kept screaming like – well, I don't know *what* screams like that. You'd be surprised how effective it is.'

'You're agents of Circle Daybreak; you're supposed to be immune to torture.' But Keller dropped the subject.

'What are you still hanging around for?' she added, as she swung her feet out of bed and carefully tried her legs. 'You're supposed to stick with her, even when she's in the house. Don't stand here staring at *me*.'

'You're welcome for putting you back together again,' Winnie said, her eyes on the ceiling. In the doorway, she turned and added, 'And, you know, it wasn't Galen she kept screaming we had to go back and get last night. It was you, Keller.'

Keller stared at the door as it shut, bewildered.

'You can't go to school,' Keller hissed. 'Do you hear me? You cannot go to school.'

They were all sitting around the kitchen table. Iliana's mother, a lovely woman with a knot of platinum hair coiled on her neck, was making breakfast. She seemed slightly anxious about her four new houseguests, but in a pleasantly excited way. She certainly wasn't suspicious. Grandma Harman had done a good job of brainwashing.

'We're going to have a wonderful Christmas,' she said now, and her angelic smile grew brighter. 'We can go into Winston-Salem for a Christmas and Candle Tea. Have you ever had a Moravian sugarcake? I just wish Great-aunt Edgith had been able to stay.'

Grandma Harman was gone. Keller didn't know whether to be relieved or frustrated. Despite what she kept saying, as long as the old woman was around, Keller would worry about her. But with her gone, there was nobody to appeal to, nobody who could order Iliana into safekeeping.

So now they were sitting and having this argument. It looked like such a normal breakfast scene, Keller thought dryly. Iliana's father had already left for work. Her mother was bustling around cheerfully. Her little brother was in a high chair making a mess with Cheerios. Too bad that the four nicely dressed teenagers at the table were actually two shapeshifters, a witch, and a vampire.

Galen was directly opposite Keller. There were shadows under his eyes – had anyone gotten any sleep last night? – and he seemed subdued but relaxed. Keller hadn't had a chance to speak to him since the dragon's attack.

Not that she had anything to say.

'Orange juice, Kelly?'

'No, thank you, Mrs Dominick.' That was what this family thought their last name was. They didn't realize that witches trace their heritage through the female line and that both Iliana and her mother were therefore Harmans.

'Oh, please, call me Aunt Anna,' the woman said. She had her daughter's violet eyes and the smile of an angel. She was also pouring Keller juice.

Now I see where Iliana gets her scintillating intelligence, Keller thought. 'Oh – thanks, Aunt Anna. And, actually, it's Keller, not Kelly.'

'How unusual. But it's nice, so modern.'

'It's my last name, but that's what everybody calls me.'

'Oh, really? What's your first name?'

Keller broke off a piece of toast, feeling uncomfortable. 'Raksha.'

'But that's beautiful! Why don't you use it?'

Keller shrugged. 'I just don't.' She could see Galen looking at her. Shapeshifters usually were named for their animal forms, but neither *Keller* nor *Raksha* fit the pattern. 'I was abandoned as a kid,' she said in a clipped voice, looking back at Galen. Iliana's mother wouldn't be able to make anything of this, but she might as well satisfy the princeling's curiosity. 'So I don't know my real last name. But my first name means "demon".'

Iliana's mother paused with the juice carton over Nissa's glass. 'Oh. How . . . nice. Well, then, I see.' She blinked a couple of times and walked off without pouring Nissa any juice.

'So what does *Galen* mean?' Keller said, holding his gaze challengingly and handing her full glass to Nissa.

He smiled – a little wryly – for the first time since sitting down. ' "Calm." '

Keller snorted. 'It figures.'

'I like *Raksha* better.'

Keller didn't answer. With 'Aunt Anna' safely in the kitchen, she could speak again to Iliana. 'You understood before, right? That you can't go to school.'

'I have to go to school.' For somebody who looked as if she were made of spun glass, Iliana ate a lot. She spoke around a mouthful of microwave pancake.

'It's out of the question. How can we go with you? What are we supposed to *be*, for Goddess's sake?'

'My long-lost cousin from Canada and her friends,' Iliana said indistinctly. 'Or you can all be exchange students who're here to study our American educational system.' Before Keller could say anything, she added, 'Hey, how come *you* guys aren't at school? Don't you have schools?'

'We've got the same ones you do,' Winnie said. 'Except Nissa – she graduated last year. But Keller – and I are seniors like you. We just take time off for this stuff.'

'I bet your grades are as bad as mine,' Iliana said unemotionally. 'Anyway, I have to go to school this week. There are all sorts of class parties and things. You can come. It'll be fun.'

Keller wanted to hit her with the pot of grits.

She had a problem, though. Iliana's little brother Alex had escaped from his highchair and was climbing up her leg. She looked down at him uneasily. She wasn't good with family-type things, and she especially wasn't good with children.

'OK,' she said. 'Go on back and sit down.' She peeled him off and tried to start him in the right direction.

He turned around and put his arms up. 'Kee-kee. Kee-kee.'

'That's his word for "kitty",' Iliana's mother said, coming in with a plate of sausages. She ruffled his white-blond hair. 'You mean Kelly, Kelly,' she told him.

' "Keller, Keller," ' Winnie corrected helpfully.

Alex climbed into Keller's lap, grabbed her hair, and hoisted himself into a standing position. She found herself looking into huge violet baby eyes. Witch eyes.

'Kee-kee,' he said flatly, and gave her a sloppy kiss on the cheek.

Winnie grinned. 'Having trouble?'

The kid had two chubby arms around Keller's neck now and was nudging her chin with his head like a kitten looking for pets. He had a good grip, too. This time, she couldn't peel him off.

'It's just – distracting,' she said, giving up and petting him awkwardly. It was ridiculous. How could she argue with baby giggles in her ears?

'You look kind of sweet together,' Iliana observed. 'I'm getting dressed for school now. You guys can do whatever you want.'

She floated off while Keller was trying to think of a reply.

Nissa and Winnie hastily followed her. Galen got up to help Iliana's mother with the dishes.

Keller tugged at the baby, who clung like a sloth. Maybe there was shapeshifter blood in this family.

'Kee-kee . . . pui!' That was what it sounded like.

'Pwee?' Keller glanced nervously at his diaper.

'He means "pretty",' Iliana's mother said, coming back in. 'It's funny. He doesn't usually take to people like that. He likes animals better.'

'Oh. Well, he has good taste,' Keller said. She finally succeeded in detaching him and gave him back to his mother. Then she started down the hallway after Iliana, muttering, 'Too bad about his eyesight.'

'I think his eyesight's just fine,' Galen said, right behind her.

Keller turned, realizing they were alone in the hall.

His faint smile faded. 'I really wanted to talk to you,' he said.

CHAPTER
7

Keller faced him squarely.

'Yes, sir? Or should I say "my lord"?'

He flinched but tried to hide it. 'I should have told you in the beginning.'

Keller wasn't about to get into a discussion of it. 'What do you want?'

'Can we go in there?' He nodded toward what looked like a small library-office combination.

Keller didn't want to, but she couldn't think of any acceptable reason to refuse. She followed him and crossed her arms when he closed the door.

'You saved my life.' He wasn't quite facing her; he was looking out the window at a cold silver sky. Against it, he had a profile like a young prince on an ancient coin.

Keller shrugged. 'Maybe. Maybe not. The bricks didn't kill me; maybe they wouldn't have killed you.'

'But you were trying to save my life. I did something that was probably stupid – again – and you had to cover for me.'

'I did it because it's my job, Galen. That's what I *do*.'

'You got hurt because of me. When I dug myself out of that rubble, I thought you *were* dead.' He said it flatly,

460

without any particular intonation. But the hairs on Keller's arms rose.

'I've got to get back to Iliana.'

'Keller.'

There was something wrong with her. She was facing the door, heading out, but his voice stopped her in her tracks.

'Keller. Please.'

She was aware that he was coming up behind her.

Her entire skin was up in gooseflesh. She was *too* aware of him, that was the problem. She could feel the air that he displaced. She could feel his heat.

He just stood there.

'Keller. Ever since I first saw you . . .' He stopped and tried again. 'You were – gleaming. All that long black hair swirling around you and those silvery eyes. And then you changed. I don't think I ever really understood what it meant to be a shapeshifter until I saw that. You were a girl and then you were a cat, but you were always both.' He let out his breath. 'I'm putting this badly.'

Keller needed to think of something to say – *now*. But she couldn't, and she couldn't seem to move.

'When I saw that, for the first time, I wanted to shapeshift. Before that, I didn't really care, and everyone was always telling me to be careful, because whatever shape I choose the first time is the one I'm stuck with. But that's not what I'm trying to say. I'm trying . . .'

He reached out. Keller felt the warmth of his hand between her shoulder blades, through her hair, through the fabric of her spare jumpsuit.

Keller shivered.

She couldn't help it. She felt so strange. Dizzy and supernaturally clear at the same time. Weak.

She didn't know what was happening to her, only that

it was powerful and terrible.

His hand remained on her back, warmth from it soaking into her skin.

'I realize how much you dislike me,' Galen said quietly. There was no self-pity in his voice, but he seemed to be getting the words out painfully. 'And I'm not going to try to change that. But I just wanted you to know, I also realize what you've done for me. I needed to say thank you.' There was something swelling in Keller's chest like a balloon. Bigger and bigger. She clamped her lips together, frightened as she had never been when fighting monsters.

'And . . . I won't forget it,' Galen was going on, still quiet. 'Someday, I'll find a way to repay you.'

Keller felt desperate. What was he *doing* to her? She wasn't in control of herself; she was trembling and terrified that the thing in her chest was going to escape.

All she could imagine doing was turning around and hitting him, like a trapped animal lashing out at someone trying to rescue it.

'It's so strange,' he said, and Keller had the feeling that he had almost forgotten her and was talking to himself. 'When I was growing up, I rejected the Power of my family. All my ancestors, they were supposed to turn into demons when they unleashed it. I thought that it was better not to fight – if that was possible. It seems unrealistic now.'

Keller could feel more than warmth now. There were little electrical zings spreading out from his hand, running down the insides of her arms. Not real ones, of course. Not the Power he was talking about, like the Power used by the dragon or Winnie. But it felt awfully close. Her whole body was filled with buzzing.

Some people shouldn't have to fight, she thought giddily. But, no, that was insane. Everybody had to fight;

that was what life was about. If you didn't fight, you were weak. You were prey.

He was still talking in that abstracted tone. 'I know you think—'

Keller's panic hit flashpoint. She whirled around. 'You don't know *anything* about what I think. You don't know anything about *me*. I don't know whatever gave you the idea that you did.'

He looked startled but not defensive. The silver light behind him lit the edges of his fine hair.

'I'm sorry,' he said gently.

'Stop being sorry!'

'Are you saying I'm wrong? You don't think I'm a spoiled and pampered prince who doesn't know anything about real life and has to be baby-sat?'

Keller was disconcerted. That was exactly what she thought – but if it were true, then why did she have this strange feeling of falling?

'I think you're like *her*,' she said, keeping her words short and brutal to keep them under control. She didn't need to specify the *her*. 'You're like this whole ridiculous family. Happy mummy, happy baby, happy Christmas. They're ready to love everybody who comes along. And they're living in a happy happy idealistic world that has nothing to do with reality.'

The corner of his mouth turned up wryly, although his eyes were still serious. 'I think that's what I said.'

'And it sounds harmless, doesn't it? But it isn't. It's blind and destructive. What do you want to bet that Iliana's mother really thinks my name is Kelly now? She can't deal with it being "demon", so she just happily changes the world to fit.'

'You could be right.' He wasn't smiling at all now, and there was something in his eyes, something lost and hopeless that made Keller feel more panicked than ever.

She spoke savagely to hold off the fear. 'You want to know what real life is like? My mother left me in a cardboard box in a parking lot. It was fixed up with newspapers inside, like something you'd use for a puppy. That was because I couldn't wear diapers, I was stuck in my halfway form – a baby with a tail and ears like a cat. Maybe that was why she couldn't deal with me, but I'll never know. The only thing I have of hers is a note that was in the box. I kept it.'

Keller fumbled in the jumpsuit's pocket. She had never meant to show this to anyone, certainly not somebody she'd known for less than twenty-four hours. But she had to convince Galen; she had to make him go away for good.

Her wallet was slim – no photos, just money and ID. She pulled out a folded slip of paper, with creases worn smooth by time and writing that had faded from blue ink to pale purple. Its right edge was a ragged tear, but the words were on the left and clear enough.

'It was her legacy to me,' Keller said. 'She was trying to pass on the truth, what she'd learned about life.'

Galen took the paper as if it were a hurt bird.

Keller watched his eyes move over it. She knew the words by heart, of course, and right now she heard them ringing in her mind. There were only twelve of them – her mother had been a master of succinctness.

> *People die . . .*
> *Beauty fades . . .*
> *Love changes . . .*
> *And you will always be alone.*

Keller could tell where Galen was by the way his eyes widened in horror.

She smiled at him, not nicely, and took the paper back.

He looked at her. And despite everything she knew about him, she was surprised at the sheer *depth* of his shock. He stared at her with those gold-green eyes that went on for miles – and then he stepped forward.

'*You don't believe that,*' he said fiercely, and grabbed her by the shoulders.

Keller was startled. He'd seen her in action. How could he be so stupid as to grab her?

He seemed to be completely unaware of his danger. There was nothing calm or hesitant about him now. He was staring at her with a kind of stricken tenderness, as if she'd just told him she had a terminal disease. It was as if he were trying to pour love and warmth and light into her by a direct connection.

'I won't let you think that,' he said. 'I won't let you.'

'It's just the truth. If you can accept that, you won't drown in life. Whatever happens, you'll be able to cope.'

'It's not all the truth. If you believe it is, why do you work for Circle Daybreak?'

'They raised me,' Keller said shortly. 'They snatched me out of the hospital nursery when they read the reports about me in the paper. They realized what I was and that humans couldn't take care of me. That's why I work for them – to pay them back. It's my job.'

'That's not the only reason. I've *seen* you work, Keller.'

She could feel warmth spreading from his hands on her shoulders. She knocked them aside and stood tall. There was a core of iciness inside her, and she hung on to that.

'Don't get me wrong,' she said. 'I don't save people out of idealism. I don't risk my neck for just *anybody* – only the ones I get paid for.'

'You mean if Iliana's little brother was in danger, you wouldn't save him. You'd stand there and watch him burn to death in a fire or drown in a riptide.'

Keller had a sinking feeling. She held her chin up and said, 'Exactly. If it meant putting myself in danger to save him, I wouldn't do it.'

He shook his head, flatly positive. 'No.'

The sinking feeling got worse.

'That's a lie,' he said, holding her eyes. 'I've seen you in action. I talked to Nissa and Winnie last night. And I've seen your *mind*. You're not just doing a job. You're doing what you do because you think it's right. And you are . . .' He paused as if to find the words, then spoke deliberately. 'You are the soul of honour.'

And you're insane, Keller thought. She *really* needed to get away now. The sinking was becoming a terrible weakness spreading through her. And although she knew that what he was saying was complete garbage, she couldn't seem to stop listening.

'You put on a good show,' Galen said, 'but the truth is that you're brave and gallant and *decent*. You have your own code, and you would never break it. And anybody who knows you sees that. Don't you know what your team thinks of you? You should have seen their faces – and Iliana's – when they thought you were dead in that rubble. Your soul is straight as a sword, and you have more honour than anyone I've ever known.'

His eyes were the colour of the first new leaves in spring, the kind you look up to see sunlight pouring through. Keller was a meat-eater and had never cared much about flowers or other vegetation, but now she remembered a line from a poem, and it froze in her mind like lightning: *Nature's first green is gold*. This was the colour the poet meant.

You could drown in eyes like that.

He was holding her arms again. He couldn't seem to

stop reaching for her, as if she were some soul in danger of being lost forever.

'Your life's been so hard. You deserve to have good things happen to you now – only good things. I wish . . .' He broke off, and a sort of tremor went through his face.

No, Keller thought. I won't let you make me weak. I won't listen to your lies.

But the problem was that Galen *didn't* lie. He was one of those idiot idealist types who said what they believed. And she shouldn't care what he believed, but she found that she did. She cared terribly.

Galen just stood there looking at her with tears in his gem-bright eyes.

Something ripped inside Keller. And then everything changed.

Keller couldn't understand what was happening at first. In panic, all she could think was that she was losing herself. Losing her armour, her hardness, everything she needed to keep alive. Some part of her deep inside was melting, flowing toward Galen.

She tried to snatch it back, but it was no good. She couldn't stop it.

With a distant shock, she realized that she had shut her eyes. She was falling, falling – and she didn't care.

Something caught her.

She felt the warmth of arms around her, supporting her. And she felt herself lean into it, relaxing, letting him take some of her weight, as if someone else were controlling her body.

So warm . . .

That was when Keller discovered something strange. That warmth could give you shivers.

Being close like this, feeling Galen warm and solid and

there to hang on to – it made a shiver of pleasure go through her.

And then she felt the true connection.

It wasn't a physical thing. The spark that passed between them connected them mind to mind. It was a riveting flash of complete understanding.

Her heart all but exploded.

It's you. The voice was in her mind, the same voice she'd heard yesterday when he had tried to save her from the dragon. It was filled with wonder and discovery. *It's you . . . the one I've been looking for. You're the one . . .*

And Keller would have told him how insane that was, except that it was just what she was feeling herself. It was as if she had just turned around and unexpectedly found herself facing a figure from one of her dreams. A person she *knew* instinctively, just as she knew her own mind.

I know you, too, Galen's voice in her head said. *We're so much alike . . .*

We're not, Keller thought. But the protest sounded feeble even to her. And trying to hang on to her anger and cynicism right now seemed silly – pointless. Like a kid insisting that nobody loved her and she was going to go play on the motorway.

We belong together, Galen said simply. *Like this.*

Warm tingles. Keller could feel the force of his love like a bright light shining at her. And she couldn't . . . resist . . . any longer . . .

Her arms came up to hold Galen back. Her face turned up slightly, but not much, because she was tall, and their lips were already only an inch apart.

The kiss was shivery, delightful, and very sweet.

After an endless time of floating in a golden haze, Keller shivered again.

There's something . . . something I have to remember . . .

I love you, Galen said back.

Yes, but there's something I've forgotten . . .

We're together, he said. *I don't want to remember anything else.*

And *that* was probably true. She couldn't really blame him. Who would want to disturb this warmth and closeness and quiet joy?

Still, they had been talking about something – a long time ago, when she had been alone. Something that had made her terribly unhappy.

I won't let you be unhappy. I won't let you be alone, either, he said.

He stroked her hair with his fingertips. That was all, but it almost short-circuited Keller's thought processes.

But not completely.

Alone . . . I remember.

Her mother's note.

You will always be alone.

Galen's arms tightened around her. *Don't. Don't think about that. We're together. I love you . . .*

No.

With a wrench, Keller pulled herself away. She found herself standing in the library on her own two feet, staring at Galen. He looked shocked and stricken, as if he'd just been slapped out of a dream.

'Keller—'

'No!' she spat. 'Don't touch me!'

'I won't touch you. But I can't let you run away. And I can't pretend I don't love you.'

'Love,' Keller snarled, 'is weakness.' She saw her mother's note lying on the floor where he'd dropped it and snatched it up. 'And nobody is making me sentimental and weak! Nobody!'

It wasn't until she was out the door that she

remembered she had left out the strongest argument of all.

He *couldn't* love her. It was impossible.

He was destined to marry the Witch Child.

The fate of the world depended on it.

CHAPTER

8

Keller was tempted to check the wards, but she knew it wouldn't do any good. She wasn't sensitive enough to the witch energies to gauge them. They'd been put up by Grandma Harman and checked by Winnie, and she would have to trust to that.

The wards were keyed so that only the Dominick family and ordinary humans could come inside. No Night Person could enter except Nissa, Winnie, Keller, and Galen. Which meant, Keller thought with a grim smile, that any lost witch relatives of Iliana's mother who came by were going to get quite a surprise. An invisible wall was going to be blocking them from crossing the threshold.

As long as nobody on the inside removed the wards, the house was safer than Fort Knox.

Grandma Harman had also taken the limo, Keller found. Sometime during the night, it had been replaced by an inconspicuous Ford sedan parked at the curb. The keys had been in a manila envelope dropped through the mail slot in the front door, along with a map of Lucy Lee Bethea High School.

Circle Daybreak was efficient.

'I didn't finish my *hair*,' Iliana complained as Nissa

hustled her to the car. 'It's only half *done*.'

'It looks terrific,' Winnie said from behind her.

And the thing was, it was true. There was nothing that could make that shimmering waterfall of silvery-gold look anything less than beautiful. Whether it was up or down, braided or pinned or falling loose, it was glorious.

I don't even think the little nitwit has to brush it, Keller thought. It's so fine that she couldn't make two hairs tangle if she tried.

'And I left my *scarf*—'

'Here it is.' Keller lassoed her. The scarf was ridiculous, crushed velvet in muted metallic colours, with a six-inch fringe. Purely decorative.

Iliana choked as Keller wound it around a few times and pulled it tight.

'A little aggressive, Boss?' Winfrith asked, extricating Iliana before she could turn blue.

'Worried about being late,' Keller said shortly. But she saw Nissa eyeing her, too.

Galen was the last to come out of the house. He was pale and serious – that much Keller saw before she shifted her eyes past him. Iliana's mother actually remained standing at the door with the baby in her arms.

'Say bye-bye to your sister's friends. Bye-bye.'

'Kee-kee,' the baby said. 'Kee-kee!'

'Wave to him,' Winfrith stage-whispered.

Keller gritted her teeth. She half-waved, keeping her senses opened for any sound of an impending attack. The baby held out his arms toward her.

'Pui!'

'Let's get *out* of here.' Keller almost shoved Iliana into the backseat.

Nissa took the wheel, and Galen sat up front with her. Winnie ran around to get in the back on the other side of Iliana.

As they pulled out, Keller saw the outside of the house for the first time. It was a nice house – white clapboard, two and a half storeys, Colonial Revival. The street was nice, too, lined with dogwoods that would be a mass of white when they bloomed. The sort of street where people sat outside on their rockers in spring and somebody was bound to have a stand of bees in the side yard making sourwood honey.

Although Keller had been all over the United States, sent from one Circle Daybreak group to another, the hospital where she'd been found had been near a neighbourhood like this.

I might have grown up someplace like this. If they'd kept me. My parents . . .

Do I hate her? Keller wondered suddenly. *I couldn't. It's not her fault.*

Oh, no, of course not, the voice in her mind said. Not her fault that she's beautiful and perfect and has parents who love her and blue fire in her veins and that she is going to be forced, whether she wants it or not, to marry Galen . . .

Which I don't care about, Keller thought. She was shocked at herself. When had she ever let emotion interfere with her job? She was allowing herself to be distracted – she had allowed herself to be distracted all morning – when there was something vitally important at stake.

No more, she told herself fiercely. *From now on, I think about nothing but the mission.* Years of mental discipline came in handy now; she was able to push everything to the side and focus with icy clarity on what had to be done.

'—stopped a train in its tracks,' Winfrith was saying.

'Really?' There was faint interest in Iliana's voice. At least she'd stopped talking about her hair, Keller thought.

'Really. It was one of those BART trains in San Francisco, like a subway train, you know. The two girls were on the tracks, and the Wild Power stopped the train dead before it could hit them. That's what the blue fire can do.'

'Well, I know I can't do anything like that,' Iliana said flatly. 'So I can't be a Wild Power. Or whatever.' The last words were tacked on quickly.

Nissa raised a cool eyebrow. 'Have you ever *tried* to stop a train?'

While Iliana bit a fingertip and pondered that, Winnie said, 'You have to do it right, you know. First, you have to make blood flow, and then you have to concentrate. It's not something you can expect to do perfectly the very first time.'

'If you want to start practising,' Nissa added, 'we can help.'

Iliana shuddered. 'No, thank you. I faint when I see blood. And anyway, I'm not it.'

'Too bad,' Nissa murmured. 'We could use the blue fire on our side today.'

They were pulling up to a charming old brown brick high school. Neither Galen nor Keller had said a word throughout the ride.

But now Keller leaned forward. 'Nissa, drive past it. I want to check the layout first.'

Nissa swung the car into a circular driveway that went past the school's oversized front doors. Keller looked right and left, taking in everything about the surroundings. She could see Winnie doing the same thing – and Galen, too. He was focussing on the same danger spots she was. He had the instinct for strategy.

'Go around the block and circle back,' Keller said.

Iliana stirred. 'I thought you were worried about me being late.'

'I'm more worried about you being dead,' Keller interrupted. 'What do you think, Nissa?'

'The side door on the west. Easy to pull up reasonably close, no bushes around it for nasty surprises to hide in.'

'That's my pick, too. OK, everybody, listen. Nissa's going to slow the car down in the right place. Slow down, not stop. When I give the signal, we're all going to jump out and go directly to that door. We are not going to pause. We are going to move as a group. Iliana, are you paying attention? From now on, you don't go *anywhere* unless Winnie's in front of you and I'm beside you.'

'And where's Galen?' Iliana said.

Keller cursed herself mentally. She wasn't used to working with a fourth team member. 'He'll be behind us – OK, Galen?' She made herself look his way.

'Yes. Whatever you say.' There wasn't the slightest hint of sarcasm in his face. He was dead serious. Absolutely miserable, earnest, and dead serious.

'And Nissa, once you've parked, you join us and take the other side. What room's your first class in, Iliana?'

'Three twenty-six,' Iliana said dismally. 'U.S. History with Mr. Wanamaker. He went to New York to try to be an actor, but all he got was some disease from not eating enough stuff with vitamins. So he came back, and now he's really strict unless you can get him to do his impressions of the presidents—'

'All right,' Keller broke in. 'We're coming to the door.'

'—and he's actually pretty funny when he does Theodore Roosevelt – or do I mean the other one—'

'*Now,*' Keller said, and pushed her as Winnie pulled.

They all made it out smoothly, although Iliana yelped a little. Keller kept a good grip on her arm as they hurried to the door.

'I don't think I *like* this way of coming to school.'

'We can turn right around and go back home,' Keller said. Iliana shut up.

Galen kept pace behind them, silent and focussed. It was Nissa's usual position when the team wasn't heading for a car, and Keller couldn't help feeling the difference. She didn't *like* having someone behind her she couldn't trust absolutely. And although the enemies didn't seem to know yet that Galen was important, if they found out, he'd become a target.

Face it, she thought. This setup is a *disaster*, security-wise. This is a horrendous accident waiting to happen.

Her nerves were wound so tightly that she jumped at the slightest sound.

They shepherded Iliana to her locker, then up a staircase to the third floor. The halls were almost empty, which was exactly as Keller had planned it.

But of course that meant they were late for class.

Nissa slid in beside them just as they opened the door. They entered as a group, and the teacher stopped talking and looked at them. So did everybody else in the room.

Quite a few jaws dropped open.

Keller allowed herself a grim inner smile.

Yeah, they were probably a bit of a shock for a small town. Four Night People – well, former Night People, anyway. A witch who was almost as small as Iliana, with a mop of vivid strawberry-blonde curls and a face like a pixie on holiday. A vampire girl who looked like cool perfection straight out of a magazine, with cropped mink-coloured hair and a strangely penetrating gaze. A shapeshifter boy who could have taken the place of any prince in a book of fairy tales, with hair like old gold and classically sculptured features.

And, of course, a panther. Which happened to be walking on two feet at the moment, in the guise of a tall girl with a tense, wary expression and black hair that swirled witchlike around her.

And, of course, there was Iliana in the midst of them, looking like a ballet dancer who had blundered in from the *Nutcracker Suite*.

There was a silence as the two groups stared at each other.

Then the teacher snapped shut his book and advanced on them. Keller held herself ready. He had a neatly trimmed beard and a dangerous expression.

It was Iliana who took him on, though. She stepped forward before Keller could draw a breath to speak.

'Mr Wanamaker! These are my cousins! Well – some of them are my cousins. They're from . . . California. Hollywood! They're here to . . . do research for . . .'

'We're really just visiting,' Keller cut in.

'A new show about a high school. Not like that *other* show. It's more of a reality-based—'

'It's just a visit,' Keller said.

'But your dad *is* a famous producer,' Iliana said. She added in an undertone to Mr Wanamaker, 'You know, like that other producer.'

All eyes, including the teacher's, fixed on Keller.

'Yes – that's right,' Keller said, and smiled while clenching her teeth. 'But we're still just visiting.' She nudged Winnie with her elbow, but it wasn't necessary. Winnie was already staring at the teacher, brainwashing him with witch power.

Mr Wanamaker blinked. He weighed the book he was holding as if he were Hamlet holding Yorick's skull. He looked at it, then he looked at Winnie and blinked again.

Then he shrugged and looked at the ceiling. 'OK. Whatever. Sit down. There are some chairs at the back. And I'm still marking you tardy.' But Keller noticed that as he returned to his desk, his posture was very erect.

She did the best she could to glare at Iliana without drawing any further attention to them. 'A famous producer?' she whispered through her teeth.

'I don't know. It was more interesting than just saying you're friends.'

You don't need life to get any more interesting, Bubblebrain, Keller thought, but she didn't say anything.

She found one thing out that surprised her, though, and she found it out quickly. Her job was made harder by the fact that everyone at the school was in love with Iliana.

It was strange. Keller was used to getting attention from guys — and ignoring it. And Nissa and Winnie both were the type that had to beat them off with sticks. But here, although the guys looked at her and Nissa and Winnie, their eyes always seemed to return to Iliana.

At break, they crowded around her like bees around a flower. And not just guys, either. Girls, too. Everyone seemed to have something to say to her or just wanted to see her smile.

It was a bodyguard's nightmare.

What do they *see* in her? Keller thought, frustrated almost beyond endurance as she tried to edge Iliana away from the crowd. I mean, aside from the obvious. But if all this is about her looks . . .

It wasn't. It didn't seem to be. They weren't all hitting on her for dates.

'Hey, Iliana, my granddaddy loved that get well card you made.'

'Illie, are you going to tie the ribbons this year for the Christmas Benefit bears? Nobody else can make those teeny-weeny bows.'

'Oh, Iliana, something awful! Bugsy had five puppies,

and Mom says we can't keep them. We've got to find them all homes.'

'Iliana, I need help—'

'Wait, Iliana, I have to ask you—'

OK, but why come to *her*? Keller thought as she finally managed to detach the girl from her fan club and steer her into the hall. I mean, she can hardly be the best problem solver in this school, can she?

There was one guy who seemed to like Iliana for the obvious. Keller disliked him on sight. He was good-looking in a carefully manicured way, with deep chestnut hair, deep blue eyes, and very white teeth. He was wearing expensive clothes, and he smiled a lot, but only at Iliana.

'Brett,' Iliana said as he accosted them in the hall.

Brett Ashton-Hughes. One of the rich twins who were having the birthday party on Saturday night. Keller disliked him even more, especially when he gave her a coolly appreciative once-over before returning his attention to Iliana.

'Hey, blondie. You still coming Saturday?'

Iliana giggled. Keller stifled the urge to hit something.

'Of course, I'll be there. I wouldn't miss it.'

'Because, you know, it would kill Jaime if you didn't come. We're only inviting a few people, and we'll have the whole west wing to ourselves. We can even dance in the ballroom.'

Iliana's eyes went dreamy. 'That sounds so romantic. I always wanted to dance in a real old-fashioned ballroom. I'll feel just like Scarlett O'Hara.'

No, Keller thought. No, no, no. No *way* is she going there. She's going to the Solstice Ceremony, where the shapeshifters and the witches are meeting, even if I have to drag her by the hair.

She caught Nissa's eye and saw that Nissa was thinking

the same. Galen and Winnie were simply watching Brett with troubled looks on their faces.

'Yeah, and I can be Brett Butler,' Brett was saying. 'Plus, the indoor swimming pool will be heated. So if you get tired of being Scarlett, you can be a mermaid for a while.'

'It sounds wonderful! Tell Jaime I said so.'

Winnie bit her lip. Keller got a fresh grip on Iliana's arm and started guiding her away.

'So it's a promise, right?' Brett called after her.

Keller *squeezed*.

'Yes, but – oh.' Iliana managed to smile and wince at the same time, her arm limp in Keller's grasp. 'Oh, Brett, there's one thing. I've got my cousin and her friends staying with me.'

Brett hesitated an instant, giving each girl on Keller's team the appraising look. Then he shrugged and flashed a smile. 'Hey, no problem. Bring them all. Your friends are our friends.'

'That *wasn't* what I was trying to tell you,' Keller said when they were away from Brett.

Iliana was rubbing her arm with an aggrieved expression. 'Then what? I thought it would be fun for you to go.'

'What do you mean, "then what"? You're going to the Solstice Ceremony that night, so you shouldn't have promised him.'

'I am *not* going to the Solstice Ceremony that night, because I'm not the one you're looking for.'

It wasn't the time to argue. Keller kept her moving down the hall.

Keller wasn't happy. Her nerves were all prickling, and she felt like a cat with its fur standing on end.

Very soon, Iliana wasn't happy, either.

'I always eat lunch in the cafeteria!'

'Not today,' Keller said, knowing she sounded as brusque and tired as she felt. 'We can't risk it. You've got to be in a room, alone, someplace where we can control access to you.'

'The music room,' Winnie said helpfully. 'I saw it on the map and asked a girl about it in English class. It's open during lunch, and there's only one door.'

'I don't *want* to—'

'You don't have a choice!'

Iliana sulked in the music room. The problem was that she wasn't very good at sulking, and you could only tell she was doing it because when she offered her cookies to Nissa, she only insisted once.

Keller paced nervously in the hallway in front of the door. She could hear Winnie and Galen inside talking. Even Galen's *voice* sounded white-faced and strained.

Something's wrong . . . I've had a bad feeling ever since we got to this school . . . and it isn't any easier having *him* around.

Part of her was worried that he might take this opportunity to come and try to talk to her. And part of her, a very deep inside part, was furious because he wasn't doing it.

Goddess! I've got to get my mind clear. Every second that I'm not in control of my emotions means an opportunity for *them*.

She was so absorbed in yelling at herself that she almost missed the girl walking past her. Keller was almost at the end of the hall, and she had to do a double-take to realize that somebody had just calmly slipped by.

'Hey, wait,' she said to the girl's back. The girl was medium-sized and had hair the soft brown of oak leaves, slightly longer than shoulder-length. She was walking fast.

She didn't stop.

'Wait! I'm talking to you, girl! That door is off limits.'

The girl didn't turn, didn't even pause. She was almost at the door to the music room.

'*Stop right there!* Or you're going to get hurt!'

Not even a hesitation in the girl's step. She turned into the door.

A thousand red alerts went off in Keller's head.

CHAPTER
9

Keller reacted instantly and instinctively.

She changed.

She did it on the leap this time. Rushing the process along, pushing it from behind. She wanted to be entirely a panther by the time she landed on the girl's back.

But some things can't be rushed. She felt herself begin to liquefy and flow . . . formlessness . . . pleasure . . . the utter freedom of not being bound to any single physical shape. Then reformation, a stretching of all her cells as they reached to become something different, to unfurl like butterfly wings into a new kind of body.

Her jumpsuit misted into the fur that ran along her body, up and down from the stomach in front, straight down from the nape of her neck in back. Her ears surged and then firmed up, thin-skinned, rounded, and twitching already. From the base of her spine, her tail sprang free, its slightly clubbed end whipping eagerly.

That was how she landed.

She knocked the girl cleanly over, and they both went rolling on the floor. When they stopped, Keller was crouching on the girl's stomach.

She didn't want to kill the girl. She needed to find some

things out first. What kind of Night Person the girl was, and who'd sent her.

The only problem was that now, as she knelt with her hands gripping the girl's arms, staring into dark blue eyes under soft brown bangs, she couldn't sense anything of the Night World in the girl's life energy.

Shapeshifters were the uncontested best at that. They could tell a human from a Night Person nine times out of ten. And this girl wasn't even in the 'maybe' range. She was giving off purely human signals.

Not to mention screaming. Her mouth was wide open, and so were her eyes, and so were her pupils. Her skin had gone blue-white like someone about to faint. She looked utterly bewildered and horrified, and she wasn't making a move to fight back.

Keller's heart sank.

But if the girl was human and harmless, why hadn't she listened when Keller had shouted at her?

'Boss, we have to shut her *up*.' It was Winnie, yelling above the girl's throaty screams. As usual, Nissa didn't say a word, but she was the one who shut the music room door. By then, Keller had recovered enough to put a hand over the girl's mouth. The screaming stopped.

Then she looked at the others.

They were staring at her. Wide-eyed. Keller felt like a kitten with its paw in the canary cage.

Here she was, sitting on this human girl's midriff, in her half-and-half form. Her ears and tail were a panther's, and she was clothed from her snug boots to her shoulders in fur. It fit her like a black velvet jumpsuit, a sleeveless one that left her arms and neck bare. The hair on her head was still a human's and swirled around her to touch the floor on every side.

Her face was human, too, except for the pupils of her

eyes, which were narrow ovals, reacting to every change of light and shadow. And her teeth. Her canines had become delicately pointed, giving her just the slightest hint of fangs.

She blinked at Galen, not sure what she saw in his expression. He was definitely staring at her, and there was *some* strong emotion pulling his face taut and making that white line around his mouth.

Horror? Disgust? He was a shapeshifter himself – or he would be if he could ever make up his mind. He'd seen her in panther form. Why should he be shocked at this?

The answer flashed back at Keller from some deep part of her brain. Only because I'm a monster this way. Panthers are part of nature and can't be blamed for what they do. I'm a savage thing that doesn't manage to be either an animal or a person.

And I'm dangerous in this form. Neither half of me is really in control.

Someone who's never changed could never understand that.

Galen took a step toward her. His jaw was tense, but his gold-green eyes were fixed on hers, and his hand was slightly lifted. Keller wondered if it was the gesture of a hostage negotiator. He opened his mouth to say something.

And Iliana came to life, jumping up and running past him and shrieking at Keller all at once.

'What are you *doing*? That's Jaime! What are you *doing* to her?'

'You know her?'

'That's Jaime Ashton-Hughes! She's Brett's *sister*! And she's one of my best *friends*! And you *attacked* her! Are you all *right*?'

It was all shrieked at approximately the same decibel

level, but on the last sentence, Iliana looked down at Jaime.

Keller moved her palm from Jaime's mouth. As it turned out, though, that didn't seem to be necessary. Jaime raised her free hand and began to make swift, fluid gestures at Iliana with it.

Keller stared, and then her insides plummeted.

She let go of the girl's other arm, and the gestures immediately became two-handed.

Oh. Oh . . . darn.

Keller could feel her ears flatten backward. She looked unhappily at Iliana.

'Sign language?'

'She's got a hearing impairment!' Iliana glared at Keller, all the while making gestures back at Jaime. Her motions were awkward and stilted compared to Jaime's, but she clearly had some idea what she was doing.

'I didn't realize.'

'What difference does it make how well she can hear?' Iliana yelled. 'She's my friend! She's president of the senior class! She's chair for the Christmas Benefit bazaar! What did she do to you, ask you to buy a teddy bear?'

Keller sighed. Her tail was tucked up close to her body, almost between her legs, and her ears were flatter than ever. She climbed off Jaime, who immediately scooted backward and away from her, still talking rapidly with her hands to Iliana.

'The difference,' Keller said, 'is that she didn't stop when I told her to. I yelled at her, but . . . I didn't realize. Look, just tell her I'm sorry, will you?'

'*You* tell her! Don't talk about her as if she isn't here. Jaime can lip-read just fine if you bother to face her.' Iliana turned to Jaime again. '*I'm* sorry. Please don't be mad. This is terrible – and I don't know how to explain. Can you breathe now?'

Jaime nodded slowly. Her dark blue eyes slid to Keller, then back to Iliana. She spoke in a hushed voice. Although it was flat in tone and some of the sounds were indistinct, it was actually rather pleasant. And the words were perfectly understandable.

'What . . . is it?' she asked Iliana. Meaning Keller.

But then, before Iliana could answer, Jaime caught herself. She bit her lip, looked at the floor for a moment, then braced herself and looked at Keller again. She was frightened, her body was shrinking, but this time her eyes met Keller's directly.

'What . . . are you?'

Keller opened her mouth and shut it again.

A hand closed on her shoulder. It was warm, and it exerted brief pressure for an instant. Then it pulled away, maybe as if revolted because it was resting on fur.

'She's a person,' Galen said, kneeling down beside Jaime. 'She may look a little different right now, but she's as much of a person as you are. And you have to believe that she didn't mean to hurt you. She made a mistake. She thought you were an enemy, and she reacted.'

'An enemy?' There was something about Galen. Jaime had relaxed almost as soon as he got down on her level. Now she was talking to him freely, her hands flying gracefully as she spoke aloud, emphasizing her words. Her face was pretty when it wasn't blue with suffocation, Keller noticed. 'What are you talking about? What kind of enemy? Who *are* you people? I haven't seen you around school before.'

'She thought – well, she thought you were going to hurt Iliana. There are some people who are trying to do that.'

Jaime's face changed. 'Hurt Iliana? Who? They'd better not even *try*!'

Winnie had been twitching throughout this. Now she muttered, 'Boss . . .'

'It doesn't matter,' Keller said quietly. 'Nissa's going to have to blank her memory anyway.' It was too bad, in a way, because this girl's reaction to the Night World was one of the most sensible Keller had ever seen. But it couldn't be helped.

Keller didn't look at Iliana as she spoke; she knew there was going to be an argument. But before it started, she had one final thing to say.

'Jaime?' She moved and got instant attention. 'I'm sorry. Really. I'm sorry I frightened you. And I'm really sorry if I hurt you.' She stood up, not waiting to see if she was forgiven. What difference did it make? What was done was already done, and what was about to happen was inevitable. She didn't *expect* to be forgiven, and she didn't care.

That was what she told herself, anyway.

Iliana did argue. Keller tried not to let Jaime see much of it, because that would only make her more scared and miserable, and the end really was inescapable. Leaving her memory intact would be dangerous not only for Iliana but for Jaime herself.

'It's death for a human to find out about the Night World,' Keller said flatly. 'And it's worse than death if the dragon and his friends think she's got any information about the Wild Power. You don't want to know what they'll do to try and get it out of her, Iliana. I *promise* you don't.'

And, finally, Iliana gave in, as Keller had known she would have to from the beginning. Nissa moved up behind Jaime like a whisper and a shadow and touched her on the side of her neck.

Although witches were the experts at brainwashing, at inserting new ideas and convictions, vampires were the best at wiping the slate clean. They didn't use spells. It was something they were born with, the power to put their victim into a trance and smooth away hours or even days of memory. Jaime looked into Nissa's silvery-brown eyes for maybe seventy seconds, and then her own blue eyes shut, and her body went limp. Galen caught her as she fell.

'She'll wake up in a few minutes. It's probably best if we leave her here and get out,' Nissa said.

'Lunch is over, anyway,' Keller said. In the quiet minutes while Jaime was being hypnotized, Keller had finally managed to convince her body that there was no danger. It was only then that she could relax enough to change back.

Her ears collapsed, her tail retracted. Her fur misted into jumpsuit and skin. She blinked twice, noticing the difference in brightness as her pupils changed, and the tips of her fangs melted into ordinary teeth.

She stood up, shifting her shoulders to get used to the human body again.

They were all subdued as they escorted Iliana back to classes. The quietest of all was Keller.

She had overreacted, let her animal senses throw her into a panic. It wasn't the first time in her life. The *first* time in her life had been when she was about three . . . but better not to think about that. Anyway, it wasn't even the first time in her career as an agent for Circle Daybreak.

An agent had to be ready for anything at any moment. Had to have radar running, in front, in back, and on all sides, all the time, and be prepared to react instinctively at the slightest stimulus. If that sometimes caused mistakes – well, it also saved lives.

And she wasn't sorry. If she had to do it over, she'd do it again. Better one nice brown-haired girl scared than Iliana hurt. Better, Keller thought with bleak defiance, one nice brown-haired girl *killed* than Iliana in the hands of the enemy. Iliana represented the future of the entire daylight world.

But . . .

Maybe she was getting too old for this kind of job. Or maybe too jumpy.

Iliana sat moodily during afternoon classes, like a fairy who'd lost her flower. Keller noticed Winnie and Nissa being extra vigilant – just in case their boss got preoccupied. She flashed them a sarcastic look.

'You waiting for me to slack off?' She poked Nissa in the ribs. 'Don't hold your breath.'

They smiled, knowing they'd been thanked.

And Galen . . .

Keller didn't want to think about Galen. He sat quietly but intently through each class, and she could tell his senses were expanded. He didn't try to speak to her, didn't even look at her. But Keller noticed that every so often he rubbed his palm against his jeans.

And she remembered the way his hand had pulled back from her shoulder. As if he'd touched something hot.

Or something repulsive . . .

Keller gritted her teeth and stared at various blackboards with dry and burning eyes.

When the last bell finally rang, she made the whole group wait in the chemistry classroom while the school emptied out. Iliana watched and silently steamed as her friends all left without her. Even the teacher packed up and disappeared.

'Can we go *now*?'

'No.' Keller stood at the second-storey window, looking down. All right, so I'm a tyrant, she thought. A nasty, unsympathetic, whip-wielding dictator who jumps on innocent girls and won't let people out of school. I like being that way.

Iliana wouldn't argue. She stood rigidly a few feet away, looking out the window herself but refusing to acknowledge Keller's presence.

Finally, Keller said, 'All right. Nissa, get the car.'

Galen said, 'I'll do it.'

The answer to *that*, of course, was, 'No way.' But Galen was going on.

'It's something useful I can do. I've been standing around all day, wishing I was trained at *something*. At least driving I can handle. And if anybody comes after me, I can run fast.'

The answer to that was still no. But Keller couldn't bring herself to say it, because she couldn't bring herself to face him for a long debate. She was afraid of what she might see in the depths of those gold-green eyes.

It would be funny if she'd managed to turn the prince of the shapeshifters off from shapeshifting altogether. Wouldn't it?

'Go on,' she said to Galen, still looking down onto the circular driveway in front of the school.

After he had gone, she said to Nissa, 'Follow him.'

That was how everyone happened to be where they were in the next few minutes.

Keller and Iliana were at the window, staring out at a cool grey sky. Winnie was at the door to the chemistry room, watching the hallway. Galen was a floor beneath them somewhere inside the school, and Nissa was a discreet distance behind him.

And standing beside the circular driveway, obviously waiting for a ride, was a girl with familiar brown hair. She was reading a book that didn't look like a textbook.

Jaime.

It all happened very fast, but there were still distinct stages of warning. Keller was aware of them all.

The first thing she noticed was a blue-green car that cruised down the street in front of the high school. It was going slowly, and she narrowed her eyes, trying to catch a glimpse of the driver.

She couldn't. The car passed on.

I should make her get away from the window, Keller thought. This wasn't as obvious a conclusion as it seemed. The Night People weren't in the habit of using sharpshooters to pick off their targets.

But it was still probably a good idea. Keller was tiredly opening her mouth to say it when something caught her attention.

The blue-green car was back. It was at the exit of the circular driveway, stopped but facing the wrong way, as if it were about to enter.

As Keller watched, it revved its engine.

Keller felt her hairs prickle.

But it didn't make any sense. Why on earth would Night People want to park there and draw attention to themselves? It had to be some human kids acting up.

Iliana was frowning. She had stopped tracing patterns in the dust on the windowsill. 'Who's that? I don't know that car.'

Alarms.

But still . . .

The car roared again and started moving. Coming the wrong way along the driveway.

And Jaime, right below them, didn't look up.

Iliana realized at the same time Keller did.

'Jaime!' She screamed it and pounded the window with one small fist. It didn't do the slightest good, of course.

Beside her, Keller stood frozen and furious.

The car was picking up speed, heading straight for Jaime.

There was nothing to do. Nothing. Keller could never get down there fast enough. It was all going to be over in a second.

But it was horrible. That giant metal thing, tons of steel, was going to hit about a hundred and ten pounds of human flesh.

'Jaime!' It was a scream torn from Iliana.

Below, Jaime finally looked up. But it was too late.

CHAPTER

10

The car coming. Iliana screaming. And the feeling of absolute helplessness—

Glass shattered.

Keller didn't understand at first. She thought that Iliana was trying to break the window and get Jaime's attention. But the window was safety glass, and what broke was the beaker in Iliana's hand.

Blood spurted, shockingly red and liquid.

And Iliana kept squeezing the broken glass in her hand, making more and more blood run.

Her small face was fixed and rigid, her lips slightly parted, her breath held, her whole expression one of complete concentration.

She was calling the blue fire.

Keller lost her own breath.

She's doing it! I'm going to see a Wild Power. Right here, right beside me, it's happening!

She wrenched her own gaze back to the car. She was going to see those tons of metal come to a stop just as the BART train on the video had. Or maybe Iliana would just deflect the car in its course, send it into the grassy island in the middle of the driveway.

In any case, she can hardly deny that she's the Wild Power now –

It was then that Keller realized the car wasn't stopping. It wasn't working.

She heard Iliana make a desperate sound beside her. There was no time for anything more. The car was on top of Jaime, swinging up onto the curb.

Keller's heart lurched.

And something streaked out behind Jaime, hitting her from behind.

It knocked her flying toward the grassy island. Out of the path of the car.

Keller knew who it was even before her eyes could focus on the dark golden hair and long legs.

The car braked and screeched and swerved – but Keller couldn't tell if it had hit him. It went skidding, half on and half off the sidewalk. Then it corrected its course and roared along the driveway, speeding away.

Nissa came dashing out of the door below and stood for an instant, taking in the scene.

Above, Keller was still frozen. She and Iliana were both as motionless as statues.

Then Iliana made a little noise and whirled around. She was off and running before Keller could catch her.

She shot past Winnie, leaving a trail of flying red droplets.

'Come on!' Keller yelled.

They both went after her. But it was like chasing a sunbeam. Keller had had no idea the little thing could run like that.

They were right behind her all the way down the stairs and out the door. It was where Keller wanted to be, anyway.

There were two figures lying on the pavement. They were both very still.

Keller's heart was beating hard enough to break through her chest.

Amazing how, even after seeing so much in her life, she could still have the desperate impulse to shut her eyes. For the first moment, as her gaze raked over Galen's body, she wasn't sure if she could see blood or not. Everything was pulsing with dark spots, and her brain didn't seem able to put any kind of coherent picture together.

Then he moved. The stiff, wincing motion of somebody injured, but not injured badly. He lifted his head, pushed himself up on one elbow, and looked around.

Keller stared at him wordlessly. Then she made her voice obey her. 'Did it hit you?'

'Just glanced off me.' He got his legs under him. 'I'm fine. But what about—'

They both looked at Jaime.

'Goddess!' Galen's voice was filled with horror. He scrambled up and took a limping step before falling to his knees.

Even Keller felt shock sweep over her before she realized what was going on.

At first glance, it looked like a tragedy. Iliana was holding Jaime, cradling her in her arms, and there was blood everywhere. All over the front of Iliana's sweater, all over Jaime's white shirt. It just showed up better on Jaime.

But it was Iliana's blood, still flowing from her cut hand. Jaime was blinking and lifting a hand to her forehead in bewilderment. Her colour was good, and her breathing sounded clear if fast.

'That car – those people were crazy. They were going to hit me.'

'I'm sorry,' Iliana said. 'I'm so sorry; I'm so sorry . . .'

She was so beautiful that Keller's heart seemed to stop.

Her fine skin seemed almost translucent in the cool afternoon light. That glorious hair was rippling in the wind behind her, every single strand light as air and moving independently. And her expression . . .

She was bending over Jaime so tenderly, tears falling like diamonds. Her grief – it was *complete*, Keller thought. As if Jaime were her own dearest sister. She cared in a way that went beyond sympathy and beyond compassion and into something like perfect love.

It . . . transformed her. She wasn't a light-minded child anymore. She was almost . . . angelic.

All at once, Keller understood why everybody at school brought their problems to this girl. It was because of that caring, that love. Iliana didn't help them to make herself popular. She helped because her heart was open, without shields, without the normal barriers that separated people from one another.

And she was as brave as a little lion. She hadn't even hesitated when she saw Jaime in danger. She was afraid of blood, but she'd cut herself instantly, even recklessly, trying to help.

That was courage, Keller thought. Not doing something without being afraid, but doing something even though you *were* afraid.

In that moment, all of Keller's resentment of Iliana melted away. All her anger and exasperation and contempt. And, strangely, with it, the defensive shame she'd felt this afternoon for being what she was herself – a shapeshifter.

It didn't make sense. There was no connection. But there it was.

The flat but strangely pleasant voice of Jaime was going on. 'I'm OK – it was just a shock. Stop crying now. Somebody pushed me out of the way.'

Iliana looked up at Galen.

She was still crying, and her eyes were the colour of violet crystal. Galen was kneeling on one knee, looking down worriedly at Jaime.

Their eyes met, and they both went still. Except for the wind ruffling Iliana's hair, they might have been a painting. A scene from one of the Old Masters, Keller thought. The boy with dark golden hair and that perfectly sculptured face, looking down with protective concern. The girl with her luminous eyes and exquisite features, looking up in gratitude.

It was a sweet and lovely picture. It was also the exact moment that Iliana fell in love with Galen.

And Keller knew it.

She knew before Iliana knew herself. She saw a sort of plaintive shimmer in Iliana's eyes, like more tears about to fall. And then she saw the change in Iliana's face.

The gratitude became something different, something more like . . . recognition. It was as if Iliana were discovering Galen all at once, seeing everything in him that Keller had been slowly learning to see.

They're both . . .

Keller wanted to think *idiots*, but the word wouldn't come. All she ended up with was *the same*.

Both of them. Idealists. Open-hearted. Trying to rescue everyone.

They're perfect for each other.

'You saved her life,' Iliana whispered. 'But you could have been killed yourself.'

'It just happened,' Galen said. 'I moved without thinking. But you – you're really bleeding . . .'

Iliana looked soberly down at her hand. It was the only thing that marred the picture; it was gory and shocking. But Iliana's gaze wasn't frightened. Instead, she looked wise beyond her years and infinitely sad.

'I . . . couldn't help,' she said.

Keller opened her mouth. But before she could say anything, Nissa appeared beside Iliana.

'Here,' she said in her practical way, loosening the carefully knotted scarf at her throat. 'Let me tie it up until we can see if you need stitches.' She glanced up at Keller. 'I got the licence plate of the car.'

Keller blinked and refocussed. Her brain started ticking again.

'Both of you, go get the car,' she said to Nissa and Winnie. 'I'll finish that.' She took Nissa's place by Iliana. 'Are you really all right?' she asked Jaime, careful to face her directly. 'I think we need to take all three of you to the hospital.'

Part of her expected to see a flinching as the dark blue eyes under the soft brown bangs met hers. But, of course, there wasn't any. Nissa's memory blanking had been too good. Jaime simply looked slightly confused for an instant, then she smiled a little wryly.

'I'm really OK.'

'Even so,' Keller said.

There was a crowd gathering. Students and teachers were running from various corners of the building, coming to see what the noise was about. Keller realized that it had actually been only a couple of minutes since the car had gone roaring and screeching along the sidewalk.

A few minutes . . . but the world had changed. In several ways.

'Come on,' she said, and helped Jaime up. She let Galen help Iliana.

And she felt strangely calm and peaceful.

* * *

Galen turned out to have several pulled muscles and lots of scrapes and bruises. Jaime had bruises and a dizzy headache and double vision, which got her actually admitted to the hospital – hardly surprising, considering how many times she'd been knocked down that day, Keller thought.

Iliana needed stitches. She submitted to them quietly, which only seemed to alarm her mother. Mrs Dominick had been called from home to the hospital. She sat with the baby in her lap and listened to Keller try to explain how Iliana had gotten cut while standing at the chemistry room window.

'And when she saw the car almost hit Jaime, she was so startled that she just squeezed the beaker, and it broke.'

Iliana's mother looked doubtful for a moment, but it wasn't her nature to be suspicious. She nodded, accepting the story.

Jaime's parents had been called to the hospital, too, and both Galen and Jaime had to give statements to the police. Nissa flashed Keller a glance when the policewoman asked if anyone had noticed the car's licence plate.

Keller nodded. She had already had Nissa call the number in to Circle Daybreak from a pay phone, but there was no reason not to have the police on the case, too. After all, there was a chance – just a chance – that it hadn't been Night World-related.

Not much of a chance, though. Circle Daybreak agents would follow Jaime and her family after this, watching from the shadows and ready to act if the Night World showed up again. It was a standard precaution.

Both Mr and Ms Ashton-Hughes, Jaime's parents, came down from Jaime's floor to speak to Galen in the emergency room.

'You saved our daughter,' her mother said. 'We don't

know how to thank you.'

Galen shook his head. 'Really, it just happened. I mean, anybody would have done it.'

Ms Ashton-Hughes smiled slightly and shook her head in turn. Then she looked at Iliana.

'Jaime says she hopes your hand heals quickly. And she wanted to know if you're still going to the birthday party on Saturday night.'

'Oh—' For a moment, Iliana looked bewildered, as if she'd forgotten about the party. Then she brightened. 'Yeah, tell her that I am. Is she still going?'

'I think so. The doctor said she can go home tomorrow, as long as she keeps quiet for a few days. And *she* said she wasn't going to miss it even if her head fell off.'

Iliana smiled.

It was well into the evening by the time they all got home. Everyone was tired, even the baby – and Iliana was asleep.

Mr Dominick came hurrying out of the house. He was a medium-sized man with dark hair and glasses, and he looked very anxious. He came around to the backseat as Iliana's mother filled him in on the situation.

But it was Galen who carried Iliana inside.

She didn't wake up. Hardly surprising. The doctor had given her something for the pain, and Keller knew that she hadn't had much sleep the night before. She lay in Galen's arms like a trusting child, her face turned against his shoulder.

They looked . . . very good together, Keller thought. They looked *right*.

Winnie and Nissa hurried upstairs and turned down Iliana's sheets. Galen gently lowered her to the bed.

He stood looking down at her. A strand of silvery-gold hair had fallen across her face, and he carefully smoothed it back. That single gesture told Keller more than anything else could have.

He understands, she thought. It's like that moment when she looked at him and discovered all at once that he's brave and gentle and caring. He understands that she cut herself to try and save Jaime, and that people love her because she loves them so much first. And that she couldn't be petty or spiteful if she tried, and that she's probably never wished another person harm in her life.

He sees all that in her now.

Mrs Dominick came in just then to help get Iliana undressed. Galen, of course, went out. Keller gestured for Winnie and Nissa to stay, and followed him.

This time, she was the one who said, 'Can I talk with you?'

They slipped into the library again, and Keller shut the door. With everything that was going on in the house, she didn't think anyone would notice.

Then she faced him.

She hadn't bothered to turn on the lights. There was some illumination from the window but not much. It didn't really matter. Shapeshifter eyes were good in the dark, and Keller was just as glad he couldn't study her face.

She could see enough of his as he stood by the window. The light picked up the edge of his golden head, and she could see that his expression was troubled and a little uncertain.

'Keller—' he began.

Keller held up a hand to cut him off. 'Wait. Galen, first I want to tell you that you don't owe me an explanation.' She took a breath. 'Look, Galen, what happened this morning was a mistake. And I think we both realize that now.'

'Keller . . .'

'I shouldn't have gotten so upset at you about it. But that's not the point. The point is that things have worked out.'

He looked bleak suddenly. 'Have they?'

'Yes,' Keller said firmly. 'And you don't need to try and pretend otherwise. You care about her. She cares about you. Are you going to try and deny that?'

Galen turned toward the window. He looked more than bleak now; he looked terribly depressed. 'I do care about her,' he said slowly. 'I won't deny it. But—'

'But nothing! It's *good*, Galen. It's what was meant to be, and it's what we came here for. Right?'

He shifted miserably. 'I guess so. But Keller—'

'And it may just possibly save the world,' Keller said flatly.

There was a long silence. Galen's head was down.

'We've got a chance now,' Keller said. 'It should be easy to get her to come to the ceremony on Saturday – as long as we can make her forget about that ridiculous party. I'm not saying use her feelings against her. I'm just saying go with it. She should *want* to be promised to you.'

Galen didn't say anything.

'And that's all. That's what I wanted to tell you. And also that if you're going to act stupid and guilty because of something that was . . . a few minutes of silliness, a mistake – well, then, I'm not going to talk to you ever again.'

His head came up. 'You think it was a mistake?'

'Yes. Absolutely.'

In one motion, he turned around and took her by the shoulders. His fingers tightened, and he stared at her face as if he were trying to see her eyes.

'And that's what you *really* think?'

'Galen, will you please stop worrying about my feelings?' She shrugged out of his grip, still facing him squarely. 'I'm fine. Things have worked out just the way they should. And that's all we ever need to say about it.'

He let out a long breath and turned toward the window again. Keller couldn't tell if the sigh was relief or something else.

'Just make sure she comes to the ceremony. Not that it should be difficult,' she said.

There was another silence. Keller tried to read his emotions through his stance and failed completely.

'Can you do that?' she prompted at last.

'Yes. I can do it. I can try.'

And that was all he said. Keller turned to the door. Then she turned back.

'Thank you,' she said softly. But what she really meant was *Goodbye*, and she knew he knew it.

For a long moment, she thought he wouldn't answer. At last, he said, 'Thank *you*, Keller.'

Keller didn't know what for, and she didn't want to think about it right now. She turned and slipped out of the room.

CHAPTER
11

'She's what?' Keller said, coming out of the bathroom, towelling her hair.

'She's sick,' Winnie said. 'Runny nose, little temperature. Looks like a cold. Her mum says she has to stay home from school.'

Well, it looks like we're having a run of good luck, Keller thought. It would be much easier to protect her inside the house.

Winnie and Nissa had spent the night in Iliana's room, while Keller, who was supposed to be asleep on the sofa bed in the family room, wandered the house in between catnaps. She'd asked Galen to stay in the guest room, and he had done just that.

'We can have a quiet day,' she said now to Winnie. 'This is great – as long as she gets well for Saturday.'

Winnie grimaced.

'What?'

'Um – you'd better go in and talk to her yourself.'

'Why?'

'You'd just better go. She wants to talk to you.'

Keller started toward Iliana's room. She said over her shoulder, 'Check the wards.'

'I know, Boss.'

Iliana was sitting up in bed, wearing a frilly nightgown that actually seemed to have a ribbon woven into the lace at the neck. She looked fragile and beautiful, and there was a delicate flush on her cheeks from the fever.

'How're you feeling?' Keller said, making her voice gentle.

'OK.' Iliana modified it with a shrug that meant *fairly rotten*. 'I just wanted to see you, you know, and say goodbye.'

Keller blinked, still rubbing her hair with the towel. She wasn't crazy about water, especially not in her ears. 'Say goodbye?'

'Before you go.'

'What, you think I'm going to school for you?'

'No. Before you *go*.'

Keller stopped towelling and focussed. 'Iliana, what are you talking about?'

'I'm talking about you guys leaving. Because I'm not the Wild Power.'

Keller sat down on the bed and said flatly, 'What?'

Iliana's eyes were that hazy iris colour again. She looked, in her own way, as annoyed as Keller felt. 'Well, I thought that was obvious. I can't be the Wild Power. I don't have the blue fire – or whatever.' She tacked the last words on.

'Iliana, don't play the dumb blonde with me right now, or I'll have to kill you.'

Iliana just stared at her, picking at the coverlet with her fingers. 'You guys made a mistake. I don't have any power, and I'm not the person you're looking for. Don't you think you ought to go out and look for the *real* Wild Power before the bad guys find her?'

'Iliana, just because you couldn't stop that car doesn't

mean that you don't have power. It could just be that you don't know how to tap into it yet.'

'It *could* be. You're admitting that you're not sure.'

'Nobody can be absolutely sure. Not until you demonstrate it.'

'And that's what I can't do. You probably think I didn't really try, Keller. But I did. I tried so hard.' Iliana's eyes went distant with agonized memory. 'I was standing there, looking down, and I suddenly thought, *I can do it!* I actually thought I felt the power, and that I knew how to use it. But then when I reached for it, there was nothing there. I tried so hard, and I wanted it to work so much . . .' Iliana's eyes filled, and there was a look on her face that struck Keller to the heart. Then she shook her head and looked back at Keller. *'It wasn't there.* I know that. I'm certain.'

'It has to be there,' Keller said. 'Circle Daybreak has been investigating this ever since they found that prophecy. "One from the hearth that still holds the spark." They've tracked down all the other Harmans and checked them. It *has* to be you.'

'Then maybe it's somebody you haven't found yet. Some other lost witch. But it's *not me.*'

She was completely adamant and genuinely convinced. Keller could see it in her eyes. She had managed to vault back into denial in a whole new way.

'So I know you'll be leaving,' Iliana went on. 'And, actually, I'll really miss you.' She blinked away tears again. 'I suppose you don't believe that.'

'Oh, I believe it,' Keller said tiredly, staring at an exquisite gold-and-white dresser across the room.

'I really like you guys. But I know what you're doing is important.'

'Well, is it OK with you if we just hang around for a

little while longer?' Keller asked heavily. 'Just until we see the light and realize you're not the Wild Power?'

Iliana frowned. 'Don't you think it's a waste of time?'

'Maybe. But I don't make those decisions. I'm just a grunt.'

'Don't you *treat* me like a dumb blonde.'

Keller opened her mouth, lifted her hands, then dropped them. What she wanted to say was, *How can I help it when you're determined to be such a nincompoop?* But that wasn't going to get them anywhere.

'Look, Iliana. I really do have to stay until I get orders to go, all right?' Keller said, looking at her. 'So you're just going to have to bear with us for a little while longer.'

She stood up, feeling as if a weight had fallen on her. They were back to square one.

Or maybe not quite.

'Besides, what about Galen?' she said, turning back at the door. 'Do you want *him* to go?'

Iliana looked confused. Her cheeks got even pinker. 'I don't . . . I mean . . .'

'If you're not the Wild Power, you're not the Witch Child,' Keller went on ruthlessly. 'And you know that Galen has to promise himself to the Witch Child.'

Iliana was breathing quickly now. She gulped and stared at the window. She bit her lip.

She really is in love with him, Keller thought. *And she knows it*.

'Just something to keep in mind,' she said, and went out the door.

'Did you get any info on the licence plate?'

Nissa shook her head. 'Not yet. They'll call us when they have anything. And a courier brought this.'

She handed Keller a box. It was the size of a shirt box but very sturdy.

'The scrolls?'

'I think so. There are wards on it, so we have to get Winnie to open it.'

They had a chance after breakfast. Mrs Dominick took the baby and went out shopping. Keller didn't worry too much about her. Just as Jaime was now being watched by Circle Daybreak agents, any members of Iliana's family who left the safety of the wards would be followed for their own protection.

They sat around the kitchen table – except for Iliana, who refused to join them and sat in the family room in front of the TV. She had a box of tissues, and every few minutes she would apply one to her nose.

'Before you open that,' Keller said to Winnie, 'how are the wards around the house?'

'They're fine. Intact and strong. I don't think anybody's even tried to mess with them.'

Galen said, 'I wonder why.'

Keller looked at him quickly. It was just what she had been wondering herself. 'Maybe it has something to do with what happened yesterday. And that's the other thing I want to talk about. I want to hear everybody's opinions. Who was in that car – Night Person or human? Why did they try to run over Jaime? And what are we going to do about it?'

'You go first,' Winnie said. 'I think you had the best view of it.'

'Well, I wasn't the only one,' Keller said. 'There was someone else beside me.' She looked toward the living room. Iliana made a show of ignoring her completely.

Keller turned back. 'But anyway, simplest first. Let's say the car was from the Night World. They cruised down the street in front of the school once before coming back. It's perfectly possible that they saw Iliana standing at the window. Maybe they were trying to determine for sure that she was the Wild Power. If she'd stopped the car, they'd have had solid proof.'

'On the other hand,' Nissa said, 'they must be pretty sure she's the Wild Power. After all, it's really beyond question.' She was looking earnestly at Keller, but she spoke loudly enough for Iliana to hear everything distinctly.

Keller smiled with her eyes. 'True. OK, more ideas. Winnie.'

'Uh – right.' Winnie sat up straighter. 'The car was from the Night World, and they weren't actually trying to run over Jaime. They were going to snatch her because they somehow knew she'd been with us, and they figured she might have some information they could use.'

'Nice try,' Keller said. 'But you were over by the door. You didn't see the way that car was driving. No way they were planning to grab her.'

'I agree,' Galen said. 'They were going too fast, and they were heading right for her. They meant to kill.'

Winnie dropped her chin into her hands. 'Oh, well, fine. It was just an idea.'

'It brings up something interesting, though,' Nissa said thoughtfully. 'What if the car was from the Night World, and they knew Iliana was watching, but they *weren't* trying to get her to demonstrate her power? What if they were just trying to intimidate her? Show what they were capable of, by killing her friend right in front of her eyes? If they knew how close she and Jaime were—'

'How?' Keller interrupted.

'Lots of ways,' Nissa said promptly. 'If they haven't snooped around that high school and talked to other kids, their intelligence system is worse than I think. I'll go farther. If they don't know that Jaime was in that music room with *us* yesterday at lunch, they ought to turn in their spy badges.'

'If that's true, then maybe it's even simpler than we think,' Galen said. 'The law says that any human who finds out about us has to die. Maybe the car was from the Night World, and they didn't know that Iliana was watching – or they didn't care. They thought Jaime knew the secret, and they just wanted to carry out a good, old-fashioned Night World execution.'

'And maybe the car *wasn't* from the Night World!' Iliana yelled suddenly, jumping off the family room couch. She wasn't even pretending not to listen anymore, Keller noted. 'Did any of you ever think of that? Maybe the car just belonged to some crazed juvenile delinquents and it's all a massive coincidence! Well? Did you think of that?' She stood with her hands on her hips, glaring at all of them. The effect was somewhat diluted because she was wearing a frilly nightgown with a flannel robe over it and slippers with teddy bear heads on them.

Keller stood up, too. She wanted to be patient and make the most of this opportunity. But she never seemed to have much control where Iliana was concerned.

'We've thought of it. Circle Daybreak is trying to check on it – whether the car's registered to a human or a Night Person. But you're asking for a lot of coincidence, aren't you? How often do people deliberately run each other over in this town? What are the chances that you just happened to be watching when one of them did it?'

She felt Galen nudge her ankle with his foot. With an effort, she shut up.

'Why don't you come over here and talk with us about it?' he said to Iliana in his gentle way. 'Even if you're not the Wild Power, you're still involved. You know a lot about what's been going on, and you've got a good mind. We need all the help we can get.'

Keller saw Winnie glance at him sharply when he said the bit about Iliana having a good mind. But she didn't say anything.

Iliana looked a little startled herself. But then she picked up the box of tissues and slowly came to the kitchen table.

'I don't think well when I'm sick,' she said.

Keller sat down. She didn't want to undo what Galen had accomplished. 'So where does that leave us?' she asked, and then answered her own question. 'Nowhere, really. It could be any of those scenarios or none of them. We may need to wait for whatever Circle Daybreak comes up with.'

Keller looked around the table grimly. 'And that's *dangerous*,' she said. 'Assuming it was the Night World that sent that car, they're up to something that we don't understand. They could attack us at any moment, from any direction, and we can't anticipate them. I need for all of you to be on your guard. If anything suspicious happens, even the littlest thing, I want you to tell me.'

'It still bothers me that they haven't even tried to get in here,' Galen said. 'No matter how strong the wards are, they should at least be *trying*.'

Keller nodded. She had an uneasy feeling in the pit of her stomach about that. 'They may be laying some kind of a trap somewhere else, and they may be so confident that we'll fall into it that they can afford to wait.'

'Or it could be that they know I'm not the one,' Iliana chimed in sweetly. 'And they're off kidnapping the real Wild Power while you guys are wasting your time here.' She blew her nose.

Keller gritted her teeth and felt a pain in her jaw that was getting familiar. 'Or it could be that we just don't understand dragons,' she said, possibly with more force than was necessary.

She and Iliana locked stares.

'You guys, you guys,' Winnie said nervously. 'Um, maybe it's time we opened this.' She touched the box Circle Daybreak had sent.

Iliana's eyes shifted to it with something like involuntary interest. Keller could see why. The box had the mysterious allure of a Christmas present.

'Go ahead,' she told Winnie.

It took a while. Winnie did witchy things with a bag of herbs and some talismans, while everyone watched intently and Iliana mopped her nose and sniffled.

At last, very carefully, Winnie lifted the top of the box off.

Everyone leaned forward.

Piled inside were dozens and dozens of pieces of parchment. Not entire scrolls but scraps of them, each encased in its own plastic sleeve. Keller recognized the writing – it was the old language of the shapeshifters. She'd learned it as a child, because Circle Daybreak wanted her to keep in touch with her heritage. But it had been a long time since she'd had to translate it.

Iliana sneezed and said almost reluctantly, 'Cool pictures.'

There were cool pictures. Most of the scraps had three or four tiny illustrations, and some of them had only pictures and no writing. The inks were red and purple and deep royal blue, with details in gold leaf.

Keller spread some of the plastic sleeves across the table.

'OK, people. The idea is to find something that will

show us how to fight the dragon, or at least something to tell us how he might attack. The truth is that we don't even know what he can do, except for the black energy he used on me.'

'Um, I can't *read* this, you know,' Iliana pointed out with excessive politeness.

'So look at the pictures,' Keller said sweetly. 'Try to find something where a dragon is fighting a person – or, even better, getting killed by one.'

'How do I know which one's the dragon?' It was an amazingly good question. Keller blinked and looked at Galen.

'Well, actually, I don't know. I don't know if anybody knows how to tell a dragon from another Night Person.'

'The one in the mall – Azhdeha – had opaque black eyes,' Keller said. 'You could tell when you looked into them. But I don't suppose that's going to show up on a parchment like this. Why don't you just look for something with dark energy around it?'

Iliana made a tiny noise that in someone less delicate would have been called a snort. But she took a pile of the scraps and began poring over them.

'OK,' Keller said. 'Now, the rest of us—'

But she never got to finish. The phone on the kitchen wall shrilled. Everyone glanced up toward it, and Iliana started to stand, but there was no second ring. After a long moment of silence, it rang again – once.

'Circle Daybreak,' Keller said. 'Nissa, call them back.'

Keller tried not to fidget as Nissa obeyed. It wasn't just that she was hoping against hope that there was useful information about the car. For some reason she couldn't define, that very first ring of the phone had made her feel unsettled.

The early warning system of the shapeshifters. It had

saved her life before, by giving her a hint of danger. But for what was about to happen now, it was entirely useless.

'Nissa Johnson here. Code word: Angel Rescue,' Nissa said, and Keller saw Iliana's eyebrows go up. 'Yes, I'm listening. What?' Suddenly, her face changed. 'What do you mean, am I sitting down?' Pause. 'Look, Paulie, just tell me whatever—'

And then her face changed again, and she did something Keller had never seen Nissa do. She gasped and brought a quick hand up to her mouth.

'Oh, Goddess, no!'

Keller's heart was pounding, and there was a boulder of ice in her stomach. She found herself on her feet without any memory of standing.

Nissa's light brown eyes were distant, almost blank. Her other hand clutched the receiver. *'How?'* Then she shut her eyes. 'Oh, no.' And finally, very softly, 'Goddess help us.'

CHAPTER

12

They were all on their feet by now. Keller's early warning system was screaming hysterically.

'I can't stand it anymore,' Iliana hissed. 'What's going *on*?'

Just then, Nissa said in a quenched voice, 'All right, we will. Yes. 'Bye.' She carefully replaced the handset.

Then she turned very slowly to face the others.

Or not to face them exactly. She was looking down at the floor in an unfocussed way that scared Keller to death.

'Well, what is it?' Keller growled.

Nissa opened her mouth and raised her eyes to look at Winnie. Then she looked down again.

'I'm sorry,' she said. 'Winnie, I don't know how to say this.' She swallowed and then straightened, speaking formally. 'The Crone of all the Witches is dead.'

Winnie's eyes went huge, and her hands flew to her throat. 'Grandma Harman!'

'Yes.'

'But how?'

Nissa spoke carefully. 'It happened yesterday in Las Vegas. She was outside her shop, right there on a city street, in broad daylight. She was attacked . . . by three shapeshifters.'

Keller stood and listened to her pounding heart.

Winnie breathed, 'No. That's not possible.'

'A couple of wolves and a tiger. A real tiger, Keller, not any smaller cat. There were human witnesses who saw it. It's being reported as some bizarre escape from a private zoo.'

Keller stood rigid. Control, control, she thought. We don't have time for grieving; we've got to figure out what this *means*.

But she couldn't help thinking about Grandma Harman's good old face. Not a beautiful face, not a young face, but a *good* one, with intelligence and humour in the keen grey eyes. A face with a thousand wrinkles – and a story to go with each one.

How would Circle Daybreak ever get along without her? The oldest witch in the world, the oldest Hearth-Woman.

Winnie put both hands to her face and began to cry.

The others stood silently. Keller didn't know what to do. She was so bad at these emotional things, but nobody else was stepping forward. Nissa was even less good at dealing with emotion, and right now her cool face was sympathetic and sad but distant. Iliana looked on the verge of tears herself, but uncertain. Galen was staring emptily across the room with something like despair.

Keller awkwardly put an arm around Winnie. 'Come on, sit down. Do you want some tea? She wouldn't like you to cry.'

All pretty stupid things to say. But Winnie buried her strawberry-blonde head against Keller's chest, sobbing.

'Why? Why did they kill her? It isn't *right*.'

Nissa shifted uneasily. 'Paulie said something about that, too. He said we should turn on CNN.'

Keller set her teeth. 'Where's the remote?' she said,

trying not to sound rough.

Iliana picked it up and punched in a channel.

An anchorwoman was speaking, but for a second Keller couldn't take in what she was saying. All she could see were the words on the screen: 'CNN SPECIAL REPORT: ANIMAL PANIC.'

And the footage, rough video from somebody's camcorder. It showed an unbelievable scene. An ordinary city street, with skyscrapers in the background – and in the foreground ordinary-looking people all mixed up with . . . shapes.

Tawny shapes. About the same size she was in panther form, and sinuous. They were on top of people. Four of them . . . no, five.

Mountain lions.

They were killing the humans.

A woman was screaming, flailing at an animal that had her arm in its mouth to the elbow. A man was trying to pull another lion off a little boy.

Then something with a white-tipped muzzle ran directly at the camera. It jumped. There was a gasping scream and for an instant a glimpse of a wide-open mouth filled with two-inch teeth. Then the video turned to static.

'—that was the scene at the La Brea tar pits in Los Angeles today. We now go to Ron Hennessy, live outside the Los Angeles Chamber of Commerce . . .'

Keller stood frozen, her fists clenched in helpless fury.

'It's happening everywhere,' Nissa said quietly from behind her. 'That's what Paulie said. Every major city in the U.S. is being attacked. A white rhino killed two people in Miami. In Chicago, a pack of timber wolves killed an armed police officer.'

'Shapeshifters,' Keller whispered.

'Yes. Killing humans openly. They may even be

transforming openly. Paulie said that some people claimed to see those Chicago wolves change. She took a deep breath and spoke slowly. 'Keller, the time of chaos at the end of the millennium . . . it's happening *now*. They can't cover this up with a 'private zoo' story. This is it – the beginning of the time when humans find out about the Night World.'

Iliana looked bewildered. 'But why would shapeshifters start attacking humans? And why would they kill Grandma Harman?'

Keller shook her head. She was rapidly approaching numbness. She glanced at Galen and saw that he felt exactly the same.

Then there was a choked sound beside her.

'That's the question – *why*,' Winnie said in a thick voice. Usually, with her elfin features and mop of curls, she looked younger than her age. But right now, the skin on her face was drawn tight, and her birdlike bones made her look almost like an old woman.

She turned on Keller and Galen, and her eyes were burning.

'Not just why they're doing it, why they're being allowed to do it. Where's the First House while all this is going on? Why aren't they monitoring their own people? Is it because they agree with what's happening?'

The last words were snapped out with a viciousness that Keller had never heard in Winfrith before.

Galen opened his mouth, then he shook his head. 'Winnie, I don't think—'

'You don't think! You don't *know*? What are your parents doing? Are you saying you don't know *that*?'

'Winnie—'

'They *killed* our oldest leader. Our wise woman. You know, some people would take that as a declaration of war.'

Keller felt stricken and at the same time furious at her own helplessness. She was in charge here; she should be heading Winnie off.

But she was a shapeshifter like Galen. And along with the ability to transform and the exquisitely tuned senses, they both shared something unique to their race.

The guilt of the shapeshifters.

The terrible guilt that went back to the ancient days and was part of the very fabric of Keller's mind. No shapeshifter could forget it or escape it, and nobody who *wasn't* a shapeshifter could ever understand.

The guilt was what held Galen standing there while Winnie yelled at him, and held Keller unable to interrupt.

Winnie was right in front of Galen now, her eyes blazing, her body crackling with latent energy like a small but fiery orange comet.

'Who woke that dragon up, anyway?' she demanded. 'How do we know the shapeshifters aren't up to their old tricks? Maybe this time they're going to wipe the witches out completely—'

'*Stop it!*'

It was Iliana.

She planted herself in front of Winnie, small but earnest, a little ice maiden to combat the witch's fire. Her nose was pink and swollen, and she was still wearing those teddy bear slippers, but to Keller she somehow looked valiant and magnificent.

'Stop hurting each other,' she said. 'I don't understand any of this, but I know that you're not going to get anywhere if you fight. And I know you don't *want* to fight.' All at once, she flung her arms around Winnie. 'I know how you feel – it's so awful. I felt the same way when Grandma Mary died, my mum's mother. All I could think of was that it was just so unfair.'

Winfrith hesitated, standing stiffly in Iliana's embrace. Then, slowly, she lifted her own arms to hold Iliana back.

'We *need* her,' she whispered.

'I know. And you feel mad at the people who killed her. But it's not Galen's fault. Galen would never hurt anybody.'

It was said with absolute conviction. Iliana wasn't even looking at Galen. She was stating a fact that she felt was common knowledge. But at the same time, now that she was off her guard, her expression was tender and almost shining.

Yes, that's love, all right, Keller thought. And it's *good*.

Very slowly, Winnie said, 'I know *Galen* wouldn't. But the shapeshifters—'

'Maybe,' Galen said, 'we should talk about that.' If Winnie's face was pinched, his was set in steel. His eyes were so dark that Keller couldn't distinguish the colour.

'Maybe we should talk about the shapeshifters,' he said. He nodded toward the kitchen table, which was still strewn with the parchments. 'About their history and about the dragons.' He looked at Iliana. 'If there's any chance of – of a promise ceremony between us, it's stuff you ought to know.'

Iliana looked startled.

'He's right,' Nissa said in her calm voice. 'After all, that's what we were doing to start with. It's all tied together.'

Keller's whole body was tight. This was something that she very much didn't want to talk about. But she refused to give in to her own weakness. With a tremendous effort, she managed to say steadily, 'All right. The whole story.'

'It started back in the days humans were still living in caves,' Galen said when they were all sitting down at the kitchen table again. His voice was so bleak and controlled that it didn't even sound like Galen.

'The shapeshifters ruled then, and they were brutal. In some places, they were just the totem spirits who demanded human sacrifice, but in others . . .' He searched through the parchments, selected one. 'This is a picture of a breeding pen, with humans in it. They treated humans exactly the way humans treat cattle, breeding them for their hearts and livers. And the more human flesh they ate, the stronger they got.'

Iliana looked down at the parchment scrap, and her hand abruptly clenched on a tissue. Winnie listened silently, her pointed face stern.

'They were stronger than anyone,' Galen said. 'Humans were like flies to them. The witches were more trouble, but the dragons could beat them.'

Iliana looked up. 'What about the vampires?'

'There weren't any yet,' Galen said quietly. 'The first one was Maya Hearth-Woman, the sister of Hellewise Hearth-Woman. She made herself into a vampire when she was looking for immortality. But the dragons were naturally immortal, and they were the undisputed rulers of the planet. And they had about as much pity for others as a *T. rex* has.'

'But *all* the shapeshifters weren't like that, were they?' Iliana asked. 'There were other kinds besides the dragons, right?'

'They were all bad,' Keller said simply. 'My ancestors – the big felines – were pretty awful. But the bears and the wolves did their share.'

'But you're right, the dragons were the worst,' Galen said to Iliana. 'And that's who *my* family is descended from. My last name, Drache, means 'dragon'. Of course, it was the *weakest* of the dragons that was my ancestor. The one the witches left awake because she was so young.' He turned to Winnie. 'Maybe you'd better tell that part. The witches know their own history best.'

Still looking severe, Winnie thumbed through the parchment scraps until she found one. 'Here,' she said. 'It's a picture of the gathering of the witches. Hecate Witch-Queen organized it. She was Hellewise's mother. She got all the witches together, and they went after the shapeshifters. There was a big fight. A really big fight.'

Winnie selected another piece of scroll and pushed it toward Iliana.

Iliana gasped.

The parchment piece she was looking down at was almost solid red.

'It's fire,' she said. 'It looks like – it looks like the whole world's on fire.'

Galen's voice was flat. '*That's* what the dragons did. Geological records show that volcanoes all over the world erupted around then. The dragons did that. I don't know how; the magic's lost. But they figured that if they couldn't have the world, nobody else would, either.'

'They tried to destroy the world,' Keller said. 'And the rest of the shapeshifters helped.'

'It almost worked, too,' Winnie said. 'But the gathering of witches managed to win, and they buried all the dragons alive. I mean, they put them to *sleep* first, but then they buried them in the deepest places of the earth.' She bit her lip and looked at Galen. 'Which probably wasn't very nice, either.'

'What else could they do?' Galen said quietly. 'They left the dragon princess alive – she was only three or four years old. They let her grow up, under their guidance. But the world was a scorched and barren place for a long time. And the shapeshifters have always been . . . the lowest of all the Night People.'

'That's true,' Nissa put in, her voice neither approving nor disapproving, simply making an observation. 'Most Night People consider shapeshifters second-class citizens. They try to keep them down. I think, underneath, that they're still afraid of them.'

'And there's never been an alliance between the shapeshifters and the witches,' Keller said. She looked directly at Iliana. 'That's why the promise ceremony is so important. If the shapeshifters don't side with the witches, they're going to go with the vampires—'

She stopped abruptly and looked at Galen.

He nodded. 'I was thinking the same thing.'

'Those animal attacks,' Keller said slowly. 'It sounds as if the shapeshifters are already making their decision. They're helping to bring about the time of chaos at the end of the millennium. They're letting the whole world know that they're siding with the vampires.'

There was a shocked silence.

'But how can *they* decide?' Winnie began.

'That's just it,' Nissa said. 'The question is, is it just the ordinary shapeshifters who're doing it, or is it official? In other words, has the First House already decided?'

Everyone looked at Galen.

'I don't think so,' he said. 'I don't think they'll make any decision yet, at least not in public. As for what they're doing in private, I don't know.' His voice was still flat; it made no excuses.

He looked around the table, facing all of them. 'My parents are warriors. They don't belong to Circle Daybreak, and they don't like the witches. But they don't like the vampires, either. More than anything, they'll want to be on whichever side is going to *win*. And that depends on which side gets the Wild Powers.'

'I think they want something else,' Keller said.

'Like?'

'They want to know that the witches are treating them fairly and not just trying to use them. I mean, if they thought that Circle Daybreak had found the Witch Child but wasn't going to promise her to their heir, well, they wouldn't be happy. It's not just a matter of having a kinship bond with the witches. It's a matter of feeling they're being treated as equals.'

Nissa's light brown eyes narrowed, and she seemed almost to smile. 'I think you've summed it up very well.'

'So what it all comes down to,' Keller said pointedly, 'is what happens on Saturday night. If there's a promise ceremony, it means the witches have found the Wild Power and that they're willing to tie her to the shapeshifters. If not . . .'

She let the sentence trail off and looked at Iliana.

There, she thought. I've put it so plainly and simply, you can't deny it now. And you can't help but see what's at stake.

Iliana's eyes were like faraway violet storm clouds. Keller couldn't tell what she was thinking. Maybe that the situation couldn't be denied but that she herself wasn't involved.

Winnie took a deep breath. 'Galen.'

Her face was still drawn and unhappy, but the burning anger in her eyes was gone. She met Galen's gaze directly.

'I'm sorry,' she said. 'I shouldn't have said those things before. I know you're on our side. And I'm not like those people who don't trust the shapeshifters.'

Galen smiled at her faintly, but his eyes were serious. 'I don't know. Maybe you shouldn't trust us. There are things in our blood – you can't get rid of the dragon completely.'

It was strange. At that moment, his eyes looked not

only dark but almost red to Keller. Exactly the opposite of their usual golden-green. It was as if a light were smouldering somewhere deep inside them.

Then Winnie abruptly extended her hand across the table. 'I know *you*,' she said. 'And there's nothing bad in your blood. I won't mistrust you again.'

Galen hesitated one instant, then reached out with something like gratitude and took her hand.

'Thanks,' he whispered.

'Hey, if *I* were the Witch Child, I'd promise to you in a minute,' Winnie said. Then she sniffled, but her smile was much more like the old Winnie's smile.

Keller glanced at Iliana almost casually and was riveted by what she saw.

The girl had changed again. Now she didn't look like a princess or an ice maiden but like a very young soldier about to go into battle. Or maybe a human sacrifice who could save her tribe by jumping into a volcano.

Her hair seemed to shine, silvery and pale, and her eyes were deep, deep violet in her small face. Her slight shoulders were back, and her chin was determined.

Slowly, staring at something invisible in the centre of the table, Iliana stood up.

As soon as the motion drew their attention, the others fell quiet. It was obvious to everyone that something important was happening.

Iliana stood there, her hands clenched by her sides, her chest rising and falling with her breathing. Then she looked at Galen. Finally, she looked at Keller.

'I'm not the Witch Child any more than Winnie is. And I think you know that by now. But . . .' She took a breath, steadied herself.

Keller held her own breath.

'But if you want me to pretend to be, I'll do it. I'll go to the promise ceremony with Galen – I mean, if he'll do it with me.' She gave a half-embarrassed glance at Galen, looking shy and almost apologetic.

'Will he ever!' Winnie said enthusiastically. Keller could have kissed her. Galen himself didn't rise to the occasion properly at all; instead, he opened his mouth, looking uncertain.

Fortunately, Iliana was going on. 'Then I'll go through with it. And maybe that will be enough for the shapeshifters to join with the witches, as long as they don't find out I'm a fake.' She looked unhappy.

She was so adamant that for a moment Keller was shaken. Could it be she *wasn't* the Wild Power? But no. Keller *knew* she was. She just hasn't awakened her power yet. And if she continued to deny it, she never would.

She said, 'Thank you, Iliana. You don't know how much, how many lives you're going to save. Thank you.'

Then the excitement got the better of her, and she took Iliana by the arm and gave her a sort of shaking squeeze of affection.

'You're a trooper!' Winnie said, and hugged her hard. 'I knew you'd come through all the time, I really did.'

Nissa smiled at her with genuine approval. Galen was smiling, too, although there was something in his eyes . . .

'There's just one thing,' Iliana said a little bit breathlessly, rubbing her arm where Keller had gripped it. 'I'll do this. I said I would. But I have two conditions.'

CHAPTER

13

Keller's excitement deflated. 'Conditions?'

'You can have anything you want,' Winnie said, blinking away happy tears. 'Cars, clothes, books . . .'

'No, no, I don't want *things*,' Iliana said. 'What I mean is, I'm doing this because I can't just stand around and *not* do anything when stuff like that is going on.' She shivered. 'I have to do anything I can to help. But. I'm still not the right person. So the first condition is that while I'm pretending to be the Wild Power, you guys have somebody out looking for the real one.'

Keller said smoothly, 'I'll tell Circle Daybreak. They'll keep looking and checking other Harmans. They'll do it for as long as you want them to.'

They would, too. It was a small price to pay.

'And the other condition?' Keller asked.

'I want to go to Jaime's party on Saturday.'

Instant uproar. Even Nissa was talking over people. Keller cut short her own exclamations and gestured for everybody to shut up.

Then she looked Iliana dead in the eye.

'It's impossible. And you *know* it's impossible. Unless you've found a way to be in two places at once.'

'Don't be stupid,' Iliana said. That small, determined chin was tight. 'I mean *before* the promise ceremony thing. I want to go just for an hour or two. Because she's one of my very best friends, and she's gotten attacked twice because of me.'

'So what? You're already making it up to her. You're saving her life and her twin brother's life and her parents' lives—'

'No, I'm *not*. I'm faking being a Wild Power when I know it isn't true. I'm acting a lie.' There were tears in Iliana's eyes now. 'But I'm not going to hurt Jaime's feelings, and I'm not going to break my promise to her. And that's that. So if you want me to go through with your little charade, I'll do it, but I want to go to the party first.'

There was a silence.

Well, she's stubborn, I'll give her that, Keller thought. Once she decides on something, she absolutely won't be budged on it. I guess that will be helpful when the Wild Powers fight the darkness someday.

But right now, it was simply infuriating.

Keller drew a very long breath and said, 'OK.'

Winnie and Nissa looked at her sharply. They hadn't expected her to give in so fast, and they were undoubtedly wondering if their boss had some trick up her sleeve.

Unfortunately, Keller didn't. 'We'll just have to work something out,' she said to her team. 'Make it as safe as possible, and stick by her every minute.'

Winnie and Nissa exchanged unhappy glances. But they didn't say anything.

Keller looked at Iliana. 'The one thing is, you *have* to be at the Solstice Ceremony at midnight. They're meeting in Charlotte, so that's about twenty minutes' drive, and we'd better leave plenty of time for safety. Say an hour at the least. If you're not there, where the shapeshifters and the witches are meeting, at exactly midnight—'

'My coach turns into a pumpkin,' Iliana said tartly. She swabbed her nose with a tissue.

'No, the shapeshifters walk out, and any chance of an alliance is gone forever.'

Iliana sobered, stared at the table. Then she met Keller's eyes. 'I'll be there. I know it, and you know why? Because *you'll* get me there.'

Keller stared at her, astonished. She heard Winnie give a short yelp of laughter and saw that Nissa was hiding a smile.

Then she felt a smile pulling up the corner of her own lip. 'You're right; I will. Even if I have to drag you. Here, shake on it.'

They did. And then Iliana turned to Galen.

She had been watching him out of the corner of her eye ever since she'd first started talking. And now she looked hesitant again.

'If there's anything – any reason I *shouldn't* do it . . .' She fumbled to a stop.

Keller kicked Galen's ankle *hard*.

He glanced up. He still didn't look like the Galen she knew. Talking about the dragons had done something to him, thrown a shadow across his face and turned his eyes inward. And Iliana's announcement hadn't lightened anything.

Keller stared at him intently, wishing she had telepathy. Don't you dare, she was thinking. What's *wrong* with you? If you mess this up, after all the work we've done and with so much at stake . . .

Then she realized something. Before, when he'd been telling the history of the dragons, Galen had looked brooding and a little scary. Now, he still looked brooding but unutterably sad. Heart-stricken – and full of such regret.

She could almost hear his voice in her head. *Keller, I'm sorry . . .*

Don't be an idiot, Keller thought, and maybe she wasn't telepathic, but she was certain that he could read her eyes. What have you got to be sorry for? Hurry up and do what you're supposed to do.

Her heart was pounding, but she kept her breathing tightly controlled. Nothing mattered but Circle Daybreak and the alliance. Nothing. To think of anything else at a time like this would be the height of selfishness.

And love is for the weak.

Galen dropped his eyes, almost as if he had lost a battle. Then he turned slowly from Keller to Iliana.

Who was standing with tears about to fall, hanging like diamonds on her lashes. Keller felt a twisting inside her chest.

But Galen, as always, was doing exactly the right thing. He took Iliana's hand gently and brought it to his cheek in a gesture of humility and simplicity. He could do that without stopping looking noble for a moment.

After all, he *was* a prince.

'I'd be very honoured to go through the promise ceremony with you,' he said, looking up at her. 'If you can bring yourself to do it with me. You understand everything I was telling you before – about my family . . .'

Iliana blinked and breathed again. The tears had magically disappeared, leaving her eyes like violets freshly washed in rain. 'I understand all that. It doesn't matter. It doesn't change anything about *you*, and you're still one of the best people I've ever met.' She blinked again and smiled.

Nobody could have resisted it. Galen smiled back.

'Not nearly as good as you.'

They stayed that way for a moment, looking at each other, holding hands – and glowing. They looked perfect together, silver and gold, a fairy-tale picture.

That's it. It's done. She'll have to go through the ceremony now, Keller thought. As long as we can keep her alive, we've recruited a Wild Power. Mission accomplished.

I'm really happy about this.

So why was there a heaviness in her chest that hurt each time she breathed?

It was late that afternoon when the second call came.

'Well, they found the driver of the car,' Nissa said.

Keller looked up. They'd moved the box full of scrolls to Iliana's bedroom when Mrs Dominick came back from shopping. Now they had them untidily spread out on the floor while Iliana lay on the bed heavy-eyed and almost asleep. She perked up when Nissa came in.

'Who was it?'

'A shapeshifter. Name of Fulton Arnold. He lives about ten miles from here.'

Keller tensed. 'Arnold. "Eagle ruler." ' She glanced at Galen.

He nodded grimly. 'The eagles are going to have some explaining to do. Damn it, they've always been hard to get along with, but this . . .'

'So it *was* connected with the Night World,' Winnie said. 'But did Circle Daybreak figure out why?'

Nissa sat down on the chair in front of Iliana's gold-and-white vanity. 'Well, they've got an idea.' She looked at Galen. 'You're not going to like it.'

He put down a piece of scroll and sat up very straight, bleak and self-contained. 'What?'

'You know all our theories about why shapeshifters are

attacking humans? Whether it's just the common 'shifter on the street or orders from the First House and so on? Well, Circle Daybreak thinks it's orders, but not from the First House.'

'The shapeshifters wouldn't take orders from vampires,' Galen said stiffly. 'So the Night World Council is out.'

'They think it's the dragon.'

Keller shut her eyes and hit herself on the forehead.

Of course. Why hadn't she thought of it? The dragon giving direct orders, setting himself up as a legendary ruler who had returned to save the shapeshifters. 'It's like King Arthur coming back,' she muttered.

On her bed, Iliana was frowning in shock. 'But you said dragons were evil. You said they were cruel and horrible and tried to destroy the world.'

'Right,' Keller said dryly. Only Iliana would think that this constituted a reason not to follow them. 'They were all those things. But they were also strong. They kept the shapeshifters on top. I'm sure there are plenty of 'shifters who'd welcome a dragon back.' She looked at Galen in growing concern as she figured it out. 'They're going to think it means a new era for them, maybe even a return to shapeshifter rule. And if *that's* what they think, nothing the First House says is going to make any difference. Even the mice are going to rally round Azhdeha.'

'You mean the promise ceremony is no good?' Iliana sat up. The interesting thing was that she didn't look particularly relieved – in fact, Keller thought, she looked positively dismayed.

'No, so don't even get that idea,' Keller said shortly. 'What it means is—' She stopped dead, realizing suddenly what it *did* mean. 'What it means is . . .'

Galen said, 'We have to kill the dragon.'

Keller nodded. 'Yeah. Not just fight it. We have to get rid of it. Make sure it's not around to give orders to anybody. It's the only way to keep the shapeshifters from being split.'

Iliana looked down soberly at the snowstorm of paper that covered her floor. 'Does any of that stuff tell you how to kill a dragon?'

Keller lifted a piece of parchment, dropped it. 'So far, none of this stuff has told us *anything* useful.'

'Yeah, but we haven't even looked through half of it,' Winnie pointed out. 'And since you and Galen are the only ones who can read the writing, the parts Nissa and I have gone through don't really count.'

There was definitely a lot of work left. Keller stifled a sigh and said briskly, 'Well, we don't need to worry about killing the dragon right now. If we can fight him off long enough to get through the promise ceremony, we can worry about destroying him afterward. Winnie, why don't you and Nissa start trying to figure out a way to protect Iliana at the party Saturday? And Galen and I can stay up tonight and read through these scrolls.'

Winnie looked concerned. 'Boss, you're trying to do too much. If you don't sleep sometime, you're going to start cracking up.'

'I'll sleep on Sunday,' Keller said firmly. 'When it's all over.'

Keller had meant that she and Galen could study the scrolls separately that night. But when everybody else headed for their bedrooms, he stayed in the family room with her and watched the eleven o'clock news. More animal attacks.

When it was over, Keller pulled out her pile of scroll fragments. It was her way of saying good night, and much easier than looking at him.

But he just said quietly, 'I'll get my half,' and brought them out.

Keller felt uncomfortable. It wasn't that she could find any fault with what he was doing. He was studying his pieces of scroll intently and letting her do the same.

But every now and then, he would look at her. She could feel his eyes on her, feel that they were serious and steady and that he was waiting for her to look up.

She never did.

And he never said anything. After a while, he would always go back to his parchments. They worked on and on in silence.

Still, Keller was aware of him. She couldn't help it. She was a panther; she could sense the heat of his body even three feet away. She could smell him, too, and he smelled good. Clean and a little bit like the soap he used, and even more like himself, which was something warm and golden and healthy. Like a puppy with a nice coat on a summer afternoon.

It was very, very distracting. Sometimes the words on the scrolls blurred in front of her eyes.

But worst of all, worse than feeling his heat or smelling his scent or knowing his eyes were on her, was something more subtle that she couldn't exactly define. A connection. A sense of tension between them that she could almost touch.

The air was buzzing with it. It lifted up the little hairs on Keller's arms. And no matter how she tried to will it away, it only seemed to grow and grow.

Somehow the silence made it worse, made it more profound. I have to say something, Keller thought. Something casual, to show that I'm not affected.

She stared at the scrolls, which she was beginning to

hate. If only she could find something useful . . .

Then she saw it. Right there on the scroll she was studying.

'Galen. There's something here – in a copy of the oldest records about dragons. It's talking about what the dragons can *do*, what their powers are besides the dark energy.'

She read from the scroll, hesitating on words that were less familiar to her. ' "A dragon has only to touch an animal and it is able to assume that animal's form, know all that the animal knows, do all that the animal can do. There is no" – I think it says "limit" – "on the number of shapes it can master. Therefore, it is a true shapeshifter and the only one worthy of the name." I told you this stuff was old,' she added. 'I think the original was written by the dragons' press agent during the war.'

' "No limit on the number of shapes it can master," ' Galen repeated with growing excitement. 'That makes sense, you know. That's what the First House has inherited, only in a diluted form. Being able to pick whichever shape we want to become – but only the first time. After that, we're stuck with it, of course.'

'Do you have to touch an animal to learn its shape?'

He nodded. 'That's how we choose. But if a dragon can touch *anything* and assume its shape – and change over and over . . .' His voice trailed off.

'Yeah. It's going to be awfully difficult to spot them,' Keller said. The tension in the air had been somewhat discharged by talking, and she felt a little calmer. At least she could talk without the words sticking in her throat.

But Galen wasn't helping. He leaned closer, peering down at her scroll. 'I wonder if it says anything else, anything about how to identify . . . wait. Keller, look down here at the bottom.'

To do it, she had to bend her head so that his hair brushed her cheek. 'What?'

'Horns, something about horns,' he muttered almost feverishly. 'You're better at translating than I am. What's this word?'

' "Regardless"? No, it's more like "no matter".' She began to read. ' "But no matter what form it takes, a dragon may always be known—" '

' "*By its horns*," ' he chimed in, reading with her.

They finished together, helping each other. ' "A dragon has from one to three horns on its forehead, and in some rare cases four. These horns" ' – both their voices rose – ' "which are *the seat of its power* are most cruelly removed by the witches who capture them, to steal from them the power of changing." '

They both stopped. They kept staring at the parchment for what seemed endless minutes to Keller. Galen was gripping her wrist so hard that it hurt.

Then he said softly, 'That's it. That's the answer.'

He looked up at her and gave her wrist a little shake. '*That's the answer*. Keller, we did it; we found it.'

'Shh! You're going to wake up the whole house.' But she was almost as shaky with excitement as he was. 'Let me think. Yeah, that guy Azhdeha could have had horns. His hair was all messy, covering his forehead, and I remember thinking that was a little strange. The rest of him looked so neat.'

'You see?' He laughed breathlessly, exultantly.

'Yes. But, well, do you have any idea how hard it would be to try and take off a dragon's horns?'

'No, and I don't care. Keller, stop it, stop trying to dampen this! The point is, we *found* it. We know something about dragons that can hurt them. We know how to fight!'

Keller couldn't help it. His exhilaration was infectious. All at once, all the bottled-up emotions inside her started to come out. She squeezed his arm back, half laughing and half crying.

'You did it,' she said. 'You found the part.'

'It was on your scroll. You were just about to get there.'

'You were the one who suggested we look at the scrolls in the first place.'

'You were the one—' Suddenly, he broke off. He had been looking at her, laughing, their faces only inches apart as they congratulated each other in whispers. His eyes were like the woods in summertime, golden-green with darker green motes in them that seemed to shift in the light.

But now something like pain crossed his face. He was still looking at her, still gripping her arm, but his eyes went bleak.

'You're the one,' he said quietly.

Keller had to brace herself. Then she said, 'I don't know what you're talking about.'

'Yes, you do.'

He said it so simply, so flatly. There was almost no way to argue.

Keller found one. 'Look, Galen, if this is about what happened in the library—'

'At least you're admitting that something happened now.'

'—then I don't know what's wrong with you. We're both shapeshifters, and there was a minute when we sort of lost our objectivity. We're under a lot of stress. We had a moment of . . . physical attraction. It happens, when you do a job like this; you just can't take it seriously.'

He was staring at her. 'Is *that* what you've convinced yourself happened? "A moment of physical attraction?" '

The truth was that Keller had almost convinced herself that nothing had happened – or convinced her mind, anyway.

'I told you,' she said, and her voice was harsher than she'd heard it for a long time. 'Love is for weak people. I'm not weak, and I don't plan to let anything *make* me weak. And, besides, what is your problem? You've already got a fiancée. Iliana's brave and kind and beautiful, and she's going to be very, very powerful. What more could you *want*?'

'You're right,' Galen said. 'She's all those things. And I respect her and admire her – I even love her. Who could help loving her? But I'm not *in* love with her. I'm—'

'Don't say it.' Keller was angry now, which was good. It made her strong. 'What kind of prince would put his personal happiness above the fate of his people? Above the fate of the whole freaking world, for that matter?'

'I don't!' he raged back. He was speaking softly, but it was still a rage, and he was a little bit frightening. His eyes blazed a deep and endless green. 'I'm not saying I won't go through with the ceremony. All I'm saying is that it's you I love. You're my soulmate, Keller. And you know it.'

Soulmate. The word hit Keller and ricocheted, clunking inside her as it made its way down. When it hit bottom, it settled into a little niche made especially for it, fitting exactly.

It was the word to describe what had really happened in the library. No stress-induced moment of physical attraction and no simple romantic flirtation, either. It was the soulmate principle.

She and Galen were soulmates.

And it didn't matter a bit, because they could never be together.

CHAPTER
14

Keller put her hands to her face. At first, she didn't recognize what was happening to her. Then she realized that she was crying.

She was shaking, Raksha Keller who wasn't afraid of anyone and who never let her heart be touched. She was making those ridiculous little noises that sounded like a six-week-old kitten. She was dripping tears through her fingers.

The worst thing was that she couldn't seem to make herself stop.

Then she felt Galen's arms around her, and she realized that he was crying, too.

He was better at it than she was. He seemed more used to it and didn't fight it as hard, which made him stronger. He was able to stroke her hair and even to get some words out.

'Keller, I'm sorry. Keller . . . can I call you Raksha?'

Keller shook her head furiously, spraying teardrops.

'I always think of you as Keller, anyway. It's just – you, somehow. I'm sorry about all of this. I didn't mean to make you cry. It would be better if you'd never met me . . .'

Keller found herself shaking her head again. And then, just as she had the last time, she felt her arms moving to hold him back. She pressed her face against the softness of his sweatshirt, trying to get enough control of herself to speak.

This was the problem with having walls so hard and high and unscalable, she supposed. When they came down, they crumbled completely, shattering into nothingness. She felt utterly defenceless right now.

Unguarded . . . vulnerable . . . but not alone. She could feel more than Galen's physical presence. She could feel his spirit, and she was being pulled toward it. They were falling together, falling *into* each other, as they had in the library. Closer and closer . . .

Contact.

She felt the touch of his mind, and once again her heart almost exploded.

You're the one. You're my soulmate, his mental voice said, as if this were an entirely new idea, and he was just discovering it and rejoicing in it.

Keller reached for denial, but it simply wasn't around. And she couldn't pretend to someone who shared her thoughts.

Yes.

When I first saw you, he said, *I was so fascinated by you. I already told you this, didn't I? It made me proud to be a shapeshifter for the first time. Aren't you proud?*

Keller was disconcerted. She still wasn't finished crying – but, yes, she was. With his warmth and passion shining into her, his arms locked around her, his mind open to her . . . it was hard not to get swept up in it.

I guess I'm proud, she thought to him slowly. *But only of some parts of it. Other things . . .*

What things? he demanded, almost fiercely protective.

Our history? The dragons?

No. Stuff you wouldn't understand. Things about – animal nature. Even now, Keller was afraid of letting him see some parts of her. *Leave it alone, Galen.*

All he said was, *Tell me.*

No. It happened a long time ago, when I was three. Just be glad you get to pick what kind of animal you'll become.

Keller, he said. *Please.*

You don't like animal nature, she told him. *Remember how you pulled your hand away when you touched my shoulder in the music room?*

In the . . . ? His mental voice trailed off, and Keller waited grimly to feel the memory of disgust in him. But what came wasn't revulsion. Instead, it was a strong sense of longing that he was somehow trying to smother. And choked, wry laughter.

Keller, I didn't pull away because I didn't like your fur. I did it because . . . He hesitated, then burst out, sounding embarrassed, *I wanted to pet you!*

Pet . . . ?

Your fur was so soft, and it felt so good when I moved my palm the wrong way against it – just like velvet. And – I wanted to – to do this. He ran a hand up and down her back. *I couldn't help it. But I knew it wasn't exactly appropriate, and you would probably break my jaw if I tried it. So I took my hand away.* He finished, still embarrassed, but half laughing. *Now, you tell me what you're not proud of.*

Keller felt very warm, and she was sure her face was flushed. It was just as well that it was hidden. It was too bad – there was probably never going to be a time to tell him that she wouldn't mind being petted like that . . .

I'm a cat, after all, she thought, and was distantly surprised to hear him chuckle. There were no secrets in this kind of soul-link, she realized, slightly flustered. To cover her embarrassment, she spoke out loud.

'The thing I'm not proud of – it happened when I was living with my first Circle Daybreak family. I used to spend a lot of time in my half-and-half form. It was easy for me to get stuck that way, and they didn't mind.'

I wouldn't, either, Galen said. *You're beautiful like that.*

'Anyway, I was sitting on my foster mother's lap while she was combing my hair, and I don't know what happened, but something startled me. Some loud noise outside, maybe a car backfiring. I jumped straight up and tried to race for my hiding place under the desk.'

Keller paused, made herself take an even breath. She felt Galen's arms tighten around her.

'And then – well, my foster mother tried to hold on to me, to keep me from being frightened. But all I could think of was danger, danger. So I lashed out at her. I used my claws – I have retractable claws in that form. I would have done anything to get away.'

She paused again. It was so hard to tell this.

'She had to go to the hospital. I forget how many stitches she needed in her face. But I remember everything else – being taken to another foster family because that one couldn't handle me. I didn't blame them for sending me away, but I always wished I could have told her how sorry I was.'

There was a silence. Keller could feel Galen breathing, and that gave her an odd sense of comfort.

Then he said quietly, out loud, 'That's all?'

Keller started, then lifted her head a little and made herself answer the same way. 'Isn't it enough?'

'Keller . . . you were just a baby. You didn't mean to do any harm; it was an accident. You can't blame yourself.'

'I do blame myself. If I hadn't been taken over by my instinct—'

'That's ridiculous. Human babies do stupid things all the time. What if a human three-year-old falls into a swimming pool and somebody drowns trying to rescue her? Would you blame the baby?'

Keller hesitated, then rested her head on his shoulder again. 'Don't be silly.'

'Then how can you blame yourself for something you couldn't help?'

Keller didn't answer, but she felt as if a crushing load was sliding slowly off her. He didn't blame her. Maybe she wasn't to blame. She would always be sorry, but maybe she didn't need to be so ashamed.

She tightened her own arms around him. *Thank you*, she thought.

Oh, Keller. You're so wonderful, and you're so set against admitting it. Everything you do . . . shines.

Keller couldn't form any words for a moment. Then she said, *Galen? When you do choose a form, choose something gentle.*

I thought you thought everybody has to be a fighter, he said, and his mental voice was very quiet.

Some people shouldn't have to be.

Then she just let him hold her.

Another endless time, while they both seemed to be floating in soft, gold fire. It flared around them and through them, joining them. Sometimes she could hardly tell which thoughts were his and which were hers.

He said, *I used to write poetry, you know. Or try. My parents hated it; they were so embarrassed. Instead of learning to be a good hunter, their son was writing gibberish.*

She said, *There's this terrible dream I have, where I look out at the ocean and see a wall of water hundreds of feet high, and I know it's coming and I can never get away in time. Cats and water, you know. I guess that's why.*

He said, *I used to daydream about what kind of animal it would be most fun to be. But it always came down to the same thing, some kind of bird. You just can't beat flying.*

She said, *One thing I always had to hide from my foster mothers was how much I liked to shred things. I thought I was being so clever when I would hide their panty hose after I used my claws on them. But when I did it on the sheer curtains one day, everybody knew.*

They talked and talked. And Keller gave herself up to it, to the simple pleasure of his closeness and the feeling that for once she didn't have to hide or pretend or defend herself. It was such a blessed relief not to have to pretend at all.

Galen knew her, and he accepted her. All of her. He loved herself, not her black swirling hair or her long legs or the curve of her lips. He might admire those things, but he loved *her*, what she was inside.

And he loved her with a sweetness and a power that shook Keller to her soul.

She wanted to stay like this forever.

There was something else waiting for them, though. Something she didn't want to think about but that loomed just outside the brightness and warmth that surrounded them.

The world . . . there's still a world out there. And it's in trouble.

And we can't ignore that.

Galen.

I know.

Very slowly, very reluctantly, Galen straightened, putting her away from him. He couldn't seem to let go of her shoulders, though. They sat that way, their eyes locked.

And the strange thing was that the mental connection

wasn't broken. They could still hear each other as they held each other's gaze.

We can never be like this again, Keller said.

I know. He had faced it as clearly as she had, she realized.

We can't talk about it; we can't even be alone together. It isn't fair to Iliana. And we have to try to forget each other and just go on.

I know, he said for the third time. And just when Keller was marvelling at his quiet acceptance, she saw tears in his gem-coloured eyes. *Keller, it's my fault. If I weren't the son of the First House . . .*

We'd never have met. And that would have been worse.

'Would it?' he said out loud, as if he needed reassurance.

Yes. She gave the answer mentally, so that he could feel the truth of it. *Oh, Galen, I'm so glad we met. I'm so glad to have known you. And if we live through this, I'll be glad all my life.*

He took her into his arms again.

'We have it, Boss,' Winnie said.

Her eyes were sparkling. Beside her, Nissa looked calmly enthusiastic.

'What?' Keller asked. She herself felt calmly alert, in spite of almost no sleep the night before. She and Galen had stayed up late, reading over the scrolls, making sure that there was nothing they had missed. They had already explained what they'd found to the others.

Now Winnie was grinning at her.

'How to protect Iliana at the party on Saturday. We've got it, and it's foolproof!'

Nothing is foolproof, Keller thought. She said, 'Go on.'

'It's like this. We put wards all around the Ashton-Hughes house, just like the wards Grandma Harman made for this house. The strongest possible from Circle Daybreak. But we put them around the house *now*, as soon as we can. We key them so that only humans can get in.'

'And we add another layer of protection,' Nissa said. 'Circle Daybreak agents posted around the house, starting now. Nothing gets in, nothing gets out that they don't know about. That way, when we go to the party on Saturday, we know it's safe.'

'We just *whisk* her from one safe place to another,' Winnie said. 'As long as we can keep her in here until Saturday night, there's no chance of any danger.'

Keller considered. 'We have to make sure the limo is safe, too. Absolutely safe.'

'Of course,' Winnie said. 'I'll take care of it.'

'And I'd want agents to check the people who go in somehow. Not just monitor. Would there be any way to do that?'

'Without the family knowing?' Nissa chewed her lip gently. 'What if we set up some sort of road crew near the front gate? There's bound to be a gate; this is a mansion, right?'

'Check it out. And we'd better get plans of the house, too. I want us all to know the place by heart before we get there.'

'City planner's office,' Nissa said. 'No, more likely the local historical society. The house is probably a historic monument. I'm on it.'

Keller nodded. 'Hmm.' She tried to think if there was anything else to worry about. 'Hmm, it sounds . . .'

They watched her, breath held.

'It sounds *good*,' Keller said. 'I think there's just the tiniest, slightest possibility that it might actually work. But I'm probably being over-optimistic.'

Winnie grinned and socked her on the shoulder. 'You, Boss? Perish the thought.'

'It's so difficult,' Iliana said. 'I mean, what can you wear to both a birthday party and a promise ceremony?'

'And a Solstice Ceremony,' Winnie said. 'Don't forget that.'

'You're trying to make things worse, aren't you?' Iliana held up one dress, then another. 'What's right for a Solstice Ceremony?'

'Something white,' Winnie suggested.

'That would be good for a promise ceremony, too,' Keller said. She was doing her very best to be patient, and finding it easier than she had expected.

The last three days had been very quiet. Iliana had agreed to stay home from school even when her cold got better. Galen and Keller had scarcely spoken in that time, and they had never been alone.

And that was . . . all right. There was a quietness inside her to match the quiet air outside.

They both had jobs to do. And they would do them as well as possible. Keller just prayed that what they did would be enough.

'White? I don't know if I've got anything white. It has to be fancy because everything at Jaime's is fancy. I hope she's really OK.'

'She's fine,' Keller said. 'You talked to her an hour ago.' To her own relief, Jaime had stayed quietly at home for the past three days, too. The last thing she wanted was for that girl to be attacked again.

But the Ashton-Hughes house, at least, was safe. For three days, it had been buttoned up tight, with Circle Daybreak agents watching every person who went through the gates. And checking them, using the same wards that protected the house. No Night Person could cross the invisible line that encircled the grounds, and no person who tried to cross and was turned back by the wards would be allowed to leave without being tracked.

All we have to do is keep her safe during the drive, Keller thought. First to the mansion, then to the meeting place in Charlotte. We can do that. I know we can do that.

She checked her watch.

'Come on, kid, it's after eight,' she said. 'We should be moving soon.'

Iliana and Winnie were both ransacking the closet.

'Pale blue,' Winnie said, 'pale lavender, pale pink . . .'

'It has to be *white*,' Iliana said.

'I'm sorry I mentioned it.'

A knock sounded on the door, and Nissa looked in. 'We're back. You guys ready?'

'In a minute,' Keller said. 'How're things at the mansion?'

'Perfect. The witches say the wards are strong.'

'Who's come in?'

'Caterers and a college band. That's all so far. All one hundred percent human according to the wards – and to Galen, who kept running up to the cars at the gate and trying to sell them Christmas Benefit teddy bears.'

Keller almost grinned. Galen would be good at that. 'The family must have thought he was crazy.'

'They never came out and complained. Nobody's come out, in fact, which makes things easy on the surveillance team.' She sobered. 'Boss, why do you think the dragon hasn't tried something yet? He's cutting it awfully close.'

'I don't know. I think . . .'

'What?'

'I think he must be betting it all on one throw of the dice. One all-out attack, fast and decisive.'

'At the party.'

'At the party,' Keller said. 'So we'd better be on our toes.'

'We've got him locked out, though. Those wards are secure.'

'I hope so.'

From the closet, Iliana squealed, 'I found it!'

She was holding a dress almost the colour of her own hair, white with some sort of sparkling thread woven in. It draped in soft folds across her hip as she held it up for Winnie's inspection.

'Perfect,' Winnie said. 'You can get engaged in that dress; you can go to a birthday party; you can celebrate the Solstice – you can probably get *married* in it if you want.'

'You can do whatever you want, but you have to do it now,' Keller said, checking her watch again.

'But do you like it? I think I bought it last year.'

'It's beautiful,' Keller said, and then, as she saw the hurt in Iliana's violet eyes: 'Really. It's beautiful. You'll look wonderful in it, and Galen will be – very impressed.'

Where had that sudden hitch in her breath come from? She had gotten over it quickly, but she noticed that Iliana gave her an odd look.

'Now, come on, everybody,' Keller said briskly, looking at Winnie and Nissa. 'Are you two ready?'

They both looked down at their ordinary outfits, then looked back up and shrugged in chorus.

'Yeah.'

'I guess they can think we're the help,' Keller said. 'Everybody check your transmitters. I want to be in constant contact once we get there.'

'Right, Boss.'

'Got it, Boss.'

Iliana had put on the dress and was looking in the

mirror. 'My hair,' she began, and then she glanced at Keller. 'I'll just leave it down,' she said. 'OK?'

'Down is fine, down is great.' Keller glanced at her watch and tightened her belt.

'Down is just right for a Solstice Ceremony,' Winnie said. She added in an undertone as Iliana started for the door, 'Don't mind her. She's always like this before a big operation.'

'It's a good thing I didn't ask her about my shoes . . .'

Keller looked around to make sure there was nothing they were forgetting. Then she looked at the other three girls. They smiled back at her, eyes alert and ready for anything. Even the smallest one, who looked like a Christmas tree angel somebody had taken down and brought to life.

'OK, people,' Keller said. 'This is it. It's show time.'

CHAPTER

15

Galen was wearing a dark sweater and pants that set off his blondness. It was casual but still appropriate for the promise ceremony later on. His eyes met Keller's briefly as Iliana said goodbye to her parents, and they both smiled. Not fake smiles, either. Simply the quiet, undemanding smiles of comrades with a job to do.

'Kee-kee!' Alex said from the door as they went to the car in the garage.

That kid is up *way* too late, Keller thought. She turned and waved.

'Blow him a kiss,' Iliana prompted helpfully. 'He likes that.'

Keller gave her a narrow sideways look and blew him a kiss.

'Kee-kee!' Suddenly, his round little face crumpled. 'Bye-bye,' he proclaimed sadly.

'Oh, that's sweet,' Iliana's mother said. 'He's going to miss you. He probably thinks you're going for good.'

'Bye-bye,' Alex said, and huge tears rolled down his cheeks. 'Bye-bye! Kee-kee! Bye-bye!' He began to sob.

There was a little silence among the group standing by the car. Winnie stared at Alex, then glanced at Iliana.

'He doesn't – he's never had any precognitions, has he?' she muttered.

'He's a *baby*,' Iliana whispered back. 'I mean, how could you tell?'

'He's just tired,' Keller said briefly. 'Come on, let's go.'

But she could hear Alex's sobbing even when she got in the car, and it seemed to follow in her head even when they had left the house behind.

They checked with the 'road crew' stationed right outside the Ashton-Hughes front gate. It looked extremely professional, with bright lights and all the accoutrements.

'All secure,' the witch in charge said cheerfully when Keller rolled down the window. He shifted his reflective vest. 'Thirty cars in, nobody out. There hasn't been one for a while – I think you're fashionably late.' He winked.

'Thirty?' Keller said. 'How many people per car?'

'Two in most of them, but some were packed.'

Keller glanced at Iliana beside her. 'And that's what they call only inviting a few people?'

Iliana shrugged. 'You haven't seen the house.'

'Anyway, it's safe,' the witch foreman said. 'No dragon has gotten in, I can promise you that. And none is going to *get* in, either.'

Keller nodded at him, and they drove on.

Iliana was right. In considering how big the party was, you had to see the size of the house. Keller had studied the plans, but it wasn't the same.

They passed something like a peach orchard on one side of the driveway, and then a carriage house that seemed to have swallowed up a dozen cars. But Nissa dropped them off by the front steps, below the stately white columns that decorated the magnificent porch.

Impressive place, Keller thought.

They walked in.

In the cavernous, softly lit entry hall, there was a girl in a dark uniform who took their coats. There was also Brett. When he saw Iliana, he pounced.

'Blondie! I thought you weren't going to make it!'

'You knew I wouldn't miss this,' Iliana said gently. But Keller thought she looked much less interested in Brett than the last time she'd spoken to him.

She's learned a lot, Keller thought. And, of course, now that she knows Galen, she sees this loser for what he is.

Brett was looking the others over in his meat-appraising way. 'So just which of these lovely ladies is your cousin? I never got a chance to ask.'

'Oh . . . that one.' Iliana pointed a random finger.

'You?' Brett's eyes ran up and down Keller's tallness and her blue-black hair. 'I never would have guessed.'

'We're sort of . . . foster cousins,' Keller said.

She didn't like Brett. That was nothing new, but somehow tonight she *really* didn't like him. There was something almost creepy in the way his eyes clung to girls, and when he looked at Iliana, it was like watching a slug crawl over a peach blossom.

'Well, come with me and join the fun,' he said, gesturing expansively and flashing a smile.

Keller almost asked 'Where?' but in a moment she realized that it was pointless. The party really seemed to be all over the house.

The entry room itself was big enough to have a party in, and it had a wide, sweeping staircase just like a proper Southern mansion. Above, on the second floor, Keller could see a hallway lined with portraits and statues.

Brett led them through room after room, each one impressive. Some seemed to be real sitting rooms; others just looked like displays in a museum. Finally, they went through one last open archway into a ballroom.

Panelled walls. Painted ceiling. Chandeliers. An ocean of floor. And the college band at one end playing music that was definitely modern. A few couples were dancing a slow dance, very near the band. They looked small enough to rattle in the enormous room. Keller almost giggled, but Iliana looked dreamy.

'It's beautiful.'

Brett looked satisfied. 'There's food over there on the sideboard. But most of the food's downstairs in the game room. You want to see that?'

'I want to see Jaime,' Iliana said.

'She's down there.'

The game room was amazing, too. Not just pool tables and darts but arcade-style video games, old-fashioned pinball machines, an indoor basketball hoop, and generally just about everything you'd find at a superior arcade.

As soon as they walked in, a guy in black pants, white shirt, and black vest offered them a tray of tiny quiches and mini-pizzas. A caterer, Keller decided, not part of the regular staff of the house. She shook her head at the food and went on looking around, keeping her senses open so she could take in everything at once.

This was the first time Iliana had been out in public since she'd gone to school last Monday, and it was nerve-wracking. The game room was much more crowded than the ballroom, and everybody was laughing and talking at once. On top of that, this old mansion had some very modern renovations. The band music was being piped into the other rooms.

'Jaime!' Iliana said as a figure emerged from the crush of people.

Jaime looked good. Her face had a healthy colour, and

her dark blue eyes were wide open and shining. Her brown hair was fluffed softly, and she was wearing a very pretty blue dress.

'Iliana.' She hugged Iliana hard, speaking in her flat but oddly pleasant voice. 'It seems like forever. How are you?'

'Fine. My cold's better, and my hand—' Iliana held up her right hand. There was a neat bandage around the palm to protect the stitches. 'It itches sometimes, but that's all. How about you?'

'I still have headaches. But I'm getting better.' Jaime smiled at Keller and the others. 'I'm so glad you all could come.'

'Yeah, so are we,' Keller said politely, feeling a stab of instinctive guilt. It was irrational, but she kept expecting this girl to look at her and say, 'You're the one who attacked me! The monster cat!'

And she wasn't glad that they had come. Her early warning system was clamouring already; she felt as if her fur was standing on end. She couldn't explain it, but there was something *wrong* about the house.

'Keep alert,' she said quietly to the others as Jaime led Iliana to the food tables. 'Remember, two of us are with her at all times. The other two can wander the house, check the perimetre, look for anything suspicious. And keep in touch.' She put a finger to her brooch.

That was when they found that their transmitters didn't work. Keller had no idea why. All any of them could hear was static like white noise.

Keller cursed.

'We'll keep in touch *physically*, then,' she said grimly. She checked her watch. It was almost nine. 'And we'll get her out of here in an hour. Ten o'clock. Just to be safe.'

'Good idea,' Galen said.

Winnie and Nissa said, 'Right, Boss.'

Keller stuck close to Iliana, telling herself that they were taking every precaution and that all she had to do was stay cool and they could get out safely. But as time went on, she only got more and more uneasy.

The dragon was going to attack.

She was certain of it.

But how? What form would the attack take? Was it going to be a battering ram of dark power like the one that had brought down the roof of the safe house? Or something tiny and sneaky, some clever way to get past the wards?

A mouse? Or an insect? No ordinary shapeshifter could turn into a bug, but it was a kind of animal, after all. Could something like that slip through the wards undetected?

What was it she was missing?

Nothing to do but keep her senses open, search every face for enemies, and be prepared for anything.

As it turned out, though, she was entirely unprepared when it happened.

Nissa and Galen were the two wandering the house at that point. Keller and Winnie were sticking with Iliana. Keller herself didn't plan to leave Iliana's side all night.

But as she was watching Jaime and Iliana laughing and chattering by one of the food tables – which offered everything from barbecue to shrimp to exotic fruit – Brett walked up chewing his lip. He was heading for Iliana, but he looked undecided and genuinely unhappy.

Keller headed him off reflexively. She preferred to keep him away from Iliana just on principle. 'Anything wrong?'

He glanced at her with something like relief in his dark blue eyes. For once, he didn't look arrogant or patronizing or even well groomed. 'Uh, there's something . . . I need to tell Iliana about . . . I guess.' He gulped, his face twisted.

'You guess?' Keller herded him into a relatively private

niche beside a video game. 'What do you mean, you guess?'

'Well, I do have to tell her. I just hate to.' He lowered his voice so that Keller had to lean closer to hear him. 'Her mom's on the phone. And she says that her little brother is missing.'

Ice water sluiced over Keller. For five seconds, she didn't breathe at all. Then she said, '*What?*'

Brett grimaced. 'He's missing from his bedroom. And, I mean, I hate to scare Iliana with it, because he's probably just crawled out the window or something – he's that age, you know? But her mom wants to talk to her. She's sort of hysterical.' He wet his lips. 'I guess we should all go over there as a search party.'

He's really worried, Keller thought dazedly, while another part of her mind, a clear, cold part, clicked through possible solutions. So there's something under that brand-name facade after all. In spite of the 'he probably crawled out of the window' crap, he's worried about the kid – and he's worried about telling Iliana, too.

Because Iliana's going to go ballistic, the cold part of her mind put in. She's going to get as hysterical as her mom and insist on rushing back there. And a search party – that would mean all of us outside the wards, crawling around between houses in the dark . . .

No. It couldn't happen. It was undoubtedly just what the dragon wanted.

But *how* had he gotten to the baby? With all those wards and the agents watching the house – how?

It didn't matter. Right now, she had to deal with the situation.

'Brett, don't tell Iliana.'

'Huh? But I have to.'

'No, you don't. I'll talk to Mrs – to Aunt Anna. I'm her

niece, remember? And I have an idea where the baby might have gone. I think he's safe, but she has to know where to look.'

Brett gawked at her. 'You have an idea?'

'Yeah. Just let me talk to her. And don't say anything to Iliana just yet.' Keller glanced toward the game room bar, which was set up like an English pub. There was a phone, but a girl with red hair was talking animatedly into it, while eating nuts from a bowl.

'It's the other line, Jaime's line,' Brett said. 'She said she called on that one first, but it was busy.'

'OK, where's the other line?'

'Jaime's room.'

Keller hesitated, looking at Iliana. Winnie was on one side of her and Jaime on the other. They were the centre of attention, something like the heart of a rose, with other people surrounding them like petals.

At least she was in full view of everyone. And somebody trying to get to her would have to go through all of them first, and that would alert Winnie.

But I wish Nissa and Galen were here to take over from me.

She glanced at her watch. Fifteen minutes before they were supposed to come back to the game room. The baby couldn't wait that long.

She forged through the crowd and touched Winnie's shoulder.

'I have to run for a minute – a phone call. Nothing to worry about yet. I'll make it fast,' she murmured in Winnie's ear.

Winnie glanced at her, surprised, but then she nodded. 'Problems?'

'Maybe. Stay alert.' Keller said it through a smile for Iliana's benefit.

When she got out of the throng, she said to Brett, 'Take me there.'

Actually, she knew where Jaime's bedroom was from the plans. But she didn't want Brett hanging around Iliana. His face alone would give away the show.

They hurried up the wide staircase. Keller's mind was racing, making plans.

I can calm her down, at least. And I can call Circle Daybreak and tell them – if they don't already know. They'll make a much better search party than humans. Iliana doesn't need to know about it at all until after the ceremony. And then . . .

Her mind stalled, and the sick feeling in her stomach grew.

No. It wouldn't be enough. She knew what she really had to do.

I have to go back there. Just me. I owe Iliana that much. I owe the whole family that much.

I'll be the best one to search. I can drive over to the house fast and see what's going on. Borrow a car from Brett. That way, when the dragon attacks – and he's *going* to attack – I'll be the only one there.

You'll be the only one dead, a snide little voice in her mind pointed out. But Keller gave it the cold shoulder.

She knew that already. It wasn't important.

You're going to risk your life – give up your life – for a baby? One who's not a Wild Power, not even a shapeshifter?

At least I'll get another chance at the dragon, she told the voice.

You're going to risk the mission, the alliance, the whole daylight world, for a single individual? the voice went on.

This was a better point. But Keller had only one thing to say to it.

I have to.

'Here.' Brett gestured at the open door of a pretty bedroom, then followed Keller when she went in. 'Um, can I help you?' He was getting over his worry and trying to cosy up to her again.

'No.'

'Oh. Well, I'll leave you alone, then.' He slid out the door, closing it behind him.

And Keller let him. Later, that was what she couldn't quite believe. That she had been stupid enough to walk into the trap and stand there while it snapped shut.

She picked up the phone. 'Mrs Dominick?'

Silence.

At first, just for a moment or two, she thought Iliana's mother might have stepped away from the phone. But then the nature of the silence got to her.

There were no sounds in the background at all. It was dead air.

Keller hit the plunger to hang up the phone. Nothing happened.

No dial tone.

She glanced at the phone cord; it was plugged into the wall. She pushed the plunger rapidly, four times, five.

Then she knew.

She'd been suckered.

In one motion, she whirled and sprang to the door.

Only to twist the handle uselessly.

It was locked.

And it was a good, sturdy door, made out of solid wood, the kind they used to make. She found this out by throwing herself against it hard enough to bruise her shoulder. It had been locked with a key from the outside, and the bolt was a good, sturdy one, too.

White icy-hot rage swept over Keller. She was more

angry than she could ever remember being in her life. She couldn't believe it – she'd been fooled by an idiot human boy. The Night People must have gotten to him somehow, must have bought him . . .

No.

Keller knew she wasn't a genius. But sometimes ideas came to her in a flash, allowing her to see a complete picture all at once where other people saw only fragments. And right now, like a bolt of lightning, realization dawned on her, and she understood.

Oh, Goddess, how could we have been so stupid?

She knew how the dragon had done it.

CHAPTER
16

We were so careful, she thought, setting up wards three days early and having agents watch the house. Nothing got inside during those three days; we were sure of that, and so we thought we were safe.

But we didn't stop to think – what if the dragon was *already* inside when we put the wards up?

Brett.

He's the dragon.

It could take on any shape, assume any animal's form, and know all that the animal knew. A human being was an animal.

So why couldn't it touch a human and know all the human knew?

It would be the perfect disguise.

And we all fell for it, Keller thought. I knew there was something creepy about him, but I just put it down to him being obnoxious. And he's been here all the time, inside the wards, laughing at us, waiting for Iliana to come.

And Iliana's with him right now.

Keller felt sure of that in her gut.

She wanted to throw herself against the door again, but that wouldn't do any good. She needed to be calm now, to think, because she couldn't afford to waste any time.

The window.

Keller tried to open it, looking down at a hedge of rhododendron bushes below. The sash was stuck, nailed fast. But it didn't matter. Glass was more breakable than wood.

She stepped back and changed.

Melting, flowing, jumpsuit becoming fur. Tail shooting free. Ears. Whiskers. Heavy paws thumping down. A single long stretch to get used to the new body and being on four feet instead of two.

She was a panther, and she felt good. Strong and mean. Her muscles were like steel under her soft coat, and her big paws were twitching to bat someone silly. That dragon would be sorry he'd ever messed with her.

With a rasping yowl that she couldn't help, she gathered herself and sprang straight at the window. The full weight of her panther body hit the glass, and it shattered, and then she was flying in the cold night air.

She got cut. Panthers actually had thin and delicate skin compared to other animals. But she was indifferent to the pain. She landed and took off running, shaking her paws in flight to get rid of little bits of glass.

She raced around the mansion, looking for a place to enter. Eventually, she found a low, unshuttered window, and once again, she gathered herself and jumped.

She landed in a sitting room with glass falling all around her onto a fine, old carpet.

Brett.

And Iliana.

She would smell them out.

She lifted her muzzle, smelling currents in the air. At the same time, she expanded her sense of hearing to its fullest.

No Iliana. She couldn't get even a whiff of her. That was bad, but she would try again from the game room, where Iliana had been last. That was where she was going anyway, because that was where Brett was.

Not Brett, she reminded herself as she loped through corridors and rooms. The dragon.

She raced through the ballroom and heard a scream. She barely turned her head to notice a girl standing frozen, just lifting her hand to point. The college band crashed to a halt, almost as one, except the drummer, who went on playing for a moment with his eyes shut.

Keller ignored them all, running at top speed and leaping down the stairs, her heavy front paws hitting the carpeted floor first, then her back paws hitting almost on either side of them. Each spring propelled her into the next.

She burst into the game room.

For an instant, she stood still, taking in the scene. She wanted to make sure with her eyes that what her ears and her nose told her was true: Iliana wasn't here.

It was true. Winnie was missing, too, and Keller couldn't smell them anywhere.

Then someone spotted her, a full-grown panther, jet black, with glowing eyes and long teeth just showing as she panted gently, standing in the doorway with her tail lashing.

'Oh, my God!' The voice soared over the babble. 'Look at that!'

Everyone looked.

Everyone froze for an instant.

Chaos erupted.

Girls were screaming. Boys were yelling. Plenty of boys were screaming, too. They saw her, and they fell over themselves, diving for the exits or for hiding places. They poured out of the room, dragging each other, sometimes trampling each other. Keller gave a loud, snarling yowl to help them on, and they scattered like chickens.

The only one Keller cared about was the Brett-dragon.

He turned and ran down a corridor. Luring her? He must be. Maybe he didn't realize she had found out yet. Maybe he had some reason for continuing the charade.

She threw her head back and gave a snarl that resounded through the house. It wasn't just anger. It was calling Nissa and Galen. If they could hear her, they would understand and come running.

Then she took off after the dragon.

As she loped down the corridor, she changed again. This time, she couldn't just try to kill him; she needed to be able to talk. But she also needed her claws, so she changed to her half-and-half form, fur shrivelling off her arms, body rearing up to run on booted feet, hair flying out behind her.

The dragon was almost at the end of the corridor when she jumped him.

She knocked him down and rolled him over, straddling him. She was braced to feel the agony of the dark power crackling through her, but it didn't come. She pinned his arms and showed her teeth and screamed in his face.

'Where is she? What did you do with her?'

The face looked back at her. It looked just like Brett, just like a human. It was sickly white, with rolling eyeballs and spittle at the corners of the mouth. The only answer she got was a moan of what sounded like terror.

'Tell me! Where is she?'

'—it's not my fault . . .'

'What?' She lifted his body and banged it down again. His head flopped on his neck like a dead fish. He looked like someone about to faint.

Something was wrong.

'She's in the bedroom with my parents. They're all asleep – or something—'

His forehead. When she shook him, his hair flew around. It was uncharacteristically messy, but the forehead underneath was smooth.

'I couldn't help it. *He* did something to my brain. I couldn't even think until a few minutes ago. I just did what he told me to do. I was like a robot! And you don't know what it was like, having *him* in the house the last three days, and feeling like a puppet, and when *he* let go a few minutes ago, I thought I was going to be killed—'

The babbling went on, but Keller's mind had disengaged.

She had lots of thoughts all at once, like layers in a parfait.

Chalk up another ability for dragons: telepathic mind control. Of weak human subjects, anyway.

Nissa was right: the Night World did know what had happened in the music room. The substitution was probably made right after that. They could have grabbed Jaime on her way back to class.

The car incident was designed to make us sympathetic and to lull our suspicions before they began. We thought of her as a victim.

The doctors at the hospital must have been controlled, too. They *had* to have been – they'd looked at Jaime's head.

Jaime's headaches have kept her at home for the past three days, so she never had to cross the wards.

Iliana trusts Jaime implicitly and would go anywhere with her without a fight.

Jaime wears a fringe.

And on the last layer, rushing at her cold and sharp as crystal: Jaimeisthedragon.

Jaime is the dragon.

A vast, silent calm seemed to have filled Keller. She felt as if there was too much space inside her head. Very slowly, she looked down at Brett again.

'Stop talking.' It was almost a whisper, but his gabble stopped as if she'd turned off a faucet.

'Now. Who's in the bedroom with your parents? Your sister?'

He nodded, terrified. Tears spurted out of his eyes.

'Your real sister.'

He nodded again.

They must have brought her in sometime, Keller thought. Certainly before we put the wards up and started checking cars, maybe even before the fake Jaime got back from the hospital.

Why they'd kept her alive was a mystery, but Keller didn't have time to worry about it.

'Brett,' she said, still in a careful whisper, 'what I want to know is where *Iliana* is. Do you know where she's been taken?'

He choked. 'I don't know. *He* didn't tell me anything, even when *he* was in my mind. But I noticed – there were some people down in the cellar. I think they were making a tunnel.'

A tunnel. Under the wards, of course. So we were made fools of *twice*.

She had to grit her teeth to keep from screaming. The floor plan of the house was a blur in her mind.

She hauled Brett up by his shirt and said, 'Where's the basement door? Show me!'

'I c-can't—'

'*Move!*'

He moved, staggering. She followed, pushing him along, until they got to a door and stairs.

Then he collapsed. 'Down there. Don't ask me to go with you. I can't. I can't look at *him* again.' He huddled, rocking himself.

Keller left him. Three stairs down, she bounded back up and grabbed him by the shirt.

'That phone call from Iliana's mother – does *he* really have the baby?' She need to know if it came to bargaining.

'I don't know,' Brett moaned in a sick voice. He was clutching his stomach as if he were wounded. 'There wasn't any phone call, but I don't know what *he's* been doing.' He threw her a desperate look and whispered hoarsely, *'What is he?'*

Keller dropped him. 'You don't want to know,' she said, and left him again.

She took the stairs very quietly but very quickly. Her senses were open, but the farther she went down, the less useful they were. They were being swamped by an overpowering sickly-sweet odour and by a rushing sound that seemed to fill her head.

By the time she got to the last step, her fur was bristling, and her heart was pounding. Her tail stood out stiffly, and her pupils were wide.

It was very dark, but details of the room slowly came into focus. It was a large furnished basement, or had been. Now every piece of furniture seemed to be broken and piled in a heap in the corner. There was a raw hole in one concrete wall, a hole that opened into a black tunnel. And the sickly-sweet smell came from piles of dung.

They were lying on the floor all around, along with giant scratch marks that had dug grooves into the tile. The entire place looked like nothing so much as a huge animal's den.

She couldn't sense anything alive in the room.

Keller moved toward the tunnel, fast but stealthy. Ripple, freeze. Ripple, freeze. Leopards could move this way across grassland bare of cover and not be seen. But nothing jumped out to attack her.

The mouth of the tunnel was wet, the soil crumbly. Keller climbed in, still moving lightly. Water dripped from the mat of roots and earth above her. The whole thing looked ready to cave in at any moment.

He must have made it. The dragon. Goddess knows how; maybe with claws. Anyway, he wasn't too fussy about it; it was meant to be a temporary thing.

The smell was just as powerful here, and the rushing sound was even clearer. There must be an underground stream – or maybe just water pipes – very close.

Come on, girl, what are you waiting for? You're a grunt, it's your job to move! Don't stand around trying to think!

It was hard to make herself go deeper and deeper into that damp and confining place. Her senses were all useless, even sight, because the bore twisted and turned so she could never see more than a few feet ahead. She was heading blind and deaf into she had no idea what. At any moment, she might reach a shaft or a side tunnel where something could attack her.

And the feel of the earth above her was almost crushing.

She kept going.

Please let her be alive. He doesn't need to kill her. He should try to make her join him first. Please, please, don't let him have killed her.

After what seemed like forever, she realized that the angle of the tunnel was changing. She was heading up. Then a current of air swirled to her, barely sniffable under the thick dragon smell, and it was fresh.

Night air. Somewhere ahead. The end of the tunnel.

A new panic invaded her.

Please don't let them have gotten away.

She threw aside all caution and sprinted.

Up, up – and she could smell it clearly now. Cold air, unfouled. Up, up – and she could hear sounds. A yell that suddenly broke off. The voice sounded like —

Galen! she thought, and her heart tore.

Then she saw light. Moonlight. She gathered her muscles and *jumped*.

She scrambled out of the mouth of the tunnel.

And there, in moonlight that hurt her eyes, she saw everything.

A car, a black Jeep, parked under a tree. The engine running but the seats empty. And in front of it, what looked like a battlefield.

There were bodies everywhere. Several were vampires in black – dark ninjas. But also on the ground were the bodies of Nissa and Winnie and Galen.

So they followed, a distant part of Keller's mind said, not interfering in the slightest with the part that was getting ready for the fight. They followed the dragon – which must have done something to Winnie to get Iliana away from her. That was why I couldn't smell anybody; they all went into the tunnel while I was upstairs with brother Brett.

She couldn't tell if they were dead. They were all lying very still, and there was blood on Winnie's head and on Nissa's right arm and back. Blood and claw marks.

And Galen . . . he was sprawled out full-length, with no signs of breathing. He wasn't even a warrior. He'd never had a chance.

Then Keller saw something that drove the others out of her head.

The dragon.

It was standing near the Jeep, but frozen, as if it had just wheeled to face her. It was holding a limp figure in silvery-white casually, almost tucked under its arm.

And it still looked like Jaime Ashton-Hughes.

It was wearing Jaime's pretty blue dress. Its soft brown hair blew gently about its face, and Keller could feel its dark blue eyes fixed on her.

But there were differences, too. Its skin was deadly pale, and something yellowish was oozing from a cut on its cheekbone. Its lips were drawn back from its teeth in a grinning snarl that Jaime never could have managed. And when the wind blew the soft hair off its forehead, Keller could see horns.

There they were. Stubby and soft-looking – or at least soft on the outside, like downy skin over bone. They were so obviously real and yet so grotesque that Keller felt her stomach turn.

And there were five of them.

Five.

The book said one to three! Keller thought indignantly. And in rare cases four. But this *thing* has five! Five seats of shapeshifting power, not to mention the black energy, mind control, and whatever else it's been keeping up its sleeve just for me.

I'm dead.

Well, she had known that from the beginning, of course. She'd known it six days ago when she first leaped for the dragon's back in the mall. But now the realization was more bitter, because not only was she dead, so was all hope.

I can't kill that thing. It's going to slaughter me as easily as the others. And then take Iliana.

It didn't matter. She had to try.

'Put the girl down,' she said. She kept her half-and-half shape to say it. Maybe she could startle it by changing suddenly when she sprang.

'I don't think so,' the dragon said with Jaime's mouth. It had Jaime's voice down perfectly. But then it opened the mouth, and basso profundo laughter came out, so deep and startling that Keller felt ice down her spine.

'Come on,' Keller said. 'Neither of us wants her hurt.' While she was talking, she was moving slowly, trying to circle behind it. But it turned with her, keeping its back to the Jeep.

'You may not,' the dragon said. 'But I really don't care. She's already hurt; I don't know if she'll make it anyway.' Its grin spread wider.

'Put her down,' Keller said again. She knew that it wouldn't. But she wanted to keep talking, keep it off guard.

She also knew it wasn't going to let her get behind it. Panthers naturally attack from behind. It wasn't going to be an option.

Keller's eyes shifted to the huge and ancient pine tree the Jeep was parked under. Or they didn't actually shift, because that would have given the dragon a clue. She expanded her awareness to take it in.

It was her chance.

'We haven't even properly introduced ourselves—' she began.

And then, in mid-sentence, she leaped.

CHAPTER

17

Not for the dragon. She jumped for the tree.

It was a good, tall loblolly pine, whose drooping lower branches didn't look as if they could support a kitten. But Keller didn't need support. As she leaped, she changed, pushing it as fast as she could. She reached the tree with four paws full of lethal claws extended.

And she ran straight up the vertical surface. Her claws sank into the clean, cinnamon trunk, and she shot up like a rocket. When she got high enough to be obscured by the dull-green needles on the droopy branches, she launched herself into the air again.

It was a desperate move, betting everything on one blind spring. But it was all she could think of. She could never take the dragon in a fair fight.

She was betting on her claws.

In the wild, a panther could shear the head off a deer with a single swipe.

Keller was going for the horns.

She came down right on target. The dragon made the mistake of looking up at her, maybe thinking that she was trying to get behind it, to land on its back again and kill it. Or maybe thinking that she might see the pale face of an innocent girl and hesitate.

Whatever it thought, it was a mistake.

Keller was already slashing as she landed. A single deadly swipe with all her power behind it. Her claws peeled the forehead off the creature in a spray of blood and flesh.

The screaming roar almost burst her eardrums.

It was the sound she'd heard before in the mall, a sound so deep in pitch that she felt it as much as heard it. It shook her bones, and it reverberated in every tree and in the red clay of the ground.

And that was another mistake, although Keller didn't know it at once.

At the same instant as she heard the roar, she felt the pain. The dark power crackled through her like a whiplash and tore her own involuntary scream from her. It was worse than the first time she'd felt it, ten times worse, maybe more. The dragon was much stronger.

And it followed her.

Like a real whip, it flashed across the clearing after her. It hit her again as she hit the ground, and Keller screamed again.

It *hurt*.

She tried to scrabble away, but the pain made her weak, and she fell over on her side. And then the black energy hit her right shoulder – exactly where it had hit the first time in the mall.

Keller saw white light.

And then she was falling in darkness.

Her last thought was, I didn't get it. I couldn't have. It still has power.

Iliana, I'm sorry . . .

She stopped feeling anything.

* * *

She opened her eyes slowly.

Hurts . . .

She was looking up at the dragon.

It had dropped Iliana; Keller couldn't see where. And it was staring down at her in malevolent fury, obviously waiting for her to wake up so she could feel it when it killed her.

When *he* killed her. He'd taken on the shape he'd been wearing in the beginning. A young man with clean, handsome features and a nicely muscled if compact body. Black hair that shed rainbow colours under the moonlight and looked as fine and soft as her own fur. And those obsidian eyes.

It was hard to look away from those eyes. They seemed to capture her gaze and suck her in. They were so much more like stones than eyes, silver-black, shiny stones that seemed to reflect all light out again.

But when she managed to drag her gaze upward, she felt a thrill of hope. His forehead was a bleeding ruin.

She *had* gotten him. Her slash had carved a nice hamburger-sized piece out of his scalp. Somewhere on the ground in the clearing were two little stubby horns.

But only two; there were three left on his head. He must have turned at the last instant. Keller would have cursed if she had a human throat.

'How're you feeling?' the dragon said, and leered at her from under the gory mess of his scalp.

Keller tried to snarl at him and realized that she *did* have a human throat. She must have collapsed back into her half-and-half form, and she was too weak to change back again.

'Having trouble?' the dragon asked.

Keller croaked, 'You should never have come back.'

'Wrong,' the dragon said. 'I like the modern world.'

'You should have stayed asleep. Who woke you up?' She was buying time, of course, to try and regain some strength. But she also truly wanted to know.

The dragon laughed. 'Someone,' he said. 'Someone you'll never know. A witch who isn't a witch. We made our own alliance.'

Keller didn't understand, and her brain was too fuzzy to deal with it. But just at that moment, she noticed something else.

Movement behind the dragon. The figures that had been lying on the ground were stirring. And they were doing it stealthily, in ways that showed they were awake and with their wits about them.

They were *alive*. She could see Galen's head lift, with moonlight shining on his hair as he looked at her. She could see Winnie turn toward Iliana and begin to crawl. She could see Nissa's shoulders hump and then fall back.

Later, when they were asked, they would all say the same thing had brought them to awareness: a deep rumbling sound that vibrated in their bones. The dragon's roar.

Or, at least, three of them would say that. Galen would always say that all he heard was Keller's scream and his eyes came open.

The surge of hope she felt made Keller's heart beat hard and wiped away the pain – for the moment, at least. But she was terrified of giving the dragon some clue.

She didn't dare look at Galen any longer. She stared at the dragon's black stone eyes and thought with all her strength, Get away.

Get away, take the Jeep, take Iliana. He may not be able to follow you. *Run*.

'Your time's over,' she told the dragon out loud. 'The

shapeshifters don't want you anymore. Everything has changed.'

'And it's changing again,' the dragon said. 'The end of the world is coming, and the beginning of a new one. It's time for everything that's sleeping to wake back up again.'

Keller had a horrified vision of hundreds of dragons being dug up and brought back to life. But there was something going on in the clearing that was even more horrifying to her.

Galen wasn't getting away. He was slithering on his stomach toward her.

And Winnie, the idiot, was beside Iliana now – but she wasn't dragging her to the Jeep. She seemed to be whispering to her.

Keller felt a hot wave of utter desperation.

What can I do?

If the dragon sees them, they're all dead. There's nothing any of them can do against him. Galen's not a warrior – he can't change. Nissa looks too hurt to move. Winnie's orange fire won't even singe the dragon. And Iliana will get swatted like a butterfly.

They can't do anything. I have to.

She was so tired and hurt, and her claws were much less lethal than in her full panther form. But she had to do it, and she had to do it *now*.

'Go back where you came from!' she shouted. She bunched her muscles and jumped.

Right for him. Straight on. That was what took him by surprise, the sheer insanity of the attack. He threw the black energy at her, but he couldn't stop her leap.

Her claws ripped into his forehead again, and then she fell back.

The dragon's scream split the heavens. Dizzy with pain and shock, Keller stared at him, hoping desperately . . .

But she'd taken only one horn off. He still had two.

He thrashed around in wounded fury, then threw the dark power at her again. Keller shuddered and lost her balance. She crashed to the ground and lay there, limp.

'Keller!' The scream was full of such raw anguish that it hurt Keller's throat to hear it. It made her heart throb hard and then fall in sick dismay.

Galen, no, she thought. Don't bother with me. You have to get Iliana away.

'Keller!' he screamed again, and then he was beside her, holding her.

'No . . .' she whispered.

She couldn't say more than that. She looked at him pleadingly with the eyes of a dumb beast. If he died, too, it would make her own death meaningless.

The dragon was still screaming, both hands to his forehead. He seemed to be too angry to attack.

'Keller, hang on. Please, you have to hang on.' Galen was dripping tears on her face.

'Run . . .' she whispered.

Instead, he did the most gallant thing she had ever seen.

He was already holding her, his shaky hand stroking the hair off her face, brushing one of her tufted ears. Now, suddenly, he gripped her hard, and his expression changed.

His jaw tightened, and a white line showed around his mouth. And his eyes . . . seemed to darken and glow red.

Too late, Keller realized.

He was taking her impression. Learning her shape.

No. You were meant to be something gentle.

Galen stood up.

And changed.

But something was a little off. Maybe it was the fact

that he had to hurry when he took the impression, or some extra twist from his own genes. Because, instead of becoming a soot-black panther, he became a gleaming golden leopard.

The same animal. Different colours. This leopard was the dark rich gold of Galen's hair, and its eyes were the incredible green of his eyes.

He was marked with perfect black rosettes, each with an even darker gold centre. His body was sleek and supple and almost seven feet long with the tail. He was a *big* leopard, at least a hundred and sixty pounds.

And before Keller had time to think, he was in motion.

A good spring. Untutored but full of the real killer instinct. The coughing yell he let out as he jumped was the kind a cat makes when its fury is too great to hold in.

The dragon whirled to face him. But it was too late. Once again, the crackling dark power hit but couldn't stop the rush. The dragon's human body couldn't fend off a hundred and sixty pounds of solid feline muscle.

Keller saw Galen swipe.

The dragon bellowed, clapping a hand to his head.

And Keller wanted to cheer.

She couldn't. She didn't have the strength left. But her heart was singing inside her with sheer pride.

You did it. Oh, Galen, my *prince*, you did it.

She saw his body falling, struck by the black energy. She saw it hit the ground and lie still.

And she was sorry that they were both going to die. But with the dragon dead, too, and Iliana alive, there would still be hope. There would be people to carry on.

Then she looked at the dragon, and time stopped, and her heart turned to ice.

He still had a horn left. The one right in the middle.

They hadn't done it after all.

He still had power. He was going to kill them now, and Iliana, too. And neither she nor Galen could do anything to stop him.

The noises the dragon was making were beyond description. He seemed to be out of his mind in pain and fury. And then Keller realized that it was more than that. He was screaming in sheer blood-lust – and he was changing.

So strange – she hadn't even thought about the dragon changing before. But she could take on most animals. She knew to go for the juncture between head and neck for rhinos, the belly for a lion.

But this . . . what it was shifting into . . .

No.

I don't believe it, Keller thought.

It looked more like a moth being born than a shapeshifter changing. It split its human skin like a chrysalis. More of the yellowish liquid she had seen on Jaime's cheek oozed from the splits. And what was revealed underneath was hard and greenish-yellow, flat, smooth.

Scaly.

The smell was the smell from the basement. Sickly-sweet, pungent, an odour to make your stomach lurch.

Powerful back legs bunched, and the figure grew and stood against the moonlit sky.

It was huge.

In her mind, Keller saw a scene from the past. Iliana, her violet eyes huge, saying, 'He can turn into a *dragon*?'

And Keller's scornful answer, 'No, of course not. Don't be silly.'

Wrong, Keller thought.

It actually looked more like velociraptor than a dragon. Too big, it was more than fifteen feet long, counting the powerful tail. But it had the same look of alien intelligence, the same reptilian snout, the same sabre-like hind claws.

It's not a mindless animal, Keller thought. It's smart. It even has things like hands on its forelegs. It's where evolution took a different turn.

And it had power. Maybe more power this way than in its human form. Keller could feel its mind even at this distance, the terrible ancient core of hatred and malice, the endless thirst for blood.

It opened its mouth, and for an instant Keller expected to see fire. But what came out was a roar that showed huge spiky teeth – and a flood of black energy. The dark power crackled around it like an aura of lightning.

Nothing – no shapeshifter, no witch, no vampire – could stand against this creature. Keller knew that absolutely.

That was when she saw Iliana getting up.

Stay down, you idiot! Keller thought.

Iliana stood straight.

There's no point, don't attract its attention . . .

'Azhdeha!' Iliana shouted.

And the monster turned.

There they were, the maiden and the dragon, face to face. Iliana looked twice as small as ever before in contrast to this giant. Her silver-gold hair was blowing loose in the wind, and her dress shimmered around her. She was so delicate, so graceful – and so fragile, standing there like a lily swaying on its stalk.

I can't watch, Keller thought. I can't see this. Please . . .

'Azhdeha!' Iliana said, and her voice was sweet but ringing and stern. 'Hashteher! Tiamat!'

It's a spell, Keller thought. Winnie taught her a spell? When they were lying there, whispering together?

But what kind of spell would Winnie know against dragons?

'Poisonous Serpent! Cold-blooded Biter! Rastaban! Anguis!'

No, they're names, Keller realized slowly. *Its* names. Dragon names.

Old names.

'I am a witch and the daughter of a witch. Mine was the hand that took your power; mine was the hand that buried you in silence. Hecate was the most ancient of my mothers. Hecate's hand is my hand now.'

Winnie couldn't have taught her that. *Nobody* could have taught her that. No witch alive today.

Keller could see Winnie's pale face watching in surprise from beyond Iliana, her eyes and mouth dark Os.

'Mine is the hand that *sends you back*!'

Iliana's palms were cupped now, and orange fire crackled between them.

Keller's heart plummeted.

Golden-orange fire. Witch fire. It was impressive, from a girl who'd never been trained, but it wasn't nearly enough. It was about as dangerous to the dragon as a firefly.

She heard Winnie's voice in the silence, small and frightened but determined.

'Aim for the horn!'

The dragon threw back its head and laughed.

That was what it looked like, anyway. What came out was a roar like all the other roars and a belch of black energy that fountained skyward. But in her head, Keller heard maniacal laughter.

Then it swung its head back down and pointed the horn straight at Iliana.

Die! it said. The word wasn't spoken but sent on a cold wave of pure energy.

'*Mine is the power of the ages!*' Iliana shouted back. '*Mine is the power—*'

The golden flare in her palms was changing, blazing white, blinding hot . . .

'—OF THE END OF THE WORLD!'

Something like a supernova was born between her hands.

The light shot up and out, exploding. It was impossible to look at. And it was no longer white but dazzling, lightning-brilliant blue.

The blue fire.

The Wild Power had awakened.

I knew it, Keller thought. I knew it all along.

Keller couldn't see what happened to the dragon; the light was simply too bright. While it flared around her, she was bathed in radiance that seemed to shine *through* her, humming inside her and lighting up her bones. She tried to lift her own hand and saw nothing but a vague rainbow shape.

But she heard the dragon's scream. Not low like the roar but high and squealing, a sound like icicles driving into her ears. It went up and up, higher in pitch until even Keller couldn't track it. And then there was a thin sound like distant glass shattering, and then there was no sound at all.

There were shooting stars in the blue-white light.

For the second time that evening, Keller fainted.

'Boss! Please, Boss, hurry. Wake up!'

Keller blinked open her eyes. Galen was holding her. He was human. So was she.

And Winnie and Nissa were trying to drag both of them somewhere.

Keller gazed up into those gold-green eyes. The exact

colour of a leopard's, she thought. Only leopards don't cry, and his were brimming with tears.

She lifted a languorous hand and stroked his cheek. He cupped his own hand over it.

Keller couldn't think. There were no words in her mind. But she was glad to be here with him, for this last moment in the moonlight. It had all been worth it.

'Boss, *please*!' Winnie was almost crying, too.

'Let me die in peace,' Keller said, although she didn't realize she was saying it aloud until she heard the words. Then she added, 'Don't *you* cry, Winfrith. You did a good job.'

'Boss, you're not dying! The blue fire did something – it healed us. We're all OK. *But it's almost midnight!*'

Keller blinked. She blinked again.

Her body didn't hurt anymore. She'd assumed it was the blessed numbness that comes just before death. But now she realized that it wasn't. Her blood was running in her veins; her muscles felt firm and strong. She didn't even have a headache.

She stared beyond Winnie to the girl in white.

Iliana was still slight and childlike, almost fairy-like of figure. But something had changed about her. At first, Keller thought she looked as distant and beautiful as a star, but then she smiled and wasn't distant at all. She was simply more beautiful than the dreams of mortals.

And *really* shining with her own light. It pooled around her in soft, silvery radiance. Keller had never seen a Wild Power do that before, not on any of the tapes.

But she's not just a Wild Power, the voice in her head whispered. She's the Witch Child.

And Goddess alone knows all that she's meant to do.

For a moment, Keller felt so awed that it was almost like unhappiness. But then Winnie's message finally sank in.

She snapped her head up. 'Midnight?'

'Yes!' Winnie said frantically.

Keller bolted upright. 'Nissa?'

'Right here, Boss.'

Keller felt a flood of relief. Nissa was the one who had seemed closest to death on the ground there. But now she was standing on her own two feet, looking cool and imperturbable, even though her shirt was bloody and in rags.

'Nissa, can you drive that Jeep? Can you figure out how to get to Charlotte?'

'I think so, Boss.'

Keller had never been so grateful to hear that calm voice in her life. She jumped up.

'Then let's go!'

CHAPTER

18

The ride to Charlotte passed in a blur. All Keller could remember was hanging on while Nissa did some of the wildest driving she'd ever experienced. They went off-road for a good deal of the way.

It was one minute to midnight when they squealed into a parking lot in front of a long, low building.

'Go in, go in!' Nissa said, slamming to a stop in front of a set of double doors.

Keller and Galen and Winnie and Iliana ran.

They burst into a large room that seemed very brightly lit. A sea of chairs with bodies sitting in them swam in front of Keller's eyes. Then she focussed on a platform at the front.

'Come on,' she said tersely.

There were a number of people sitting at a table on the platform, facing the audience just like any ordinary panel, with glasses of water and microphones in front of them. But Keller recognized some of the people as she got closer, and they were anything but ordinary.

That little dumpling-shaped woman with the round face was Mother Cybele. Mother of all the Witches, just as Grandma Harman had been Crone. With Grandma

Harman dead, she was the witches' leader.

The tall girl with the lovely features and the café au lait skin who sat beside her was Aradia. The blind Maiden of the Witches mentioned in the prophecies.

And that regal-looking man with the golden hair and beard, sitting by the queenly woman with flashing green eyes . . .

They could only be the leaders of the First House of the shapeshifters.

Galen's mother and father.

There were others, too, important people from Circle Daybreak, but Keller didn't have time to focus on them. Mother Cybele was on her feet and speaking. She must have been a little short-sighted, because she didn't appear to see Keller and the others coming up on the side. Her voice was slow and concerned.

'I'm afraid that since it's now past midnight—'

Keller glanced at her watch. 'It's just midnight now!'

Mother Cybele looked up, startled, over her glasses. Every head on the panel turned. And every face in the audience was suddenly fixed on Keller's group.

A low murmur like the humming of bees began, but it swelled very quickly to something like a muted roar. People were pointing openly as Keller ran up the steps to the stage.

She glanced back at the others and realized why. They were a pretty sad-looking bunch. Every one of them was dirty and ragged. Winnie's strawberry-blonde hair was dark red with blood on one side. Galen's sweater was in shreds. And she herself was filthy from the tunnel and all the dirt she'd encountered in the clearing.

Only Iliana looked reasonably clean, and that was probably because the glow kept you from focussing too closely.

Mother Cybele gave a little cry of joy that sounded quite young, and she dropped the index cards she'd been holding. Aradia stood up, her beautiful blank eyes turned toward them, her entire face shining with joy. Galen's parents looked extremely startled and relieved.

But some guy in a dark suit grabbed Keller's arm as she reached the top of the steps.

'Who are you supposed to be?' he said.

Keller shook him off and stood with her hair swirling around her. 'We're the people who're bringing you the Wild Power,' she said. She spotted Nissa just coming in the door and beckoned to her. 'And we're also the ones who killed the dragon.'

The big room fell so silent that you could have heard a paper clip drop.

'Well, actually, *she* killed the dragon,' Keller said, pointing to Iliana.

Aradia said in a hushed voice, 'The Witch Child. She's come to us.'

Iliana walked slowly up onto the stage and stood straight. 'I didn't kill it alone,' she said. 'Everybody helped, and especially Keller and Galen.'

Galen's father's golden eyebrows went up, and Galen's mother gripped her husband's arm. Keller glanced sideways at Galen and saw that he was blushing.

'They fought it and fought it until they were both almost dead. But then, when I used the blue fire, they got better again.'

She said it so simply, speaking to Mother Cybele alone, or so it seemed. She didn't look in the least self-conscious, or in the least arrogant.

I suppose she's used to having everybody looking at her, Keller thought.

Mother Cybele actually clasped her little soft hands

together and shut her eyes. When she opened them again, they were shining with tears.

But all she said was, 'Welcome, my child. Grandma Harman's last words were for you. She hoped you would find your power.'

'She did,' Keller said. 'Winnie helped her.'

'I didn't help her do *that*,' Winnie said candidly. 'What she did back there and what she said. I just tried to show her how to use the orange fire. But when she started talking—' She shook her curly head. 'I don't know where she got all that stuff about Hecate.'

'It just came to me,' Iliana said. 'I don't know. It was as if somebody was saying it to me, and I was just repeating it.'

But who could have said it? Keller thought. Who else but somebody who was there the first time, when the dragons were put to sleep? Who else but Hecate Witch-Queen herself?

Even though she'd been dead thirty thousand years.

It's time for everything that's sleeping to wake back up again.

Keller realized that she was hearing a noise from the crowd. At first, she thought that they were muttering in disbelief again, or maybe in annoyance at these people who were standing on the stage and chattering.

Then it got louder and louder, and she realized it was applause.

People were clapping and cheering and whistling. It was echoing off the ceiling and walls. And just when Keller thought it couldn't possibly get any louder, a new wave would come and prove her wrong.

It took a long time for Mother Cybele to get them all quieted down. Then she turned to Keller and said formally, 'So you've completed your mission?'

Keller realized that it was a cue. And in the midst of the

dizzy happiness she'd been feeling, something twisted in her heart.

She kept it from showing on her face. She kept herself standing erect.

'Yes,' she said to Mother Cybele. 'I've brought the Witch Child.' She swallowed hard.

'And here is the son of the First House of the shapeshifters,' Galen's father said. He stepped over to Galen and took his hand. His face was stern but glowing with pride.

Galen's face was pale but set. He looked at Keller – for just one moment. And then he looked straight out at the audience with unseeing eyes.

Mother Cybele looked toward Iliana. To take *her* hand, Keller supposed, and join it with Galen's. But Iliana was holding some whispered conversation with Aradia.

When she finally turned around, Iliana said, 'I want Keller to do it. She's the one responsible for all this.'

Keller blinked. Her throat was so swollen, it was impossible to swallow again. But she wouldn't have thought it of Iliana. Really, it seemed so pointlessly cruel to make *her* do it.

But maybe she doesn't understand. That's it, she doesn't realize, Keller thought. She let out a careful, shaky breath and said, 'OK.'

She reached for Iliana's hand –

And felt a stab in her palm.

She looked down, astonished. Iliana had a *knife* in that hand, a perfectly serviceable little knife. She had cut Keller with it, and Keller was bleeding. In fact, Iliana seemed to be bleeding, too.

'Sorry,' Iliana hissed. 'Ick, I hate blood.'

Then, grabbing Keller's hand again, she faced the audience and raised it up high.

'There!' she said. 'Now we're blood sisters. And she's already been like a sister to me, because she saved my life over and over. And if *that's* not good enough for an alliance between the witches and the shapeshifters, I don't know what is.'

The entire audience gaped at her. Mother Cybele blinked rapidly.

'Are you saying . . .' Galen's father looked incredulous. 'Are you saying that you won't marry my son?'

'I'm saying that *she* ought to marry your son – or promise to him, or whatever they want. She's the one he's in love with. And I don't see why you should make him miserable for his whole life just because you want the shapeshifters tied to the witches. Keller and I are tied together, and we always will be. And Galen, too. Why can't that be enough?'

A sound was starting from the crowd again. Keller's heart seemed to soar on it. But she was still staring at Iliana, afraid to believe.

'But . . . what if the witches don't agree to it?' Galen's father said feebly.

Iliana stamped her foot. She actually did.

'I'm the *Witch Child*. They'd better listen to me. I didn't go through all of this for nothing.'

Then the crowd was thundering applause even louder than before, and the wave seemed to sweep Keller right into Galen's arms.

Sometime later, in the middle of a lot of hugging and kissing, Keller whispered to Iliana, 'Are you sure?'

'I'd better be sure, don't you think? Or Galen's going to be pretty upset.'

'Iliana—'

'I'm sure,' Iliana whispered. She squeezed Keller. 'I

really do care about him. I guess I'm sort of in love with him, too. But I saw. I saw his face in the clearing when he thought you were dead. And I heard the way he said your name. And then . . . I knew, you know? The two of you were meant to be. So I'm sure.'

'A leopard?' Galen's mother said, shaking out her topaz-coloured hair. 'Why, dear, that's wonderful. Your great-great-grandmother was a leopard.'

'You gave up being a bird for me,' Keller whispered in his ear.

'I think I could learn to like running,' he murmured, and took the chance to touch his lips to her cheek.

'No, ma'am, I'm really sorry I woke you up,' Keller said. 'Yes, ma'am, I do know how late it is.' She strained to hear the voice on the other end of the phone. She had a finger in her ear to try and block out the noise of the wild celebration around her, but it wasn't doing much good.

'Because I honestly don't think it's funny,' Iliana's mother said. 'The baby is just fine; he's been in his bed all night. Why would you think he wasn't?'

'Well, ma'am, it's hard to explain . . .'

'And now he's awake, and he's going to start crying – well, he's not crying. But now he wants to eat the phone . . . Alex!'

A voice on the other end squealed and said distinctly, 'Kee-kee!'

'Yeah, it's Kee-kee,' Keller said, startled. 'Um, I'm glad you're OK, kid. And, see, I didn't go bye-bye after all. So you may think you're pretty smart, but you still have something to learn about precognition, hotshot. Right?' Keller added, 'You know I thought for a minute once that you might be the Wild Power. But I guess you're just a good old-fashioned witch baby.'

Iliana, who was passing by, gave her a very strange look. 'Keller, are you having a conversation with my baby brother?'

'What *exactly* did the dragon say?' Mother Cybele asked anxiously. Although she looked like a big dove and her eyes were always kind, there was a firmness about her plump chin that Keller liked.

'I asked who woke him up. And he said' – Keller reached for the exact words – 'he said, "Someone you'll never know. A witch who isn't a witch. We made our own alliance." '

'A witch who isn't a witch,' Mother Cybele repeated.

Aradia's face was sober. 'I wonder who that could be. And where they are now.'

Mother Cybele said quietly, 'Time will tell.'

'The police are already inside,' Nissa said, holding the cell phone to her ear as she talked to Keller. 'I guess the kids at the party called them when they saw a panther. They've found the family . . . Mr and Ms Ashton-Hughes and Jaime and Brett. They're taking them to the hospital.'

She snapped the phone shut. 'We'd better send some witches to the hospital. But as long as they're alive, they have a pretty good chance, don't you think? After all, we've got a Wild Power with healing fire. Now, can't you relax and try to enjoy yourself?'

It was two days later. Keller was sitting in a sunny alcove in the safe house where Iliana and Galen and the others had been brought to protect them from the Night World. And to give them a chance to recover.

It was nice to be still for a while. To sit and read . . . and think. And it was even nicer to be able to do it with Galen around.

He came in the door quietly – he always moved cat-quietly now. She smiled at him. He looked so wonderfully dear with his golden hair and fairy-tale looks and leopard-green eyes.

'I wrote you a poem,' he said, sitting down beside her. 'Well, no, that's not true. I kind of stole what your mother wrote and made it into . . . something. I don't know what. But I think maybe it's what she really meant to say, after all.'

Keller blinked at him, then looked down at the piece of paper he gave her.

> *People die . . . so love them every day.*
> *Beauty fades . . . so look before it's gone.*
> *Love changes . . . but not the love you give.*
> *And if you love, you'll never be alone.*

'Actually, I was going to say, 'And you will always be alone . . . so don't rely on others for your happiness, but don't stop loving, either, because then you'll end up empty and alone instead of alone and strong and able to give without worrying about what you're going to get back.' But that was kind of long, and it didn't scan,' he said.

Keller stared down at the paper blindly.

'I'm sorry,' he said. 'If you don't like it—'

Keller threw her arms around him, and her tears spilled over. 'I'm going to burn the other one,' she said. 'And I love you. Kiss me.'

He grinned. 'Yes, Boss.'

And he did.

One from the land of kings long forgotten;
One from the hearth which still holds the spark;
One from the Day World where two eyes are watching;
One from the twilight to be one with the dark.

Out now . . .

NIGHTWORLD
L.J. Smith

The Night World is a secret society of vampires, werewolves, witches and creatures of darkness – a place where it is too dangerous to fall in love . . .

Read the first compelling volume of:
SECRET VAMPIRE, DAUGHTERS OF DARKNESS AND ENCHANTRESS

In *Secret Vampire*, Poppy is dying. Her best friend, James can offer her eternal life – as a vampire. One kiss and she sees into his soul. But can she follow him into death . . . and beyond?

In *Daughters of Darkness*, there are three sisters with a secret, on the run from their cruel and ruthless brother. Can their new human friend Mary Lynette resist the powerful charm of their brother – and save the sisters and herself from a deadly fate at the hands of a werewolf?

In *Enchantress*, Blaise is irresistible. She's lethal. She bewitches boys for sport. Then she meets a boy who matters to her cousin, Thea. They become rivals in love. It's Thea's white magic against Blaise's black magic. They're both breaking the rules. But it's Thea who risks expulsion from the Night World . . .

A stunning new supernatural series . . .

THE BEAUTIFUL DEAD

By Eden Maguire

Not alive. Not dead. Somewhere in between lie the Beautiful Dead . . .

Book 1
Jonas

Something strange is happening at Ellerton High. Jonas, Arizona, Summer and Phoenix. All dead within a year.

Jonas Johnson is the first to die, in a motorbike accident. But there are many unanswered questions, and the three deaths that follow are equally mysterious. Grief-stricken, Darina can't escape her heartache, or the visions of her dead boyfriend Phoenix, and the others who died. And all the while, the sound of beating wings echoes inside her head . . .

Are these visions real? Or do the Beautiful Dead only exist in Darina's traumatised imagination?